A Kiss . . . Interrupted

He touched his mouth to hers again. Her hands closed into fists against his chest, but she didn't push him away. . . . Shivers of excitement broke free and crept over her breasts, settling in her belly. She'd never known kissing a man could be so pleasurable. The last time, her only time, had been . . .

Suddenly she felt his body tense and he jerked his mouth away from hers as a voice from out of the darkness called out to him: "Take your hands off her, or I'll blow you away quicker'n a tumbleweed in a tornado."

Diamond Wildflower Romance

A breathtaking line of searing romance novels . . .
where destiny meets desire
in the untamed fury
of the American West.

RECKLESS RIVER

TERESA SOUTHWICK

DIAMOND BOOKS, NEW YORK

This book is a Diamond original edition,
and has never been previously published.

RECKLESS RIVER

A Diamond Book/published by arrangement with
the author

PRINTING HISTORY
Diamond edition/July 1994

ISBN: 0-7865-0018-2

Diamond Books are published by The Berkley Publishing Group,
200 Madison Avenue, New York, NY 10016.
DIAMOND and the "D" design
are trademarks belonging to Charter Communications, Inc.

PRINTED IN THE UNITED STATES OF AMERICA

10 9 8 7 6 5 4 3 2 1

To my mother, Gladys, who always told me I could do anything I set my mind to.

To my father, Frank, the Irishman from whom I inherited a love of language.

To my husband, Tom, for his unwavering love and constant faith and support. And the idea for this book.

And last, but most definitely not least, to my critique group: Susan, Jolie, Denise, and Stephanie. Without each of you the writing would still be just a dream.

one

Colorado River, Arizona Territory
May 1881

"Lady, we both know you're not going to shoot. So put away the pistol and we'll talk—"

Instantly a gunshot shattered the hot desert stillness.

Half a second later Jeff Tanner felt ghostly fingers of air as the bullet whizzed by his ear. He ducked to his right, barely avoiding the shot. If she'd come half an inch closer, he'd be dead.

His throat went dry, as parched as the sand that stretched all the way to the craggy mountains on either side of the railroad track. Two feet behind him, his Pullman waited imposing and dignified, out of place in this desolate land.

"Put that damn thing away before you hurt someone." His tone was hard, each word spoken through gritted teeth and meant to intimidate.

Another shot rang out and his hat flew off. He ducked, then straightened, glaring at her. She stood only ten feet away. The acrid stench of gunpowder lingered in the air, mingling with the smell of swirling dust. He didn't need more proof that she meant business.

"All right. You've got my attention. What do you want?"

"I want you to do something about Slonneger." The woman angled the barrel of her gun to his left toward the man beside him, swaying drunkenly. "I only have two rules on my boat, no drinkin' and no smokin'. He broke both."

Each word was tough as nails and backed up by lead. She was small, hardly as tall as the underside of his jaw, Jeff estimated. And she couldn't weigh more than a hundred pounds, soaking wet and wearing those denim pants. Her black-streaked cotton shirt caught a gust of wind and billowed out behind her like a sail. A floppy brown hat secured by rawhide thongs beneath her stubborn chin hid most of her hair.

Jeff was a shade over six feet and weighed close to two hundred pounds. The man she'd hustled at gunpoint was a good inch taller and probably outweighed him by fifty pounds. And she faced them both down without batting an eye. She had guts. That glimmer of respect irritated him, and he pushed it away.

She might be no bigger than a minute, but she was holding a gun. He'd underestimated her once today when he'd left his Colt .45 inside his Pullman. His fingers curled tightly into his empty palm. Misjudging her again could be fatal. He picked up his hat and poked his finger through the bullet hole in the crown.

An awed murmur rose from the semicircle of men behind her. Attracted by the commotion, a small group had gathered outside his private railroad car. His eyes narrowed as he stared at them. He didn't know if they were with her or not. Then he dismissed the crowd and concentrated on her.

"Last I heard, drinking and smoking wasn't a hanging offense." Jeff watched her like a hawk, waiting for the slightest move that would warn him.

"It is on a steamboat. He nearly burned up the *River Belle*."

"So you're going to shoot him?"

"Not a riverman alive would blame me. But shooting's too good for the likes of him. I brought him to you." A corner of her mouth turned up. Then she balanced her slight weight evenly on both feet and tightened her hands around the grip, aiming her weapon directly at him.

Angry words hovered on the tip of his tongue, but instinct shouldered them aside and one thing hollered out loud and clear: *Don't rile a woman holding a loaded gun.* Her shots had come too close for comfort, and he didn't know if it was skill or luck—or a little of both. Until he did, he'd take it slow and easy. "Why?"

"You're that railroad bigwig here to build the bridge."

He nodded. "So?"

"He works for the railroad. Your foreman stuck him on my riverboat . . ."

His brows rose. "Now hold on. You're telling me you run a steamboat?"

She lifted her gun a fraction until it pointed directly at his heart. "You don't believe me?"

He pushed the crown of his hat down and felt the bullet hole. She'd proved she could shoot. His guts told him she was just as competent at everything else. "Just wanted to make sure I heard right. My ears are still ringing."

"You heard right."

"Why did you get stuck with him?"

"Because he couldn't pull his weight with the construction crew. Even though he doesn't know a mudbank from a stern-wheeler, I was willing to give him a chance—until today." Her eyes narrowed in the shadow of her hat brim.

"What happened?"

"He got drunk and tossed a lighted cigarette. It hit the wooden deck and caught like dry prairie grass. If I hadn't had my buckets full—" Her lips pulled tight. The wind caught a wisp of long black hair and blew it into the corner of her mouth. She took one hand off the gun grip only long enough to quickly brush the strand away. "When it comes to my boat, I don't give second chances."

Jeff glanced at the man beside him and frowned. Unable to remain upright, the drunk had fallen on his ass and sat in the hot sand, grinning like an idiot.

"If what you say is true"—he shot another quick, disgusted look at Slonneger—"you have my word that he won't come near your boat again—drunk or sober."

Steam billowed from the train engine behind him, sticking his shirt to his back. It was hotter than hell. Sweat trickled from beneath his wide-brimmed black hat and made his forehead itch, but he resisted the urge to wipe it. The midday sun blistered his shoulders through his white linen shirt. Heat wavered up from the desert in the ten feet that separated them as Jeff waited, his eyes cutting into her.

She met and held his gaze, taking his measure, and he shifted uneasily. He wasn't used to that. Men—rich, powerful, important men, bigger and tougher than she— flinched from his stare. And ladies batted their lashes, flirting, not ever looking directly at him, never honest and straightforward. This little bit of a woman didn't seem intimidated in the least. For the third time in the last ten minutes, admiration flashed through him.

"What are you going to do about the damage to my boat?"

"I'll see that it's repaired good as new."

Finally she nodded and lowered the muzzle of her gun until it pointed directly into the sand. "Fair enough."

Jeff slowly released his breath and flexed his shoulders, easing the tension that waited coiled within him. Then he shot a look to two men in the crowd and nodded toward the drunk sitting in the sand. "Get him out of here."

He was used to having his orders obeyed without question and hardly noticed when Slonneger was hoisted to his feet, one arm draped around each man, then led away. The remainder of the crowd stayed and gawked. He returned their stares until the men looked at the ground and shuffled uneasily. Finally, one by one, they turned away, and in seconds the group dispersed.

Then he focused on the woman. The show was over and they were alone.

"What's your name?" He pushed his hat back and wiped the sweat from his forehead with his forearm. Then he pulled the brim level with his brows, shading his eyes from the blazing sun.

"Murphy."

A flicker of awareness flared through him. "I have a contract with B. E. Murphy—of Murphy's Colorado River Navigation Company." He pointed at her. "You know anything about that?"

"Everything, Mister Jefferson Tanner." She looked smug. "I'm B. E. Murphy. In my letters I said I'd be here to take you upriver to Hardyville."

He believed she could run a steamboat, but letting her ferry him up and down the river in it was something else again. He moved closer, considering her. He was near enough to smell the faint fragrance of lavender. The shadow of her hat had hidden her face before, but now he could see the streaks of soot that slashed the soft skin on her cheeks. He raised his gaze a notch and read her eyes— the biggest, bluest, most beautiful eyes he'd ever seen. Hostility swirled in their depths, sizzling like the blue flames that mixed with yellow and orange in a wood fire. His gut clenched as if he'd been sucker-punched and he hauled in a deep breath. The hot air scorched his lungs.

"I thought B. E. Murphy was a man," he said.

"You thought wrong."

"So I see." He stared openly, his gaze moving from the top of her head, over her small waist, and down her shapely legs. "What does B. E. stand for?"

"None of your business."

His brows drew together in a frown and he inched closer, towering over her. She needed to learn who was boss. "I own the railroad company that contracted your steamboat to help build this bridge. That damn well makes it my business."

Her chin lifted slightly, a subtle challenge. "The *B* stands for Breanne. Bree's good enough."

"And the *E*?"

"Expert."

The corners of his mouth twitched, and he smoothed his mustache with his thumb and forefinger to hide the movement. "An expert shot or steamboat captain?"

"Both."

He laughed then. Eyes as blue and wide as the Arizona sky and an ego to match. He liked that. She was gutsy and cool-headed. In her shoes he'd probably have shot Slonneger first and asked questions later. That was the fourth time since she'd whizzed lead past his ear that he'd admired her spirit. Something told him B. E. Murphy would be a lot more interesting than he'd expected.

He held out his hand. "Glad to meet you, Murphy."

She hesitated, studying him warily. Finally she placed her hand in his. "Wish I could say the same, Tanner."

Her grip was firm and her palm hard. This was not a woman who sat around and stitched samplers all day. Only the smallness of her hand and the slender, graceful fingers set her apart from a hardworking man. She pumped his arm once, then quickly withdrew and jammed her fist in the pocket of her trousers. He knew that she didn't like him much. Instinct told him her animosity ran deep.

Jeff made up his mind to find out what was at the bottom of it.

"My throat's parched. How about you?"

"I'm fine." She brushed the back of her hand across her dry lips.

He scanned the shiny black Pullman beside them and smiled with satisfaction. In his thirty-four years he'd known the frustration as well as the gratification of working with his hands to build something, but in his wildest dreams he'd never imagined having a private railroad car at his disposal. That was pleasure—pure and simple. Too bad he couldn't keep it with him.

He'd only used the coach for transportation to the Territory. The bridge construction would take close to six months, barring complications, and one of his partners had need of the Pullman. But the luxury was his for a bit longer.

"Why don't we go inside for something to drink? After that, I want to see what it'll take to repair your boat."

She watched him uneasily. Spirit swirled in the depths of her blue eyes as she regarded him.

"Let's skip the drink. You wanted to see the boat. Follow me."

"Whoa. I have to get my gear off the train. It's almost ready to leave."

"You mean you're really staying?"

"I already told you, I've got a job to do." He glanced to his left. Below that shallow, sandy bluff the Colorado River flowed, hell-bent for the Gulf of California. He intended to break her legendary spirit; he aimed to see a bridge built to span her treacherous muddy waters.

"Why you? Couldn't you hire someone else so you don't have to get your hands dirty?"

"I could." He'd thought about it. But there was a primal satisfaction in building where nothing existed before, something elemental in a man doing it with his own two hands. Excitement stirred his blood at the challenge; he hadn't felt that for a long time. It was a risky undertaking, but he wouldn't be where he was today if he couldn't face a gamble without flinching. "I have my reasons for handling this project personally."

Still holding her gun, she rubbed the bridge of her dirty nose with a knuckle. "A person can always hope. You've got five minutes to get what you need off the train before I leave for Hardyville without you. I have a schedule to keep."

"I'm paying you. I make the schedule." He met and held her hostile gaze, and the air between them sizzled as hot as the blazing sun. "Come inside. Jeremiah can get you a cold drink."

Her shoulders tensed and her chin lifted sharply. "Who's he?"

"My porter." He saw her skepticism. "It's cooler. Wouldn't you like to get in out of the sun?"

"This isn't anything. Wait a couple weeks. You'll think you died and woke up in hell. Maybe even go back where you came from." Her look was hopeful and there was sarcasm in her voice.

With his thumb and forefinger Jeff smoothed his mustache as he studied her. Her eyes never left his, measuring, mistrustful—afraid to turn her back. They'd only just met. What could she possibly have against him? She licked her lips and brushed the perspiration from her forehead with grimy fingers, leaving more black streaks.

"How about a glass of lemonade?"

Her hand went still, half covering one eye. The way her full lips tightened into a straight line told him she didn't much like the fact that she wanted that drink. So, she had a weakness, wasn't quite as tough as she pretended. He sweetened the pot.

"It's cold—best tasting stuff this side of the Colorado," he said.

"You just got here. How would you know?"

He turned his head from side to side, gazing at the wide open desert. About two hundred yards away, a city of tents housing the men hired to build the bridge was the only sign of civilization in the vast barrenness of the landscape. "Just a wild guess."

She looked at him skeptically. "It's cold, you say?"

He nodded. "Real cold."

"How?"

He wiped the sweat from his forehead and glanced at the fierce fireball sun. Then he played his trump card. "Ice."

Her eyes widened, and she bit her lip. He'd won this hand.

She nodded. "All right. One glass. Then I want to know what you intend to do about my boat."

He looked at her gun and held out his hand. "Would

you mind giving that to me? I think we'd all be a lot safer."

"Yeah, I mind. I feel a lot safer *with* it." She stuck the pistol in the front of her trousers and glared at him, daring him to take it.

Jeff noticed again her small waist and slender legs encased in the tight-fitting denim. It was the most curvaceous shape he'd ever seen in a pair of pants. But then, where he came from, women wore dresses.

His threatening grin refused to be tamed. He was mighty curious to see what was underneath all that soot on her face. If those magnificent eyes were any indication, she was quite a beauty. A dip in his private tub would be one way to separate her from her gun. Then maybe she'd quit acting like a man and remember how a woman was supposed to behave.

He pointed to the train steps. "After you."

"No. You first."

He noticed the rigid set of her shoulders, her suspicious glance. Nope, he suspected she'd find a way to keep that gun with her—come hell or high water. Was it all men in general she felt the need to protect herself from, or him in particular?

"We'll go together." He took her upper arm and hustled her aboard before she changed her mind and left without him.

Inside, Bree stopped smack in the center of the car and wrenched her arm from his grasp, then waited for her eyes to adapt to the dark, airless interior. Smoke from the fire must have addled her more than she'd thought; otherwise she'd never have stepped foot in here. But she hadn't—at least not willingly. He'd practically dragged her inside. And she definitely didn't want to be alone with him.

She was glad she hadn't let him take her gun. A long time ago she'd learned not to turn her back on a man; none of them could be trusted. No matter how rich or handsome—and she grudgingly admitted Tanner was both—she couldn't let her guard down for a minute. Not even with kin.

Her hand tightened on the handle of her pistol, and the hard surface dug into her palm, steadying her nerves. If he tried anything, the slightest unseemly move . . .

Then her eyes adjusted, and her breath caught in her throat. She inched backward a step, her heavy boots scraping on the wooden floor. Never in her life had she seen such richness.

Tanner moved alongside her into the center of the Pullman. The motion stirred the heavy air, and she caught a whiff of the smoky smell that still clung to her clothes and hair. The back of her hand was grimy from grease and mud. She'd never wanted a bath as badly as she did now.

She cleared her throat, struggling to hide her unease. "Nice place y'got."

"Thanks." He grinned and amusement crinkled the corners of his eyes.

He was laughing at her. Probably thought she had no business so close to such elegance. That's one thing they saw eye to eye on. Embarrassment burned her cheeks as hot as the fire she'd just put out on her boat. If there was any justice in the world, she'd be able to hide it from him.

She'd had just about all she could stand of snooty, westbound Eastern passengers who looked at her strangely, funning behind her back. She knew what they said about her doing a man's job and saw how they turned up their noses because she dressed like a man.

Those people passed through her life, and she never saw them again. They couldn't hurt her. But she had a contract with Tanner; she had to work with him for as long as it took to build that blasted bridge. If he laughed at her— well, it just might make her wish the bullet hole she'd put in the crown of his hat had gone an inch or two lower.

Her work—her life—was the riverboat. She wore pants because it was comfortable and she couldn't afford to worry about getting soiled. In the elegance of his Pullman every sooty streak seemed branded into her skin, as if no amount of scrubbing could ever wash it away, as if she tainted his fancy car just by her very presence. It had been a mistake to come inside. She longed to be back in the world she knew.

"I think I'll wait outside." She quickly turned away.

In her haste she bumped against the chair beside her and gasped, fearful that she'd ruined it. The shiny material caught her eye and touched a deeply buried core inside her. With a trembling hand she reached out to stroke the green brocade, aching to know what something so beautiful felt like.

Her dirty fingers curled into a fist just a half-inch away. Her bullet had missed Tanner's ear by about as much. Even though she wished he'd never come to the Territory, she wouldn't have hurt him, any more than she'd deliberately soil something so pretty. She'd never felt quite so . . . what was that word her stepmother always used? *Gauche*—that was it. For the first time she knew what it meant.

He took her arm and pulled her farther away from the door. "What's your hurry? You haven't had that drink yet."

Her head turned from side to side until she was nearly dizzy from trying to see everything in the car at once. The walls were paneled in dark pine, and several crystal chandeliers lined the ceiling. It was so lovely—so perfect. Her small steamboat couldn't hold a candle to the furnishings, in fact didn't have any—except the mattress she kept in the wheelhouse. But that didn't count. Even the bigger *Elizabeth*—well, there was no comparison.

He pointed to the back of the car. "There's more."

Bree jumped; she'd forgotten he was there. Curiosity had gotten the better of her need to escape.

"Seems bigger when you're inside." She swallowed hard staring in the direction he indicated.

Straight ahead through open double doors, she could see the side of a bed and, beyond that, the edge of a brass tub peeking out from behind a dressing screen. Her mouth went dry. She forgot her urgency to flee, her thirst, and even that she was alone with a man. She took a step toward the tub, like a honeybee to a flower's nectar.

Such indulgence, she thought, and on a train. She could hardly believe it. To be able to immerse herself in water, warm water without a current or the icy bite of melted mountain snow, any time she felt like it, and still get to where she was going. She'd sell her soul for just one bath in that tub.

She thought of her *River Belle* and felt like a traitor. Maybe her boat didn't have such conveniences, but *Belle* had proved herself on the Colorado more than once. The river had been here long before the railroad, and would be around long after.

While she battled her envy, the door at the far end of the car opened and a man appeared, silhouetted against the blinding sunlight. As he walked briskly forward, she darted a quick look to Tanner, then pulled the gun free of her waistband. "You low-down—"

"What the hell are you doing? For God's sake, not again." Irritation whipped Tanner's words until each one was like a lash against her skin. He cursed loudly.

From the corner of her eye she saw him move. Before she could react, an iron grip closed around her wrist and wrenched it toward the ceiling. Automatically her index finger squeezed the trigger and a deafening roar filled the car, followed by the tinkle of breaking glass. Then the gun was forcefully removed from her hand.

Her chest heaving with fear, Bree backed away from him. Something hard behind her knees stopped her. With a firm shove Tanner seated her in the chair she'd just admired. She started to rise, and he pushed her down again.

"Stay put," he growled. His expression was ruthless. He had the look of a man who did what he wanted regardless of the consequences, the cold-hearted air of a man others didn't cross.

"Let me out of here." Panic quickened her breathing as

she tried to get up again and he stopped her. His hand was heavy on her shoulder and fingers of steel bit into her.

"S-sir, is everything all right?" The newcomer's voice shook.

Bree stared at the Negro man, immaculate in his spotless white shirt so stark against his dark skin and black suit. His brown eyes were wide with fright, an exact reflection of her own, she was sure. Tanner put her gun in his waistband, his furious look daring her to make a move for it. Then he crossed his arms over his broad chest. "Everything's just fine, Jeremiah. The lady would like some lemonade."

"Yes, sir, Mr. Tanner. Right away." With one last uncertain glance, the servant left them alone.

"What in bloody hell is wrong with you? I've never in my life raised my hand against a woman, but, lady, you sorely test my patience." Exasperation wrapped around his words, convincing her that he'd reached his limit. He planted his boots wide apart as he glared down at her.

Bree named herself every kind of fool for ever coming into his blasted car. Without her gun she was trapped for sure. When they were standing outside in the wide-open Arizona desert, he'd seemed . . . manageable. Now, in these close quarters, he dwarfed his surroundings and loomed over her menacingly. He was a big man, powerfully built. The sleeves of his white linen shirt were rolled to his elbows revealing wide, strong forearms that looked more like a blacksmith's than a tycoon's.

Defiantly she raised her gaze to his and refused to let him see her fear. In his tanned face, green eyes glittered harshly, eyes the color of wild desert grass after a sudden violent rain. Wavy brown hair framed his face, curling down his neck, and a thick mustache gave him a sinister air. His nose was slightly crooked, and a certain pleasure stole over her that he'd probably had it broken. She'd give a month's pay to shake the hand of the man who'd done it.

Beside him, gold-braided ropes confined the thick green velvet drapes and caught the glint of the sun. She blinked, then stared at the width and harnessed power in his chest, and her satisfaction faded. Dark hairs peeked through the open neck of his shirt, reminding her that he was a man and they were alone. Swallowing hard, she braced herself, ready to fight him with every ounce of strength she possessed, knowing it would be like trying to hold back the storm-driven river.

"I . . ." She only managed a hoarse croak and cleared her throat. She hated the weakness and him for causing it. "I want out of here."

He stared at her, and she knew the exact moment that he smelled her fear and the nature of it.

His nostrils flared slightly and his eyes narrowed. "Did you think I lured you inside to compromise your virtue?"

Her face burned with the truth of his question, but she wouldn't look away. His gaze took in her appearance down to her worn brown boots and back up again. "The thought never crossed my mind."

"It's a good thing," she snapped. Although she was relieved, his words still stung.

With a dirty finger she traced a streak of soot on the leg of her denims and tried not to care. But she had feelings, same as every other woman. Long ago she'd hardened herself to the slights about her work and her femininity. Only something about Tanner made the insult more painful, and that made him a man to stay away from. She longed to be back on her boat. On the river the danger wasn't personal. Her skill and knowledge of her craft gave her the upper hand, and that's the way she liked it.

"Why are you in such an all-fired hurry to leave? I promised you lemonade, and you're going to get it—with ice." The last words were nearly shouted.

Bree flinched. She glanced at the door where the porter had disappeared, then looked him in the eye. "Two against one. I don't like unfair odds is all."

"Odds are only important in poker and fistfights." He looked around the car, then raised one dark brow questioningly. "We're not gambling, so I guess we must be fighting. The question is why."

"You're here, aren't you?"

"Thank you. It's clear as mud now." He closed his eyes briefly and released a long, restrained breath. "You've had a burr under your saddle since you laid eyes on me. I want to know what you're so riled about." He sat down in the matching wingback chair across from her.

She thought about denying his accusation, but it wasn't her way. Direct and to the point was how she'd achieved hard-won respect from the men on the river, and she wasn't about to play false with this railroad man. "I don't like you, Tanner. Nothing personal. It wouldn't matter who came to build the bridge. I'm river—through and through—and you're railroad. The two don't mix. It's as simple as that."

"It's about the bridge, then?"

She nodded. "As soon as it's finished, Murphy Navigation will be out of business."

"That's ridiculous."

"Is it? Since the railroad came to Yuma in seventy-seven, we've lost half our trade. The railroad can haul freight farther, faster, and cheaper than we can on the river. The bridge is the final straw. After that there'll be nothing left for us. You're a businessman. Think about it. Would you roll over and play dead for the outfit that planned to destroy everything you worked your whole life for?"

The porter entered the car's sitting area and placed a tray containing two glasses of pale yellow liquid on the cherrywood table between them. "Will there be anything else, sir?"

"Thank you, no, Jeremiah. Is my gear ready?"

The black man nodded and looked uncertainly out the window at the desolate landscape, broken only by scrub brush and sand. "I don't know who's gonna do your shirts, sir. Not the way you like 'em."

"I'll survive. Thanks, Jeremiah. You can go now. Pleasant journey." He smiled at his servant. When the door at the far end of the compartment closed, Tanner turned back to her.

Bree looked at the fine clothes he wore, the perfect even stitches in the linen shirt, the fashionable cut of his brown trousers. She'd never seen anyone dressed just so before. A wistful feeling tightened in her chest. He'd never look twice at a woman like her. As quickly as it came, she pushed the thought away. In the Territory every ounce of energy was used to survive, and that meant work, from sunup to sundown. Her own clothes were made to hold up to soot and soil, grease and mud. That's the way it was, and that's the way she wanted it. She picked up her glass and took a sip.

"Why did you accept my contract, Murphy?"

Bree heard the words but couldn't answer, too caught up in the sweet-sour taste of her drink. Liquid from heaven and so cold it made her head hurt. But she didn't care. Every lesson in manners she'd ever learned deserted her. She gulped her lemonade down, then rolled the remaining ice around before tipping her glass once more to slide a cold chunk into her mouth, puffing out her cheek. She looked across the table and caught him grinning at her.

Sheepishly she spit the ice into her empty glass, then placed it on the tray. She looked longingly at the remainder, then dragged her gaze back to him. "Thanks."

"Glad you enjoyed it. Now I'd like an answer."

"I forgot the question."

"If you're against the railroad expansion, why did you take the bridge contract?"

"Money." And Cap's drinking, she thought bitterly. If her father hadn't taken refuge in a bottle of whiskey after her mother's death, they'd be a darned sight better off, in spite of the railroad. The course of her life had taken bends and twists that she'd never expected. But she'd learned to cope, and she'd fight with every ounce of her energy to keep Murphy Navigation from bankruptcy.

"Money?" he asked, repeating the word.

She nodded. "If we had any choice, you'd have to find someone else to help build the bridge."

"I see." He rubbed the frown lines between his brows. "At least I know where we stand. All I ask is a fair and competent day's work."

"I never give less." Her reputation as an able riverboat captain might soon be all she had. She wasn't about to jeopardize that because she didn't like the boss. She'd do a good job for the devil himself just for the pride of work well done.

He stood up and hefted the carpetbag by the door, then grabbed his hat from the brass tree and stared at the bullet hole in the crown. "Let's go see what's left of your boat."

She took one last look around, noticing the broken crystal on the floor. Guilt stabbed her square in the chest. In less than an hour she'd shattered a beautiful chandelier and made Swiss cheese of his hat. It bothered her more than she cared to admit. "I'll pay for the damages."

"Never mind that." He poked his finger through the hole in his hat's black crown. "I did like this hat, though. Just got it broken in."

"I'm responsible. I'll make it right."

Green eyes met and held hers, narrowing slightly. "If you insist, I'm sure there's some way you can pay me back." A slow half-smile creased his face, revealing very white teeth below his mustache. Then he was out the door.

Uneasy, she shook her head. She didn't think he was talking about money.

two

"Give me a hand up." Bree curled her fingers over the roof of a structure in the stern of the *River Belle*. They were moored parallel to the rocky shore, and Jeff could see nothing in either direction but winding river and the cottonwoods that grew along it. The sun blazed down, a blinding ball of golden fire in a cloudless blue sky. Sweat trickled between his shoulder blades and wet his shirt, sticking it to his skin.

With his back to the embankment, he examined the wall boards beside her, singed black from the fire. The stench of smoke still clung to them, hovering in the air and clogging his throat with every gust of wind. Three wooden buckets were strewn on the deck as if hastily tossed aside. The desert heat had long since evaporated the water used to extinguish the flames, leaving behind dark, muddy stains.

Bree bent her knees, then impatiently looked over her shoulder. "Come on, Tanner. Give me a boost."

"What the hell . . ." Jeff looked from her to the small cabin she evidently wanted to climb. The top of it was over her head, but he'd have to duck to stand inside.

"I want to make sure the fire didn't weaken the wheelhouse." She grinned at him. "Don't look so worried."

He realized it was the first time he'd seen her smile. Her straight white teeth gleamed, and dirty face or no, the effect dazzled him. He could almost see her tension ease and watched her mistrust melt away. She was at home on her boat, no question about that. Relaxed and in control, completely natural. Not like she'd been in his Pullman. He cupped his hands, and she placed a boot into them, hoisting herself up as he lifted.

"Be careful." He had a disturbing image of her falling through because of the damaged boards and breaking her fool neck. He was glad he'd told Slonneger that the railroad would no longer require his services.

She crawled around, carefully studying the roof, unknowingly giving him a fascinating view of her shapely derriere enfolded in the worn, soft denim. The pitch and roll of her rounded backside mesmerized him until he wasn't sure he could lift a finger to help if she did fall. When she moved from his line of vision, he released the breath he'd been holding.

On deck Jeff braced his boots wide apart against the dip and sway of the surging river beneath. The small, flat-bottomed boat seemed flimsy protection against the swift current farther out in the muddy Colorado. He judged the total length of the craft at about sixty feet, including her sternwheel. She was about twelve to thirteen feet across the beam. Toward the bow, a boiler and smokestack left little deck space on either side.

"She's sound." Bree sat on the edge of the cabin with her legs dangling over the side. Her streaked white shirt had gathered more soot from climbing up the wall, and the hot wind blowing against her molded the cotton to her breasts. She was round and soft in all the right places. B. E. Murphy was a sight to behold.

She started to turn on her belly to slide down.

"Wait." Enough of her monkeyshines, he thought. He put his hands around her small waist and was surprised at her softness. When was the last time he'd held a woman without the constrictions of whalebone and petticoat? His thumbs explored the area below her breasts, and he felt her feminine curves, the ribs that God had given her, not laces and stiff, unforgiving stays.

Directly behind him, the side of the boat gave way to the shore. One false step and they'd be overboard and possibly crushed between the bobbing craft and the unyielding riverbank. He eased her down, very close to his body, and felt her tense as her hands balled into fists on his shoulders. Her slender body, pressed against him from chest to knee, drove the steel barrel of her gun into his abdomen. He'd forgotten about it.

"Let me go." When her boots touched the deck, she pushed against him, and instantly he released her.

She sidestepped him, then braced her feet several inches apart. With her small hands still clenched into fists like a prizefighter, she faced him squarely. Her startling blue eyes narrowed, creasing her forehead with a frown. She obviously didn't trust him, and it was more than just her quarrel with the railroad.

"I guess you want this back." He held her gun out, handle grip first.

She grabbed it, then stared at him questioningly before tucking the barrel in her denims. "Thanks." Her shoulders relaxed as she inclined her head toward the doorway of the cabin. "The wheelhouse seems solid. Some sanding and a coat of paint and I think she'll be good as new."

She moved forward and stepped on the blackened part of the deck, placing all her weight on the circular spot where the fire had apparently started, then spread to the wall of the wheelhouse.

Jeff added his weight to hers. She was slight, not big enough to confirm that the damaged area would hold a man. The burned layer crumbled to ash beneath the combined punishment. He dropped to one knee and pressed the charred wood. It disintegrated into fine black soot beneath his fingers. "Looks like this needs replacing."

She nodded. "*Belle* has a pretty thick hide, but when the

river goes down, she'll need every inch of bottom she can get."

He looked across the boat, at the red-brown water racing past. He knew that as summer gave way to winter, the river would drop to a fraction of what it was now. "I guess come November, you hole up until the spring thaw."

"Yep." She nodded her head emphatically. "Some rivermen claim they can travel upriver on a heavy dew. But I wouldn't try it."

For some reason he was pleased that she didn't take chances. "Glad to hear it."

"*Belle* needs at least twenty-two inches of water."

He blinked and tapped his palm against the side of his head. "You know, I think that gunshot a while ago affected my hearing. I could have sworn you said this boat can run in less than two feet of water."

"Nothin' wrong with your ears. That's exactly what I said. And she can do it with thirty-five tons of freight."

"I heard about this, but I thought it was an exaggeration."

"Rivermen never joke." She looked at his expression and laughed. "The Colorado's dangerous, can't take her lightly. We might brag and stretch the truth from time to time, but we never take anything for granted when our boat's at stake."

"Not so very different from railroad men."

"Maybe, maybe not." She shrugged. "But like I said before, river and railroad don't mix."

"I aim to change that by building the bridge. And I'd best get to it."

"Since Slonneger's drunk as a skunk, you'll have to crew for me. But I can still get you to Hardyville."

He reached into his back pocket and withdrew a freshly laundered handkerchief. Then he leaned over and dipped it into the river before handing the dripping cloth to her.

"What's this for?" Her brows drew together in confusion as she squeezed the excess water from the square.

"Your face. I'd like to have a good look at you."

"Why should you care what I look like?"

"I only have your word that you know how to run this thing," he said, flinging his arm out to indicate the boat. "I'm a gambler, but I'm not stupid. I'd like a little more to go on—like how old you are, how long you've been operating a steamboat. Do you have any credentials?"

"Twenty-one, three years, I took a test and have a license." She wrapped the handkerchief around her neck. "Thanks. That feels good."

Then she pressed the cloth to her face, and when she removed it, one layer of soot was gone. Her skin was smooth and tan, with a sprinkling of freckles across her cheeks. Her turned-up nose was peeling and the newly exposed skin already burned pink. A hazard of working outdoors. The New York ladies would be shocked. But he was intrigued and more interested than he should be. Maybe it had been a mistake to clean her up.

She pulled her hat more firmly down over her black hair. "Stand in the bow and keep watch."

"I never said I was going upriver with you."

"It's a long walk. Without water you won't last long." She looked him up and down, gauging something. "Man your size—about twelve gallons ought to do it. Can you carry that much?"

He gritted his teeth and the muscle in his jaw tensed. "Guess my options are limited."

"Reckon so." Her dark brows drew together like a thunderhead. "Tell me something, Tanner. If you'd known I was a woman, would you have signed that contract?"

He shook his head. Her hand closed around the dirty, black square of cloth that used to be his handkerchief and squeezed until the blood left her fingers.

"Don't get me wrong, I'm sure you know how to run this boat. But this job won't be as easy as going from port to port. We'll be transporting heavy steel girders and beams from one side of the river to the other when the current is as high as it gets. It will require a great deal of physical strength, which frankly, Miss Murphy, you don't have."

Her mouth tightened in a straight line. Her whole body practically vibrated with indignation because she couldn't refute his statement.

She let out a long, slow breath. "Fact is, we still have a contract."

"My agreement is with Murphy Navigation, and you're not the only riverboat captain with the company."

"But I'm the only one . . ."

He held up a hand. "There's nothing you can say to change my mind. Just get me to Hardyville."

She bit her lip and studied the top of a jagged peak across the desert floor, then nodded. "Best settle this later. You'll still have to crew for me. The water's high, so there's not much chance of running aground. But the sandbars are always shifting. The river runs smooth over 'em. If you see that, call out. Tell me which side—port is left, starboard is right. I'll do the rest." She put her hands on her hips and raised a dark, delicate brow. "Think you can handle that, Tanner?"

"Yeah."

"Good. I'll make sure there's enough fuel for the trip, then stoke the boiler."

"Aye, aye, Captain." He saluted and started to the front of the boat. The swift-moving river current caught his eye, and he studied it for a moment. "I'm a strong swimmer. I could always jump overboard and get to shore if necessary."

She scowled at him.

"That was a joke, Murphy." He pulled his hat lower and started to turn away.

"Hey, Tanner. You married?"

Surprise lifted his brows as he stared at her bland expression. "No. Why?"

She shrugged. "Just wanted to know if there'd be anyone to claim the body," she said, leaning over the side to gaze at the fast-moving muddy water. "That is if there's a body to find. Get caught up in that current, could wind up in the Gulf of California." Then she grinned.

He smoothed his mustache. "I thought rivermen never joke."

"Who's joking?"

Her laughter carried to him as she bent to a stack of wood in the middle of the boat. She opened the metal door of the boiler and started tossing the split logs inside. When the fire burned hot enough, she went to the stern and pulled in the plank, then released the lines holding the boat fast.

After Bree entered the wheelhouse, the deck beneath Tanner's boots vibrated as the boat sputtered to life. A plume of black smoke sprinkled with sparks poured from the solitary stack as the engine settled into a rhythmic chukety-pow.

Jeff watched the distance from the embankment widen as more and more of the reddish-brown river separated him from solid land. Pushed by the paddle wheel churning in the stern, the bow of the boat sliced through the muddy water on its journey upstream. He turned his face into the wind and watched for sandbars, just as he'd been told.

When the town came into view, Bree headed the boat toward shore, then caught a glimpse of her passenger. Casually standing in the bow, one foot braced on the edge of the boat, he leaned forward, his shoulders as wide as a mountain, his pose very male. He looked as if he'd spent years on a steamboat. The idea irked her and she thought about running aground, just for the sheer pleasure of seeing him pitch headfirst into the river. Good sense prevailed, and she brought the craft parallel to the bank instead. She secured the bowline to an iron ring on the west shore, then looked at him.

"You can open your eyes now, Tanner."

"On the contrary, Captain. I never shut them. Had to be able to see where to jump . . . just in case." He grinned at her.

She tried to ignore his teasing. The games and undercurrents rippling between her and Tanner made her uncomfortable. "Do you want to go to your office first or the boardinghouse?"

"Office."

She nodded. "I'll show you where it is."

He grabbed his carpetbag from the wheelhouse. When he came out, he watched her fill the last of the three buckets and set it beside the others on deck.

"Expecting another fire?" He lifted one eyebrow.

"I'll shoot the next person who brings liquor or smokes aboard my boat." She eyed his bag suspiciously.

"I swear there's nothing in here but shirts, pants, under—"

"I believe you," she said quickly.

"So what are the buckets for?"

"None of your concern. Let's go."

Jeff followed her across the plank. She was all business, direct and to the point. Did she ever flirt? Did she know how? He'd never met a woman who didn't cozy up to a man and bat her lashes. And Bree Murphy had the longest, thickest lashes he'd ever seen. What surprised him was that she didn't seem to be the slightest bit interested in using her feminine wiles.

He'd heard that men outnumbered women five to one in the Arizona Territory. She must have them underfoot like locusts in a wheat field. Maybe she was already spoken for, though he hadn't seen a ring on her finger. Or maybe she was putting on an act. Females had their methods. Appearing disinterested and dressing like a man might be her way of getting noticed.

With a start, he realized it was working. He couldn't remember the last time he'd spent so much time trying to figure out a woman. They'd always plainly shown their feelings—never made a secret of their attraction to him.

His wealth made him a prize catch, and that made him cautious.

A hundred yards to the left of the *River Belle*, Jeff saw the ferry dock. Straight ahead a well-worn path carved the mesquite-covered bluff in two. They tramped through the rocky sand, and at the top, he got his first good look at the town.

Hardyville, set about three hundred yards from the river, wasn't quite what he'd expected the bustling center of trade on the Colorado River to look like. One row of wooden buildings lined the street parallel to the river. Straight ahead stood an adobe building with a sign above that said "Murphy Navigation Company." To the right of that he saw Cactus Kate's Saloon. The post office, a restaurant, and a mercantile continued down the line to the livery stable and harness shop.

He propped his boot on a rock, then rested his forearm on his knee and looked around.

Bree studied his slow, easy smile and tried not to notice the way his mustache gave him a rugged, rakish—and dangerous—air. Was his dark brown hair as soft as it looked? His eyes crinkled easily at the corners as if the smile were frequent and familiar. Most of all, as she looked at him, she fought the strange sensation in her stomach, like the way it dropped to her toes when *Belle* rushed hell-bent for leather over the river's rapids.

She wanted to smile back at him, tempted to let her guard down just this once. But she didn't dare. She wasn't about to get friendly with a railroad man. Especially one like Tanner who could charm the sting from a scorpion's tail with that lazy grin of his.

"Nice place y'got here." There was a teasing edge to his voice.

He was echoing her words in the Pullman. Judging by that railroad car, Hardyville wasn't the kind of place he hung his hat—even one with a bullet hole in the crown. Guilt stabbed through her at the thought of what she'd done, but she pushed it away. He was here to build that blasted bridge, and it didn't much matter to her whether or not the accommodations were to his liking.

She pointed straight ahead to the structure between the big storage building on her left and the saloon. "I fixed up a small office in Murphy Navigation for you. Figured it was either that or Cactus Kate's. The steamboat company's a lot quieter."

"Appreciate it."

She shrugged. "You're payin' for it."

"So I am."

She turned and scanned the river in both directions. "Cap's not back from Ehrenberg yet. He should be here before long."

She tried to keep the anxiety out of her voice, but it wasn't easy. The well-known knot of worry pulled tightly in her abdomen, then settled in like an unwanted visitor fixin' to spend the evening.

With her hand shading her eyes, she studied the position of the sun. It would be dark in a couple of hours. A good steamboat captain knew better than to be on the river then, and her father was the best. Unless he'd been drinking.

If he stopped for a whiskey before he started back . . . But he'd promised her he wouldn't. If only Charles weren't with him. Her stepbrother didn't have the instincts of a riverman. If financial circumstances hadn't forced her to accept the railroad contract, she'd be crewing the *Elizabeth*. But if wishes were horses, beggars would ride. She drew in a deep breath, then let it out slowly before walking the short distance to the office.

"Here it is." She opened the door for Tanner and followed him inside.

The building was narrow, twenty-five feet deep and divided into four rooms. The steamship company occupied the ones on the left and the remaining two on the opposite side of the hall were rented by a merchant.

She stopped at the second door. "You'll be using my . . . this office."

Bree resented giving anything up for him. But as she'd said, he was paying for it. She recalled cleaning her things out of the scratched and scarred desk against the far wall, and the almost overwhelming temptation to leave him a snake or lizard in one of the drawers. Nothing deadly, just a reminder that he was in Arizona Territory now. Only the fact that she couldn't stand creepy, crawly things had spared him.

The leather chair she'd ordered all the way from San Francisco sat in front of the desk. She couldn't imagine how Tanner was going to fit his big muscular body into her chair. The thought of him squeezing himself uncomfortably into that space pleased her immensely.

Tanner ambled over to the desk and sat on the corner. He sniffed, then opened the middle drawer and looked inside. He pulled out a bar of soap and grinned. "A welcoming present?" His smile broadened when he put the bar to his nose and inhaled. "Lavender. My favorite. That was real thoughtful."

"It's mine." She grabbed the soap from his outstretched hand, and instantly the fragrance of flowers replaced the odors of stale cigar smoke and dust. "Riley must have put it there for me," she said.

"Who's Riley?" His green eyes narrowed.

"A friend."

"If that's your desk, then this must be your office?"

She nodded. "It's yours now."

"Where will you go?"

"I'll share space with Cap."

"There's no need. I'll be dividing my time between here and the bridge site. We can both use it."

"No." The thought of being cooped up in here with him was more than she could stand.

"If I say we're going to share the place, then that's the way it's going to be."

. As easy as that, he expected his command would be obeyed. Well, she was accustomed to giving orders, too. She reckoned he wasn't used to dealing with the rivermen, and that was just one more in a growing list of things that they needed to get straight. But the stubborn set of his square jaw told her this wasn't the time to argue with him.

Tanner opened his carpetbag and pulled out a photograph depicting five people, then placed it on the desk. The simple act made him seem human. A man with flesh-and-blood ties to the race and not just someone with a steel heart. She didn't want to be interested in him or wonder who the people were to him. But her curiosity got the better of her.

She nodded toward the desk. "Who are they?"

He picked up the framed picture and smiled fondly. "My family." He pointed to a man with graying hair and a mustache. "My father, Joe. Mother says his name is boring, always calls him Tanner." When he met her gaze, the amusement in his eyes told her he was thinking that she called him that, too. Well, Jefferson *was* a mouthful. "She's partial to strong names. My younger brother Jack here is Jackson Andrew." He paused and stared at her.

She thought for a minute. "You mean as in the President, only reversed?"

"Smart girl. And our little sister is Cady Elizabeth." He waited again.

"Elizabeth Cady Stanton?"

"The suffragette, right."

She moved closer beside him to study the formal portrait. His arm brushed against her shoulder, and a tingling sensation sluiced all the way to her fingertips. She didn't want to think about that, or the warmth that spread through her. Taking a step away, she crossed her arms over her breasts. "I think I'd like your mother. What's her name?"

"Frances. She'd like you, too."

"What about your name?" In spite of herself, Bree was intrigued by this family, especially the handsome man beside her. "Since you're not called Benedict or Arnold, I can't imagine who she named you after."

"My middle name is Thomas."

"Thomas Jefferson. Hmm. You have a powerful lot to live up to."

He replaced the frame on the desk and stared at it for a moment. "That I do. What about your family?"

She hesitated. "I have an old tintype taken when my father was courting my mother. . . ."

She walked over to the wooden file cabinet she'd pushed into a corner and very carefully pulled out a ragged-edged copper-colored daguerreotype. Holding it gently by the corner, she stared at the likeness, and a lump settled in the back of her throat. After running her index finger over the face, she handed it to him. "Mama died when I was thirteen."

Jeff took it from her. "She was a beautiful woman. You look a lot like her."

Bree touched the front of her hair, the wild strands that wouldn't stay put.

For an instant she met his gaze and her cheeks burned. Then she looked down at the tintype and brushed a nonexistent particle of dust from it. He'd called her beautiful, in a backhanded sort of way. But all the same, the compliment kindled a glow in her belly that spread to her arms and legs and settled in her chest. "There's just me and Cap now. Sort of. He remarried."

"Must have been hard on you."

She shrugged. "Mary's all right, means well. It's her son . . ."

"You have a stepbrother?"

Why in the world was she telling him this? All the man did was put out a picture of his family and she was blabbing her life story. "Charles is with Cap on the *Elizabeth*."

He snapped his fingers. "The *E* stands for Elizabeth."

He grinned and placed the tintype beside the one of his own family. "Breanne Elizabeth, a beautiful name for a beautiful—"

"It was my mother's middle name."

"My sister's, too."

Bree reached over and moved her mother's likeness to the other side of the desk. He smiled and nodded as if he knew what she was thinking. The idea that he could read her thoughts made her uneasy, and she lifted her chin a fraction. They *were* worlds apart. He'd best not forget it.

He pointed to the scented bar still in her hand. "I don't mind if you keep your soap in our desk."

"Feel free to borrow it, Tanner. The girls in Cactus Kate's are loco about lavender. Could be you'll have to beat 'em off with a stick."

His look was lazy and amused. Green eyes flicked over her from neck to knee. "I'll keep that in mind—if the need arises."

Angry heat burned her cheeks. His implication embarrassed her, and she was fresh out of clever retorts. He was the most infuriating man she'd ever met. One of these days she was going to shake him out of that confident calm. It might not be tomorrow or the next day, but she'd do it, or die trying.

A faraway sound caught her attention, and she opened the window above the desk.

"Something wrong?" he asked sharply.

She cupped a hand to her ear and froze. "Did you hear that?"

"What?" He listened intently. "I don't hear anything."

A part of Bree always waited for the distinctive noises of the other steamboat. When Cap was especially late and she listened hard, she often mistook the wind for the swish of the boat's paddle wheel.

"Thought I heard Cap coming. Guess not." She looked at Tanner's shirtfront. Black streaks decorated the once spotless material. "You're a mess."

He looked down at his chest, then back up at her with a raised brow. "Yeah. Wonder how that happened, Murphy."

He knew as well as she did how he'd gotten dirty. If he hadn't held her so close when he'd helped her from the top of the wheelhouse, he'd still be clean as a whistle. It was his own blasted fault. But she remembered the feel of his big hard body next to hers, the corded strength and rippling muscles as he'd lifted her down. Next to him, she'd felt small and feminine. No man had ever made her feel so much like a woman. She'd been as much afraid of that as the dangerous flicker in his eyes at the contact or what she thought he might do next.

A sound carried to her again, and she held herself stone still to listen. This time she was sure.

"What is it?" Tanner asked.

"Cap's back."

Relief coursed through her. But along with that was an uneasy feeling. As much as she disliked the ever-expanding railroad, soon she'd have to do battle with Tanner for her right to work on the bridge project. She wasn't looking forward to that. He seemed like a man who didn't alter his course once he'd set it. Somehow, she had to change his mind.

three

Boots rang in the hall before two men entered the office. Jeff pushed his hat away from the edge of the desk, then turned his back to it and watched Bree throw herself into the arms of a ruddy-faced, gray-haired man. Ten to one that was her father. Not very big, he was only a couple inches above her height. The other man was taller, younger, somewhere closer to Bree's age, and wiry. Jeff didn't usually make quick judgments about a man, but something about this one stoked his suspicious nature into full steam.

The two men stood in front of him, with the shorter one in the middle and Bree to his right. The smell of sweat and ash and dust filled the room, and Jeff wiped his brow. The warm breeze from the open window died, and the added body heat made the room stifling.

"You must be Jeff Tanner. Sean Murphy," the short, beefy man said, holding out his wide, work-roughened hand. His booming voice bounced off the four walls, and Jeff was certain they could hear him all the way to Cactus Kate's.

Jeff shook the man's outstretched palm. "A pleasure, Mr. Murphy."

"Everybody calls me Sean. I see she got you here in one piece." He glanced at his daughter. "What happened to *Belle*?"

"Fire, Cap. I told you Slonneger was trouble."

35

"Not anymore," Jeff said, folding his arms across his chest. "He's not with the railroad anymore. The boat will be fixed good as new. I gave my word to your daughter."

Sean's thick white brows drew together as he contemplated the words, then nodded. "Fair enough." He clapped a leathery hand on the shoulder of the man to his left. "This is my stepson, Charles Perkins."

Jeff assessed the man dressed in black trousers, shirt, vest, and hat. Only the shiny silver band around its crown disrupted the severity of his appearance. Perkins removed his hat to brush the sweat from his brow. Slicked straight back from his forehead, his blond hair was tied at his nape with a thin leather thong.

"Tanner."

"Charlie." Jeff held out his palm, and the other man hesitated a second before shaking it.

Jeff's father had always said you could judge a man by the strength of his handshake, but Jeff questioned the reasoning now. Perkins's grip was firm and sure. It was his eyes that gave Jeff pause. Pale blue, almost colorless, there was something sneaky and underhanded in his gaze.

"Now that the howdys are over, why don't we have that whiskey we didn't have time for in Ehrenberg?" Charlie smiled at Sean, then flicked a look in Jeff's direction. "Care to join us, Mr. Tanner?"

"Your mother will be waiting supper," Bree said.

"She won't mind. A few drinks won't hurt anything. You must be parched, Sean."

The older man licked his lips and glanced at the door.

Bree threaded her arm through her father's and looked up at him nervously. "Cap, there's something we need to get straight. Tanner doesn't think I can handle taking heavy loads of supplies back and forth across the river at the bridge site. I thought maybe you could set him straight."

The older man looked at him sternly. "Truth is, Mr. Tanner—"

"Jeff, please."

"All right, Jeff. She's as good as most men on the river, better than some. But now that you mention it, I've been thinkin'. Maybe it *would* be better if I take the railroad job. Bree, you and Charles can handle the rest of the work on the river."

If he hadn't been looking directly at Bree, Jeff would have missed the almost imperceptible shake of her head. Instead of standing between the two men, she'd deliberately moved to the outside, next to her father.

"Can't Charlie work with me?" Jeff asked.

Sean shook his head. "He's not licensed to captain a steamboat." He stepped forward and took Jeff's arm, leading him across the room and out of earshot. "Jeff, I think it'd be best if I work with you. Bree's just a might touchy when it comes to the railroad. She wouldn't say anything, mind you—"

Jeff lifted a brow but decided to keep his mouth shut. No point in shattering a man's illusions. "Do you think she can handle the job?"

"She's smart as a whip. Been on the river with me since she was fourteen and learned faster than anyone I ever saw. Works hard, too." He shrugged. "Decision's yours."

Jeff turned back and studied Bree and her stepbrother. He didn't much like the way the other man stared at her, like a wolf sizing up his next meal. Bree's hands fluttered constantly, nervously, always coming back to the gun grip sticking out of her denims. Finally she crossed her arms beneath her breasts and looked away from Charlie.

Jeff recalled the look in her eye when she'd told him of her father's remarriage. She'd only said three words concerning her misgivings about the union, "It's her son." He remembered the way her blue eyes had darkened nearly as black as precious sapphires. He hadn't been sure then, but he knew the emotion now. Fear. He'd bet money on it.

As much as she disliked the railroad's intrusion in the Territory, she'd rather help him build the bridge than work with her stepbrother. Only hours ago she'd held off him and Slonneger, both of them twice her size, with only a pistol. Yet she was afraid of Charlie.

Jeff knew his reasons for wanting a man to do the job were sensible and sound. He considered her fine-boned frame and had a disturbing image of shifting girders and beams crushing her. Every business instinct he had objected to having her on the project. This was his chance to solidify his reputation.

He was young compared to his partners. But he'd had the money and they'd needed the capital. It had taken several years and some fast talking to convince them his idea was a good one. He'd barely managed to win their approval and knew they were still skeptical, waiting for a false step.

One slip-up and he'd be relegated to a passive role in running the railroad. This bridge was a daring and dangerous undertaking. If he succeeded, he'd have the power to do whatever he wanted. If he failed . . . The thought of a silent partnership grated on him.

He moved closer to the desk, and Bree looked up. "So what's the decision, Tanner?"

"I think the choice is pretty clear, little sister. And I've always wanted to work with you." Charlie smiled.

Jeff watched her move a fraction of an inch away from Charlie. Something deep in his gut responded. His protective instincts stirred to life, rusty and unfamiliar. He knew what he had to do. It made about as much sense as spitting into the wind.

He looked down at Bree. "You can try it."

Though she didn't make a sound, Jeff sensed her sigh of relief. Her shoulders sagged slightly as the tension trickled away. "Thanks, Tanner."

"Don't make me regret it."

She nodded. "It's time to get you settled at the boardinghouse. Last I heard, it was nearly full."

"What about that drink, Sean?" Charles looked at the

older man, then his glance slid to Jeff, swirling with hostility.

Bree protectively hooked her arm through her father's. "Your mother's probably been cooking all afternoon, and if we don't get there soon, it will be ruined."

"She's right, Charles. We better hightail it up there before your mama has our hide."

"One drink, Sean. I can handle Mother."

The setting sun glinted off the younger man's silver hatband, and Jeff took a step forward. He could see what was happening, and he didn't like it one damn bit. "Another time, Charlie."

The younger man shrugged. "Sean likes a whiskey or two at the end of a trip."

"Not always," Bree said, tossing her braid over her shoulder. With her arm still looped through her father's, she pulled him out the door.

Charlie shook his head slightly as he stared after her, his eyes fixed on the feminine sway of her backside. He rubbed the back of his hand across his mouth. "She's somethin'. Ain't she?"

Jeff picked up his hat and studied the hole in the crown. "Yeah. Somethin'."

Jeff wiped his boots on the porch mat, then followed Bree and her father into the adobe boardinghouse. The front door needed a coat of whitewash, and the wood showing through was gray, all the moisture sucked out. The outside stairway leading to the second story was in pretty much the same condition. When he closed the front door, the knob wiggled in his hand.

"Mary?" Sean's voice reverberated off the white adobe walls. "Wonder where that woman's got to. Bree, you show Jeff around, and I'll find her." The thump of his boots on the wooden floor faded as he headed down the entry hall that ran the length of the downstairs.

Bree pointed to a room on her left, and the foot of a bed

showed through the partially open door. "That's the master bedroom. Guest rooms are upstairs." She indicated the stairway straight ahead, then pointed across the hall. "Parlor, dining room, and kitchen are all on that side."

Jeff poked his head into the sitting room. Heavy velvet curtains covered windows that faced the front of the house. Rays of sunlight shone through the material where it was coming apart. A brocade-covered settee hugged the far wall, and the low pine table in front of it couldn't hide the threadbare condition.

He looked past the open French doors at the far end of the room. A long pine table surrounded by eight chairs filled the center of the dining room while a sideboard sat against the wall. His gaze shifted to Bree, standing in the center of the hall with her hands in the front pockets of her denim trousers. "This is nice."

"Used to be. Cap built it in seventy-five, before the railroad came through. It was a showplace then, when everything was new. Now . . ." She shrugged. "We take in boarders. Your room's upstairs. Follow me."

"I'm right behind you."

A runner covered the dark wood treads, and beneath his hand Jeff felt grooves and splinters on the matching banister. Slowly he climbed each step, staring over his shoulder as he pictured the place brand new. It would take time and money to maintain this house the way it was meant to be, especially out here. From what she'd said, the Murphys had neither. Guilt gnawed at the edge of his mind. But he crushed the feeling before it took hold.

Progress was inevitable, and the railroad was part of it. Power and profits were the keys; people had to let go of the old and find a place to fit in the new. He couldn't be accountable for every one of them.

When they reached the landing, he accompanied her down the long hall to the last door on the right. She opened it. "This is your room. It better do. The rest are all taken."

Jeff peeked over her head, pleased to find the accommodations clean and neat. He walked in and dropped his carpetbag on the pink and blue quilt covering the bed. Centered on the long wall the four-poster faced a matching dark pine armoire. In the corner sat a wooden rocking chair and a table with several worn books scattered on top. Lace curtains allowed the evening breeze in, and the smell of lavender floated around him.

"This'll do fine." The familiar scent made him vaguely uneasy. "Where's your room?"

She leaned a slender shoulder against the doorframe and looked at the toe of her boot before meeting his eyes. "You're in it."

He shook his head. "I can't take your room. You just said there was nothing else available."

"Don't worry about me, Tanner. I'll find somethin'." She shrugged and almost smiled.

"What? Cactus Kate's?"

"Nope. Too noisy. Hard to sleep."

He walked to the bed and picked up his carpetbag. "I'll find someplace else."

"You can't," she said sharply, pushing herself away from the door.

"I sure as hell can. Watch me." He started to move past her. She put her hand on his arm to stop him. He looked down at the slender fingers that gripped his sleeve. There was something desperate about the gesture, something that tugged at his conscience.

"I'll sleep on *Belle*."

He shook his head. "Not good enough. A woman alone on a boat in a three-saloon town. Forget it."

"I do it all the time. I can take care of myself."

He pulled himself up to his full height and towered over her. "That's debatable."

"I have my gun."

"And a lot of good it will do if some drunk gets the

drop on you when you're asleep. You'd never get a shot off."

He started out the door, his boots scraping on the wood floor. He felt both of her hands on his arm this time and stopped again. That's twice she'd touched him in the last two minutes. Either she'd had a sudden change of heart about railroad men, or something was going on that he didn't understand. Sucking in a long breath of air, he turned and let it out slowly.

"Tanner . . ." She released her hold, then hesitated.

He shifted his bag to the other hand. "What?"

"Don't go. Please." She spoke the last word through clenched teeth as if it had been wrung from her by force. Looking up at him, her blue eyes flashed.

He stood captivated by the clear, beautiful blue depths. "Why? Give me one good reason."

She bit her lip and crossed her arms over her chest, then met his gaze squarely. "We need the money."

Pride stiffened her spine straight as a fireplace poker. He knew the truth of her words. He'd seen the proof in the run-down condition of the boardinghouse. The thought of her on that boat unprotected went against his better judgment. But part of him felt somehow obligated to help. He noticed the rigid set of her shoulders, the slight lifting of her chin. Offering money was out of the question.

"There must be someplace in the boardinghouse for you to sleep. What about Charlie's room? Let him take the boat."

She looked at the room next to hers and something crept into her eyes, something he couldn't name. He thought she paled some. "Charles always stays in his room."

Her stepbrother's selfishness made him angry. "You mean no one's asked him to give it up?"

"No one's asked me. I *prefer* to sleep on *Belle*."

"Why?"

Her gaze flicked to her brother's door. "Fresh air." She

reached out to take his bag. "Besides, I'm not really alone. Riley watches out for me."

He brushed past her and put the carpetbag back on the bed. She followed and stopped beside him. "That's the second time you mentioned Riley. Who is he?"

"A friend."

An unpleasant feeling settled in his gut, something he didn't want to examine too closely. But he couldn't suppress his curiosity about this friend she was so fond of. "That's what you said before. How do you know he'll look after you? What makes you so sure?"

"My father saved his life."

"Oh?" He crossed his arms over his chest and waited.

"Riley used to prospect for gold in the hills, still does when he's not looking out for me. He came into town once with a pretty fair amount of gold dust. A couple of no-good drifters tried to separate him from it, and Cap stepped in to even the odds." She shrugged and leaned against the post at the end of the bed. "He's been around ever since."

"I still don't like it. If he can't protect himself from a couple of drifters, how's he going to take care of you?" He lifted a brow in question.

Before she could answer, a tall thin woman entered the room. She smelled of fresh-baked bread and furniture polish. Strands of gray-streaked blond hair clung to her damp forehead, and she pushed them away. "Welcome, Mr. Tanner. I'm Mary Murphy. I do apologize for not being here to greet you when you arrived. I was at the general store getting some things for supper."

"Glad to meet you, Mrs. Murphy." Jeff removed his hat and nodded politely. "No pardon necessary. No way you could've known when I'd arrive. Besides, Bree has taken good care of me." He poked his finger through the hole in his hat before tossing it on the bed. Beside him, he felt Bree stiffen, and when he glanced at her, the embarrassed flush in her cheeks made him smile.

Mary Murphy's face was flushed, too, probably from her trip to the store in the late afternoon heat. Just below the fine lines around her left eye, a star-shaped scar stood out red and angry against the blush. The mark didn't look like a recent injury. But he wondered about it all the same.

"I see Bree has acquainted you with your room. It's one of the nicest we have. If there's anything else you need, just let me know." Mary's faded blue eyes were friendly and her smile shy. "I do hate to run, but dinner needs work yet. We'll eat when Charles gets here. Sean said he's having a drink at the saloon." She frowned for a moment, then the expression vanished as she looked at her stepdaughter. "Bree, you're a sight, child. Why don't you clean up and put on that pretty cotton dress your father brought you? The last time you wore it, Charles couldn't take his eyes off you."

Beside him, Jeff heard her soft intake of breath. When he looked, her knuckles on the spindle post were white.

"I'll see if I can find it, Mary."

"It's hanging in the master bedroom closet with the rest of your things." The woman smiled at Jeff. "I'll see you at dinner, Mr. Tanner."

"I'm looking forward to it," he said. His stomach rumbled, reminding him he hadn't eaten since late morning. If Charlie didn't get here soon, there wouldn't be anything left for him, and Jeff found the thought greatly satisfying.

When the woman was gone, he turned to Bree and laid a hand on his carpetbag. "It's time we settled the question of where you're going to sleep."

She lifted her shoulders slightly. "It *is* settled. Why are you making such a fuss about this, Tanner?"

He wished he knew the answer to that. But from the minute she'd aimed her pistol and shot his hat, nothing about Breanne Murphy had been clear to him. "My mother taught me that a gentleman never takes a lady's bed."

She grinned. "You mean there's rules for a situation like this?"

He smiled back. "Just a general one and Mother would tan me good if I broke it. *I'll* sleep on the boat."

Her eyes opened wide in shock, then she laughed out loud. "You? Whatever will you do without your soft mattress and feather pillow?"

"I'll have you know that I used to lay track for the railroad." His eyes narrowed. Her insinuation that he'd never seen a hardened, outdoor life irritated her. He recalled the endless months of backbreaking labor, working fourteen-hour days.

"You? Laid track?" Her look was scornful. "Why? Spying on the employees? Makin' sure none of 'em were doggin' it?"

"I needed the money for my last year of college."

Surprise lifted her dark, delicate brows. "But you're rich."

"I wasn't always. My mother's father had money. When she chose to marry a struggling merchant, he disowned her." His mouth tightened briefly. "He wouldn't loan me the money to finish my education, so I got a job with the railroad."

He'd made it sound simple, but the old bitterness stirred and stretched behind his breastbone when he remembered his mother's humiliation at the hands of her own father. She'd never have asked him for anything for herself, but her children were something else again. And the selfish old bastard had turned her away, his only child. It was the only time he'd seen her cry. Jeff could stand anything but the sight of a woman's tears.

So he'd gone to work. Railroads crisscrossed the country like stitches on a brawler's face. Getting a job had been easy. He clenched his fist as he recalled the blisters on his hands from swinging a sledgehammer to drive the thick spikes into the steel rails, raw spots so sore he could hardly hold the wooden handle. He remembered aching muscles, hurting in places he didn't even know he had until he pulled himself out of his bedroll. But he'd stuck with it, wouldn't give the old man the satisfaction of seeing him quit.

The experience had hardened him, inside and out. Grueling physical labor and living outdoors held no concern for him. And he'd show this smug little miss that she wasn't the only one who knew how to work.

"Well, Tanner, you're just full of surprises. If you weren't born to money, someday you'll have to tell me who you robbed to buy the railroad. I don't have time right now." She turned on her heel and headed for the door. In the entry she stopped and looked back, hugging the doorjamb from breast to knee. "We have an important guest for dinner, and I've been ordered to spruce up for the occasion." She started to leave, then poked her head in the room. "By the way, the mattress is pretty comfortable—mostly—but watch out for that spring on the left side." Then she was gone.

He'd never met a woman who left him speechless or got the upper hand, or made him so furious he wanted to throttle her. By God, if she wanted to sleep on that damned glorified raft, he wouldn't stop her.

But he looked at the bed, and his anger slipped away like a fool's fortune. He pictured her curled up on the soft mattress and wondered what she slept in. A cotton nightrail trimmed with lace at the sleeves and neck? No, she didn't seem like the lace type, although she was the only woman he'd ever met who wasn't. Maybe she wore nothing.

Sweat popped out on his forehead and he swallowed hard as he scanned the length of the quilt. God almighty. He'd spent more time wondering about Miss Breanne Murphy than any other female he'd ever known—and he'd only known her for a day. She wasn't his kind of woman, and he intended to put her out of his mind, starting now.

Bree leaned her back against the river side of *Belle*'s wheelhouse and felt the dry wood splinters pulling at her dress. She stared at the sky. It was like a blanket of gold dust with an embroidered crescent moon. There wasn't enough light to reflect on the water, and she could only see the ripples of current from the soft glow of her lantern, shining through the window behind her.

She turned her face into the warm breeze and closed her eyes, savoring the pleasant sensation. It was good to be here, and she was glad she'd refused to let Tanner stay in her stead. What was it about him that made her bristle so?

She was ashamed of herself now. Especially since he'd agreed to let her work with him on the bridge project. No man had ever treated her like a lady, and her confusion had made her lash out. Conscience advised an apology for her rudeness; pride dug in its heels. Pride won out.

He was here to build the bridge, nothing more. When the job was done, he'd be gone and she'd never have to put up with Jefferson Tanner again. Good riddance.

But would that truly be cause to celebrate? She'd found herself watching him at dinner. He'd charmed her stepmother outrageously, politely held Mary's chair and complimented her cooking until she thought the woman would swoon. And he'd hardly looked in her own direction, never even said a word about her dress. Damn his highfalutin hide!

But hell was too grand for the likes of him. The only good thing about finishing that bridge would be that he'd go away. But so would their business. If only he'd leave the river be. If only she'd never laid eyes on him.

She heard the crunch of rocks on the embankment, and the hair at her nape prickled with apprehension. The sound of sliding stones and sand carried to her on the wind as someone came closer. Whoever it was made enough noise for a herd of jackasses, obviously making no effort at stealth. That should have made her feel better, but fingers of fear slithered over her scalp. Reaching into the wheelhouse, she picked up her gun and cocked it.

Boots thumped on the gangplank, and when the boat

dipped, she was certain her visitor was a big man. She heard his heavy breathing, felt his hesitation to catch his breath after climbing down the bluff. Her gun hand shook, and she gripped the handle with her other to steady it. She waited.

"Bree? Where are you?" The voice was familiar. Deep tones washed over her and sent her jitters packing as her shoulders sagged with relief.

Then anger replaced nerves.

Tanner! That mangy, two-bit tenderfoot had frightened her half to death.

"What in blue blazes are you doing here?" She rounded the wheelhouse and crossed the boat's beam to face him. Just a step away, she could smell cigar smoke on his clothes and something else, something masculine that she'd come to identify as the man-scent of him. Goose bumps skittered down her arms, and her legs felt weak as a newborn colt's. She released the gun's hammer and replaced the pistol in the wheelhouse.

"I could've killed you." Her words were hardly more than a breath of wind.

"I'm glad you didn't." He turned his head and searched the boat from one side to the other. "Where's Riley?" His tone was mocking.

"He's around. Somewhere."

"Somewhere wouldn't do you a bit of good if my intentions had been less than honorable."

"I was ready."

"So I noticed." In the lantern light she saw his white teeth flash. "But at least you didn't shoot at me this time. I must be making progress."

There was more truth in his words than she cared to admit. "What do you want, Tanner?"

"I came down to make sure you were all right."

"I was just fine till you got here."

"What is it about me that bothers you?" His husky voice sent heat to every part of her.

"Not a thing. You just spooked me, is all."

He shoved his hands in his pockets and looked up at the stars. "Nice night. It's cooler down here by the river. I can see why you wanted to sleep outdoors."

Comfort was only part of the reason, but he already knew more than she liked. She wasn't about to tell him anything else. Pressing against the wheelhouse, she put her hands on the wood behind her to cushion her back, then crossed one ankle over the other. She felt his gaze on her, studying her, then he moved beside her in an exact imitation of her position. Their shoulders brushed, and she could feel the regular rise and fall of his chest, hear his even breathing. Her lungs felt about ready to burst, and she took a deep draft of air.

Silence stretched between them. Only the gurgling of the water where the boat's side interrupted its flow broke the quiet. Both of them stared at the sky as if it were the most fascinating sight they'd ever seen.

Bree's nerves pulled as tight as a fiddle string. She felt obligated to say something, but shyness gripped her in an unyielding vise. If he'd been a riverman, or a prospector, or someone from around these parts, she could have found as many topics of conversation as there were stars in the sky. But he was a rich Easterner and she had nothing in common with him. She closed her eyes for a second. Please go away, she prayed.

He cleared his throat. "Nice night."

She looked over at him. "You already said that."

"Oh." He shifted and crossed his arms over his chest. "But it really is pleasant."

"I know."

She looked out over the river and clamped her lips tightly together. Without encouragement, maybe he'd leave her be. But the air between them hummed with electricity. She felt it as surely as she felt the warm breeze on her face, the rocking of the boat from the river's current.

"Why is it that we have nothing to say to each other unless we're fighting?" His voice was husky.

Because we're different as night and day, she thought. "Got me, Tanner. Why do you think that is?"

"Can't say why for sure, but I think it's more than just the bridge."

"Oh?"

"Yeah. You're afraid of something."

She pushed herself away from the wooden wall and stood in front of him. "I'm not afraid of you."

"Then maybe you're afraid of this."

Before she knew what was happening, he took hold of her upper arms and pulled her to him. Every instinct cried out in fear, pleaded for escape. But his fingers were like iron, his chest beneath her palms as wide and solid as the walls of the Grand Canyon. He lowered his head and touched his mouth gently to hers. His lips were soft, undemanding.

He raised his head and turned her so that the lantern illuminated her profile. His back faced the riverbank as he studied her, leaving his own features in shadow. Ever so slowly, his hands moved up and down her bare arms, the friction creating sparks that warmed her body from head to toe. Her heart fluttered wildly, and only a fraction of the fear remained. Somehow she knew he wouldn't ask more than she was willing to give.

He touched his mouth to hers again. Her hands closed into fists against his chest, but she didn't push him away. In her palms she squeezed the material of his shirt. His wiry mustache tickled her upper lip, and shivers of excitement broke free and crept over her breasts, settling in her belly. Her blood raced through her veins and pounded in her ears until she felt light-headed. She'd never known kissing a man could be so pleasurable. The last time, her only time, had been. . .

Suddenly she felt his body tense and he jerked his mouth away from hers as a voice from out of the darkness called out to him: "Take your hands off her, or I'll blow you away quicker'n a tumbleweed in a tornado."

four

There was no mistaking the hard, deadly double-barreled shotgun jabbing him between the shoulder blades. The owner's hoarse, whispery voice had sent chills down Jeff's spine. In the air around him the odor of sweat blended with whiskey and cigarette smoke.

Jeff took exception to a gun in his back, but if he tried anything, there was a better than even chance Bree would get hurt. That left him no choice. Lifting his hands from her shoulders, he raised his arms high to signal he'd gotten the point. All he could do was buy some time, start the gunman talking until he could figure out a way to get the drop on him.

He turned, keeping himself between Bree and the gun. "Can we discuss this?"

"We ain't talkin' until you git away from that little girl."

"Riley." Bree stepped out from behind him.

"You all right, Miss Bree? If this polecat hurt you, I'll—"

"I wondered where you were." She put her hand on the man's forearm, gently urging him to lower the shotgun. "I'm fine."

Jeff stared at the wiry little man. A battered black hat covered his hair, but his white beard gleamed in the lantern's glow. Dark eyes burned like coals, and wrinkles creased his weathered face like boundary lines on a sur-

51

veyor's map. Jeff couldn't make a guess at his age. He could be anywhere from fifty to ninety. Way too old for Bree.

"Had me a couple drinks in the saloon."

"Anything else? That pretty brunette still serving whiskey for Kate?" There was a teasing note in her voice.

"Now, hold on, missy. Don't you be askin' questions about things a lady has no right t'know." He belched loud and long.

"I won't, if you'll stop doin' that in front of me."

"Sorry."

"Me, too."

The old man peered at Jeff in the dim light, making no effort to hide the fact that he was taking his measure, then he looked back at Bree. "There's questions t'be asked, and I reckon I'm gonna start. Who is he? And why was he all over you like stink on—"

"Riley." There was a warning tone in that single word.

"You get my meanin'."

"Loud and clear," Jeff said. "I'm with the railroad. Jefferson Tanner."

"You're a railroad man and she let you that close? You all right, boy? Don't see no bleedin'." Riley stared from him to Bree.

"I'm fine, although my hat's a little the worse for wear."

He shook his head in wonder. "You're mighty lucky she don't miss."

Jeff rubbed his ear recalling the zing of her bullet whizzing past, then held out his hand. "Bree told me about you. Pleased to make your acquaintance."

"Likewise. Name's Riley O'Rear." His grip was firm as he looked Jeff square in the eye. "What'd she say about me?"

"You nosy thing." The affection in Bree's tone was unmistakable. "I told him you'd shoot a man in the back, then pick his pockets clean as a vulture'd pick bones."

"You're not too old t'take over my knee, missy." His harsh words were punctuated by cackling laughter.

"But you're too old t'try it."

"I'm not." Jeff saw the barrel of the shotgun lift a fraction. "But I wouldn't."

"Didn't think so." He looked at Bree. "You stayin' on *Belle* tonight?"

"Yup. Boardinghouse is full up."

He nodded. "It's time I turned in. But I'll be close by." His gaze rested on Jeff. "So don't go gettin' any ideas."

"No, sir." He couldn't suppress a grin.

The old man straightened to his full height. "You funnin' with me, boy?"

"Never."

"Better hadn't. Make Swiss cheese out of you quicker'n a goosey coyote can pounce."

Jeff put up his hands again as if the gun were still in his back. "I don't doubt that for a second."

Bree kissed the old man's leathery cheek just above the whiskers. "Good night, Riley. And thanks."

"No need t'thank me, girl." With a last quelling look at Jeff, he left them as quietly as he'd come. A slight lift of the boat told Jeff the craft was relieved of Riley's weight.

"He's quite a character. A friend, you say?"

"The best. I trust him with my life."

Jeff remembered the look in the old man's eyes. There was an edge of fierceness that hinted at a hard life, like he'd faced death square on and lived to tell about it. After that, there was nothing left to fear. Riley O'Rear was someone to be respected, and Jeff was glad he watched over Bree. Maybe now *he* could get some sleep.

"It's getting late," he said.

"Yup."

"Guess I'll go back to the boardinghouse."

"Suit yourself."

So they were back to square one with nothing to say. For a split second he considered kissing her again. Didn't need words for that. And B. E. Murphy had about the softest, sweetest lips he'd ever tasted. But he had the feeling that somewhere beyond the circle of lantern light on the steamboat there was a shotgun aimed at his head. There was no way on God's green earth he would kiss her now, no matter how much promise he'd sampled. But there would be a next time. He was sure of it.

He started toward the gangplank. "Good night, Murphy."

" 'Night, Tanner."

"Don't let the bedbugs bite."

"No bedbugs on the river. Just rats—the two-legged kind."

This time he'd be damned if he'd let her have the last word. He stood on the edge of the boat. She was behind the wheelhouse, and he couldn't see her, but every instinct told him she was listening. "By the way, Murphy. I can see why Charlie couldn't take his eyes off you in that dress. See you in the morning."

"Not if my luck improves."

The words drifted to him on the warm breeze, and a broad grin split his face. He hated to agree with Charlie about even one thing, let alone two. But she really was somethin'.

Bree's arm ached from sanding down the burned wood on the wheelhouse wall. She stopped and brushed the damp wisps of hair off her forehead with the back of her hand, then rubbed the sore muscle. A fine black dust covered her forearms. The sandpaper was limp and nearly worn out, about like she was.

It was already midmorning. The blue sky was cloudless, and the sun grew hotter every minute. She'd been at it since the crack of dawn. The rumbling in her stomach reminded her she hadn't eaten breakfast. She'd found it impossible to go up to the house for food and face Tanner after what had happened.

Thoughts of his kiss had kept her awake most of the night. Even now, remembering how firm and warm his mouth had been and the way his mustache had tickled her upper lip, set her stomach to fluttering something fierce. Damn him! Why had he done it?

Surely he was toying with her, just to see if she was any different from the ladies back home. He'd probably laughed long and hard after he'd returned to his room. Her brows drew together. It would never happen again. She'd rather be tarred and feathered than give him a few laughs at her expense.

Her stomach tightened with hunger. She looked over her shoulder at the embankment, wondering if she dared go to the boardinghouse yet. The sight of building supplies at the river's edge pricked her curiosity again. She was mighty interested to know who had arranged for lumber, sanding materials, paint, and tools to be delivered to the steamboat dock bright and early this morning.

A sneaking suspicion took hold and wouldn't let go. If she was right, she'd have a few choice words for Tanner.

She turned back to her work. Only a small portion of black remained. The rest of the wood was solid, mostly just smoke-blackened. As soon as she finished, she could start on the floorboards that needed replacing.

She'd deliberately put that part off, doubting her ability to do the work. She was a riverboat captain, not a carpenter. But they didn't have the money to hire labor, so she expected she'd just have to learn.

"Good morning."

Only two words and she knew Tanner's voice. "Was good," she said. Her hands trembled.

His velvet tones washed over her skin and made her feel as if he'd touched his lips to hers again. For a second she closed her eyes and shook her head, trying to chase away the unsettling recollection.

What a ninny she was. Why couldn't she forget about it? He probably had. He probably kissed women all the time. She desperately wanted to pretend it had never happened, and hoped he'd do the same. "What are you doing here?"

"You know, Murphy, if I were you I'd be nice to me."

She could hear the laughter in his voice. "Aren't you going to look at what I brought you?"

"If you mean the supplies, I've got a bone to pick with you about that." She turned.

He waited by the gangplank, his hat pulled low on his brow. Guilt sliced through her when she noticed the bullet hole in the crown. A man with all his money should have more than one hat, she thought irritably. Dressed in white cotton shirt and denim work pants, he looked like an everyday, hardworking man. Well, maybe that wasn't exactly true.

His teeth flashed white in the shadow of his hat brim, and his shirtsleeves, rolled up past his elbows, revealed strong, tanned forearms. He stood with his legs braced wide apart. His muscled thighs strained against the material of his pants, reminding her of the trunks of the cottonwood trees fixed deep in the mud at the river's edge, defying the powerful pull of the current. Her throat went dry. He was the furthest thing from ordinary she could imagine.

A quiver began in her belly and spread. Must be lack of food, she reckoned. No other explanation. Her gaze fixed on the tray he held, covered with a white cloth napkin. Her mouth started watering.

"If you tell me that's not food, I swear I'll shoot you dead."

His deep laugh bounced off the river's bluffs and carried in the clear morning air. "It is. Mary said you'd be hungry and too busy to stop and eat. Permission to come aboard, Captain."

"Permission granted."

The thump of his boots sounded on the plank before he stepped easily into the stern. He confidently carried the food without spilling a morsel, and she wondered what other odd jobs he'd done to pay for college.

She groaned inwardly. On top of everything else, he was formally educated. Just one more difference between them. In the Territory teachers were hard to come by, and the few brave souls who ventured out hadn't lasted long. Her only schooling had been at her mother's knee coupled with an unquenchable desire to read. When she was little, she'd begged her father to bring her books back from his travels. He'd hardly ever come home empty-handed.

Tanner inched his way along the narrow deck past the wheelhouse. His long, brown fingers curved around the edge of the tray, and she recalled the restrained strength in them when he'd held her last night. Instead of the fear she'd expected, he'd aroused sensations she'd never felt before, had thought never to experience. He'd awakened feelings she wanted to know again. And the thought tugged at her heart. Feelings like those for a man like him were dangerous and best forgotten.

He lifted the tray a fraction. "Where do you want this?"

"On the deck, between the wheelhouse and the boiler."

When he placed it there, she stepped over it and sat cross-legged on the deck, the tray in front of her. With her back to the river, she uncovered the food. Bacon, biscuits, potatoes, and eggs filled the tin plate. She picked up a biscuit and took half the flaky roll in one bite. Seconds later the rest was gone.

Her stomach rumbled loudly, and she looked up to see if he'd heard. He sat on the edge of the boat across from her, elbows resting on his knees, hands dangling between his legs. What was he thinking? Were her table manners lacking? Was he comparing her to the women where he came from?

An Eastern lady would probably take dainty little tidbits and lift a pinky in the air while she did it. But this was a steamboat, not a fine restaurant. Out here a body could starve eating that way. Folks worked hard and had to keep up their strength. Food was gobbled up before you could reach for a second helping.

She took a forkful of eggs and a small bit of bacon and stared at the distant rugged rock formations over his left shoulder as she chewed. At least now she had an excuse for not saying anything to him. Even *she* knew it wasn't polite to talk with her mouth full.

He waited until she'd swallowed, then pushed his hat back on his head. "So what's the bone you have to pick with me?"

She glanced at the pile of supplies on the riverbank. "I have a sneaking suspicion you sent all that lumber and paint down here."

"I did."

She stared at him, waiting for him to explain. Several moments passed and he remained silent, never taking his eyes from hers. Finally she looked away. "Why?"

"I told you I'd make her good as new."

"I know you did but—"

"But you didn't believe me." His lips tightened, nearly disappearing in his thick mustache.

She looked again at the stack of things on the sandy riverbank and her heart sank. Everything was brand new and first class. Murphy Navigation couldn't pay for those materials. She'd intended to replace the boards with used lumber and nails. Paint could wait for the time being. Sandpaper was cheap.

"Murphy, we need to get something straight. I don't say anything I don't mean."

She stared at a bird soaring through the air, black and graceful against the clear, blue sky. After taking a bite of potatoes, she chewed slowly, then swallowed. "Neither do I."

"Then we'll get along just fine." He removed his hat and ran splayed fingers through his thick brown hair.

"I wouldn't go that far."

His eyes narrowed. "What's bothering you?"

She pushed away her empty plate and pointed to the supplies on the riverbank before crossing her arms over her chest. "This doesn't feel right."

"Why not?"

She flicked her gaze over the paint and two-by-fours. "Feels like charity."

"Well, it's not."

"It's just that—" She took a deep breath, then looked up at him. "Murphys take care of what's theirs, and they don't do it with handouts."

"You think the railroad makes a profit by giving things away? I have a job to do, and I need this boat in working order to do it. Hardyville is the freight center here on the river. With a constant flow of supplies for the bridge, I need to be able to get back and forth to the site. I intend to see that *Belle*'s fixed proper, with first-rate materials. The bill's going to the railroad."

"Still feels wrong, Tanner."

He stood and took a step toward her and pointed. "Right or wrong, I'm in charge and we'll do things my way," he said.

The muscle in his cheek contracted angrily as he stared her down. Bree placed an elbow on her knee and rested her chin in her palm, studying him. He looked ready to explode. His green eyes blazed with fury as his index finger aimed steady in her direction after punctuating each furious word. She figured he probably meant what he said. Besides, the boat meant more to her than her pride.

"You win."

He blinked. "What?"

"We'll do it your way." She extended her hand, and he helped her to her feet. "I didn't know how much it meant to you, is all. Now that I do"—she shrugged—"I'm not an unreasonable person. You should have said something before, Tanner."

He groaned and clenched his fists. "Murphy, give me a reason, just one—a real good one—why I shouldn't strangle you."

"Because you'd be hanging from the end of a rope before you knew what hit you."

He released a huge breath. "Yeah?"

She grinned. "Yeah. The only judge we have in these parts knows Cap real well. He runs a combination saloon, brothel, post office, and general store."

"That's real convenient."

She stared at the tray for a second, then looked up at him. "Now answer me something. You don't like me any better than I like you. Why are you so set on helping me with the boat?"

"Call it protecting my investment."

"I thought your money was in railroads."

"Some is. But the first rule in business is never give your competition too much information."

His answer was vague. He didn't seem like the sort of man to beat around the bush. It gave her an uneasy feeling. "There are rules in business?"

"Yup, just like in beds." He pulled his hat low over his eyes. "Speaking of beds, yours was mighty comfortable. Slept like a baby last night. How about you?"

"Fine," she lied. She crossed her fingers behind her back. That made the falsehood a fib and didn't carry the same weight when the Almighty was judging who'd go up to heaven and who'd go the other way.

But her lack of rest had nothing to do with the thin mattress in the wheelhouse. She hadn't been able to shake the memory of his lips on hers or his hand heating the skin on her arms and everywhere else he touched. At first light she'd started putting *Belle* back together. Work always kept her from thinking unpleasant thoughts. And Tanner was definitely an unpleasant thought.

Beside him on the deck, she saw her three empty buckets. Glory, with everything else crowding her mind, she'd completely forgotten to fill them this morning.

"Since we're doing this your way, hadn't we best get started?" She slid between him and the wheelhouse. Her shoulder brushed his chest, and she shied away from the contact.

"You're a little skittish this morning. Sure you slept all right?"

"Just fine."

She couldn't meet his gaze. Instead, she bent over and picked up one of the buckets, dipped it into the river, then carried it across the boat's beam to the other side of the wheelhouse.

He never said a word, but Bree felt him watch her. She grabbed the second one and repeated the ritual. When she started to reach for the third, he snatched it from her and filled it.

"All right. I give up. What's the water for?" He took a step and stood beside her, then studied the river water he'd just pulled up. "Looks more like mud to me."

"It is. Takes hours for the red silt to settle so it can be used."

"Why three buckets? What's it for?"

She wrapped her arms across her chest. "Lots of things."

"Like what?"

"You know, Tanner, if you keep stickin' your nose where it doesn't belong, two bits to a dollar you're gonna lose it."

"I reckon that means you're not going to tell me."

"I reckon that means it's none of your business."

He set the bucket beside the other two. "Just makes me more curious."

She shrugged. "Can't help that."

"Well, maybe there's something you can help." He stared at the blackened part of the deck. "This needs fixing."

With a long, easy stride he crossed the gangplank, then returned with a collection of tools and supplies. He went down on one knee, then pulled a pair of worn leather gloves from the back pocket of his pants and slipped his big hands into them. After selecting a crowbar, he wedged it into the sliver of space between the boards, and the corded muscles in his forearms tensed and contracted as he started to lift.

A high-pitched squeal filled the air and set her teeth on edge as the plank came apart. The nails curved at a painful angle, and he pulled them away from the cross-beam below until the board broke free. He tossed it on the riverbank and set to work on the next one.

Bree was horrified. She felt as if he'd ripped her heart out. Who did he think he was? Maybe he'd laid track for the railroad, but this was different. This was *her* boat. She wouldn't let just anyone work on *Belle*. Like a she-cat protecting her babies, she put herself between him and the area of the deck he'd started to remove.

"What do you think you're doing?"

He braced an elbow on his knee and looked up at her. "That should be pretty obvious. I have to pull off the burned planks before I can replace them."

"You?" Bree stared at his clenched jaw and narrowed eyes. She didn't care if he was angry. That didn't give him the right to just step in and take over without so much as a by your leave. "You're not tearing apart this boat unless it's over my dead body."

"That could be arranged." He stood and glared down at her. "Murphy, I'm getting real tired of this. There's work to do, so get out of my way. If you want to help, start painting the wheelhouse."

He'd demanded to know what qualified her to pilot a steamboat. By God, she'd get the same respect. Nobody worked on her boat unless he knew what he was doing. "What makes you think you can fix her?"

He flexed his shoulders as if they hurt, then took a deep breath and exhaled slowly. "I studied engineering in college. Before that, I built trestle for the railroad. I think I can handle this. An apprentice carpenter could replace that flat deck."

She glanced over her shoulder at the blackened boards. It didn't look so easy to her. She turned back to him and bit her lip. "You're set on this?"

He nodded. "Until she's shipshape, you're not taking

her out on the river. And I can't afford to have this boat out of commission."

It pricked her pride that she couldn't make the necessary repairs herself, but she had to admit he was right. Besides, she *was* anxious to get back on the river. "There's no way I can change your mind?"

He shook his head.

"All right, Tanner. But one false move, and . . ." She hooked her thumbs into the waistband of her jeans. "I'm watching you."

"Yeah. Let's get to work." He pulled his white cotton shirt over his head and tossed it on top of the wheelhouse.

Bree's heart jumped and heat swept over her body like a prairie fire, stealing all the air from her lungs. She stared at the broad expanse of flesh and rippling muscles, then swallowed hard. A mat of dark hair spread over his chest and flat midsection, before narrowing to a vee that disappeared into the waistband of his pants. He was tall and tanned, and she wanted to touch the smooth skin covering his shoulders and the wide contours of his upper arms. Was his skin soft and warm from the sun?

She remembered touching him the day before, stopping him from walking out of the boardinghouse. She'd felt the harnessed power under her fingers, but then his brawny strength had been hidden from sight. Now she knew what he looked like beneath the cloth. In these parts, when the weather heated up, workmen stripped to the waist all the time. But she'd never seen such a man before. The sweat-slickened skin over his powerful upper body glistened, and she couldn't look away. He was a sight to behold.

"Are you gonna watch me all day, or are you gonna help?"

Bree instantly turned away. He'd caught her staring at him. Her cheeks burned and she pulled the sandpaper from her back pocket. "I think I'll finish this, then start painting," she said without looking at him.

Behind her, she heard him chuckle. That grated on her more than the sound of the planks being removed.

Jeff stood back and admired his work. The smell of sawdust and paint filled his nostrils. He'd missed working with his hands.

He glanced over at Bree, just putting the finishing touches of red color on the wheelhouse. She'd labored as hard as he had. A grudging respect filled him. Maybe he'd been wrong about her ability to handle the bridge project.

He remembered their earlier disagreement and was still annoyed. He wanted to hear her admit she was wrong about his carpentry skills. "What do you think, Murphy?"

"About what?" She turned her head. Scarlet streaks crossed her cheeks and nose and the front of her blue cotton shirt. She looked like an Indian painted for war. The image suited her. Seemed like she was always itching for a fight.

"*Belle.* How does she look?" He pointed to the deck.

Still holding a paintbrush between two fingers, she rubbed her nose with the back of her hand. She looked at the wall she'd just finished. "Looks good."

"I mean the deck."

"Oh." She glanced over. "It's not black anymore."

"Is that all you've got to say?"

She walked toward him, a spattered can in one hand, the brush in the other. "What do you want me to say?"

"Thanks would be a good start."

She placed a boot on the new wood, lighter in color than the weathered planks surrounding it. Placing all her weight on the deck, she nodded with satisfaction. The tools he'd used were stacked beside the wheelhouse wall. "Seems solid."

"Are you ready to admit you were wrong about me?"

"Maybe. If we don't sink on the way to the bridge site. You ready to go?"

He nodded. "You're a stubborn woman, Bree Murphy."

She grinned, flashing even white teeth. "Thanks."

five

Jeff glanced at the *Elizabeth*. She'd left hours before them with a load of supplies and was already docked at the bridge site. Beams and girders were tied on a barge attached to the bigger steamboat. He watched as a parade of men working in pairs unloaded the heavy construction materials. With luck, the job would be completed by nightfall, or else they'd have to finish in the morning. It was too dangerous to continue without adequate light. One slip and a man could lose an arm or a leg, or worse.

On the bluff the city of tents glowed beneath the red and orange sky. In the stern of the steamboat Bree started to slide the gangplank from the boat to the embankment. Jeff took the other side of the board and helped her push it into place.

He looked at her. "Well?"

She met his gaze. "Well what?"

"We didn't sink."

"You don't miss anything, do you, Tanner?"

"Isn't there something you wanted to say to me?"

Her smooth forehead puckered thoughtfully. "Go home?"

He grinned. "C'mon, Murphy. Give it up. I did a good job fixing this boat, and you know it."

"This was one short trip. If it lasts awhile, then maybe . . ."

"Murphy." His voice held a warning note.

"You win." She held up her hands in surrender. "I'll admit you did a good job, Tanner."

"Now, was that so hard?" he asked, lifting a brow.

"You have no idea." She glanced around. "I wonder where Cap is."

Just then he saw Dan McGee, his construction foreman, cross the *Elizabeth*'s gangplank and shove a fistful of papers in his back pocket. The man waved.

Bree returned the gesture, then cupped her hands to her mouth as she called out, "Where's my father?"

He pointed to one of the cabins aboard the bigger steamboat. "We just finished taking care of the purchase orders. Now I have to help get this stuff unloaded."

Jeff pulled his leather gloves from his back pocket. "Need an extra pair of hands, Dan? Sun's goin' down fast."

The big, bearded man grinned. "Yeah, boss. Think you can handle it?"

"Watch me." He looked at Bree. "Are you going to see your father?"

She nodded.

Frowning, he studied her small-boned, slight figure. "Don't go wandering through camp by yourself." That was another reason he'd wanted a man for this job. She was the only woman for miles around. It wouldn't take much to turn a bored railroad crew into an ugly mob. He was glad she had a gun and knew how to use it.

"I don't plan to."

"Good." He started to walk away, then hesitated. Something wasn't right. He had yet to give her a direct order and have her obey it without an argument. What was she up to? "That was too easy. *Why* aren't you planning to go into camp?"

"Because I'm leaving right after I see my father."

"What do you mean?"

"I have to get back to Hardyville to pick up the mail for

the fort, then deliver it. Should have gone there this morning, but with the fire and the repairs and gettin' you here, I was delayed."

"Boss, you comin'?" The railroad foreman watched from the riverbank. Behind him, two men placed a beam on the rising stack of wood.

"You go ahead, Dan. I'll be with you shortly." He looked back at Bree. "*You're* not going anywhere."

"Look, Tanner, if you're worried about gettin' back to the boardinghouse, don't. You can spend the night on the *Elizabeth*. The cabins are decent, bigger than *Belle*'s, and I'll be back in the morning to pick you up." She shrugged, then started to go ashore.

Jeff reached out and grabbed her upper arm, turning her around. She jammed her hands on her hips, and rebellion radiated from her in waves. The faint odor of turpentine clung to her clothes. He planted his feet wide apart in the stern, and she waited on the gangplank. They stood nose to nose, and her eyes glittered with defiance.

He'd just about had it with her suggestions that he was soft. "I'm not worried about where to bed down tonight. I *am* concerned about you. You can't navigate that river alone, and I'm not going with you. It'll be too dark to see in an hour. I thought you were concerned about the safety of this steamboat."

"I wouldn't do anything to endanger *Belle*. The moon will be full tonight. That's enough light." She exhaled slowly as if she were gathering the pieces of her patience together to deal with a disobedient child. "Look, Tanner, you're a businessman. You can understand contracts and deadlines. I have an agreement with the army to deliver mail to the soldiers at Fort Mojave. I intend to fulfill that obligation."

"Then I won't stop you."

"I knew you'd see it my way."

"As long as you fulfill it tomorrow morning."

"What?"

"One more day won't make any difference."

"It makes a difference to those men. They're expecting letters today. Mail from home's about all they have to break the monotony. I have a responsibility to get it there on time."

"My first responsibility is building this bridge. I can't risk the boat or you. If you're smashed up on a sandbar somewhere, you'll be no good to anyone. The army can wait."

"Well, I can't. It's my boat. I made the schedule, and I intend to keep it." She jumped down from the gangplank. "I'm going now before I waste any more daylight jawin' with you. Get out of my way, Tanner."

"Don't make me pull rank on you, Murphy. You're staying."

"I'm going."

Jeff looked at the deck beneath his boots, then met her icy blue gaze. She was determined to meet her schedule because Murphy Navigation couldn't afford to lose the army contract. He wasn't prepared to lose her. Those stakes were too high for him to throw in his hand. He had to put all his cards on the table.

"You're not going—not in my boat."

"Your boat?" Her eyes widened, then she laughed. The sound was tinged with hysteria, and there was a note of fear mixed in. She snickered until tears ran down her cheeks. She swiped at the moisture with her palms, then sniffled. "I always thought you were crazy, Tanner. Now I know for sure."

"I'm serious, dead serious."

"What are you talking about? Cap owns the *River Belle*."

"Not anymore. Murphy Navigation was bought out by a holding company of the railroad."

"What are you saying?" Her voice was hardly more than a whisper before she swallowed hard. She clenched her fists as her body went rigid with shock.

"In simple terms—I own Murphy Navigation."

"Liar." Her eyes were like twin blue flames and burned with an inner intensity.

There was pain, too, and he could only guess at how deep it went. "I may be a lot of things, but liar isn't one of them. If you don't believe me, ask your father." His voice was hard.

"Bet on it, Tanner." She turned away and raced over the gangplank to the *Elizabeth*.

Bree stormed into her father's cabin on the lower deck of the larger steamboat. Hot and heavy, the air inside pressed against her like the blackness of perdition, or maybe the ominous feeling came from within her. She'd just faced the devil, and his hellish words were branded into her mind.

Cap sat with his back to the door at a small desk built into the wall, his gray head lowered as he wrote in his log book.

She took a deep shuddering breath and blurted out her fears. "Tell me he's lying, Cap. Tell me the railroad doesn't own us."

Sean Murphy flexed his shoulders as if they pained him. Then he turned to face his daughter. "He's not lying."

"Why didn't you tell me? I had a right to know. I've practically been running every—" She stopped and bit her lip. "Cap, you shouldn't have kept this from me."

"I only wanted to protect my little girl." Sadness tinged his tone.

"I'm not a little girl. I don't need you to spare me." She stopped as thoughts raced through her mind, then turned crystal clear. "It all makes sense now. I never understood why you insisted we sign the contract with the railroad. I always knew it wasn't just the money. We never had any choice because Tanner owns us."

He rubbed a trembling hand across the silver bristles on his chin. "They tell us what t'do now. I'd hoped things would improve. I'd planned t'buy back the company so's you'd never have t'know."

He buried his face in his hands. Dark brown spots dotted the backs, and white hair sprinkled the skin, stopping at his knuckles. She'd never thought of her father as old, but for the first time she could see it. Behind him on the desk she saw the half-filled bottle of whiskey and the full tumbler beside it. Another glass, empty now, but showing an amber ring in the bottom, told her that someone had shared a drink with him.

"Does Mary know?"

He looked up and shook his head. His light blue eyes were glazed and bleak with self-pity.

Her stomach knotted. "What about Charles?"

His gaze lowered and skittered away. "He'll be the head of the family soon."

"How could you? You trust me to captain a steamboat, but not to run the company, our company?" She laughed, but there was no humor in it. "Or should I say the railroad's company?"

"You need a man, child. No one will deal with a woman. You know that, too, or you'd have signed your full name to that contract."

Tears burned at the back of her eyes, but she wouldn't give in to them. As angry as she was, she refused to contribute to his humiliation by letting him see her cry. He was her father, and no matter what, she loved him. His shoulders, always so wide and strong when she was a little girl, slumped now. He needed her strength, not her blame.

She went to him and put her arms around him, then smoothed the coarse hair at the back of his head.

His hand came around her waist and squeezed. "Can you forgive me?"

"It's not your fault. If it weren't for the railroad, business would be as good as it ever was."

She blamed Tanner. Expanding the railroad was all he could see. He didn't give two hoots about anyone else as long as he got what he wanted. Making money was all that mattered to him. Bitterness grew within her until it pushed out everything else. And he'd tried to tell her he was worried about her. Horse manure. All he cared about was risking *his* property. *Belle.*

The steamboat belonged to her. Tears still burned, hotter and thicker now. She took a deep breath, trying to steady her reeling emotions. "I have to go, Cap." Her voice cracked. "I'll see you later."

Before he could say anything, she was gone.

It was pitch dark when Bree finally stepped aboard her steamboat, and only by following the lights of the *Elizabeth* had she found her way. She'd wanted to be alone and had walked into the hills. With her back propped against a rock, she'd watched the sun go down, taking her spirit along with it.

She'd thought over everything her father had told her, trying to decide what hurt the most. She'd known all along the business was going down quicker'n a mine shaft in a cave-in. Cap must have sold out before she'd taken over the paperwork.

In the past year his drinking had steadily increased, forcing her to do more and more. The humiliation of selling to the railroad had probably pushed him to the edge and made his drinking worse. What bothered her was that he'd seen fit to tell Charles while she knew nothing. And the idea of her stepbrother heading the family was something she couldn't even bring herself to think about. Cap had a lot of good years left, and it would be a cold day in hell before she'd listen to anything Charles had to say.

After entering the wheelhouse, she lighted her lantern and hung it on a bent, rusty nail, then dragged her buckets of water into the center of a small space. The odor of cookfires and frying bacon from the railroad camp was trapped inside. She pulled tightly closed the blankets she'd hung on ropes across the window above the wheel and the doors on either side of the structure. With a huge sigh she placed her pistol beside the mattress on the floor.

The comfort of any small stirring of air was closed off, but so was the danger of prying eyes. The thought sent prickles of apprehension slithering across her shoulder blades and down her arms. She picked up her gun and flipped the cylinder open, making sure it was loaded and ready. When she replaced it, she glanced around the small space, judging the distance to her weapon from every corner. Confident that she was safe, she let out the breath she'd been holding.

From a small cabinet beside the wheel, Bree pulled out a metal washbasin containing her lavender soap, a cloth, and a copper pitcher. She knelt on the wooden floor and checked to make sure the mud had settled to the bottom of the buckets, then skimmed water from the top.

After pulling off her boots, she removed her paint-streaked cotton shirt and hung it on a nail beside the lantern. She untied her braid and ran her fingers through it to untangle the length. Then she piled it on top of her head and secured the mass with pins. Several loose strands tickled the back of her neck and shoulders. Her muscle were tight as wet rawhide drying in the sun, and she tipped her head from side to side to loosen the tension. Outside, the wind whistled down the channel of the river and pressed the blankets in. Waves slapped the side of the boat.

With her chemise open to the beginning of the hollow between her breasts, she drew the soapy moistened cloth over the hot sticky skin on her chest. As her eyes closed, she pictured Tanner's Pullman car with the wonderful brass tub. She tried to imagine the sensation of sitting in it with so much warm water that her breasts would be covered. Was it big enough for her to stretch her legs out? Two bits to a dollar it was. Probably custom made to fit him, and he was a big man. If she sat in it, there might even be room to spare. Glory, what a luxury.

A vision of the tub's owner flashed into her mind, his

roguish grin, the memory of his mouth moving seductively across hers. She remembered his solid chest, the rock-hard contours beneath her hands. She'd wanted to uncurl her fists, explore the expanse, but something had stopped her. She was afraid of the strange, exciting shivery feeling in the pit of her stomach. Only danger from the river had ever made her heart race that way—until Tanner's kiss.

Distracted, she dragged the wet cloth around her neck and shoulders, then tossed it in the basin. Water sloshed over the side, staining the wood floor with dark spots. A sudden draft of air on her back caused her scalp to tingle as goose bumps raised on her arms.

She turned and saw Charles standing in the doorway, one hand braced on the frame, the other holding up the blanket. He'd entered from the river side of the boat, hidden from the shore. The look in his eyes chilled her to the bone. Hunger, raw and primitive, burned in his gaze, and he touched the tip of his tongue to his top lip.

"Evening, little sister." His voice was lazy and low.

"Don't call me that."

He smiled. "But that's what you are."

Her heart thundered against her ribs and roared in her ears. She had to keep her wits about her. "Where's Cap?"

"Sean is blissfully asleep. He finished off his bottle of Joy Juice. When that didn't do the trick, I fetched him some Red Disturbance. Did you know that stuff'll raise a blister on a rawhide boot?"

"You know I don't like you encouraging him to drink."

His small, pale eyes were like slits when he grinned. "But he needed it. Sean can't stand to see you unhappy. You're his weakness, Breanne, not the liquor."

"What are you talking about?"

"He told me you know about selling the company."

She nodded. From the corner of her eye she searched for her gun and gauged the distance. It was to her left. If he made a move, she'd lunge to the side. Her feet began to tingle from her cramped position, and she shifted sideways to allow the blood flow back into her lower legs. She massaged her denim-clad thighs to speed up her circulation. If the need arose, she had to be fast.

"What do you want, Charles?" She tried to keep her voice steady. She hated the way his grin broadened, as if he could smell her fear and fed on it.

"Sean said you didn't take the news well. I came to comfort you, make you feel better." He took a step inside and let the blanket drop back into place before resting his shoulder against the wall. His thumbs hooked into the pockets of his black wool pants, and his fingers pointed casually downward, toward his groin.

"Get out of here." Bree reached for her weapon.

Like a cat, Charles moved at the same time and placed a pointed-toed boot over her pistol, just an inch from her trembling fingers.

He looked down at her, white teeth gleaming in the lantern light, eyes cold as the darkest winter night. "Shame on you. That's not very sisterly."

"Didn't mean for it to be. I want you to leave."

"And I will, just as soon as I do what I came to do." He lifted his foot and, with one movement of his slanted heel, sent her gun sliding into a corner behind him.

Bree scrambled to her feet. Panic filled her belly and grew until it became a great black beast clawing at her insides. Her breath came in gasps. Before she could back away, his hand snaked out and pulled the pins from her hair. The dark mass tumbled around her face, and she shook it away.

A scream gathered in her chest and pushed at the back of her throat. Cap was close by. Would he hear her over the sound of the wind? Was Charles lying, or was Cap really too far gone from the liquor? Raucous laughter and shouts drifted from the railroad camp on the bluff. She couldn't expect help from there.

Frantically her mind raced, searching for a weapon. Only her basin of water stood between them. With her toe she caught the metal lip and flipped it up, splashing soapy water on his pants and boots.

"Sonofabitch!" He looked down at the sopping material clinging to his legs.

In a flash she was out the other side of the wheelhouse. Her bare toes stubbed painfully against something, and she heard the rattle of tools.

Bree bent and blindly searched with her hand until she found the crowbar Tanner had used earlier. When Charles followed her, she lifted the curved piece of iron with both hands.

"If you take one step closer, it'd give me great pleasure to b-bash your skull in." Her breasts heaved with the effort and the terror swelling within her.

Charles smiled. "Could you explain that to Mother?"

"I'd tell her the truth." Her voice was a whisper.

"What truth, Bree? That I came to comfort you and got crowned with a crowbar for my efforts?"

"Go away."

"I don't aim to fight you. Why should I? Soon I won't have to." His nearly silent laughter crawled over her skin and burrowed inside her, making the blood run cold through her veins. "You should have told me you didn't want to talk about it. Good night, little sister."

His carefree whistling floated back to her on the night air. When the echo of rattling stones and sliding sand from his climb up the riverbank had died away, she lowered the crowbar. Shivering started in her limbs and quickly spread to every part of her body.

Before she collapsed, she darted into the wheelhouse to find her gun. If he decided to come back, she wanted to be ready. She saw the pistol wedged beneath the corner of her mattress and grabbed it. Then she sank to the floor and braced her back against the wall. She looked from one door to the other.

Fear surged through her, and she felt like a young girl again, that same terrified child he'd tormented years before. She'd grown up since then and learned how to take care of herself. She'd thought everything was under control. That had been her mistake; her guard had slipped. But it had been so long ago, and he'd done nothing else, until tonight. Why now? What had pushed Charles to approach her again?

A wave of apprehension shook her. He'd managed to get to her. Her stubbornness, her skill with a gun, the careful precautions she'd taken, none of it had kept her safe from him. She felt as helpless as a willow branch tossed in the storm-swollen river. She pushed her hair out of her eyes and held her pistol in both hands.

It was going to be a long night.

Jeff crossed the gangplank and dropped his bedroll on deck. The thump of his boots rang through the night air. It was hot and dry, and his nerves were on edge. Ever since he'd seen Charlie swagger into camp and pull out a deck of cards, saying he had an itch that needed to be scratched, something had eaten away at him.

Jeff couldn't forget how the man had looked at Bree yesterday, the craving in his eyes. He remembered Bree's fear, as real as if she'd placed it in his palm, and her relief that she didn't have to work with her stepbrother.

Tonight, after watching for a while and trying to figure out how Charlie was manipulating the cards, he'd made up his mind to check on her. In fact, he planned to stand guard on *Belle*. If he knew the men in the railroad crew personally, he'd have assigned one of them. But knowing a man that well would take time, and right now he only trusted himself. He was sure Bree couldn't stand the sight of him, but that didn't lessen his determination to watch over her.

He'd despised himself for telling her the condition of her company. But she'd pushed him into it, damn stubborn woman. If she hadn't been so set on traveling after dark, he'd have let things stand, and Sean could have broken the news when he saw fit. Jeff couldn't risk losing the boat, and the thought of her wrapped around a sandbar did things to his gut that he didn't want to think about. A crack of light outlined the wheelhouse, and he moved closer.

"Murphy?" He pushed the blanket aside and poked his head in. He saw her sitting against the wall.

She sat cross-legged on a thin mattress, her long black hair tumbling around her face in a mass of wild curls. Her shirt was gone and her chemise gapped open, the thin, lace-trimmed straps sliding down her arms and exposing her creamy shoulders. The dainty pink ribbons at the top hung loose, revealing the pale swell of her breasts in the lantern's glow. The inviting valley between could make a saint forget himself—and he was no saint.

While his heart rate increased, his gaze slid across the tight denim pants, and he wondered about the slender legs encased there, what the delicate limbs looked like. Her small feet were bare. Her wild femininity slammed him in the gut like a runaway locomotive. The sensuous sight tightened his groin and made him heavy with longing.

But when he looked into her huge blue eyes, he saw her fear, and his desire withered instantly. If he hadn't been so preoccupied with her charms, he'd have instantly noticed her raised gun, aimed directly at him, and the crowbar beside her.

"What's wrong?" he asked.

The sound of his voice seemed to startle her. She shivered, then blinked. "Tanner? What are you doing here?"

"I wanted to make sure you were all right." He saw the overturned basin, her lavender-scented soap and cloth resting beside it, dark spots on the wooden floor where water had spilled. "What happened?"

"N—Nothing." She bit her lip, then glanced around, and finally her gaze lowered to the front of her open bodice. She sat up straighter and shifted her shoulders away from him, placing her bosom in shadow. With the pistol still in her hand, she tried to pull her chemise together over her breasts and tie the ribbons.

He'd give anything to know what had spooked her and knew for certain that he'd be the last person she'd tell.

"It would be easier if you put your gun down." He made his voice as gentle as he could.

She shook her head and continued to struggle with the task. He looked around and grabbed her shirt from beside the lantern, then went down on one knee in front of her.

"Here. Let me help."

He gently pushed her shaking hands aside and stared into her wide eyes. A sigh escaped her, and she briefly lowered her lids.

He slipped the shirt around her shaking shoulders, and she let him take the gun while she put her arms into the sleeves.

He handed the pistol back. "Do you want to tell me what happened?"

"No."

"All right, then. Are you ready to tell me what the water's for?"

A hint of a grin turned up the corners of her full lips, and her pale cheeks colored a little. "You're the nosiest man I ever met. You're not gonna drop it, are you?"

"Not nosy. Persistent." He grinned. "I didn't get to own the railroad by taking no for an answer."

She returned his smile, but he thought her lip quivered slightly before she caught the corner in her small teeth. "The water is for washing."

"I figured that much out, what with soap all over the place 'n' all. Why three buckets?"

"Takes that much by the time the mud settles out."

"You know there are places in the world where women actually put mud *on* their faces."

"Really?" Her eyes widened, then the spark sputtered and died. "You're fibbing."

"I swear. They say it's good for the complexion." Hers

was flawless, except for the freckles across her nose. He missed her spirit and sparkle and traced the delicate line of her jaw with his forefinger because it was either that or kiss every freckle on her face. "Apparently Colorado River mud works wonders. You'd better guard the secret. If word gets out, women will flock to these parts."

"You're teasing me."

He held his hand up, palm out. "May lightning strike me if I'm telling a falsehood."

A small smile turned up the corners of her lips. Then she settled back against the wall and gripped her gun until her knuckles turned white. The wary expression returned. "It's late. I'm leaving at first light. If you're comin' with me, you'd better go back to camp and get some sleep."

He'd get some rest, but he wasn't going anywhere. Someone had frightened her badly. He wasn't about to leave her alone tonight. "I'll be outside."

Her eyes widened and she opened her mouth to say something. He touched his index finger to her soft, full lips. "Save your breath. I'm keeping watch tonight. Now go to sleep."

She studied him for several moments, then nodded. A small, sad sigh escaped her as she slid down on the mattress and curled up, facing the wall.

"Sleep well." On impulse he leaned over and kissed her temple. He felt her tense. "You'll be safe tonight. I promise."

Jeff stood and started outside.

"Tanner?"

He lifted the cover in the doorway and stopped. "What?"

"Thanks."

"Don't mention it."

He spread his bedroll in the stern, by the gangplank, and settled in. Thoughts swirled through his mind, keeping rest at bay. Bree didn't frighten easily, and she'd been scared tonight. It would be worth his shares in the railroad to know who'd spooked her. He'd give a good deal more to have ten minutes alone with the bastard—no questions asked. If one of the railroad employees was responsible, there'd be hell to pay. If someone else had terrorized her—and he had a gnawing suspicion he knew exactly who that someone might be—there'd be the same hell, but he'd take greater satisfaction in delivering the punishment. One way or the other he intended to find out who had been here tonight.

six

Bree eased *Belle* up to the riverbank and secured the lines through the big iron ring there to hold the boat fast. It was almost noon and hot as blazes. She brushed the back of her hand across her forehead to wipe the dampness away before sliding the gangplank to the shore. Now that she was back in Hardyville, she could do something about the plans that had kept her awake most of the night. Between the panic of Charles's unexpected intrusion and learning that the railroad owned Murphy Navigation, sleep had been fleeting.

Even now she shivered at the thought of her stepbrother. She was thankful to be out in the open with the sun beating down warm and reassuring on her shoulders and, as much as she hated to admit it, grateful for Tanner's powerful presence. On top of everything else, her feelings for him couldn't be put in a neat, tidy box and easily stored away.

On the one hand, he made her feel safe and she appreciated him standing guard the previous night. *But he'd bought out her company and never said a word.*

The fact that she didn't own *Belle* still shocked her, and only Cap's confession had convinced her that Tanner had spoken the truth. Taking orders from that infernal railroad man because she had a contract with him was one thing; taking orders from him because he owned Murphy Navigation stuck in her craw. She'd do anything to buy the company back.

That meant hard work and long hours, but she'd do it. She was used to backbreaking labor. The hard part would be asking Tanner—her boss—for the opportunity to buy back Murphy Navigation. It was something she dreaded; she was afraid the words would stick in her throat.

She glanced at Tanner in the bow of the steamboat, the black smokestack between them as he secured the other line. His white cotton shirt stretched tight across his back, and the muscles bunched and rippled as he completed the task.

Swallowing hard, she reminded herself again that he was her boss. She had no right thinking of him as a handsome man; she had to push away thoughts of him that did odd things to her insides. With that shivery sensation in her abdomen again, it would be hard to suppress her pride and beg a favor.

Bree cleared her throat. "Mr. Tanner?"

Jeff looked over his shoulder, then stood and walked along the narrow deck, stopping in front of her. The wind fluttered the brim of his hat, and he pulled it more securely on his head. "Let's get something straight, Murphy."

"I thought we *had* everything straight." She stared at the bullet hole in the crown of his hat and guilt pricked her. Would she have shot at him if she'd known he owned her lock, stock, and barrel?

"Not quite. What's this 'mister' business?" He smoothed his mustache with a thumb and forefinger, then folded his arms across his chest and looked down at her. "When *you're* that polite, it makes me want to look over my shoulder all the time."

She shrugged. "You're the boss. I know my place."

"What exactly is your place?" He shifted his stance.

The sun's rays flashed from behind his large frame, and she placed a hand to her forehead, shielding her eyes from the glare. "I work for you."

"Most of my employees call me Jeff. Besides, I thought we were friends." Something glittered in his green eyes.

She bit her lip. Was he thinking about the kiss they'd shared the other night? Right this minute he was close enough to reach out and touch her. If he did, she'd probably melt against him now the way she had then. Out here in the Territory, there was one woman for every five men. Why did he have to be the one who affected her that way?

She liked to think she had enough sense to keep her distance. Not only because he paid her wages, but because they were too different ever to see eye to eye.

"What do you want me to call you?" She looked down at the deck.

Jeff glanced up at the cloudless blue sky and sighed. "As long as there's no *Mister* in front of it, you can call me anything you want."

"Anything?" A small smile pulled at the corner of her mouth.

His teeth flashed white in the shade from his hat. "Anything within reason." He rubbed the back of his neck, then stared down at her. "Look, Murphy, I'm sorry I broke the news about your company that way."

Bree looked at the river to her left and watched the current race by, dimpling over the sandbars and lapping against the bend of the channel. "It wasn't your place. Cap should have told me. But sooner or later I had to know."

"I'm sure he had his reasons."

"He did. I suppose I should give you fair warning that I plan to buy it back."

"Is that a fact?"

She nodded and swallowed the lump in her throat. "I want you to let me use *Belle* so I can increase my freight contracts. I plan to save the extra money until I have enough."

His brows drew together. "I'd have to be crazy to agree to that."

At least he hadn't laughed. "Then I guess the answer's no."

Jeff studied her expression. He was relieved that she seemed more like herself after what happened last night. Her small, stubborn chin lifted in the air and her hands clenched into fists on her hips. She was determined; that much he could tell. But some of her fire had been extinguished, and she made him think of an orphan, floating free without ties. The idea pulled a gentleness from him that was unfamiliar. He was accustomed to rooting out the weakness in people and using it to his advantage.

His disclosure about her company had pricked her pride and taken something from her. He missed the spirited give-and-take between them. He wished he could change things back.

Before yesterday she'd have told him she planned to blow up the bridge, and him with it. But now he could see the price she paid for her respect to him, the uncertainty she hid behind her bravado. And he admired her determination to get her company back, even though it would be like swimming against the mighty current of the Colorado. He'd have done the same in her shoes. How could he deny her the opportunity?

As long as she knew her first obligation was to the railroad, in her free time she could haul as much freight as she could carry. The holding company would receive a percentage of all the business she contracted. Seemed fair.

But Bree already worked long and hard. Because of the change in her circumstances, she intended to increase the hours she put in. That bothered him. Even so, he couldn't deny her the chance she wanted. He'd asked a favor once and been denied. He studied the glow sparking and coming alive in her eyes. He couldn't douse that fire in her.

"As long as you're available when I need you, you can do what you want on your own time."

"Fair enough." She looked over at the river, then stared him in the eye. "Thanks, Tanner."

"Don't mention it." He rubbed the bridge of his nose. "How do you plan to increase your—our business?"

"My first stop is Cactus Kate's. A while back she wanted us to carry supplies and other"—she cleared her throat uncomfortably—"goods from Yuma."

"You turned her down?"

She nodded.

"Why? Something wrong with Kate?"

"Nope. In fact, Kate's always been a good friend to me, like a mother in some ways." She looked away for a moment, and her cheeks grew pink. When she met his gaze again, her eyes were troubled. "She watches out for Cap. . . . It's just that we were too busy before."

"But not anymore?"

"Nope. Not since the railroad came through," she snapped.

"Then why does Kate need the steamboat?"

"Right now the railroad only goes as far as Yuma. Supplies need to be hauled from there to towns downriver."

He frowned. "But if business was so bad, why didn't you pursue the contract with Kate before this? What is it you're not telling me?"

She shuffled her feet. "I don't approve of Kate's cargo."

A becoming pink crept into her cheeks, and he was sure the sun hadn't put it there. Now that she knew he was her boss, she had to tamp down her temper. She was like a stick of dynamite with a hissing fuse about an inch away from kingdom come.

"What's wrong with the cargo?"

"The woman runs a saloon, for goodness' sake. What do you think her cargo is?" She hesitated and looked down at the toe of her boot.

"Spell it out for me." Slaves were outlawed. Stolen goods? What could a saloon owner ship that was so distasteful?

She put her hands on her hips and glared up at him.

"Look, you get a percentage no matter what. What do you care if I haul pianos or—liquor."

"Liquor? What's wrong with that?"

She met his gaze and the color in her cheeks deepened. "I'm not even gonna waste my breath explaining it to you. The only thing you understand is making money, and you don't care who you hurt in the process." Her brows drew together before she turned away.

"Seems to me you'll be doing the same thing." He couldn't restrain the defensive words and regretted them as soon as he'd spoken. This was about her father. He'd seen Sean, or rather seen him passed out, in his cabin the night before with an empty bottle of whiskey beside him. "You don't make people drink, Bree. They're bound to do it no matter what."

"That doesn't make it right."

"But you're going to get the contract from Kate anyway?"

She sighed, a sound so big it seemed all the air left her and she'd fold in on herself. "I don't have a choice anymore. Kate understands how I feel."

He tugged on the braid hanging over her breast. "For what it's worth, those goods would find their way into town no matter what. You haul freight; you don't force people to use it."

"Don't be nice to me, Tanner." Without looking up, she pulled her hat over her dark hair and walked away.

Jeff lowered the heavy canvas bag of mail that he'd slung over his shoulder and waited on the landing, surveying Fort Mojave situated on the east bank of the river. He glanced over his shoulder and watched Bree dragging her sack before she stopped beside him. "This isn't the most impressive military fortress I've ever seen," he said.

She paused to catch her breath. "Doesn't have to be. Mojaves are peaceable enough. Every so often the army sends some bloodthirsty, wet-behind-the-ears officer out here who stirs up trouble."

"Sounds like you don't have any more use for the army than you do for the railroad."

She shrugged. "That's true. But Kane is different."

"Who's Kane?" he asked, keenly studying the compound. He'd have liked it a lot better if he hadn't heard the respect in her tone when she mentioned this Kane character.

The main adobe structures stood in an L-shaped formation with two long buildings he assumed were the barracks. Adjacent to them were small individual houses with children playing in front, no doubt the officers' quarters. Enlisted men wouldn't be allowed to bring their families. Structures scattered on the bluff overlooking the Colorado included the corral, laundry, and blacksmith. Men in blue uniforms, gold stripes running the length of their pant legs, moved back and forth.

He looked down at her and repeated his question. "Who's Kane?"

"Captain Carrington. He's the post commander."

"Sounds like you two are mighty thick."

"Kane is all right." She glanced up at Jeff, lifting thick, dark lashes, then hefted her canvas sack with an effort. "C'mon, Tanner. You were so all-fired eager to come along, you might as well meet everyone."

He accompanied her on the long landing, slowing his stride to hers. Her breathing became labored and she stopped once to rest. She'd insisted on carrying the heavy bag and had protested when he'd grabbed one, said it was her job and he should leave it be. Since ignoring her seemed to work best, that's what he'd done.

He watched her struggle with the heavy mail sack, cursing her stubborn pride. Maybe her Captain Carrington could convince her to graciously accept help. He looked around, wondering which of the adobe houses belonged to the commander and how his wife, if he had one, fared in the harsh, isolated environment.

Bree crossed the rocky dirt and stopped at a building sitting all by itself. When she stepped beneath the overhang, her boots thumped on the wooden walkway, and she plopped her sack down, dragging it the rest of the way.

The young, blond private guarding the door took an eager step forward. "Mail, Miss Bree?"

She nodded. "That's right."

"Hot damn." He blinked and then froze. "Sorry, ma'am. What I meant to say was hot diggity. It's just . . ."

"I understand. I would've been here yesterday." She looked over her shoulder at Jeff and lifted one dark brow before turning away. "But I ran into a spot of trouble. Are you waiting for a letter from someone special?"

Above the uniform collar his neck turned red, and the color crept into his still-smooth cheeks. "Could be. Any of 'em smell like rosewater?"

"Could be. Why don't you get a couple of men to unload the rest from the boat. Is the captain inside?"

He nodded. "Yes, ma'am. Go on in. How many sacks are there?"

"Two more."

The soldier opened the door, and she walked into the post commander's quarters, pulling the bag behind her. Jeff followed, then lowered his mail sack beside hers to the plank floor in front of the cluttered desk. The man behind it looked up and nodded in greeting.

The officer stood and grinned at Bree. "Afternoon, Captain."

She smiled warmly and slipped her hat off, letting it dangle down her back by the rawhide thongs. "Same to you, Captain."

His gaze shifted past her to Jeff. The officer's brown eyes darkened slightly and narrowed as he considered the stranger. Jeff moved in front of the desk and extended his palm. "Name's Tanner. Captain Carrington?"

The man nodded and took Jeff's hand, his eyes never wavering, his grip firm. "Mr. Tanner. I didn't realize that Bree had taken on hired help." The officer pulled a wooden ladder-back chair from a corner of the small office and held it while Bree sat down.

"Tanner's with the railroad, Kane."

"I *own* the railroad." Jeff wasn't normally given to boasting; his need to do so now puzzled him. And he wondered why the captain's gentlemanly attention to Bree bothered him. "I'm here to build the bridge."

"I see."

Jeff had to admit the captain cut a dashing figure in his blue uniform with the gold buttons down the front of the jacket. The man was tall, about his own height. His square jaw was clean-shaven, and his wavy black hair stopped an inch short of his collar. Carrington's appearance was impeccable, even out here in the middle of nowhere, and Jeff suspected he was a by-the-book officer.

Glancing at Bree, Jeff noticed her casual, friendly smile as she talked with the other man. She trusted him. Her manner was relaxed, completely the opposite of the way she acted in his own presence. But then, Kane Carrington hadn't bought her steamboat company, and he wasn't building the bridge that would deal the death blow to river trade. The two of them were compatible; they understood this Territory and the way of life here. The idea ate away at him like a nagging toothache.

"Captain, have you been at the fort long?" Maybe his tour was nearly over, Jeff thought.

"A little over a month."

"How long do you expect to be here?"

"At least a year. But with luck, maybe there'll be a small war or trouble with the Indians somewhere else that will necessitate a transfer." The officer grinned, showing even white teeth against his tanned face.

"You don't like it here in the Territory?" Maybe he'd be around less than the usual amount of time.

"I've never seen a more inhospitable climate." Kane glanced at Bree and winked. "Although Bree brightens up this barren landscape considerably."

Jeff sat on the corner of the captain's desk and looked at her. A blush stained her creamy cheeks, and she stared at her clasped hands as if they were the most interesting sight since steam navigation.

"How does your wife like it here, Captain? Must be pretty isolated for a woman."

"I'd never subject a woman to this kind of life. I'm not married."

"Then there's someone special waiting for you at home?" Jeff touched the mail sack with the toe of his boot. "Perhaps there's a letter from her in one of these bags."

Kane's expression tightened as he shook his head. "Nope. Nobody in particular I'm expecting to hear from."

Jeff felt something hot curl and coil in his chest. "You must get mighty lonely out here."

"A man can be lonely in a crowd." The captain blinked as if bringing himself back from somewhere else, then rested his gaze on Bree. "Speaking of crowds, I'll be in Hardyville this evening—Saturday night in town is about all these soldiers have to look forward to. Takes a firm hand to keep 'em in line. Mind if I stop by the boarding-house for dinner, Bree? Mary's pot roast is about the best I've ever tasted."

She smiled. "I'd be mad if you didn't come by, Kane. The usual time?"

The officer nodded, then looked at Jeff. "Will I see you there, Tanner?"

"Doubt it. I've got a lot of paperwork to catch up on." He pulled his pocket watch from his trousers and clicked open the case back cover. "You ready, Murphy? We have a schedule to keep."

She stood up and shot him a puzzled glance. "Since when are you so worried about being on time?"

Since he'd met Kane Carrington. Twenty-four hours ago

he'd been concerned about her safety, not about the nature of her acquaintance with another man. He refused to call it jealousy. She wasn't the kind of woman to make a man possessive. But there was a part of him that wanted to keep her away from the handsome army officer, a part of him that wanted for himself the same easy, relaxed give-and-take the other man enjoyed with her.

"Let's go." He nodded to the other man. "See you around, Carrington."

"Count on it, Tanner." He grinned at Bree. "See you tonight."

She smiled in return. "I'll tell Mary to expect you."

Jeff tossed down the rest of the whiskey in his glass and waited for the fire to burn down his throat and hit his belly. The bottle beside him on the scratched table was only three fingers down, and he knew it would take a lot more before he'd feel nothing. He slid lower in his chair and felt the curved back and wooden spindles dig into his shoulder blades.

Cactus Kate's was crowded with soldiers, prospectors, and some familiar faces from the bridge site. In front of the cigarette-scarred and brawl-damaged mahogany bar, circular tables crowded the smoky room, and the odor of sweat and lantern heat filled his nostrils. He'd been there since sundown, skipping dinner at the boardinghouse and drinking to forget why. So far, he was stone sober and damn hungry.

Jeff stared through the haze and watched Charlie rake in another pot at the poker table. He'd only lost a hand or two all evening, and Jeff knew he was cheating. At this distance he couldn't tell how, but he knew it all the same. He felt it. But he hadn't decided yet whether or not he wanted to get involved.

"Mind if I take a load off?" Riley sat in the chair across from him.

"Suit yourself."

"Have you figgered it out yet?"

"What?"

"How Charlie's cheatin'. Seen ya' watchin'."

"Either he's using his own deck, or he's reading the cards in the reflection of the spilled drinks on the table. Can't tell which unless I get closer, and I don't aim t'get that close without a damn good reason."

The old man grinned, showing spaces where some of his teeth were missing. "Sized 'im up right quick, didn't ya', boy?"

Jeff shrugged. "I've seen my share of gamblers—honest and dishonest. Doesn't take long to tell which ones you have to watch out for."

"And just where did a dandy like you do all this gamblin'?"

Jeff sat up straighter and glared at the man. "I'm fed up with everyone assuming I'm citified."

"Don't get riled, boy. All I asked was where ya' learned t'play cards."

"When I laid track for the railroad, there wasn't much to do besides drink liquor and play cards." He glanced ruefully at the whiskey-filled bottle beside his hand. "Found out real quick that drinkin' had its drawbacks, but cards didn't give you a hangover the next day. I usually got lucky."

The old man's eyes narrowed. "How lucky?"

He shrugged. "Lucky enough to buy into the railroad when the time was right."

"Whether or not yore citified remains t'be seen, but there ain't no brag in ya'." Riley nodded emphatically. "I like that."

"Thanks." Jeff grinned, then stared into the amber liquid as he turned his glass between his palms. "What did Charlie do to Bree?"

The old man's look was wary, watchful. "How do you know he did anythin'?"

"I can feel it. She's afraid of him, and I think he's the

reason she packs a pistol. Did he pay her a visit last night on the *River Belle*?"

"Don't know 'bout that. As fer th' other—you'll have t'ask her."

Something told Jeff that asking Bree would be as useless as a boxcar without an engine. He glanced at the poker game in progress and saw Charlie rake in another pot. "I don't trust him."

Riley nodded. "Listen t'yer gut. Man needs t'trust his instincts."

Jeff heard the saloon's swinging wooden doors creak, and he peered into the dense smoke, squinting slightly until the newcomer came close enough to identify. The dark blue uniform and shiny gold buttons emerged through the haze, and he recognized Kane Carrington. He had no business bringing Bree to a place like this. The man had eaten supper at the boardinghouse and surely planned to spend the evening with her. Jeff's lips thinned as anger exploded in his head.

"You look ornery as a hedgehog rolled up the wrong way." Riley followed Jeff's look, then cackled gleefully. His black eyes danced. "Yer competition just sashayed in, boy. Did ya' know how much the ladies love them fancy duds and all them gold geegaws?"

Jeff blinked as Riley's laugh penetrated the red fog clouding his brain. He watched the officer walk up to the bar, then rest his boot on the brass rail along the bottom. No one followed, and Jeff released his breath when he realized Carrington was by himself. Relief oiled through his gut, easing the tension. Where was Bree?

He glanced across the room and watched Charlie nod slightly with satisfaction as he looked at his cards. At least *he* was here where Jeff could keep an eye on him. But Riley was sprawled in the chair across from him grinning like an idiot, and that meant Bree was probably by herself.

Jeff pushed aside his drink and stood. "See you around, old man."

"Two bits to a dollar she's on *Belle*." Riley scratched

the gray whiskers on his chin. His gaze focused on a brunette wearing a red satin dress and black feathers in her
hair. "Tell 'er howdy and I'll be along—presently."

"What makes you think I'm going to find Bree?"

The old man grinned. "Instinct."

Jeff started to leave and saw Carrington heading for
Charlie's poker table. The officer had said he'd only been
at the fort a short time. Should he warn him?

Although he was none too pleased about Bree's acquaintance with Carrington, Jeff disliked Charlie and his
cheating ways more. He tried to ignore his conscience, and
cursed himself soundly when he couldn't.

He tapped Kane on the shoulder, just below his gold ep-
aulets. "If you're after a game of poker, look for another
table."

Carrington turned and his eyes narrowed. "Appreciate
the warning. How's he doing it?"

Jeff shrugged. "Can't say for sure. I just know."

"I owe you one, Tanner."

Satisfied, Jeff nodded and walked out of the saloon.
He'd rather have Carrington owe *him* than the other way
around.

After sponging herself off, Bree pulled her jeans back
on, then slipped her blue cotton shirt over her chemise.
She left the buttons undone, trying to catch every bit of
breeze against her moist skin to cool off.

On the river side of the wheelhouse, she crossed the narrow deck and poured the lavender-scented water into the
current slapping the side of the boat. The nearly full moon
reflected on the flowing stream before her, and she released a heavy sigh of relief.

She'd half-expected Charles to interrupt her like he had
the previous night and had almost put off bathing. But the
appeal of washing away the day's dust and grime was too
tempting. She was determined that he wouldn't force her
to give up the sheer pleasure of this nightly ritual.

Besides, she and Kane had passed Cactus Kate's on their way to the boat. She'd seen Charles there playing cards. The only thing he fancied more than stalking her was gambling. And she was fairly certain she'd have time to clean up before he lost interest in the game.

Tanner was in the saloon, too. She'd stood on tiptoe and looked over the swinging doors before Kane had teased her away. She'd seen the handsome railroad man with his bottle of whiskey, green eyes glittering as he took in everything going on around him. She's seen the way Kate's girls had ogled him as they walked by and wiggled their behinds. Irritation spiraled in her belly. But why should she care if he took a shine to one of them?

Before she had a chance to ponder further, she heard the thump of boots on the gangplank. The boat dipped toward shore as a man boarded, and she started to reach for her gun.

"It's Tanner, Bree."

Her empty hand closed into a fist that she pressed against her lips before she let her shoulders relax. "Over here."

He crossed the boat's beam and rounded the wheelhouse. "You all right?"

"Yeah. Why?"

"I saw your Captain Carrington in Kate's. Riley was there, too, and I—well, I wanted to make certain everything was—quiet." He glanced inside and apparently the condition of the wheelhouse satisfied him. He nodded, then looked at her standing beside the doorway. Without moving, she could reach out and touch him.

The lantern hanging on the inside wall sprinkled a golden glow through the opening between them. She saw his gaze lower to her breasts and heard his quick intake of breath. The warm breeze caressed her bare skin above the chemise, and she lifted her hands to pull her shirt closed.

"Don't," he whispered, raising his palm.

His heated gaze cast a spell that held her motionless. With his index finger he gently stroked the pink ribbons dangling between her breasts. He smelled of whiskey and smoke and masculinity, and her heart beat painfully against her ribs. She couldn't seem to draw enough air into her lungs. Her legs trembled and she leaned against the wall for support.

"Tanner . . ." The word was no louder than a sigh, and she didn't realize she'd said his name until his hand froze. He stepped closer and his body blocked the light spilling from the wheelhouse.

"Don't be afraid." His voice was fierce and husky.

She shook her head. "I'm not."

He slipped the shirt from her shoulders and ran his hands down the length of her bare arms, sending heat to every part of her body. He touched the ribbons again.

"You're a puzzle, B. E. Murphy. Sharp as a cactus on the outside. Soft and pretty and pink on the inside." He rubbed the end of the ribbon between his fingers.

Her breath caught as she waited, spellbound by his nearness. Would he touch her the way a man touches a woman? Would he walk away before she knew what it felt like? Should she *send* him away and protect herself from the dangerous feelings he stirred up inside her?

If she feared for her life, she'd know exactly what to do. But she knew as surely as the morning followed the dawn that she needn't be afraid of this man. Instead of being reassured, that knowledge made her feel bare and unprotected. She didn't know how to combat his assault on her senses, how to fight his invasion of her soul.

He stared at the satin bow holding her chemise together, then shook his head and dropped the end of the ribbon as if it burned his fingers. "It's getting late. I'd better go. I'll send Riley down to watch out for you."

Pain expanded in her chest and pressed against her heart. "Don't bother. I don't need anybody."

The lantern behind him hissed and flickered before the light went out. She watched him walk away. Inside her, the tiny flame of hope died.

seven

Jeff took a black string tie from the drawer in the armoire and stared in the mirror on the inside of the door. He turned up his white linen collar and slipped the narrow string beneath. It was Sunday, and Mary Murphy kindly, but firmly, asked her boarders to remember the Lord's day at dinner. He assumed that included her stepdaughter and found himself eagerly anticipating the meal. He hadn't seen Bree in a dress since the first day he'd arrived. Twice, he'd seen her in far less, and the memories still burned, hot and raw as a swig of whiskey clear through to his gut.

Someone knocked on his door, and he pulled his dangerous thoughts back to the present. When he answered, Bree stood before him in a high-necked, short-sleeved blue cotton dress. Her hair hung like black silk around her shoulders, and curly wisps teased her forehead and cheeks, wild and free, framing her small face and making her blue eyes seem enormous.

She looked down and cleared her throat. "Sorry to bother you, but I need something from my—the armoire."

"Help yourself." He held his arm wide, motioning her inside. What could she want? Since he'd been here, besides the books on the table, he hadn't come across anything of hers in the room.

She walked past him, and he saw that her hair fell

nearly to her waist. Why had he never noticed that before?
Because by braiding it and wearing a hat, she'd done her
best to hide her glorious tresses.

She stooped and pulled out the bottom drawer. He'd
never looked in there; his belongings fit just fine in the top
part of the armoire. After reaching way into the back, she
found what she wanted, then started to rise. He held out
his palm to assist her, and she hesitated before ignoring it
and standing herself.

"Thanks, Mr.—"

"Don't say it. Are we back to that blasted formality
again?"

"You tell me." Her voice was hardly more than a whisper. She dropped her fist to her side and buried it against
her hip in the folds of her dress.

Her tone was distant, wounded, just like last night when
she'd said she didn't need anyone. She might as well have
said she didn't need *him*. That should have pleased him,
but it didn't. This subdued young woman standing quietly
before him made him uneasy.

"I thought we'd reached an understanding." He closed
the armoire and leaned a shoulder against it.

"We did. I work for you, that's all. When you don't
need the *River Belle*, you go your way and I'll go mine."
Her gaze lifted from the middle of his chest to his face.

Jeff sensed the anger and hurt simmering beneath her
reserved exterior. He wanted to see just a fraction of her
usual spirit. He could handle her temper—he suspected it
was a facade she'd perfected to survive in a man's
world—but this uncharacteristic coolness bothered him.
And he wasn't sure why.

Maybe because he'd seen her fire, tested the surface of
her desire with his kiss. He guessed there was more, so
much more, beneath this distant disguise she'd taken on.

Jeff fought the urge to pull her against him and find her
passion again. He wanted to kiss her until she was warm
and soft and responsive in his arms. And that was why

he'd left her so abruptly last night and why he was relieved that she'd avoided him today.

He didn't dare see her alone. The temptation to touch her was more than he could handle because he didn't know if he could stop there. And he'd sworn he'd never hurt her.

He knew she didn't trust men, and he wanted her faith. Something told him she was innocent—and there was a part of him that wanted desperately to taste her innocence—but he wouldn't break his word. He couldn't give her anything; the only solution was pushing her away.

But he wasn't sure he had the strength for that. All he knew was that seeing her quiet and reserved troubled him. That was wrong for her somehow, and he wanted to change it.

He looked at her fist, pressed tightly against her side. "What are you hiding in your hand?"

She took a step back. "Nothing."

"Can't be nothing. It was important enough for you to come up here and ask me for it."

"What do you care?" She drew back several more steps until the spindle on the bed halted her.

He pushed away from the armoire and followed until he stood directly in front of her, trapping her between himself and the four-poster. "I care about you."

"I'll believe that when snakes sprout wings. You don't care what happens to anyone on the river. If you did, you'd . . . Oh, never mind. It doesn't matter anymore."

A warm breeze fluttered the lacy curtains in the opened window to his right. Bree blinked and lifted her fist to brush strands of hair away from her face.

"It does matter." He took her small hand and held it in his palm. Through her fingers he saw a length of blue satin. He was the last person she wanted to see right now, but she'd come to his room for her ribbon. The thought pulled at him.

She tried to wrench away. "I haven't time for this, Tanner. Mary needs help."

He tightened his grip, not enough to hurt the fine bones of her hand, just enough to keep her there. When she stopped resisting, he pried open her fingers and lifted the shiny satin. "This must be mighty important to force you up here to face me."

"No." She shrugged and looked out the window, squinting against the glare of the sun. "Just wanted to get it out of your way, that's all. I forgot about it until I put on this dress. It matches."

"I see that." Her blue-black hair rested across her breast. He lifted a strand and rubbed the silky softness between his fingers. "It will look beautiful in your hair.'

Bree turned her head to the side, pulling away from his touch. "It's none of your business what I do with this ribbon or anything else. The sooner you get that through your thick skull, the better. Now get out of my way."

Jeff heard the door close in the room beside his. Heavy boots sounded in the hall. He looked over, and Charlie stood in the open doorway.

"Is this a private party, or can anybody join?" Dressed in a black shirt and pants, he leaned against the frame, an insolent look in his pale eyes. A slight smile slashed his face, like a knife mark through fresh dough.

"It's not a party at all." Bree grabbed her ribbon. "Supper's ready. That's the other reason I came up here, Tanner. Come and get it."

She hurried from the room. When she passed him, Charlie moved slightly, letting his elbow brush her breast. Jeff watched her back stiffen, then she lifted her skirt slightly and increased her pace. Her stepbrother's grin grew broader.

A blaze of fury exploded in Jeff's head. He clenched his hands into fists, suppressing the urge to beat the self-satisfied smile from the other man's face.

After the sound of Bree's light, running steps faded

down the stairs, Jeff moved closer to the man standing in his doorway. He stayed just out of reach, not trusting himself to control his temper. "I want to talk to you, Charlie."

"What about, Tanner?"

"About what happened the other night on *Belle*, at the bridge site."

Charlie straightened and folded his arms across his rangy chest. "Don't know what you're talkin' about."

"Somebody was there—with Bree. Somebody frightened her badly, and I aim to find out who." Jeff watched the other man closely, judging his reaction.

A look of shock, then exaggerated innocence screened his features. "Breanne didn't say a word about it to me—and she tells me everything. Are you sure about this?"

"Yeah, I'm sure. Then you don't know who was there?"

Charlie shook his head, then rubbed his palms over the hair slicked back from his forehead. He tugged on the leather thong at his nape to tighten it. "If you find out who it was, let me know. Nobody scares my little sister and gets away with it."

He was lying. Jeff knew it as surely as he knew death followed a rattler's fangs. But he couldn't prove anything, and Bree wouldn't talk about it. Riley had told him to trust his instincts. His gut told him to make sure Charlie never got her alone again.

Jeff touched the knob and started to pull the door closed. "Supper's ready. Let's go."

Charlie turned and headed down the hall. "You're in for a treat, Tanner. Nobody makes better fried chicken than Mother."

After turning the key, Jeff put it in his pocket and followed. He trusted Charlie Perkins about as much as a sidewinder spooked from under a rock.

Jeff descended the stairs and crossed to the dining room. Sean sat at the head of the table with Mary to his left and his daughter on the right. With her back to him, he could see that Bree had confined her thick hair using the light blue ribbon.

Charlie rounded the table and kissed his mother's cheek, next to the star-shaped scar just below her eye. "Mother, everything looks wonderful, as usual."

"Thank you, dear. I'm lucky to have a son who appreciates me so." She smiled warmly at him, then nodded to Jeff. "Mr. Tanner." She held out her left hand and indicated the chair beside her. "Would you do me the honor?"

"My pleasure, ma'am. Sean." He nodded to the older man as he passed Charlie, who moved to the other side of the table and sat next to Bree. Jeff's gut tightened, and he gritted his teeth. Simmer down, he cautioned himself. The man wouldn't try anything here at the family dinner table. But he saw Bree stiffen and hunch her shoulders forward when Charlie's elbow grazed her upper arm.

The table, covered with a yellowed Irish linen cloth, held fried chicken, steaming mashed potatoes and gravy, biscuits, and green beans. The china had been fine once, but now cracks and chips marred the delicate plates. When Mary passed him the chicken, he noticed a permanent stain on the material where the platter had rested. The Murphys had seen abundance in the past, but times had changed. He silenced his conscience; he wasn't responsible for their decline in fortunes.

Mary cleared her throat. "It seems we're just family tonight—and of course you, Mr. Tanner."

"I'm delighted to be included," Jeff said. "Where's everyone else?"

"Cactus Kate's." Sean placed a biscuit beside his gravy and potatoes.

Jeff nodded. Sunday evening in the saloon was about what he'd expect from the other boarders. "I guess they probably didn't get up early for church this morning, either."

Mary shook her head as she handed him the basket filled with rolls. "There isn't one yet, a church, I mean.

We have services at Bellmore's restaurant. That reminds me. There's to be a dance next Saturday—a fund-raiser to build a church. That new reverend's just a ball of fire. Says we need a real building that's just for the Lord so's we can nourish our souls as well as our bodies."

Bree finished chewing and swallowed. Excitement shone on her face, and her eyes sparkled like sapphires. "A dance sounds like fun. But how is it supposed to raise money?"

"All the women are asked to bring a boxed dinner to raffle off. And that Reverend Howard"—Mary shook her head, and laughed—"he's a sly one. The gentlemen have to pay for a dance with the lady of their choice."

Charles looked at Bree and licked the chicken grease from his lower lip. "Sounds like my kind of shindig. What do you think, little sister?" He stared at her, and his eyes glittered like a hungry wolf.

Bree lifted her fork, and her hand froze halfway to her mouth. She darted a look at her stepbrother, and all the pleasurable anticipation faded from her expression.

Mary glanced from her son to her stepdaughter. "Why, that's a fine idea, Charles. I think you should escort Breanne and bid on her basket."

The way he plays cards, he'd have enough money, Jeff thought. Then he saw Bree's face. Fear, raw and unmistakable, stirred in her eyes and tightened her mouth. She reminded him of a cornered deer poised for escape, every nerve and muscle recoiling from Charlie. A frown marred the smooth skin of her forehead as she shifted slightly, closer to her father.

"I'm too busy to go."

"You wouldn't want to disappoint Mother, now, would you, Breanne?" Charlie put down his fork and stroked her bare forearm with his index finger. "Surely one evening . . ."

"It's just a church social. I don't really care about going."

"Nonsense, child." Sean wiped his face with the napkin and put it on the table beside his empty plate. "You work too hard. One night can't hurt—young girl like you should go to a dance every now and then."

Charlie smiled, an arrogant, smug expression. "Then it's all settled. I'm looking forward to it."

Bree pushed her plate away, her dinner half-finished. Jeff waited, willing her to speak up, silently urging her to refuse to go with him, but she didn't. A protective feeling broke loose within him, and he wanted to step between her and Charlie Perkins. The man wasn't any kin to him, and he didn't much care whose feathers he ruffled as long as he kept her safe. But he was an outsider, walking a tight-rope between the railroad and the rivermen. He'd bide his time and find another way.

Mary smiled indulgently at her son. The scar on her cheek lifted and blended with the laugh lines at the corner of her eye. "I know you two will have a fine time."

Bree wiped her trembling lips, then put down her napkin. "Supper was good, but I'm stuffed. Mary, would you mind if I took a walk?"

Her stepmother nodded, and Bree hurried into the hall. Jeff excused himself and followed. He saw her grab her pistol from the table by the front door just before she left the house.

Outside, Jeff blinked several times and squinted against the late afternoon sun. He saw Bree walking briskly down the worn path and started after her.

He caught her arm and halted her. "I'm going with you."

"You don't even know where I'm headed."

"To the river. That's where you always go when you're upset."

"What makes you think I'm—"

"Quit, Bree. I saw the look on your face when they pushed you into going to that dance with Charlie."

"They mean well."

"Let's go this way." He took her arm and led her up the dirt footpath and into the hills behind town. They walked in silence, and finally stopped beside a pile of boulders surrounded by tumbleweeds. The sun sat on the top of the mountain, an orange circle of fire. There wasn't much daylight left.

Jeff sat down on a rock. He took off his string tie and stuffed it in his pocket, then loosened his collar and rolled up his sleeves. In the distance wisps of cotton clouds glowed red-orange and gold, outlined with purple where the moisture in them lingered.

Bree stood to his right, watching the brilliant sunset. His gaze rested on her profile. "Don't go with him."

She looked puzzled. "What?"

"Tell Charlie you won't go to the dance with him."

"I can't." She stared at the sunset again, frowning.

"Can't—or won't?"

"You don't understand, Tanner."

"Enlighten me."

"Mary's been good to me, tried hard to take my mother's place. I owe her for that. And—it's only a dance." She shrugged and looked into the distance. After brushing a strand of hair from her eyes, she dropped her hand to her side, and her fingers closed into a fist. "It's just one night, for a good cause. There will be lots of other people there." She bit her lip and looked at him. Apprehension clouded her face, and her voice was hardly more than a whisper. "I have no choice."

"There's always a choice."

"Not always."

Frustration twisted his insides. He reached down and grabbed a handful of rocks beside him.

A rustling noise scratched at the edge of his mind, but the red mist of anger screened it out.

Bree's gaze shifted to his left. She gasped and stiffened, as the color left her face. She lifted her gun in his direction. "Don't move."

"Now, wait a minute . . ." Then he heard the ominous rattle.

Her hands tightened on the handle of the pistol; her eyes narrowed as she aimed and squeezed the trigger. The explosion reverberated through the hills and bounced off the rocks. While he waited for his ears to stop ringing, Jeff looked beside him and saw the long, thick body of a snake and the deadly rattles on the tail.

"I hate snakes." She lowered her gun hand. Then she grinned. "You're lucky I hate 'em more than railroad men."

He took a deep breath and released it long and slow. He looked at the reptile, the ragged, bloody place where the head used to be. "Nope. Lucky you're good with that gun."

She nodded. "I have to be." She planted her hand on her hip.

"Practice much?" He'd missed seeing this spunky side of her.

"Now and then." She turned away from him and brushed strands of hair from her eyes. The blue ribbon had slid down, almost to her waist, and hung at the end of the thick, dark length. "See that three-armed cactus over there?"

He nodded. "Yup."

She lifted her pistol and gripped the handle in both hands. Four shots, one right after the other, rang out. When he looked past her, Jeff saw the prickly green arm fall slowly, then dangle precariously from the trunk of the saguaro.

He grinned. "That's good shooting."

"Good?" She looked over her shoulder and raised a dark brow. "Just 'good'?"

"Damn good."

"That's better." She smiled, then a perplexed expression crossed her face. "If I was a lousy shot, or just a smidgeon slower, all my troubles would be over."

"How do you figure?"

She pointed the barrel of her gun at the mutilated snake. "If that rattler had struck, you'd be buzzard bait now, and the bridge would be just a bad memory."

He picked up the long body and held it out to her, grinning when she shrieked and backed up a step. He tossed it behind him into the thick clump of tumbleweeds. "Thanks, Murphy. I guess I owe you one."

"Darn right you owe me. You could pay me back by going home." She looked at him hopefully.

Jeff smiled broadly. "You know I can't do that."

But he had something in mind to repay her. Exactly how he'd pull it off, he wasn't certain. But he always made good on his debts.

After the sun went down, Bree allowed Tanner to accompany her to the steamboat. She stood on the gangplank and looked at him. He dropped his hand from her elbow after steadying her, then backed up a step onto the riverbank. As the sun's glow faded behind the jagged mountains, he stood silhouetted against the horizon. She could hear his breathing, smell the masculine scent of him, but she wasn't near enough to touch him without moving forward.

The distance between them settled her nerves. She struggled to still her shivery insides and prayed that he wouldn't see how much his close call with the deadly rattler had unsettled her. She had a vision of him suffering a lingering, painful death from the snake's bite. She exhaled slowly, a shuddering breath.

"You're not cold, are you?" he asked abruptly.

"No. It's just when you get close to the river, the breeze picks up the coolness from the water."

"Oh."

All this attention made her as jittery as a long-tailed cat in a room full of rocking chairs. She wasn't accustomed to a man, such a handsome man, paying her any mind. It set her aglow from the pit of her stomach to the tips of her toes. If that wasn't enough, sometimes she thought he could read her mind. Though she'd refused to say, somehow, he sensed her fear of letting her stepbrother escort her to the church fund-raiser. He also knew Charles had been on *Belle* the other night and had frightened her.

He obviously thought she was crazy to go with Charles. But she'd handle it; somehow she always did. She couldn't talk about her fears to anyone; she'd die if it got back to Mary. She wouldn't hurt the other woman that way. And as for the dance ... A tremble began in her stomach and rippled through her, settling in her knees. She swayed on the gangplank.

"You sure you're all right?" he asked.

"Fine."

In the short time they'd stood and talked, the sun's rays had faded, and now stars shimmered above them.

She stared up and sighed.

He followed her gaze. "I've never seen such a sky. In New York there are too many lights to see the stars shine that bright."

"I saw a dress in a catalog once—came all the way from San Francisco." She glanced at him shyly. Darkness hid his expression and gave her the courage to go on. "It had fuss and flounces and jet and beads all over. Couldn't tell from the picture, but I bet it sparkled like gold dust. I imagined it to be the prettiest thing ever. But two bits to a dollar it's not anything compared to the glory of an Arizona sky filled with stars."

"You'd win that bet, Bree." His voice was husky.

He stepped closer. She could feel the heat of his body, his breath stirring her hair. Sensing the coiled tension in him, she knew he was going to touch her. But she couldn't think, couldn't move.

He went still, suddenly alert, and looked past her, peering into the darkness beyond. "Do you smell smoke?"

She looked around, then spotted the glow of a fire upwind along the river. "Riley's bedding down for the night."

"Good. Guess I'd better head back, then."

"Guess so. 'Night, Tanner."

When the sound of the scrape and rattle of rocks from his footsteps died away, she touched her fingers to her trembling mouth. Unhappiness settled like a stone on her heart. Maybe tomorrow she'd be glad he hadn't kissed her, but right now something cracked wide inside her, a gaping emptiness that couldn't be filled. In the morning she could explain away her need for his touch, tell herself that she was better off. But in the dark of night a fierce and piercing loneliness surrounded her. No man had ever made her feel this way, and she wished she'd never laid eyes on Jefferson Tanner.

Jeff headed toward the campfire just below the riverbank. Stepping over the rocky uneven dirt, he moved closer and saw the white beard and battered black hat. Light glinted off metal as Riley saw who it was and slowly lowered the shotgun. The old man was ready for trouble, and Jeff was glad he watched over Bree, for more reasons than just her protection. If he hadn't known someone was watching, he'd have kissed her—the worst thing he could've done.

"Care t'set a spell?" Riley pointed to the empty space beside him on the fallen cottonwood trunk.

Jeff nodded and sat down. Hard and rough, the dead tree bit into his backside as he looked around the makeshift camp. In the small circle of firelight a bedroll and canvas sack were the only provisions visible. The moon had risen, and he could plainly see the *River Belle* and the outline of Bree's lantern around the blanket over the wheelhouse door. The gangplank he'd just left stretched clear and open from the riverbank to the boat, and Riley could have hit him dead on if he'd wanted to. No one could get past without being seen.

"Somethin' eatin' you, boy?" The old man opened a leather pouch, then stuffed a pinch of tobacco into his cheek.

"What did Charlie do to her, Riley?"

"If'n she wants ya' t'know, she'll tell ya' herself, but I aim t'see he never catches her alone again."

"He did last week, at the bridge site."

Riley spit a brown stream into the fire beside the dented tin coffeepot, and the flames sputtered and hissed. His eyes narrowed to black slits as his hand tightened on the deadly gun across his knees. "You certain?"

"All I know for sure is someone was there and she was scared. I'd lay odds it was Charlie." Jeff picked up a stick and poked the embers. "Is he the reason she carries that gun?"

"Yup. I taught her how t'shoot like a man—better, maybe."

"Then I owe you my thanks." Jeff laughed. "She saved my life a while ago. Killed a rattler."

"That what all the commotion was about?" He stopped, puzzled. "She coulda' done that with one shot. I heard five all told."

"She killed a cactus, too, showing off. Interesting woman." Jeff grinned at the memory, then his brows drew together as a frown creased his forehead. "Why are Mary and Sean pushing Charlie at Bree?"

"Mary's hopin' for a weddin' b'tween them, sorta settle Charlie down." Riley shifted the tobacco chaw from one side of his mouth to the other, and his cheek bulged. "Don't judge her harsh. She had a hard life with Charlie's dad. He was a bad 'un. My guess is she wants a strong woman fer her son, a lady t'keep him on the straight 'n' narrow. And Sean wants his girl taken care of."

It made sense if they didn't care about her being happy. Bree Murphy was the most fearless, capable women he'd ever met. She and Charlie shared an interest in steamboats; marrying her would keep the business in the family. He exhaled deeply and looked up at the black sky. The smoky glow from the fire blurred the blanket of stars until they disappeared. "Can't you talk to her father? Make Sean see that he's not right for her."

"Ain't my place to convince him different."

"It damned sure is. For God's sake, man, you're sitting here with a shotgun to protect her. Did you know they pushed Bree into going to the church social with him?"

Riley spit into the fire again. The lines on his forehead deepened. "Hadn't heard. Jest hafta' stick close to her."

"Sean should know what's going on."

He shook his head. "Missy made me promise not t'tell her pa. Said she won't give him another reason t'drink."

"Then talk to Bree. Convince her not to go. She'll listen to you."

"There's not a body in these parts kin make Bree Murphy do nothin' she ain't of a mind t'do. Leastways, it ain't me." The old man speared him with a look. "What about you? You tried talkin' her out of it?"

"Yeah. She wouldn't listen. Says it's only a dance and she owes Mary." He raked his fingers through his hair. "Somebody has to make them see that Charlie's wrong for her."

"One skirmish at a time, boy. What're you aimin' t'do about the church shindig?"

"I'm the last person to try to tell her anything. She can't stand the sight of me."

The old man sighed. He shook his head, and the glow from the fire turned his white whiskers orange and gold. "You got a lot t'learn about women. What they say and what they *feel's* two diff'rent things."

"What are you trying to tell me?"

"For somebody smart enuff t'make more money than the Almighty hisself, you're slow as mud, boy. Bree Murphy packs a pistol—reminds Charlie t'keep his distance. She wears pants t'make him forget she's female, but she's all woman—through and through. She's sweet on you. Somethin' tells me you feel the same."

Jeff stared at the old man beside him, suppressing the desire to laugh. Bree, sweet on him? Ridiculous. More than once she'd threatened to blow his head clean off.

Him—sweet on her? Impossible. She wasn't even close to the kind of woman he envisioned in his life. Besides, he was practically spoken for, although he hadn't actually said anything to Emily. He thought of his partner's daughter, pretty enough in a plain, pale sort of way. He tried to picture her shooting the head off a rattler. This time he did laugh.

"Somethin' funny, boy?"

With an effort Jeff controlled his laughter, then rested his elbows on his knees and stared into the fire. "I was just thinking about a friend back home."

"This—friend—wear skirts?"

Jeff glanced at the old man and wondered if Riley O'Rear could read his mind.

"Yeah, Emily's a lady."

"Mind you recollect somethin', son. Clothes don't make a person. It's what's inside."

Jeff thought of Bree in her blue cotton dress, pistol in her hand. Skirt or pants, she was more woman than any female he'd ever met—and with all her heart and soul she backed whoever or whatever she cared about. Besides her father, the river and her boat were the most important things to her.

He tried to picture her playing hostess at a business dinner. The thought made him smile. He could see her threatening to shoot someone who disagreed with him. On the other hand, her fierce kind of loyalty was a rare treasure. Any man would be lucky to have her.

Any man but him.

"You gonna answer my question?" The old man glanced at the boat and shifted the shotgun resting across his knees.

"Forgot what it was."

"You sweet on Bree?"

"Nope. Just don't want to see her hurt."

"So what're you gonna do about it?"

Jeff looked at Riley and glowered. "What makes you think I plan to do anything?"

"Ain't stupid, boy. Ain't blind, neither. You're smart as a whip and watchin' over her same's I am. 'Tain't often I'm wrong about a man, and I reckon you got somethin' up yer sleeve."

"You're imagining things, old man."

Riley snorted. "Not hardly. And I'd like t'know how yer plannin' t'keep that snake from takin' her t' the church shindig."

"Don't know yet. But I've got a week to figure it out. And one good turn deserves another."

eight

Bree walked away from the boardinghouse and kicked the pebbles in her path. The warm breeze billowed her cotton blouse behind her while loose tendrils of hair escaped the knot on her crown and tickled her bare neck. Dusk encompassed her as the night sounds commenced; one by one lights appeared in the buildings along Hardyville's main street. She jammed her hands into the pockets of her jeans as her spirits sank lower than the sun behind the jagged shadowy hills.

She'd just seen Mary and tried on the dress her stepmother had altered for her to wear to the church social the following night. How could she tell the woman she'd rather take her chances with a pit full of snakes than be alone with Charles?

If only she'd held her tongue at Sunday dinner. "Dumb, dumb, dumb," she muttered to herself. "I'm half-witted as a magpie, with a mouth to match."

But when talk of the dance had come up, she could only think about the sheer pleasure of seeing other people. It'd been so long; excuses to socialize were few and far between. And she looked forward to seeing friends, hearing the latest news, kicking up her heels. She loved music and missed it sorely. But now she was stuck with Charles.

If she was a good liar, she could go to Mary with some

excuse. But Bree knew the other woman would be suspicious and demand to know what was wrong.

She needed to talk to her father. She didn't have to come right out and tell him why she'd rather not be alone with her stepbrother. That would only add to Cap's problems. But if she pleaded nerves, or a sprained ankle, even female complaints, Mary would never have to know the truth.

"And maybe I'll flap my arms and fly away." Bree took aim with her toe and booted a good-size rock out of her way.

She felt the jolt up to her knee and ruefully acknowledged that if she didn't think of something soon, that sprained ankle wouldn't be a fib. At the bottom of the rise she noticed a light in the window at the steamboat company. Why was Cap still there this time of night? Well, no matter. Now was as good a time as any to approach him.

She entered the front of the building and inched her way down the hall. Cap's office was dark. Next door the lantern's glow spilled into the corridor. Must be Tanner working. She peeked into the room and saw him sitting bent over the desk. Scattered papers covered the part she could see; his broad back and shoulders hid the rest. A few sheets littered the floor around him. In the far corners of the room, shadows danced and swayed from the flickering light beside him. He was the last person she wanted to see. His close call with the rattlesnake had proved that her feelings for her boss were more than business. They had to work together, but after hours, she did her best to steer clear of him. As she turned to slip away, her boots scraped on the wooden floor.

Tanner straightened and pushed his chair around, checking the room behind him. "Somebody there?"

"Just me." She stepped out of the gloomy hall and leaned against the doorframe.

"Bree?" He flexed his shoulders and tipped his head from one side to the other, stretching his strong neck. His thick brown hair was mussed, as if he'd dragged his fingers through it countless times. "What are you doing here?"

"It's my office, too."

He blinked, then rubbed the bridge of his nose. "So it is. I just didn't expect to see you. With all this paperwork I've lost track of time." He glanced to the desk on his right and shook his head. "I hate it as much as you hate snakes."

She studied the untidy pile spread every which way beside his elbow. "I can see that. If we're sharing this office, just where do you expect me to work in that mess?"

"Sorry. Didn't know you had work to do. I'll clean off your half." He started to shuffle scraps together, then looked at her. "Pushing a pen won't be so bad with you here to talk to."

Did that mean he was happy to see her? The warmth of his gaze melted her reserve like a hot knife through butter. Her stomach flip-flopped and her heart knocked against her ribs. Then she remembered why she'd come. "Don't bother. I was just looking for Cap."

"He's at Cactus Kate's."

"Then I'll see him there."

His brow lifted. "Must be mighty important."

"It is." She looked at the floor, then started to turn away.

"Have anything to do with the dance tomorrow night?"

Her head snapped up. "What I have to say is between my father and me. It's no concern of yours, Tanner."

"That's true. But something tells me you're having second thoughts." He leaned back in his chair and folded his arms across his chest. "Stay. Talk to. me."

She almost escaped out the door, but she made the mistake of glancing up at him. He smiled at her, a soft, slow smile that made her stomach quiver and turn upside down—a smile that said "trust me." A smile that showed her she couldn't trust herself. Green eyes met and held hers. Awareness sizzled through her like burning gunpowder. She was drawn to him, his undeniable masculinity. She blinked, breaking the spell, and reminded herself not to let her guard slip.

In her experience men were not to be trusted. She had to stay one step ahead all the time, and she could only rely on herself. Was Tanner any different from the other men she knew? He saw Charles for what he was; he knew her fear and tried to help. But so did Riley. Her attraction to the handsome railroad man was more than just gratitude. And that gave him the power to do her greater hurt. She studied him—his broad chest, the lazy grin and dark shadow of whiskers that covered his square jaw, the hard angles of his face—and was pulled to him as surely as if he'd thrown a lasso around her waist and tugged on the rope.

Slowly she approached him and stopped in front of the desk. Beside her he sat in the chair, the bigger one from her father's office. Hers sat in a shadowed corner, and hauling it over would imply staying awhile. She didn't intend to do that. But somehow, where Tanner was concerned, all her plans washed away, like driftwood on the Colorado.

The cautious side of her wanted to leave, to get out while she still could. The woman side of her wanted to stay near him. Excitement crackled between them. He might be dangerous, but he made her tingle all over and feel alive. And that was better than the empty feeling inside. She couldn't tear herself away—not just yet.

"If you need to talk, maybe I can help." He smoothed his mustache with his thumb and forefinger.

"No. I need to speak to Cap—alone."

"That'll be a trick. My guess is he's with your stepbrother. I heard Charlie offer to buy him a drink."

"Oh." She leaned her hip on the edge of the desk and wondered what Charles was up to. Why couldn't he leave Cap alone?

Distractedly, she brushed some papers aside and cleared a place to sit on the desk. With her hands braced on the top, she slid backward and dangled her boots over the side.

The scent of perfume caught her attention, and she took a closer look at the papers beside her. On the stack of invoices and business correspondence rested a personal letter handwritten in a lovely, flowing style. She guessed that he'd been reading it when she surprised him, and she'd bet everything she owned that it was written by a lady. Curiosity worried the edges of her mind like a persistent itch. But she looked away and folded her hands in her lap.

She glanced around the room, trying to control her nosiness. When her gaze slid to the side again, she forced herself to look away. What did she care if the entire pile was from women? Maybe his sister or his mother wrote.

No matter how much she might want to know who'd written, a double team of oxen couldn't drag the question from her. His ego was already the size of Arizona, and she wouldn't give him the satisfaction of asking whom the letter was from.

She glanced again at the note and read the signature at the bottom: "Fondly, Emily." A twinge rippled through her, two parts jealousy, one part irritation. That wasn't his sister's name, and certainly his mother wouldn't inscribe it that way. The individual letters curled and flowed, forming words in a graceful feminine composition. Her own scrawl was big and boxy and plain. Cap could read it without his spectacles. And wasn't that the point? Writing was meant to be read, not framed and hung on the wall.

She glanced at Tanner, the amused expression on his face. Could he read her thoughts?

Before she could stop herself, the question was out of her mouth. "So, who's the letter from?"

He spread his long fingers wide and touched the tips together, forming a steeple. "Emily Hollingsworth."

"She from back East?"

He nodded. "My partner's daughter."

"She married?"

He shook his head.

Deep inside her, an ember of hope dimmed. "What does she do?"

"She runs her father's house."

She watched him intently, waiting for more. "That's all?"

"It's a big house—a job in itself. She directs a full staff of servants, plans daily menus. And if there's a dinner party, it's usually for several hundred people. That's a lot of work."

"Can't be so hard." But she tried to picture that many people at a formal get-together. Two hundred? All at the same time? That was more than the entire population of Hardyville. Her eyes opened wider. She couldn't imagine a home big enough to hold that number of guests. "Why would you want to eat with so many people?"

"Constructing a successful business is like building anything. You plan, put together a firm foundation and a sturdy frame and solid walls to weather the storms. Elaborate dinner parties with the right people are the finishing touches. Then success—and power—are unquestionable."

She shook her head, amazed at how complicated it was. "But why so many?"

"Plain, old-fashioned common sense." He grinned. "It's best not to slight anyone. You never know when you might need a favor. Besides, I'd rather have my competition where I can keep an eye on them. That's better than giving them the chance to plot behind my back."

She stared at the toe of her boot. He might as well live on the moon, for all she knew about his fancy way of life. But his lady friend probably fit his world like a custom-made kid glove. "And Emily knows how to put together one of these elegant dinner parties?"

"She went to school to learn how to manage a large household. Normally a woman waits until she marries to take on the responsibilities of lady of the house. But Emily stepped in when her mother died." There was a faraway look on his face. Then he nodded. "Yeah, Emily's just about the most efficient hostess I know."

She remembered him telling her about working his way through school. Maybe his lifestyle was less sophisticated than Emily's. "You have a big, fancy house and a bunch of servants, too?"

He grinned. "Yeah. It's pretty big."

"You have anyone to take care of it for you?"

"Right now my family lives there with me. Mother runs the house. My sister, Cady, helps when she's home from boarding school."

Bree remembered the fine furnishings in his private railroad car and realized his house must be a hundred times more grand. She'd known his way of life was different from hers, but she hadn't understood how different until now. She couldn't imagine going to school to learn how to take care of a home. Although it didn't sound very much like a home to her. Sounded more like a palace—stiff and stodgy and uncomfortable.

"I guess Emily knows all there is to know about running your house. If you were to marry her, that is."

"I suppose she could take care of it at that."

Bree's heart sank and the small spark of hope spit faintly before it sputtered out. She couldn't compete with Emily, even if she wanted to.

A sharp ache formed in her chest as she remembered the feel of his mouth on hers. She'd yearned to experience the sensation again, to test her heated response. That was something they didn't teach in boarding school. She'd stake her reputation as a steamboat captain on it. She sighed. Her good name and high regard in river navigation was all she had and probably all she ever would have. Even if she was lady enough to make him look at her twice, he was already taken.

Jeff studied her pensive expression.

She seemed to feel his gaze and looked at him. "So are you?"

"Am I, what?"

"Going to marry Emily?"

He rubbed the back of his neck. He didn't intend to discuss his personal life with Bree. He wished she'd never seen Emily's letter, then wondered why he should care that she had.

"It would be a smart move, Tanner. Keep all those little trains in the family."

"Maybe."

Funny, he'd once thought the same about her and Charlie, about keeping the steamboat business under one roof. Before he'd met Bree Murphy, he'd been certain that Emily Hollingsworth would make him a perfect wife. She was a woman equally at ease with politicians and businessmen. She was right in so many ways. But if Emily was so suitable, why couldn't he get Bree Murphy out of his mind? He knew the answer. A man could never be satisfied with cool efficiency when he'd tasted fire.

He respected Bree's directness, had come to expect nothing less from her. There were depths and layers to her that he could only begin to imagine. A man could spend a lifetime discovering her mysteries. The thought fascinated him. He watched her and studied the open inquisitiveness in her big blue eyes. Her thick black hair looked different tonight, the braid missing. The upswept tresses revealed her graceful, slender neck, and he took a deep breath, aching to know how she tasted.

What was she thinking? From the moment they'd met, she'd appeared indifferent, hostile. But now he wondered.

He'd always enjoyed a challenge, thrived on it, wouldn't be where he was today if he shied away from a risk. In fact, except for the pain his mother had experienced, he could almost thank his grandfather for turning his back when he'd needed money. A man could afford to take a chance when he had nothing to lose. And he'd learned to take chances, an attribute that served him well in business. He'd learned to spar with adversaries and best them, as if the deal were nothing more than a game.

Since his arrival in Arizona, he'd hardly thought about Emily and certainly hadn't missed her. When he wasn't busy with construction of the bridge, it was Bree who occupied his thoughts. Even when he was engaged in business, she had a way of sneaking into his mind. After casually shifting her position on the desk, she touched the edge of his letter and her smooth forehead puckered thoughtfully. She seemed exceptionally interested in Emily.

He wondered if she was really as indifferent to him as she seemed. Was Bree jealous? The thought pleased him.

Did she wear her hostility to hide her tender feelings the way she wore jeans and boots to conceal her femininity? Her act might work with other men, but he wasn't buying it. He'd seen the delicate pink ribbon that closed her chemise over her creamy breasts. He's sampled the warmth of her lips that hinted of fire beneath the surface. And he knew something else, too. He wanted her.

Blood pounded through his veins and raced to his groin. The ache spread and settled like a rock in his gut. He'd promised not to hurt her. But what if she wanted him, too? What if she needed him the way he needed her?

The lantern behind her outlined the lush fullness of her breasts beneath her loose shirt. The top button was carelessly undone, and sweat formed on his brow as his gaze roamed higher over the pale column of her neck. He wanted to release the hair curled and twined and piled on her head. He wanted to see the black silk free and flowing, framing her bare shoulders, slipping through his fingers.

"Your hair's different. I like it."

Shyly she lowered her eyes and touched the wisps at her ears. "Mary helped me. She said it would look good with the dress I'm wearing to the dance."

"You're set on going?"

She nodded.

"Then go with me." He stood up and moved closer to her. The sweet, clean fragrance of her surrounded him. Her female scent made him want her the way man has wanted woman since the beginning of time.

"I already agreed to go with Charles."

"No. Mary suggested it and you didn't disagree."

"Tanner, I can't—"

"You're going with me." He put his hands around her waist and lifted her down. "And this is why."

Jeff lowered his mouth to hers. His arms encircled her in a fierce grip, holding her close against him. He kissed her hard and urged her lips open, then searched the inside of her mouth with his tongue. With his body he tried to tell her what he couldn't put into words. He wanted her; he'd take care of her. He tightened the protective circle of his embrace. He would keep Charlie away from her, and he didn't give a damn who he offended.

He lifted his head and stared at her. Her lips, moist and slightly swollen from his rough kiss, were parted. He felt her breasts swelling against his chest, her breathing harsh like his own.

"Tanner, I think—"

"That's your problem, Murphy. You think too much. You were on your way to the saloon, right? Well, let's go together and break the news to Charlie. I owe you a debt, and it's time to pay up."

Jeff didn't give her a chance to protest but grabbed her hand and pulled her along with him. His long stride made it hard for her to keep up, and he heard her trying to catch her breath, but he didn't slow down. He was sick and tired of trying to think of a way out of this mess. He wanted action. He craved it; he could taste it. His blood raced at the thought of it. He had a message for Charlie that was long overdue.

The thump of their boots on the wooden walkway was drowned by the sound of laughter and music in Cactus

Kate's. Jeff pushed open the swinging doors and stood there with Bree beside him while his eyes adjusted to the bright lights and smoke.

Through the haze he spotted the two men at the long bar across the room. In his black pants and vest, with the stark white shirt beneath, Charlie looked like a dandy, arrogant and self-confident. His dark hat with the silver band was pulled low on his forehead. As they watched, Sean threw back the amber liquid in his glass, then staggered slightly as he wiped the back of his hand across his mouth. Charlie grabbed his arm and steadied him, then poured another shot into Sean's glass.

"Charles knows how little it takes. Damn him." Bree yanked her hand away. "I have to get my father out of here."

"Let's go." Jeff put his arm around her shoulders, pulling her close, protecting her from the rowdy, jostling men as they moved through the crowded saloon. The smell of smoke and liquor and sweat mingled together. As they crossed the wooden floor, he heard the quiet that followed them like trampled virgin prairie grass.

They stopped in front of the other two men. The soldiers on either side backed away several steps. Before Sean could lift the whiskey to his mouth, Bree put her hand on his arm. "Don't, Cap. Let me take you home."

Charlie looked at her, and surprise flickered briefly in his light blue eyes. "Don't be a stick in the mud, little sister."

She glared at him. "How dare you?"

Her stepbrother shrugged. "What's the big deal? He's a grown man. He wanted it."

"You did the inviting," Jeff said, anger twisting inside him.

Charlie slowly turned his gaze away from Bree and narrowed his eyes. "He could've refused. This is no concern of yours, Tanner. Butt out."

"Charles, you know he can't . . ." Bree stopped pleading, and her fingers, extended in supplication, curled into her palm. "Why am I wasting my breath? I'm taking him home." She gripped her father's arm. "C'mon, Cap. Let's go."

"Jus' one more." Sean held up his thumb and forefinger with a space in between. "A little one."

"You've had enough."

"Don't be so bossy, Bree. Let him have another," Charlie said.

Sean brushed a hand across his face as he looked down at his daughter and tried to focus. "Maybe I should see if Mary's got s-supper on th' table."

Bree nodded and smiled. "That's a fine idea."

Jeff noticed two of his railroad construction crew in the milling crowd. He angled his head toward the intoxicated man, and the workers stepped forward and looped Sean's arms over their shoulders, leading him from the saloon. Bree shot Jeff a grateful look and started to follow.

"Not so fast." Charlie moved suddenly, blocking her path as her father was helped through the door. He stared at her, and something cold and dark filled his eyes. "You think you've won this round. Don't you, little sister?"

"That's not the point . . ." She backed away from him and bumped into Jeff, standing in front of the bar. He put his hands on her shoulders and felt her tremble.

Charlie took a step forward. "That's *exactly* the point, Breanne. But I'm not one to hold a grudge. You've had your way tonight. Tomorrow is mine."

Jeff gritted his teeth, and the muscle in his jaw contracted while he reined in his temper. He wanted to lace his fingers around the other man's neck and squeeze, but he smiled pleasantly.

"About the dance tomorrow." He felt Bree grow rigid and squeezed her shoulders reassuringly. "She's going with me."

The younger man's mouth thinned to a straight line as

he took a step forward. Jeff let go of Bree and moved in front of her.

Charlie's eyes hardened to ice. "The hell you're going with her. It's all arranged. Mother's—"

Jeff held up a hand. "A gracious woman like your mother would be the first one to suggest that Bree make a stranger welcome. I wasn't sure if I could make it to the dance." His gaze locked with the other man's. "I decided I can."

Charlie's slender fingers twitched, then curled into fists at his sides. His body tensed like a rope stretched too tight and ready to snap.

Without looking, Jeff knew the crowd parted, then he smelled the cloying odor of perfume and perspiration. He felt a hand on his arm but still wouldn't take his eyes from Charlie.

"A little disagreement, boys? Maybe you could settle it somewhere else. Don't want any trouble in my place."

Jeff glanced to his right. So this was Cactus Kate. Her whiskey-colored eyes regarded him with weary worldliness as she planted her fists on ample satin-covered hips. There was a sparkle of female interest in her expression, an approval he was accustomed to from women. Above the low-cut neckline of her red dress, generous breasts threatened to overflow. When she glanced at Charlie, distaste showed plainly in her face.

"Sure. We can go outside," Jeff said, turning his most charming smile on her.

Charlie pulled a deck of cards from his pocket. "There's a civilized way to settle this. A hand of five card stud, winner take all."

"Jeff, no . . ." Bree moved beside him and put a hand on his arm. Worried blue eyes pleaded with him.

"It's all right, darlin'," Kate said, her smoky voice loud and authoritative.

"But, Kate—he doesn't know how Charles—"

"Don't you worry." She glanced around the smoky,

crowded room, then smiled at Bree. "Honey, your business is riverboats, mine is men. And that one"—she pointed to Jeff—"can take care of himself."

"It'll be all right." Jeff nodded thanks to the saloon owner, then smiled and briefly covered Bree's hand with his own. After that he pushed thoughts of her from his mind. He didn't want any distractions, and she definitely kept a man's mind on her instead of business. "How about gentlemen's poker. At least one of us is—a gentleman, I mean."

"Right this way, gents." Kate led them to an empty table on the far side of the room. "Win or lose"—she gave each of them a stern look in turn—"don't either of ya' start trouble that'll break up my place. That clear? I'll send over drinks—on the house."

Jeff sat down with his back against the wall. Charlie took the wooden chair across from him as a crowd of men gathered around, three and four deep. Bree pressed through the crush of bodies and stood at Jeff's elbow, arms wrapped around her waist as she bit the corner of her lip.

Jeff watched the other man, holding the deck of cards as if judging its weight. He knew Charlie planned to cheat and considered asking for another deck, then decided against it.

Charlie inserted his thumbnail into the center of the stack and cut it, then slipped the bottom half on top with one practiced movement. He started to deal.

"Wait." Jeff evenly met his gaze. "I want to cut."

"I already did."

"Humor me," Jeff said coldly.

Charlie looked at the men gathered around, then wiped the sweat from his forehead as he put the deck on the round table between them. Jeff lifted one card from the top and slid it beneath the pile. If he was right and the deck had been stacked, he'd get the hand Charlie intended for himself. If not, he'd play the cards he got and take his chances. He waited, eager for the showdown, anxious to see what Charlie's next move would be.

The younger man looked at the deck, then met Jeff's gaze and brushed his chin and upper lip with his forearm. While he hesitated, grumbling rose from the crowd surrounding them. Charlie darted a look around, then flexed his shoulders. His hands shook slightly.

Jeff laced his fingers together and rested his wrists on the table. "You gonna deal 'em or should I just take Bree?"

"You sayin' I'm cheatin'?"

Jeff shook his head. "I'm sayin' deal 'em or fold."

Cactus Kate placed a glass of whiskey in front of each man.

Charlie wiped his hand on his pants, then dealt out five cards to each of them. He picked up his drink and took a sip. As he set it down, the glass slipped from his fingers, splashing the contents across the table and soaking the cards between them.

"Sorry, Tanner."

"I'll bet. Too bad. I had a feeling about those cards."

"Can I have another deck, Kate?" Charlie smiled apologetically and looked up as the saloon owner brought over a rag to wipe up the mess and another stack of cards. A predatory gleam flashed into his eyes, a victorious look that twisted Jeff's insides with rage. He wanted to show up the bastard for the cheating snake that he was.

"Here, Tanner. You deal." He handed over the fresh deck.

Jeff dispersed five cards to each of them—one down, four showing. Charlie had a pair of deuces and a pair of fours. His own pile had two queens, a three, and a five of diamonds.

The younger man grinned as he fiddled with the corner of his hidden card. "Ready t'fold yet, Tanner?"

"Nope. I'll ride these to the end of the line."

Charlie turned over a queen and his smile grew wider, arrogant and triumphant.

Without moving his eyes from his opponent, Jeff lifted his card and with a flick of his wrist, he exposed it. A murmur went up from the gathered crowd. Charlie's gaze went from exultation to shock to fury in a split second. "I don't believe it, Tanner. Three ladies."

Jeff glanced at Bree. "Four."

He stood up and held out his hand.

Charlie's flinty eyes never wavered as he stood. He ignored the gentlemanly gesture and downed the rest of his whiskey. "You won this hand, but don't bank on the next one. And there will be a next time. My daddy always said, don't get mad, get even—and stay on top."

"Words to live by," Jeff said.

Then the man glanced at Bree. "Another time."

When Charlie was gone, the crowd dispersed and they stood alone. Jeff looked down at her beside him. "Are you mad?"

She looked surprised. "Why should I be?"

"Because I interfered."

"I'll make an exception this once. Just don't make a habit of it."

He pulled himself to his full height and cleared his throat. "Miss Murphy, I'd like permission to call for you tomorrow evening at six?"

Her smile was dazzling. "Permission granted."

nine

"May I carry your dinner basket?" Tanner's voice was mannerly, but there was something else there, too. A huskiness Bree didn't quite understand. Anticipation crackled in the air, raising goose bumps on her skin. She was going to the dance with the handsomest man in the Territory. Even though she knew he was doing it because he was beholden to her for shooting the snake, she was excited—and scared. What if she made a fool of herself in front of him?

"It's not heavy. I can do it."

He sighed. "I know you're capable. But allow me." He took the wicker hamper from her.

Self-consciousness made her shy and tongue-tied. She darted a look at him in his black wool coat and trousers, with the fine white linen shirt and string tie. His thick dark hair was neatly combed, the waves slicked into submission, at least for the moment. He smelled good, too, like shaving soap and cologne. Her own light blue cotton dress, with one petticoat beneath, was a hand-me-down from Mary, altered to fit. She was plain and unrefined. He was confident and sophisticated.

He took her breath away.

Only, he had someone special back home waiting for him. And that someone had a name—Emily—a lady who fit in his world. The gap between her and Jeff seemed insurmountable, even if she *wanted* to cross to his side.

The warm evening breeze lifted the dust from their footsteps and swirled it around them as they walked from the boardinghouse to the main street of Hardyville. It was a small town and reminded her of his remark about the lights from the big city blotting out the stars. She couldn't imagine how many buildings there must be to produce so much radiance. She thought about the number of people who worked and lived in all those buildings. It was frightening.

"Bree, you're so damned independent, I even have to fight you to carry the picnic basket. Why can't you accept help, freely given, like a normal woman?"

"Normal for Arizona—or normal for New York?"

"Normal for anywhere." There was no disapproval in his tone, merely curiosity.

She looked at him and waited for her defensive anger to rear up. When it didn't, she felt naked and vulnerable. She owed him for putting himself on the line in the card game and winning her away from Charles. But that didn't mean she had to confide in him. The less he knew about her, the easier it would be to protect herself from him.

She shrugged. "I just do what's necessary to get by. It's not normal or otherwise. I'm just me."

"You're a special woman."

Bree studied him, unable to form words for the lump lodged in her throat. She looked into the warm green eyes gazing down at her as her heart slammed against her breastbone. She hoped he couldn't hear the pounding or see how easy his charm turned her to mush.

"Where'd you learn to play cards like that, Tanner?" she asked, deliberately turning the conversation away from herself.

"Laying track got pretty boring. Cards were easy to carry around." He shrugged. "We gambled a lot to keep from going crazy."

She thought about that and smiled. "I guess in a roundabout way, I should be grateful to the railroad."

His eyebrows lifted in surprise. "Oh?"

"If it hadn't been for your know-how, I'd be here with Charles." She shivered. "So I did accept your help."

"Not willingly."

"Does it matter? Point is you showed Charles up for the cheat he is in front of half the town, and I need to thank you for that." She stopped as they got to the boardwalk on the main street and hesitated before stepping up. Beside her, she touched the wooden two-by-four supporting the overhang and rubbed up and down with her thumb. He stood in the dusty street, his lean, rugged face inches from her own. Finally she met his gaze. On impulse she leaned over and kissed his firm, freshly shaved cheek. "You didn't have to bring me to the social. What you did last night was enough. Thank you."

"You're welcome," he said with a slow half-smile that melted her insides. "I didn't *have* to bring you tonight. I wanted to." He shifted the basket from one hand to the other, then placed a booted foot on the wooden step. After resting his forearm on his knee, he looked at her. "How did Mary take the change in plans?"

"Charles told her that he backed out because you were a stranger in town. He acted as if the whole thing was his idea." She shuddered. The wind billowed her skirt out around her, and she smoothed it down before turning her troubled gaze to his. "I wish I had my gun."

He put the basket down and took both of her hands into his large warm ones. He squeezed gently. "He's not going to get near you, even if he has the nerve to show up."

"I wouldn't put anything past him."

"Forget about him." He touched her chin with his index finger and lifted until she met his gaze. "You look lovely tonight, Miss Murphy. We're going to have a good time."

She smiled in spite of her misgivings. His teasing grin was impossible to resist for very long. She knew because she'd tried. "You look very nice yourself."

His face changed, grew hard somehow, hungry. Charles

always watched her with a similar look. But on Tanner, the expression didn't frighten her. Just the opposite. The intensity in his eyes excited her. The wanting she saw there reflected a corresponding need within her and constricted her breathing as surely as a whalebone corset.

"Then, I take it you're not embarrassed to be seen with me?" His voice dripped over her like honey, warming her until she thought she might dissolve into a sweet puddle at his feet.

"Oh, no," she whispered softly, then glanced away quickly before looking him in the eye again.

"The feeling is mutual. Very mutual."

His gaze traveled from the top of the curls piled on her head, down her plain, cotton dress stopping at her thin, black slippers. Then he looked into her eyes, and the intensity in his expression told her more truly than words of his approval. For the first time ever, she felt beautiful.

He held out his arm. "I suggest we proceed to the social, Miss Murphy."

She placed her hand in the crook of his elbow, then carefully lifted the hem of her long dress as he escorted her along the boardwalk to Bellmore's restaurant. The setting sun turned the evening sky bright orange, with tinges of pink and purple thrown in for good measure. She wondered if the Almighty had created this night just for her. Happiness swelled in her until she didn't think there was room for more.

And it would have been so different if Tanner hadn't won the poker hand last night.

She stumbled over an uneven plank and gripped Tanner's arm for support. The powerful muscle tensed as he stopped and waited for her to steady herself.

"You all right?"

"Yes. It's just that I'm used to my boots. In these thin-soled slippers, I can feel every rock and pebble."

He smiled. "I like that."

"What?" she asked, puzzled.

"That you say exactly what you think. You're honest as the day is long and you don't hide anything. A person always knows where he stands with you."

Well, that was something anyway. He liked that she spoke her mind. She studied the hard planes of his face, the square jaw and thick, dark brows. He was the best-looking man for miles around, and his masculinity was undeniable. She'd have her work cut out for her at the social tonight. Every unmarried young woman within traveling distance, and probably some who were already spoken for, would be after him like cats chasing a rolling ball of yarn.

She'd have to do more than blurt out whatever popped into her head to hold off all those females. The affair was a fund-raiser, but Lord, how she dreaded the bidding. She was assured of at least two dances, but after that ... It would be humiliating if no one else would pay for her company.

Inside the restaurant pushed-back tables hugged the wall to the right. On the other side of the room, checkered gingham cloths covered a long board supported by two sawhorses on either end. The makeshift table was quickly filling with dinner baskets. A small platform had been hauled inside and sat in the corner for the musicians—a fiddler, guitarist, and washboard player.

Jeff placed the basket beside the others, then looked around the room. Men and women greeted each other as if they hadn't met in years, then milled about in couples and sometimes larger groups. It was warm inside, and he noted the informal attire of the other men. He removed his tie and coat and slung them over a chair back, then rolled up his sleeves. He hated dressing for formal occasions. These people knew how to have a good time.

He watched Bree move a few feet away to hug a red-haired woman who appeared to be in her forties. Next, a young man tapped her on the shoulder, and she smiled at him warmly. Across the room someone called out her name, and she turned and waved, unable to work her way through the crush.

He'd never seen this side of her—this social, outgoing part of her nature. Obviously, she was well liked. The throng parted briefly, and he saw her stepbrother across the room. When their eyes met, Charlie nodded in salute, his cold, raw-boned features fixed in a taunting grin that didn't reach his eyes.

Jeff moved beside Bree and protectively circled her waist with his arm. She glanced up at him, and he was sure she hadn't seen Charlie yet. Her smile was gay and vivacious, full of feminine delight in visiting with friends. Nothing clouded her bright, beautiful face, and he wanted to keep it that way.

He scanned the room and spotted Riley not far from the punch bowl. Their eyes locked in silent communication, a commitment to safeguard Bree. He turned her away to give her a few more minutes of peace.

Just then a tall man with thinning brown hair artfully arranged across his scalp stepped on the platform. "Excuse me, everyone. For those of you I haven't met, I'll introduce myself. I'm Reverend John Howard." He held his hands out at his sides. "And this is my church—at least for now. The Lord doesn't mind where we gather to worship, but I do. With your generosity and help, before long I'll have the funds to build a church in Hardyville. Right now, I'd like to have all the ladies come forward. To make this fund-raiser interesting, you gents have to bid on the lady of your choice for a dance."

Jeff watched all the women, giggling and nervous at being on display, line up shoulder to shoulder on the platform with their backs to the musicians. Bree took her place as if she were facing the executioner's ax.

Bree wondered if anyone could hear her knees knocking. In front of her a sea of masculine faces blurred together. She didn't trust the strangers, and the ones she knew didn't fit her notion of the ideal man. Would one of them pay anything for a dance with her? Or would they still see her as the crazy river woman who wore pants and carried a gun? She'd done her best all these years to make them think that, to push them away. Now she was afraid she'd been too successful, and Tanner would witness her humbling.

The reverend pointed out Matilda Kramer, a rail-thin woman with snapping black eyes. "What'll you give for this fine specimen of womanhood, Sam?"

"Two bits!" roared a portly man with round, ruddy cheeks.

"Can you spare it, Sam Kramer? Wouldn't want you t'go hungry or nothin'." The woman scowled. Her dark gaze lowered to the belly hanging over his waistband, then raised to the suspenders straining at his shoulders.

"Now, Tildy, you know we got expenses. I do what I can." He moved forward sheepishly and paid his coin, then took his wife's elbow.

Bree watched the couple move to the side and wondered if it would be worse to have a low bid or none at all. Either way she'd be shamed.

Beside her, Amy Bellmore looked into the whistling crowd of men and waved shyly.

Tall, blond-haired Luke McLaughlin came forward holding out a small rawhide pouch. "Reverend, I don't know how much dust is in here, maybe a buck, buck fifty, but I aim t'give you every last ounce for Miss Amy." He glared at the group around him, daring any man to outbid him. Then he jammed the sack of gold dust into the clergyman's hand, grabbed Amy around the waist, and lifted her down from the platform.

Bree laced her fingers together in front of her, thinking how lucky Amy was to inspire such devotion.

Finally the reverend put his hand on her shoulder. "What am I offered for a dance with this lovely lady?"

"Got me a dollar. Reckon I'll buy her first dance." Riley reached into his pocket and retrieved a coin.

Bree smiled at him. She should have known he'd never let her down.

"Twenty dollars—gold." Charles shouldered through the crowd and stood in front of her.

She froze. Twenty dollars! Where had Charles gotten that kind of money? Then her blood ran cold, and fear prickled at the nape of her neck. No one would pay more than that for her. She couldn't bear the thought of being close to him, not even for one dance. But there didn't seem to be any way out. She swallowed hard and started to move toward him.

"Not so fast." Jeff pulled some bills from his pocket and counted several. "Will a hundred dollars buy her dances for the whole night, Reverend?"

Bree heard a gasp from the crowd. After that it was quiet as death, and she could feel everyone looking at her. A hundred dollars? For her?

Charles's eyes narrowed. "Always tryin' to throw your weight around, Tanner. It won't work. The bids are one dance at a time."

"Can you best that amount?" the reverend asked.

When her stepbrother hesitated, the clergyman held up his hands as if to placate the two men. "I don't think the Lord would mind bending the rules for the evening. If the lady's agreeable?"

Bree nodded slowly, her eyes wide. She could hardly breathe. When Tanner moved forward, the crowd parted. She took the hand he offered, then stepped from the platform, grateful that he stood between her and Charles. When she found the courage to peek around Tanner's tall form, she saw her stepbrother's back as he left the fundraiser.

She and Tanner stood by themselves. The other women stared, and Bree was uncomfortable being the center of attention until she recognized envy in their expressions. She felt special. She wanted to press the feeling to her and hold it in her heart forever. She glanced up at the man beside her and forgot about everyone else; they were the only two people in the room.

Jeff smiled as he stood with Bree waiting for the music to begin. Moments like this made the hard work and long hours worth it. He'd shown Charlie up because he'd had the money and power. But he knew he'd have used his fists if that was the only weapon he had to keep Charlie away from Bree.

The first strains of music started, and Jeff took her in his arms, letting his unpleasant thoughts drift away. Her radiant face and huge sparkling blue eyes captivated him. Jeff savored the moment—it belonged to him. Charlie wouldn't try anything more tonight, not in front of so many people. So Jeff planned to enjoy the feel of her soft body. Her rounded breasts, flattened against his chest, sent his blood roaring through his veins.

She tipped her head back and looked up at him. "A hundred dollars?"

He grinned. "The music is better than I expected. I've been to fancy balls from Boston to—"

"A hundred dollars!" she said.

Money was the last thing he wanted to talk about. Their feet barely moved, and he felt her slim legs pressed to his through the light material of her dress. When was the last time he'd danced with a woman, appreciating the curves of her body, without battling crinolines and petticoats?

"Is it warm in here? Or is it just me?" he asked.

"I can't believe it. A hundred dollars?"

"Will you quit saying that. It's not a big deal."

"No? Do you have any idea how long and hard most people in these parts have to work to earn that kind of money?" Her eyes narrowed suddenly. "Why, Tanner? Why'd you pay so much?"

Why indeed? he wondered. For one thing, he intended to use this very public social to his advantage. He'd bought all her dances for the whole night. She couldn't escape him without drawing attention to herself; he'd wager

far more than his hundred dollars that she wouldn't risk
that. How did the very independent Miss Murphy feel
about being at his mercy? Mad as hell, judging by the suspicious glitter in her beautiful eyes. How did *he* feel about
it? He figured he was probably out of his mind to tempt
fate by being with her, but he couldn't help himself.

Jeff felt a tap on his shoulder. Riley stood beside them,
scratching his silver whiskers. The worn, wide-brimmed
hat rested on his head, even in the Lord's house. The old
man reached into his vest pocket and handed Bree two
gold coins. "I guess you'll be wantin' these back. Your
dance card is full, missy."

Her face turned pink. "Riley, I . . ."

He shook his head and cackled. "Take care of her,
sonny."

"I intend to," Jeff said, grinning.

So the very independent Miss Murphy had taken steps
to make sure someone would dance with her. He looked
around. The place was full, with men outnumbering the females, and she was the most beautiful woman there. Obviously she hadn't thought anyone would buy a turn around
the room with her. He found that refreshing. The women
he knew were raised from the cradle expecting men to
court them.

He pulled her closer. "Have I told you how lovely you
look tonight?"

"Yes. But I wouldn't shoot you in the foot if you told
me again." Her face clouded for an instant, then her eyes
narrowed. "You didn't answer my question, Tanner. Why
did you pay so much on my account?"

He wished he knew the answer to that. He told himself
it was to keep Charlie away from her. Only deep in his gut
he knew there were other reasons, reasons that had nothing
to do with her stepbrother and everything to do with himself. But he wasn't going to talk about them—especially to
her.

"You're a wonderful dancer. Where did you learn?" he asked.

Her features softened and a faraway look replaced her curiosity. "My mother taught me. She was born and raised in the South, before the war. She always said that a young lady should be versed in all the social graces." She stopped and tipped her head sideways to stare at him. "You changed the subject—again. I want to know why you paid a small fortune and what you expect in return. I'm not the kind of woman you can buy in Cactus Kate's, you know."

"I know." No one who worked in a saloon looked as sweet and innocent as she did.

The curls piled on top of her crown danced and teased her neck. He watched, fascinated with the pale creamy column, wondering if it would feel like satin against his lips. How could he tell her why he'd bought every dance when he wasn't sure himself? He just knew he couldn't stand the thought of anyone else touching her, dancing with her, except himself.

Jeff readjusted his hand on her slim waist and his chest tightened at the thought of her this close to anyone but him. He'd never felt so strongly possessive or protective of a woman before—not even Emily.

"I paid a hundred dollars to prove to Charlie once and for all that he's lost. Besides, you saved my life. I owed you."

"Oh."

Jeff could hear the disappointment wrapped around that one small word. Had she expected something different? What could he say? He'd be gone soon. Because of that he had no right to be here, to hold her like this, no right to stand in her way for a chance at happiness. Men were a dime a dozen in the Territory, and most of them were looking for a woman. She'd have no trouble finding someone. He had no right to enjoy the curve of her waist, the softness of her breasts, her small hand grasping his so trustingly. But he couldn't resist a night with Bree all to himself.

His mind rebelled at the thought of her being with anyone but him. But the railroad was his life, the river was hers. She needed someone who understood and loved it the way she did. He shouldn't prevent her from finding that man. He looked around the room at the unattached males who watched, hungry to hold her just for a short while. His arm encircling her waist tensed protectively. He wouldn't give her up.

And he couldn't keep her himself.

But he'd be damned if he'd watch a roomful of prospectors and soldiers ogle her with undisguised lust. He knew if he looked in a mirror, the same need would burn in his own eyes.

He stopped dancing and took her hand, leading her from the crowded room. "Let's get the hell out of here."

"But—"

"Not one word. I bought your company for the evening."

"You paid for dances."

"We can dance anywhere."

"What about the music?" She pulled away from him.

"Damn the music." He seized her wrist and led her outside onto the boardwalk.

Bree heard his boots pound on the wooden planks as his swift strides set a pace that nearly made her run to keep up. He tugged her down the steps and headed toward the river. Every stone and grain of sand dug into the bottom of her feet through her dainty shoes. Nothing slowed him down until she pulled free and stopped to empty the sand from her slipper. He waited, but she felt his impatience. Finally he swung her into his arms and kept going.

"Put me down," she said. He ignored her. And when he slid and stumbled over the uneven track, she was forced to put her arms around his neck for balance.

When he stopped by the riverbank, she heard his accelerated breathing, felt the rapid rise and fall of his wide chest. His warmth seeped through her thin cotton dress, penetrating her body as surely as a well-aimed arrow. His muscled arm was like a steel band beneath her knees.

She felt as if she'd been the one physically exerting herself, her panting breath a near-match for his.

"Put me down," she whispered again, hearing the lack of conviction in her voice.

He removed one arm from under her legs and let her slowly slide down his length until her feet touched the sandy shore. His other hand at her waist held her prisoner against him. She could feel his muscled thighs through her petticoat and his wool pants. She couldn't have escaped, even if she'd wanted to.

He took her hand in his and began to move, waltzing to a melody in his mind. "The wind will be our music."

An air of expectation surrounded her, pressing against her skin, setting every nerve vibrating. "Why did you bring me out here? What do you want from me?"

He stopped. In the moonlight she saw his dark brows move together, deepening the lines on his forehead.

"I wish I knew." He stared at her, his face tensing. "That's a lie. I want you all to myself. And I've wanted to do this all night." He lowered his head and pressed his lips to hers, hard and hungry.

One dance was over and another begun, the rhythm as old and primitive as the beginning of time. Instinctively her mouth opened to him. His tongue stroked hers, imitating the more intimate act of mating. Velvet fire flashed through her, and she followed his example, begging him to consume her. A moan built in the back of her throat, and when it burst forth, her chest contracted.

"Oh, God, Bree . . ." he whispered.

He looped her hand around his neck and put his other arm around her waist, holding her more tightly to him. He was big and male, and she gave herself up to the sensations he evoked in her. His mouth, teasing her ear and burning a trail down her neck, ignited a blaze that spread to her belly like wildfire. Her blood flowed hot through every part of her, and a pulsating ache settled between her thighs. Overwhelming need gripped her—a sensation of waiting and wanting held her spellbound.

Bree felt the hard ridge of his arousal pressed to her, and she pulled away slightly, shock waves rippling through her.

"I won't hurt you. Don't be afraid," he said in a hoarse, guttural voice.

"I'm not." Her arms were still around him, and behind his neck she automatically crossed her fingers to render the lie harmless. It wasn't truly a falsehood. She feared the power of the feelings churning within her, but she wasn't afraid of Tanner.

"Come with me," he said. He gently took her wrists from around his neck and led her farther down the embankment to a cluster of rocks. He sat down on one and pulled her onto his lap. The proof of his feelings pressed hard and insistently against her thigh. She smelled the warm air, the muddy river, and the man. Her heart pounded so fast and furiously she thought it might just stop. Lord, but it was difficult to breathe.

His fingers hesitated on the top button at the back of her dress. She didn't say anything, and he worked it free. She felt his practiced touch and held her breath. One by one he freed the closures, and her bodice sagged lower as her sleeves slipped down her arms before she freed herself from the material. The top of her dress pooled in her lap while his soft lips caressed her temple, his strong fingers squeezed her waist, and the night breeze stroked the exposed flesh of her chest, above her chemise.

His hand trembled and his ragged breathing stirred the wisps of hair near her ear. "Bree, you're so sweet and soft. Your hair is like silk. And your skin ... like the finest satin."

His words went straight to her heart, and she wanted to

give him everything. An ache throbbed between her thighs and spread to her belly and her bosom. Only his touch could ease the need he'd aroused in her. With shaking fingers she pulled the satin ribbon on her chemise, opening it to free her breasts to him.

"Please, Jeff," she whispered, her voice hoarse.

"Are you sure about this, Bree? Really sure?"

Maybe she was making a fool of herself. "Don't you want me?"

"Want you?" His laugh was harsh. "More than you could know. But I need you to be sure."

"I'm sure." Her erect nipples waited, desperate for the comfort only he could give her. "Please . . ."

His hand slid slowly upward from her waist, and she held her breath in anticipation. She sensed he was telling her his intentions and giving her the choice to stop him. But she had neither the will nor the desire to end his intimate touch, the contact that set her on fire.

His mouth captured her upturned lips, and she felt the moan that vibrated in his throat. His chest rose and fell rapidly.

She squirmed in his lap and pressed herself against him, needing to be closer and not sure how.

When his big hand closed over her breast, she gasped at the potent pleasure that flooded through her. Instead of fear, she felt the need to know more. She arched her back, offering herself freely to his touch. His fingers gently toyed with her nipple, making it tight and hard and hot. The soft flesh around the peak knew the exquisite torture of his caress. He lowered his head and took the mound in his mouth, letting his tongue glide over her skin until she thought she'd die from the sheer pleasure of it. When he lifted his lips, the breeze from the river dried the moisture there, and she shivered with delight.

His hand danced on her thigh, and the hem of her dress slowly crept up. Then his warm fingers curled into her pantalettes, the only material that kept her from the joy of feeling his hand on her flesh. She wanted more. She writhed in his lap as her breathing grew labored.

He groaned at her invitation. "Bree, come with me to my room."

His raspy voice scraped against her skin, raising tingles everywhere. "Oh, Jeff ... I ..."

"I need you. I've never known anyone like you."

Bree froze in his arms. "What?"

"I want you. You're not like any woman I've ever met."

So, that was it. He was only curious. She was an oddity to compare to the soft and dainty women he knew back East. And it had almost worked. Shame and bitterness lumped together in her chest, and she tried to push herself away from him.

"What's wrong?" He tightened his hold.

"Let me go."

She pushed with all her strength against his chest, but she couldn't make him let go. If he didn't release her, he'd find out just how different she was from the women he knew. Did he think that because he paid her wages and had bought a dance he had the right to more? She'd thought him unlike any other man. He'd certainly fooled her. She'd begun to think he cared for her just a little. How wrong she'd been. How foolish. He owned the railroad; he was rich. He'd proved that tonight with his wad of money. She'd been an idiot to believe that someone like him could be interested in a woman like her. The pain cut deeper, nicking a corner of her heart, setting up permanent residence in her soul.

She pressed her palms against his chest once more, and with surprisingly little resistance this time, he let her go. She jumped off his lap and pulled her dress up to cover her exposed breasts. How could she have been so stupid to think he cared about her? He'd never have taken such liberties with a lady. If she *were* a lady, she would have stopped him. She wanted to die.

"What's gotten into you?" His voice was angry, frustrated.

"Nothing. You've had your dance, and I have an early run to Ehrenberg tomorrow."

"I don't think so." He exhaled a long breath and straightened, his body tensing. "I've got things to do in the morning. When I'm working, you're working."

"Since when do you need me on Sunday?"

"Since now. You'll have to go another time."

"I promised Kate. There's a shipment, and she wants me to fetch it right away."

"I have to go to the bridge site."

"Why?"

"Because I want to speed up the construction."

"The sooner it's done, the sooner you can leave?"

"Something like that. You'll have to postpone your Ehrenberg run. It's my boat. I need it."

She rubbed her cheek. If he'd slapped her, it couldn't have been more painful. Would he be in such a hurry to leave the Territory if she'd given in to his demands just now? Anger wrapped around her and she saw red. She hated that he had the power to control her life—in so many ways.

"It's my day off and I'm going to do what I have to do. If you don't like it, fire me."

"Now, hold on—"

"You hold on. We both know you can't fire me. You don't know the first thing about riverboats."

She glared at him, then turned her back. With one hand she lifted her skirt before stomping away. She was furious, too enraged to stop when the rocks bit into the soles of her feet.

"I'm not finished talking to you. Where do you think you're going?" he shouted.

"To *Belle*. We won't be here come sunup. If you need a ride to the bridge, rent a horse."

"You're bluffing."

"You're the poker player, Tanner, not me. We'll see who's bluffing."

ten

Bree picked her way through the boxes of cargo stacked on deck and frowned. Liquor filled those crates, and she felt like a hypocrite. She reminded herself that Cap would drink whether she had taken this contract or not. She was doing it to save Murphy Navigation. But her conscience still troubled her.

In the stern she stopped and wiped the perspiration from her temple, then let her hat dangle down her back. The breeze cooled her damp forehead, and she treasured the sensation.

Propping her boot on the gangplank, she studied the straggling street of adobe houses that made up the shipping community of Ehrenberg. Tanner's arrival had kept her so busy, she hadn't made a run here for a while. She shook her head. It hadn't changed and didn't look much different from Hardyville. The town had fewer structures and people, but this place was still an important ferrying point for West Coast passengers and river cargo. But like Hardyville, it would be just a memory when the bridge was finished.

She had to make as much money as she could for as long as possible. And that was why she'd fought with Tanner last night. She sighed heavily. That wasn't completely true. If they hadn't quarreled about this trip, it would have been something else.

Thoughts of Tanner kindled her banked anger, but part of the hurt leaked through. For a while he'd made her feel pretty and feminine. Then he'd asked her to his room. Not because she was different from any lady he'd ever met, but because he didn't think she was a lady at all. In a way, she was almost grateful to him. She'd let her guard down. It didn't take a kick in the head from a jackass to remind her that she couldn't trust him, just a moonlight kiss from that mule-headed railroad man—and the invitation that followed.

Bree looked at the sun and judged the hour at just a little after noon. Where were the passengers? If Riley didn't come back with Kate's "upstairs girls" soon, she intended to leave without them. The river was treacherous at night. She wanted to get home before dark.

She was not looking forward to seeing Tanner again, after deliberately disobeying his order. He wasn't the sort of man who took kindly to having his authority challenged. Let him fire her. She'd find another way to get *Belle* back.

A cloud of dust swirled at the top of the bluff just before she saw Riley, followed by three women. They slipped and skidded down the path, sending rocks and sand sliding as they struggled with their carpetbags. Bree moved back and rested against the wheelhouse as the new arrivals crossed the gangplank with the old man's assistance.

He pointed to a tall auburn-haired, brown-eyed woman. She was dressed in a cotton skirt and a blouse unbuttoned low enough to reveal a fair amount of her curves and cleavage.

"This here's Ginger. And that pretty little angel is Sally."

Bree studied Ginger's fair skin, powdered and made up with an artificial blush. Perspiration dotted her nose and trickled down her cheeks, taking the paint with it.

Ginger pulled blond, blue-eyed Sally protectively to her side. The younger girl wore a calico dress, low cut but less daring than her companion's blouse. They both stared at Bree warily while Ginger spoke. "Sally only serves drinks and entertains downstairs. She don't do no private stuff."

"My job is to get you to Hardyville, nothing more. Take that up with Kate when we get there." She hesitated for an instant, then held out her hand. "Bree Murphy."

Something about the woman's protective manner toward the other girl earned Bree's respect. She didn't know anything about these two women except that they were going to work for Cactus Kate. Out here the only way to judge others was by gut instinct. There was a bond of loyalty between them; she admired that. It was good enough for her.

Ginger took her hand. "Pleased to make your acquaintance, Cap'n."

Bree smiled, pleased the woman didn't question her right or ability to be in charge of the boat. She pointed to a place in the bow where they could sit on some boxes for the trip upriver, then turned her attention to the third woman.

She wore a traveling suit of dark green wool with a small felt and feather concoction perched at a jaunty angle on the side of her golden-brown hair. The hat was obviously for fashion because it sure wouldn't keep the sun off her face. She was younger than Sally, not more than eighteen or nineteen. There was a mischievous expression in her pretty green eyes. The girl was stunning, and Bree felt a momentary twinge of jealousy. Something made her think of Tanner. It would be hard for any man to resist a woman like this even if she could be bought.

Although Bree was the first to admit she knew next to nothing about clothes, she'd seen enough San Francisco catalogs to know the woman was expensively dressed. Apparently the profession paid better than she'd thought.

The girl stared openly at her, gazing from the top of her head to the tips of her boots. It wasn't a condescending look, merely curious.

Bree bent to release the stern lines, then glanced over

her shoulder. "You'd be more comfortable if you'd take off that jacket, roll up your sleeves, and find something to keep the sun off your head before you keel overboard from heat stroke."

"I'd be cooler if I could dress like you. You don't happen to have an extra pair of trousers I could borrow?" She arched her delicate brows questioningly. "Never mind. But thank you for the advice," she said sweetly. "It *is* awfully warm. I wasn't sure it was proper to remove my traveling jacket, but I guess it's better to be practical than dead."

Bree watched her move to the bow and sit in the shade from the crates.

Since when did saloon girls worry about propriety? She shook her head, then entered the wheelhouse. "Riley, release the bowlines!" she shouted.

He nodded. When they were free, Bree turned the wheel and guided the steamboat into the deepest part of the channel. She'd have to be careful. By this time in August the Colorado was hardly more than a trickle. Only vigilance and caution would keep them from running aground. Summer rainstorms would help some, but from now on the river would be at dangerously low levels until the spring thaw. No matter who held the paper, *Belle* was hers, and she'd never do anything to jeopardize her boat.

She could hardly believe it had been such a short time since Tanner had set foot on her boat and turned her life upside down. How long before he left again? As soon as the construction was finished, he'd be a memory, too. That brought a stab of pain.

To distract herself from her thoughts, Bree watched the three women sitting on cargo in the bow. Ginger and Sally and the pretty young one chatted away as if they'd known each other since the cradle. But saloon girls always formed fast friendships. They had to. Decent women wouldn't give them the time of day, forcing them to turn to each other for companionship.

As much as she hated to admit it, Bree envied their

friendship. Normally the passengers stared, openly disapproving of her. But not these three. She longed to join them. Her social nature and craving for female companionship drew her, but she couldn't leave the wheel. Although the *putt-putt* noise of the steamer's engine filled her head, snatches of conversation drifted to her. She listened carefully and heard Green-eyes say something about the East.

Why should that surprise her? Certainly eastern cities had their share of ladies of easy virtue. Lots of them. In fact, it made sense that they'd take their trade to the Territory. There was money to be made here, even in their line of work. Especially in their line of work.

Bree had never seen a more diverse-looking group. But their success in Hardyville was none of her business. Her responsibility was to get them there; after that, they were Kate's problem. She'd have enough to handle when Tanner got hold of her. And she had no doubt that he was pacing the riverbank right now planning to wring her neck. Well, she was none too happy with him, either.

Bree was exhausted by the time she docked the steamboat. The sun was beginning its descent behind the hills, and she'd set out before dawn to avoid Tanner. After what had happened with him the night before, she hadn't slept much. All she wanted now was her sponge bath and rest.

When the sound of the engine died, she heard a cheer go up from the men gathered on the riverbank. Word of her cargo had already spread. There was more than enough business for the three women to share and make a lot of money to boot.

Bree stepped out of the wheelhouse and spotted Tanner in the front of the group waiting expectantly on the riverbank. Even in the waning light, she could see the scowl on his face. His mouth tightened in a grim line as he separated from the crowd and swiftly moved toward the gangplank.

She turned her back on him and walked toward the bow to say good-bye to her passengers. In town they probably wouldn't have the opportunity to get to know each other. She regretted that; those three looked real friendly. Maybe they would cross paths sometime. The town wasn't that big, and Bree didn't much care if anyone approved of her friends. Most people didn't approve of her captaining a riverboat.

She'd learned a long time ago that a person did whatever was necessary to survive. Far be it from her to judge Sally and Ginger and Green-eyes. She suddenly realized she didn't know the girl's name. Whistles and hoots filled the evening air from the milling men, impatient to get a look at the new skirts in town.

"Welcome to Hardyville, ladies." Bree pointed to the riverbank.

Sally stepped closer to Ginger, and the auburn-haired woman patted her arm reassuringly. The gesture spoke volumes, and there was no doubt the sweet little blonde would be guarded carefully. Bree smiled. Cactus Kate was about to meet her match in Ginger.

"Where's the saloon?" Sally asked, a slight tremor in her voice.

"Up the path and to your right. You can't miss it. I'd bet any of those gents would be happy to direct you." Bree saw the anxious look on the girl's face and could have kicked herself. Her tone softened. "Most of them just want someone to talk to. They wouldn't hurt a fly." She spotted Riley securing the bowlines. "And if you have any problems, you tell Riley."

The man looked up and nodded, a big grin adding creases to his weathered face. "Anyone gives you grief, you let ol' Riley know."

Bree went back in the wheelhouse while at the front of the boat the three women gathered their belongings before disembarking. Green-eyes rolled down her sleeves and slipped her traveling jacket on, then straightened the perky, impractical little hat on her head. Her waist-length hair had long ago fallen from its knot. She seemed unconcerned as she gathered her reticule and carpetbag.

Bree felt the boat tip, and she knew without looking who had come aboard. Her shoulders tensed at the heavy sound of boots on the wooden deck. Then Tanner's big body filled the doorway, blocking out the light before he eased inside.

He planted his feet wide apart and crossed his arms over his chest. "Where the hell have you been?"

"I told you I was going to Ehrenberg to pick up a shipment for Kate."

"And I told you I needed you today."

"I agreed to take this job because you never work on Sunday. I wasn't going to break my word to Kate just because you were getting even with me. Your nose is out of joint because I wouldn't go to your room last night."

"That's not true." He shifted his weight, then fixed his gaze on a point somewhere over her shoulder.

She shrugged. "It doesn't matter anyway."

"I ought to fire you."

"Probably." Bree stared at him defiantly, refusing to look away.

"If I didn't need you for the project . . ." Glittering green eyes glared into hers. The anger was familiar, but there was something else there that made her uneasy. A barely harnessed tension emanated from him and pulled at the tightness in her abdomen. She pushed the thought aside. Something told her she was off the hook this time. But she knew she couldn't push her luck again.

"So what's it gonna be, Tanner? Do I still have a job?"

He shoved his hands in his pockets and looked down at his boots. He glanced up and let out a long breath. "For now. But if you ever pull a stunt like this again . . . I want your word."

She leaned her back against the big wheel.

A scuffling noise outside the wheelhouse directed their

attention to the women passing by. "Bye, Bree. Nice meetin' ya'." Sally and Ginger peeked in and smiled.

The last passenger followed, her back to the doorway as she struggled with her carpetbag. "Good-bye, Miss Murphy. I hope I'll see you again, in town perhaps," she called over her shoulder, her face concealed by the evening shadows.

"I'm sure we'll run into each other again."

Tanner glanced through the doorway as the woman passed, a puzzled expression on his face. Then he shook his head and glared at Bree. "Since when do you socialize with strumpets?"

"What business is it of yours who I socialize with?"

He smoothed his mustache with his thumb and forefinger. "Why are you itching for a fight?"

"What makes you think I'm—" She stopped, realizing he was right. She was still mad at him for the way he'd treated her last night. But why should he care if she was acquainted with ladies of easy virtue? In the moonlight he'd acted as if that's what he wanted. Regaining her self-control, she squared her shoulders and released a long breath. "I'm too tired to fight with you."

"You wouldn't be if you hadn't gotten up before the Almighty to avoid me."

"You'd have tried to stop me."

"Damn right."

She rubbed the weary ache from her eyes with both fists, then looked at him. "I'd like you to leave so I can clean up."

"I will," he said, moving beside the wheel as he stared thoughtfully down at her. With his index finger he gently traced her jaw, then lifted her chin. "When I'm sure we have a truce."

The unexpected tenderness in his voice belied the warlike words, and Bree's heart fluttered wildly. Not now, she thought. If he was nice to her, she knew she wouldn't be able to resist him. She brushed past him and left the

wheelhouse to collect her water buckets and her composure, but Tanner followed her.

On the gangplank the green-eyed lady stood hesitantly
while three or four men shoved and shouldered each other
away in their zeal to assist her from the boat.

Finally one big man prevailed and held his hand out to
her. She took it, then turned to wave one last time.

Behind her, Bree heard Tanner say one brief, crude
curse word. Then she felt his hands on her shoulders as he
stopped her and moved in front before proceeding along
the deck of the boat.

"What the hell is she doing here?" he muttered, stomping angrily toward the stern.

The young woman looked over her shoulder. Recogni-
tion flashed across her face. "Jeff—"

He stopped beside the plank and glowered at the big
stranger holding her hand. "Let her go or I'll break your
arm."

Bree watched, bewildered by the exchange. He acted as
if he knew the girl.

"What in God's name are you doing here?" Jeff picked
up the carpetbag resting next to her. Then he looked at the
other man. "Buster, unless you've got a death wish, let her
go. Now."

The man released her wrist and shifted his position on
the gangplank to face Tanner. "You got no right—"

"I've got every right." Jeff glared at him.

"Why? You paid for her already?"

Tanner's hands clenched into fists. "She's not a saloon
girl."

"Me? A saloon girl?" She laughed, then a sweet smile
turned up the corners of her mouth. "Oh, Jeff. I didn't expect to find you so easily. I've missed you so much." She
threw her arms around his neck, and he hugged her to him,
embracing her fiercely.

Bree remembered the conversation between the three
women on the boat, the remark about the East. Was it pos-

sible she wasn't with the other two? Judging by the way
he was squeezing her, Tanner knew this one pretty well.
Jealousy seized Bree in a grip as tight as the one he had
around the pretty young woman. Emily?

Tanner put her away from him and looked at the subdued crowd of men on the riverbank. "Show's over. Take
my word for it, she's not one of Kate's girls." A warning
clung to every word.

Almost as one, the men eased back, then turned and
drifted away, up the hill to the saloon. Tanner encircled the
woman's waist with his arm and turned toward the wheelhouse, where Bree waited. She should have known that
someone so expensively dressed was not in the same line
of work as Ginger and Sally. But the woman's friendly
ways had made her jump to conclusions.

She watched them, especially Jeff's possessiveness of
Green-eyes. What would it be like to belong to him, to
have his regard and protection? Oh, he'd stepped between
her and Charles, but he'd never shown any sign that attention from other men bothered him.

Behind *Belle* the setting sun's golden rays shone on the
two faces so close together. One masculine, the other feminine, identical pairs of green eyes stared at her.

He looked down at the young woman. "I ought to blister your backside, Cady Tanner."

Bree moved forward. "She's your sister?"

Cady nodded, her eyes twinkling with mischief. "I bet
you thought I was with Ginger and Sally."

"No," Bree said a little too quickly, crossing her fingers
behind her back. "I never thought that."

Cady laughed. "It's all right. They were very nice.
Thanks to them, the trip wasn't tedious at all. The time
just flew by."

Jeff looked from one woman to the other, piecing together what had happened. He hadn't gotten over Bree's
blatant disobedience—or the fact that he hadn't fired her
for it. Now he'd come to find out that she'd brought his

innocent little sister downriver with a couple of whores and permitted her to speak to them for hours. Anger surged through him, heating his blood to boiling.

"I can't believe it, Murphy. You let my sister associate with those women?"

"How was I supposed to know she was your sister?"

"Jefferson Tanner, what's gotten into you?" Cady pushed his arm from around her waist and stared at him, astonished.

Jeff ignored her and took a step toward Bree. "I can't believe you thought Cady was one of them." He gestured wildly, indicating the saloon where the lights had just flickered on. He added beneath his breath, "I should have fired you when I had the chance."

Bree recoiled and drew in a deep breath. "How in blazes was I supposed to know she wasn't with them?"

"Does she look like them?"

Raucous laughter from Cactus Kate's saloon floated down to the river, and he cringed. If he hadn't been here, Cady would have been whisked away by that horny pack of men. She'd have been helpless to stem the tide of their lust.

Beside him, Cady turned slightly, showing him the expression in her eyes. She reminded him of their mother when she'd made up her mind about something. "Jeff . . ."

Righteous indignation suffused him, and he ignored the rebellious expression on her face. "And as for you. You know better than to associate with women like that."

Cady's chin lifted stubbornly. "Quit being such a prig. I didn't know they were saloon girls. I've never been inside one, so how could I? And even if I had known, it wouldn't have made any difference. That's the most fun I've had since putting frogs in the headmistress's bed at boarding school."

He glared from one young woman to the other and rolled his eyes. He couldn't handle Bree Murphy alone;

now his little sister had sided with her. He had the uneasy feeling that he was badly outnumbered.

A thought suddenly occurred to him. He'd never received word that Cady was coming. Surely his mother would have notified him if she'd known. "Do the folks know where you are? Why aren't you in school?"

She glanced at her feet, then looked him in the eye. "Summer holiday."

A blast of hot wind caught her skirts, throwing her off balance. He touched her elbow to steady her. "If anyone needs time off, I'd lay odds it's the headmistress."

Cady giggled. "Poor woman has turned awfully gray since I enrolled."

"I guess we need to find a place for you in the boardinghouse." He glanced at Bree, leaning against the wheelhouse. The stiff breeze had stirred up the waters of the Colorado rocking the boat, and he braced his boots wide apart for balance.

Jeff had learned the hard way that he couldn't tell this stubborn river captain what to do, but he'd be damned if his sister would sleep on this blasted boat with her. There was a point when a man had to put his foot down. "I'm going to telegraph Hollingsworth and get the Pullman out here." He took his sister's arm and started to guide her across the gangplank. "And I need to telegraph Mother."

Cady stopped and obstinately planted her hand on her hip as she stared up at him.

"Don't give me that look," he said. "She'll be beside herself. I need to let her know where you are and that you're all right."

"What makes you think she doesn't know?"

"From the day you were born, you couldn't fool me, Cady. Mother has no idea you're here, does she?"

She shook her head, grinning without remorse. "If I'd told her, she wouldn't have let me come. I planned to wire her when I arrived."

Blatant disobedience. Bree had done the same thing

only that morning. He was surrounded by impulsive, pig-headed women. And Cady didn't seem the least bit concerned about what she'd done. She knew he couldn't stay angry with her. And their mother was so far away at the moment, Cady had no reason to worry about any punishment from that quarter.

"It was nice meeting you, Cady," Bree said. "I hope I'll see you again soon." Her lips curved slightly, then she disappeared into the wheelhouse.

He still hadn't settled things with her. He pointed at his sister. "Don't move."

Through the doorway he saw Bree pull the washbasin from the cupboard beside the wheel. She looked up at him. "Forget something, Tanner?"

"I want your word that you won't take off again like you did this morning." He wanted more than her word. That was his problem.

"If I hadn't, your sister wouldn't be here now."

It didn't sweeten his temper that she was right.

She'd also come too close to the truth when she'd accused him of wanting her to work on Sundays for selfish reasons. But it wasn't because she'd refused to go to his room. Jeff couldn't forget the way the men at the dance had looked at her—wanting her. An instinct, deep and primitive, had driven logic clear from his mind. He wanted her with him so he'd told her he needed her and the boat. When he'd discovered them both gone, he'd been furious.

All day he'd prowled Hardyville restlessly, angry at her but mostly missing her. Last night he'd tossed and turned, unable to sleep for the ache in his loins. Even now the passionate anger in her eyes made him eager to take her right here, right now.

But it wasn't just pleasure he wanted. He'd wanted her in his bed to forge a bond with her as strong as steel and as old as time. He'd wanted to mark her as his own so that no other man would dare touch her.

"I need you," he said, clearing his throat of the huskiness. "I can't do this job without you."

"Really?"

"Really?" Cady asked from the doorway.

He glanced over his shoulder at his sister, then back at Bree. He nodded. "I need this boat and a good captain. You're the best I know."

Bree traced the wooden spindles of the big wheel beside her. "Careful, Tanner. That kind of flattery will turn my head."

"What do you say?" he asked, ignoring her sarcasm.

"Would this be a good time to ask for a raise?" Her finely arched brows lifted hopefully as a small smile teased her full lips.

"No."

"Then I'll agree to stay under one condition. I don't work on Sundays. Ever."

"Fair enough."

"Mary is an awfully good cook," Cady said, closing the boardinghouse door behind her. "Bree, it was very gracious of your parents to take me in without notice. And the next time I see Mr. McLaughlin, I must remember to thank him for moving to the saloon and giving up his room for me."

Tanner stood next to his sister and draped an arm protectively across her shoulders. "Don't flatter yourself. Cactus Kate's is next door to the restaurant. It gave him a good excuse to be closer to Amy Bellmore."

Cady elbowed him in the ribs. "Thanks, Jeff. You make me feel ever so good. I'm glad I moved heaven and earth to visit you in the wilds of Arizona."

Bree smiled at the playful exchange and envied their easy relationship. It was something she and Charles had never shared.

The hot wind pushed the curtain into the front room through the open window, and voices drifted out as the other boarders conversed with her parents. She thought she saw a shadow block the light for an instant, but then it was gone.

"Bree, won't you change your mind and share the room with me?" Cady asked.

"No, thanks anyway."

Hadn't she already had this conversation with one member of the Tanner family? But Jeff's invitation had had nothing to do with sleeping. That much had been clear. She was unsophisticated, but she wasn't stupid. And she never made the same mistake twice. She wouldn't let him close again.

Tanner removed his arm from Cady's shoulders and playfully tapped her nose. His affection for his younger sister was obvious. Bree had liked her right away. She couldn't dislike anyone who called that arrogant railroad man a prig. But sharing a room was something else again. Cady was a paying guest and entitled to her privacy. Besides, her brother was sleeping under that roof, too. Keeping her distance from Tanner, especially at night, was self-preservation, pure and simple.

"How long will you be staying, Cady?" Bree asked.

"I'm not sure."

"The fall term at school will be starting soon. You can't stay very long." Tanner leaned against the post opposite Bree.

"I'm not going back to school."

"The hell you're not."

Apparently she wasn't the only one he tried to boss around, Bree thought with a smile.

Cady's shoulders squared as her eyes pleaded with him to understand. "Jeff, you don't know what it's like there. All those girls come from old money."

"Old money, new money. What difference does it make? It all spends the same."

"Shows what you know. Old money buys a higher place in society. I'm at the bottom of the ladder. And those stuck-up girls never miss an opportunity to rub my nose in it." She lifted her chin defiantly and looked at him. "I'm finished with that finishing school."

So Cady Tanner didn't fit in, either. A wave of protectiveness for the younger girl swept over Bree. Clothes, money, the work you chose—didn't matter what the reason was. Being left out hurt. She stared at Cady's brother, waiting for his reaction, preparing to come to the girl's rescue if necessary.

Tanner crossed his arms over his chest. "There are ways to work your way up socially."

"If you want to," Cady said, bitterness in her voice.

"What does that mean?"

"Nothing." His sister sat down on the top step, her skirts spread wide around her, elbows on knees, chin resting in her hands.

Tanner lowered his big body beside her. "Why did you come, Cady? Don't tell me for a holiday. Arizona Territory isn't the most relaxing place to visit. I know you. Something's on your mind. Why did you move heaven and earth to get to me?"

She tossed a long strand of golden-brown hair over her shoulder and looked him straight in the eye. "For Emily. I came to set a date for your wedding."

eleven

Stunned, Bree stared down at Tanner sitting beside his sister on the porch. She hadn't realized how much she'd come to trust him, until this moment of betrayal.

Red-hot fury exploded inside her. He *was* engaged to Emily. He'd flat out lied to her. Just last night he'd almost persuaded her that he cared. She'd nearly gone upstairs with him, taken in by a handsome face hiding a deceitful heart. Equal parts of shame and anger mixed together until a knot of humiliation tightened inside her. She couldn't stand the sight of him; the pain of betrayal was too great. She started down the front steps.

Tanner quickly stood. At the same time his hand shot out and gripped her upper arm. "Where are you going?"

"To *Belle*." She pulled at the fingers forming an iron ring around her arm, trying to free herself.

He tightened his hold. "Not so fast."

"I can't abide the sight of you any longer, Tanner."

Cady stood and held up her hand. "Bree . . . wait."

Bree glanced at the other woman. "Sorry. I know he's your brother. But I won't hold that against you."

Jeff glared at his sister. "Cady, go to your room."

"You can't send me away like a child."

"You've caused enough trouble for one day. Go upstairs. I want to speak to Bree alone. You and I *will* talk about this later." A muscle in his lean jaw jerked angrily.

165

"Bree, I . . ." Cady's troubled gaze skipped from one to the other, before a helpless look crept into her eyes. She turned away, and her petticoats rustled as she slipped through the front door.

Bree tried again to wrench her arm free. For her efforts, she felt a sharp pain from her elbow to her collarbone. "Let me go, Tanner. I can't abide liars."

"What are you talking about?"

"You know good and well. You told me you'd never even thought about marrying Emily."

"I did say that." His voice was calm, controlled.

At least he owned up to the untruth. Behind him in the boardinghouse window, the lantern's glow highlighted the masculine angles of his profile and cast the shadow of his mustache across his jaw. Half his features were visible, the other half obscured. And she didn't trust anything about him, not even the part she could see.

"You're engaged to her. I call that a bald-faced lie."

"It would be if I had asked Emily to marry me. I haven't."

"Then why is your sister here to set a date for the wedding?"

"I haven't any idea. But I damn well intend to find out." He glanced over his shoulder at the front door. His lips compressed into a grim line, nearly hidden by his mustache.

"Why would Cady say it if it wasn't true? And please release my arm."

His brows drew together, carving a furrow in his forehead. "Do you promise to stay and hear me out?"

She hesitated and he tightened his grip.

"You can run, but it won't do you any good. I'll follow and I guarantee you're going to hear what I have to say, whether you want to or not. Are you going to stay put?"

She studied the obstinate expression on his face and decided to get it over with, here and now. She nodded and he loosened his grip.

She crossed her arms beneath her breasts and lifted her chin. "Only because I'm curious to see how you plan to talk your way out of this."

He hooked his thumbs in his waistband. "I don't know why Cady came all the way out here. Emily's been a good friend to her. Because of the partnership, our families have been thrown together a lot, and Emily's taken my sister under her wing."

Cady and Emily—two against one. She didn't blame his sister. It made perfect sense for Cady to want her best friend and her brother to marry, especially when they were perfectly suited.

"Cady must have had some inkling that there was an occasion to set a date for."

He sighed and ran his fingers through his dark hair. "Cady sometimes tries to make things the way she wants them to be. She's impulsive, in case you haven't noticed." He grinned fleetingly.

"Do you take me for a fool? She wouldn't have come all this way if she didn't believe there was a good reason. Why can't you admit you were trying to pull a fast one, Tanner?"

"A fast one?" he asked, rubbing the back of his neck.

Bree laughed sarcastically. "Does Emily know what kind of man you are? Does she know that her fiancé kisses other women and tries to get them up to his room?"

"That's not true."

"You're denying that you asked me to go upstairs?" She couldn't believe he'd lie to her face. "I was there, Tanner. I know what you said and what you wanted."

"I'm not denying that. I'm telling you that I'm not promised to another woman. If I were, I'd never have kissed you."

Just a kiss? That's not the way she remembered it. She recalled his strong, sure hand on her breast, and even now her body betrayed her. The tingles in her stomach spread to her limbs, and she braced her feet in the rocky dirt at the bottom of the steps to keep her knees from buckling. Her face burned. She hated that she knew him for the liar he was and still her skin begged for his touch.

"You did a whole lot more than kiss me."

"I know exactly what happened," he said huskily. "I was there, too. But I am not engaged to anyone."

"Maybe not yet, but you're splitting hairs." She wasn't sure if she was more hurt because he'd pretended to care for her, or angry at herself because she'd fallen for his lies. "You're going to ask Emily to marry you. Aren't you?"

He jammed his hands in his pockets and hesitated to answer. Would he deny it again? Would he twist the words and try to make a fool of her?

Finally he let out a long breath. "Plans have a way of changing." He stared down at her and reached out a hand to her cheek.

She saw the intensity in his face and backed up a step. He wouldn't burn her again.

Jeff gritted his teeth, waiting for her response. Why had it been so hard to admit to her that he'd probably marry Emily? If he had any sense at all, he'd walk away from Bree right now and let her believe he was a two-faced bastard. That would be best for both of them.

Her shoulders slumped, and she wearily rubbed her forehead. All the rage seemed to drain out of her. "I had you pegged before I ever laid eyes on you. All you care about is yourself and what you want. People's feelings don't matter to you."

"I care about you. I care what you think."

She shook her head. "You have a funny way of showing it."

"Whether you believe it or not, it's the truth."

"You wouldn't know the truth if it bit you in the behind."

"When you simmer down and look at this rationally, you'll see everything more clearly."

"I'm calm, Tanner." She looked up at him and there was

sadness in her eyes that cut clean and deep. "You may be able to push other people around and make a bundle of money doing it. But you can't use me, then try and sweet-talk me into believing that you're anything other than a low-down, cheating, two-timing skunk."

"Don't spare my feelings. Give it to me straight."

"Quit, Tanner. Your charm's wasted on me."

Bree could call him names and try to persuade herself that she didn't care about him, but he knew better. He'd felt her fiery response to his kiss. His body had absorbed the trembles that rippled through her at his touch. And he wouldn't rest until he made her admit what she'd felt. If he had to, he'd shake her bodily from that unnatural composure she'd gathered around herself. He was sick and tired of cool, sophisticated women who put on airs for show and hid their honest emotions.

Bree was different. That's what had drawn him to her in the first place.

"I guess you're tired. I'll walk you to the boat and you can get some sleep. We'll talk about this in the morning."

"Go to hell, Tanner." Her voice drifted to him from the blackness beyond the circle of light as she headed down the path to the river.

Every nerve in his body pulsated with the need to go after her. He wanted things settled. But common sense intervened and warned him to patience. She needed time, only he didn't have much time left. The bridge was more than half-finished. He'd be leaving soon. He released a long breath as he entered the boardinghouse.

Charlie stood in the entry, a knowing smile on his angular face. Jeff's insides twisted with suppressed rage. The son of a bitch was responsible for Bree's mistrust of men. If not for him, Jeff knew he'd have been able to discuss everything with Bree more rationally. His hand clenched into a fist. *Give me a reason*, he thought.

The younger man smoothed the right side of his already slicked-back hair with a slender hand. "Trouble?"

"Nothing I can't handle."

"Once Bree's made up her mind about something, she won't change it. She won't have anything to do with you now."

So he'd heard everything. Jeff reined in his temper. If he lost it, that weasel face would be unrecognizable. "And you think she'll give you a second look?"

"No question about it." Charlie grinned smugly. Without another word he turned and walked toward the rear of the house.

Jeff controlled his urge to follow and beat the hell out of him. He watched the other man's back and wished he could keep an eye on his own—and Bree's. Anger drained away and apprehension replaced it. Just one more reason to show Bree how wrong she was about him. If he couldn't get close to her, it would be that much harder to protect her.

He was here to build a bridge, for God's sake. How hard could it be to span the differences between him and that stubborn woman?

Jeff started up the stairs. There was another stubborn woman up there, and he needed a word or two with her as well.

Cady shifted her position on the pink and blue quilt covering her bed and looked around. The room was clean and airy, though a little smaller than Jeff's. She bounced once and found the mattress firm, although the dresser and chiffonier across from it had seen better days. The comfortable room reminded her of its owners, who had welcomed her so graciously. Her acceptance here had been instantaneous; she didn't have to struggle to belong.

Only Charles made her uneasy. She'd taken to everyone else right away. But Bree's stepbrother gave her the jitters. Something about him sent chills down her spine. But she wasn't concerned for herself. The man had hardly taken his eyes off Bree.

The scrape of boots outside in the hall sent a ripple of apprehension down the back of her neck.

"Cady, I want to talk to you."

She heard the tension in her brother's voice and heaved a sigh. Best get it over with. The sooner they talked, the better she'd feel.

"Come in, Jeff."

But when she saw the dark expression in his eyes, the deep, angry grooves between his brows, Cady wished she could put the interview off indefinitely.

He glared at her, then stomped past and sat in the chair beside the writing table in the corner. "What do you mean coming here to set a date for my wedding? I've never even proposed to Emily."

"I had no idea how hot the desert could be," she said, smiling brightly, sitting Indian-style on the bed.

"When and if I ask Emily to marry me, I'll damn well set the date myself," he said furiously, jabbing his finger at her.

"The mountains are spectacular, so different from the East. I didn't expect to find anything beautiful in the terrain here."

"I thought you came out here to talk about Emily. Why the hell are you discussing scenery?"

"Shame on you," she said, shaking her head. "You know Mother hates it when you swear."

"Damn it, Cady," he said. "If you don't quit beating around the bush, I'm going to do a lot more than swear." He leaned forward in the chair as if he intended to carry out his threat. Then he looked at her and shook his head, a grin turning up the corners of his mouth. "I forgot how you exasperate me."

"And how much you missed me?" she asked hopefully.

"Not enough to put up with this nonsense." He crossed his arms over his chest. "Come on, Cady. It's not like you to interfere. Why are you really here? You've run away from home, haven't you?"

She bit her lip and nodded. "I had to. I hate boarding school. I'm not going back. Mother says I'm too young to know what's best and refuses to change her mind. Father adores her and won't listen to anything except what she wants."

"It's the most exclusive school in the East. You're going back—and you'll finish."

"Just because it's expensive doesn't mean it's good for me." She tipped her head to the side and studied him. "I know you're paying for it, and I appreciate what you're trying to do. That's why I had to come. I had to talk to you face to face and make you understand that finishing school is not what *I* want."

"It's the only way you're going to make a place for yourself in society."

"That's Mother's dream, and yours. It's not mine. You're still trying to prove something to Grandfather because of what he did to you and Mother." She tapped her lips with her forefinger. "You know something? You're very much like him—domineering, arrogant, and snobbish."

A dark look crossed his face. Her barb had hit its mark. "I'm nothing like that dictatorial bastard!"

"Don't you see? You're trying to make me do what you want just the way Grandfather did with Mother." She lifted her chin and looked at him, silently pleading for his understanding. "Are you going to cut me off without a penny, too?"

His eyes glittered. "Then you wouldn't have to go back to school."

She nodded eagerly.

"Not a chance." He relaxed in the chair and rested a booted ankle across the opposite knee. "The fact that you associated with those two women on the boat trip proves you have a lot to learn."

"At least Ginger and Sally talked to me. It's not like that at school."

"You're exaggerating."

"Maybe a little. But all that's important to those girls at school are clothes and parties. There's more to life than that."

"And that's why you're in school. To learn about making a life in proper society."

"I don't want to receive someone's card on a silver tray. I can't pretend to be nice to shallow, pretentious people who bore me to tears. I have nothing in common with them." Cady was afraid she'd never convince him. She only had one argument left, and she was gambling everything on the fact that he really, truly cared for her. "Jeff, I have no friends there. They make fun of me because I grew up without money."

"Damn them!" Then he looked at her and his anger dissipated. He sighed and dragged his fingers through his already disheveled hair as he shook his head. "You should have told me."

"Does that mean . . ."

He nodded. "I'll write the headmistress." He smiled sheepishly. "You didn't have to come all this way to wrap me around your little finger. You could have written. I'd have understood."

She smiled. "No, you wouldn't. You're as stubborn as I am. Emily *was* an excuse to come in person and disarm you with the Tanner charm."

He grinned briefly. Then the smile faded, and a thoughtful look replaced it as he steepled his fingers and touched them to his chin. "You've caused a whole pile of trouble."

"Bree's angry?"

"Furious."

Cady had seen the other woman turn pale when she'd mentioned his marriage. In that instant she'd realized that Bree was in love with Jeff. She'd seen their fight on the boat and wondered about the powerful feelings running between them.

"Are you in love with her?"

Instantly he glanced up and a wry smile curved his mouth. "In love with B. E. Murphy?" He considered the question for a moment, then laughed, a little too loudly. "I think the desert sun has fried what few brains you have, my dear little sister."

"Then what trouble have I caused?" His sarcasm didn't faze her in the least. It only meant she was on the right track. "If you don't care about Bree, what harm have I done?"

"Bree thinks I lied to her. Since we work closely together, that concerns me." He stopped, hesitating as if he'd given too much away, and a hooded expression covered his eyes. He'd say no more about Bree. "Now I have to worry about you, and I'm too busy to nursemaid you."

"I never asked you to. I can take care of myself."

He looked uneasy. "You'll have to until the Pullman arrives from San Francisco day after tomorrow." His eyes narrowed. "Stay away from Charlie. In fact, I think I've got another job for Riley."

"The old man who helped Bree on the boat?" she asked.

He nodded. "And stick close to Mary. I'm certain you'll be all right since Charlie will be upriver with Sean. Even so, I think I'll have Riley keep an eye on you."

"I'll be perfectly fine. I can take care of myself."

"That's questionable. If I hadn't been there at the dock, you would've landed yourself in a lot of trouble by associating with Ginger and Sally." He held up a hand to forestall her retort, then crossed the room and stopped in front of her. A tender expression filled his eyes. "I'm glad you're here, Cady. In spite of all the trouble you've caused, it's nice to see family."

"Does that mean you forgive me?" She smiled up at him.

"Not yet." He smoothed his mustache between his thumb and forefinger, and she knew he was fighting a grin. "But it's getting late. I have to be up early in the morning, or Captain Murphy will leave without me."

"I'm sorry if I made things difficult for you, Jeff. I'll explain the misunderstanding to Bree."

He shook his head. "It doesn't matter." He kissed her forehead, then left the room.

Cady scrambled off the bed and locked the door after him, then leaned against it, thoughtfully touching a finger to her lips. Some instinct had driven her to the Territory—and Jeff. Boarding school was in the past now, and for that she was grateful. There were some things that couldn't be taught in school, and love was one of them. Her big brother didn't know it, but he desperately needed her help.

Jeff surveyed the wooden trestle as Bree guided the riverboat beneath the bridge construction on their way upstream to Hardyville. The project was more than half-finished, on schedule and within budget, definitely worth all the hard work and long hours. He touched the frayed edges of the bullet hole in the crown of his hat as he pushed it low on his forehead, shielding his eyes from the descending sun. The boat slowly churned through the water, kicking up the smell of mud around him. Closer to the riverbank where the water had receded, the dried sandy dirt cracked and curled in a reddish-brown geometric design. He stood in the bow with a willow switch, measuring the depth of the current in the shallow parts of the river. Beneath his boots the deck vibrated and the hoarse hum of the boat's engine filled his head. He glanced back at Bree and watched her mouth tighten. She still wasn't ready to talk to him.

Behind her he watched the bridge under construction growing smaller as they chugged upstream. For the hundredth time he calculated the load factor a moving train would place on the rails supported by that wood. Had he built in enough safety factor? He nodded confidently.

Douglas fir had been chosen for its durability; it could take the most weight before shattering. He'd been in on the design and planning of the structure, had insisted on rivets every three inches though other engineers had thought the number excessive.

He'd supervised the project from the foundation up. If that was weak, the bridge would never be sound, no matter that the finest materials had been used. The structure was as solid as he could make it, and a sense of pride swelled in his chest.

After he completed this project, he'd have the railroad business at his feet, and his partners seeking *his* counsel. Only on this bridge—his bridge—could the trains get to San Francisco without taking a longer, roundabout route. Profits would increase, and his reputation and power would be unquestioned. He just wished his grandfather were still alive. The old man would never know how wrong he'd been.

The boat engine's steady hum sputtered for a second, then resumed an uninterrupted rhythm. He glanced over his shoulder at the smokestack and black metal housing covering the steam-driven engine. Behind it, in the wheel-house, he saw Bree. Her brow puckered delicately as she turned the big wheel slightly left, then right, as she guided *Belle* up the Colorado. He could feel her concentration. She was as serious about her work as he was about his. What would happen to her after the bridge was completed?

Last night she'd told him he didn't care about people. She was wrong. He cared about her.

A part of him hoped she was mistaken about the effect that the railroad expansion would have on river trade. But the businessman in him knew what the future held for Murphy Navigation. Was there anything he could do to help them? He immediately dismissed the thought. B. E. Murphy wouldn't take help from the railroad. Her damned, stubborn pride wouldn't let her take anything—especially from him.

She'd hardly said two words all day. She'd taken *Belle* back and forth across the river, relaying orders, transporting supplies and even himself if the crew on one side or the other needed a hand. But she wouldn't speak to him unless it had to do with work. And for once the bridge construction wasn't the wrinkle that had her britches in a bunch. This was personal and had everything to do with the fact that she thought he was engaged to someone else while he dallied with her.

If Jeff lived to be a hundred, he'd never forget the pain he'd seen in Bree's eyes. He'd never forgive himself for putting it there.

Perspiration collected on his forehead, and he wiped it away, then brushed his hand down the side of his pants. The calluses across his palm caught the material along his thigh. All his life he'd worked his tail off to make something of himself. He'd sweated through heat the devil himself couldn't tolerate and toiled in cold that numbed him to the bone. He'd swung a sledgehammer until the blisters on his hands bled and studied until his eyes ached and the words blurred. The only thing that had kept him going was his obsession to make his grandfather eat his words. Now that he had success, he intended to ensure that no one would take it away.

A certain amount of luck had come to him, but mostly he'd followed his plan. And Emily was part of it. She was his calling card on the silver platter of society, the spike that would drive him firmly into financial security and give him the power to maintain it.

Emily's father had hinted that a marriage would unite the partnership. Jeff considered it a sound business decision; she was part of the plan.

And everything had gone accordingly, until he'd met Bree Murphy. From that moment he'd acted purely from instinct—a man's gut reactions to a woman he had to have. Without conscious thought, he'd pursued her, determined to win her—obsessed only with what he wanted. He'd never thought about her feelings or what would happen when he won her. He deserved every name she'd called him—and then some.

Cady had told him he was domineering, arrogant and snobbish. She'd forgotten selfish. If another man had treated his sister as callously as he'd treated Bree, Jeff would have strangled him with his bare hands.

Bree had no one to defend her honor. Her father had his own difficulties with the bottle, and Charlie was her biggest problem. Jeff had taken on the role of her champion, but some protector *he* was. He'd hurt her the most.

He'd deliberately set out to win her trust. When he finally had it, he'd let her down. The damndest part was he didn't know why he hadn't left her alone in the first place. But now that the damage was done, it was important that he make things right between them. He had to convince her that he'd never meant to hurt her, never wanted this to happen.

He lived his life by blueprint, and he'd never needed a plan more than he did now.

Jeff squatted in the bow and dipped the willow branch, noting that the water level was low—real low. He glanced over his shoulder. "Hey, Murphy . . ."

"Turn around, Tanner, and watch where we're going."

So much for getting through to her. He stood and moved down the right side of the craft, closer to the wheelhouse, checking the depth of the current again. The muddy stick indicated that the water was hardly deeper than the twenty-two inches she'd bragged she needed to safely operate the steamboat.

He looked at her through the doorway. "What happens if we run aground?"

Her gaze flicked to him for an instant, then concentrated on the channel ahead. "We stop moving."

"Okay." He took a deep breath and willed himself to patience. "Let's try this again. I meant, would *Belle*'s underside be damaged?"

She tossed her braid over her shoulder and shook her

head. "Not unless we hit a big boulder. And that's unlikely. The river's so shallow, you can see everything." She turned her disapproving gaze on him. "If you keep your eyes open and point us in the right direction."

"If we stopped moving," he asked slowly, "how would we get the boat out of the mud?"

"We couldn't, at least not alone. We'd probably be stuck here all night." She shrugged. "The river might rise enough to get her going again. But most likely she'd be stuck until Cap came lookin'. There's a winch on the *Elizabeth* to pull her out."

"I see."

"What's the matter, Tanner? Nervous?" A small, self-satisfied grin turned up the corners of her mouth. "Don't worry. All you have to do is keep watch and let me know if the current gets low. I'll do the rest."

"That's my plan, Captain." He moved forward, grinning.

Jeff watched the riverbank as they passed. On the bluff he studied the random ocotillo cactus, surrounded by desert scrub and sand. The landscape never changed, and he marveled that she knew where she was at any given time.

She probably knew every needle on every prickly pear. He could only judge their progress by time. He checked the sun. Brilliant blue sky slowly surrendered to the pink and gold of approaching dusk. According to his calculations, they were about halfway between the bridge and town.

He slowly lowered the peeled willow switch to take soundings of the river level. "Channel's getting shallower. Turn her to the right a little!" he shouted over his shoulder.

Jeff saw her nod, then felt the bow shift closer to the riverbank. He backed up several steps and braced himself. Then he heard a scraping sound at the same time the boat came to a lurching halt. The sudden stop threw him forward, but he shifted his right boot to counterbalance and managed to stay upright.

The engine's *putt-putt* died, and in the quiet that followed, only the whistle of the warm wind surrounded him. He heard a muttered curse and turned toward her, bracing himself again.

She raced to the bow and looked over the side into the mud. "Idiot railroad man! Something wrong with your eyes?"

"My sight is just fine, thanks." He crossed his arms over his chest and smiled down at her.

Bree pushed her hat back on her head, and her blazing blue eyes widened with comprehension. "You did that on purpose. Damn you! How dare you take a chance with my boat?"

"It's my boat and I don't take chances. We weren't traveling fast enough to do any damage. You said so yourself. But it appears we're stuck. How long do you suppose it'll be before Sean comes looking for us?" He lifted a brow and looked down at her.

She glared at him, then turned away and stomped furiously across *Belle*'s thirteen-foot beam. Bree might be quivering with anger, but this was the only way Jeff could think of to get her alone. He wanted to talk to her without interruption. And by his calculations he had until midmorning of the following day. She walked back and stopped in front of him, crossing her arms beneath her breasts. "You think I'm going to sit here all night and do nothing?"

"What choice do you have?"

"I can go for help."

"Oh, no, you don't." He looked at the sun's position on top of the mountain. "It'll be dark in less than an hour. You can't go gallivanting through the desert at night."

"I'd sooner take my chances with the snakes and scorpions than with you, Tanner. At least I know what to expect from them."

"No way I'm letting you off this boat. If you didn't die of thirst, you'd likely lose your way."

The gold and pink rays of the setting sun highlighted her profile as she bit the corner of her lip. He'd counted on her practicality to work in his favor. She let out a long breath, then removed her hat and let it hang down her back.

She sat on the edge of the boat, helplessly dangling her hands between her knees, and looked up at him. "Why did you do this to me, Tanner?"

"I need time to convince you that I'm not the bastard you think I am."

She laughed bitterly. "Eternity wouldn't be long enough."

twelve

After sponging the day's dirt from her hands, face, and arms, Bree put her shirt back on and left the wheelhouse. She hung her lantern on the outside wall, then leaned her shoulder against the hard surface. The sun had crawled down the backside of the mountains, leaving the peaks a-glow and the higher sky a light purple. As daylight disappeared, one by one the stars twinkled and blinked as they came out to play.

She glanced at Tanner in *Belle*'s bow. Bare from the waist up, the muscles of his back rippled and bunched as he drew her towel over his wide shoulders, then hung it around his neck after washing up. Yearning welled within her. She should have taken her chances on foot. It was risky, but at least that way she *had* a chance. Staying aboard was more dangerous to her than the desert—down deep inside where the critters couldn't sting or make her bleed.

Only Tanner could hurt her there.

She swallowed hard and tightly closed her eyes, trying to resurrect her anger. But it had marched through her like an avenging army, and in its wake there was only profound sadness.

All because she cared about Jefferson Tanner. The truth made her a fool. But the fact was undeniable.

She'd thought about it all day. It's a wonder she hadn't

grounded the boat without Tanner's help. She hadn't been able to think of anything but him. And she finally realized there was a reason she'd reacted like a she-wolf protecting her cubs at the news of his engagement. She'd begun to hope that there was a chance, just a small one, that he cared for her. Now that she knew he couldn't, the pain squeezed her chest, and she bit her lip to keep from crying out.

She'd always known that they were from two different worlds and in the end he'd likely choose someone from his. But he'd deliberately set out to make her trust him. It had worked, even better than he knew. She thought the sun rose and set on Jeff Tanner. She'd never met a man like him and knew she never would again.

All she had now was her pride. He'd never know how she felt about him.

But what defense did she have against his devastating smile and easy charm? She took inventory of her arsenal. Anger had deserted her; she hadn't the energy to fight him. Running away was out of the question, and murder was against the law. She could only continue to ignore him. Maybe it would be enough to hold him off until Cap found them.

In the bow with his back to her, Tanner reminded her of a conquering warrior—feet braced wide apart, arms crossed over his chest as he stared up at the star-sprinkled sky. Beside him, fingers of lantern light licked and danced over his perfect male body. Her heart pounded and her breath caught. If she put both her hands around his upper arm, she couldn't span the powerful muscle. She longed to explore the wide curve of his shoulder, touch his strong neck and the thick dark hair curling down.

Her mouth went dry. Lord, it was going to be a long night.

He'd said he needed time alone with her. Well, she needed something from time, too. She needed to speed it up, make it go faster until he was gone forever. Until she could forget him.

He turned to look at her, and she tried to make herself invisible, pressing her back into the wheelhouse wall. It was the section he'd replaced after the fire. The boards seemed to bend and give and fold her inside, pulling her further under his spell. He'd whittled a place in her life, carved a spot for himself in her heart. And somehow she knew that even after he left, she wouldn't forget him.

He'd always be there, a part of her memories, her mind, her soul.

Squeezing her eyes shut, she tried to block out his handsome face, his masculine body. Then she heard his bare feet slap on the deck planks, the sound growing louder as he closed in on her. She felt the heat of his body beside her. In spite of herself her lips turned up at the corners. His heated skin carried the fragrance of her lavender soap. Then her smile faded as she recognized the underlying scent of man.

Her female core melted in response, and she knew her meager fortifications would never hold up if he touched her.

"Can I talk to you?"

His breath fanned her face. His deep tone surrounded her and her brows drew together, her forehead puckered, as she tried to close her eyes tighter. *Keep him out.* But he didn't have to lay a finger on her. His voice, his breath, his warmth penetrated her, touching her in places that his hands never could.

She opened one eye and glanced warily at him, then slid her back down the wall and sat cross-legged on the deck. "We should get some sleep."

"Not yet. I want to ask you a favor."

"A favor?"

"For my sister." He crossed his arms over his chest. "When my private car arrives tomorrow, I want to move her to the construction site. She'll be the only woman there, and I can't be with her every minute. Would you stay with her? She'll be safe with you."

So, all he wanted was a companion for his sister. "Why should I do anything for you?"

"It's not for me. Besides, you and Cady seemed to hit it off."

Bree shrugged. "Maybe. But if I'm there, how will you get from Hardyville to the construction site?"

"For the time being, I'll bunk in with Dan at the site."

"I like Cady." She'd never admit it, but the offer was tempting. All the months he'd been there, she'd been living on *Belle*. She missed the security of four walls around her, and solid ground beneath her feet at night.

"You'll be comfortable there. The beds are soft," he said.

Oh, he was a devil. She yearned for a real mattress and smooth sheets against her skin. Her resolve cracked a little. Then her gaze strayed to the solid wall of his bare chest, and her breath caught. "I don't think I can stand being that close to the bridge."

"It's got a tub."

"The bridge?"

"Of course not. The car. You saw it yourself—the shiny brass one."

"A tub?" She hesitated, licking her dry lips. She'd forgotten about that. "Is it a big tub?"

"Big enough for a little thing like you to sit in and stretch your legs out."

"Hmm. That big." She raised an eyebrow. "How deep?"

He grinned. "Deep enough for the warm, soothing water to cover you all the way to your . . ." His gaze lowered to her breasts, then raised just a fraction. ". . . neck."

For a second she considered bluffing her way through this, then discarded the notion. She could almost see him tossing his winning hand on the table and raking in the pot. The lure of that brass tub was more than she could resist. She hated that he knew it.

"All right. I'll stay—but only for Cady." Is this what it felt like to be a fallen woman? She'd sold her soul for brass in the shape of a tub instead of coin.

He stuck his hands in his pockets. "Good."

"If that's all, then we should get some sleep."

"Not yet, Bree. There's something else I want to say."

"Make it quick."

Sitting in front of her, one leg bent upright with his wide wrist resting on his knee, his big body seemed to fill the narrow deck. "I don't know how to begin."

"Try the truth."

"The truth is I'm sorry. I should have told you all about Emily. My behavior was inexcusable." He took a deep breath. "I care for you. I'd never deliberately hurt you."

"But you did hurt me, Tanner. Why?" Below the husky whisper, she heard the quiver in her voice and bit her lip.

Jeff closed his eyes for a second, then swallowed hard and looked into her face. He hesitated, weighing his words. Then his shoulders relaxed as he seemed to give in to whatever thoughts warred within him. "I can't stay away from you. It's as simple as that."

She knew she should let it drop, stop him there. But she needed to know more. "Why?"

He laughed. "I wish I knew."

She stiffened and started to draw away. He reached his hand out and cupped her cheek. "I didn't mean it like that. See what you do to me? I feel like an adolescent schoolboy." He stroked her neck. "Beautiful Bree . . ."

His closeness would have been difficult enough to resist under normal circumstances, but along with his sincerity she had no weapon against him. The combination was more destructive than dynamite in demolishing the wall around her heart. But maybe she was her own worst enemy. The intensity in his eyes, the touch of his fingers, made her feel beautiful. She wanted so badly to believe everything he said. Did he take prisoners? She fervently hoped so, because she had already surrendered.

"You mean a lot to me. If you believe nothing else, believe this—I'd never purposely hurt you. Emily's not—"

"Don't." She held up her hand to stop him.

She didn't want to hear about anyone else. Not now. This was her time; he'd given it to her. Rivers and rails, right and wrong, good and bad—she pushed it all away. Nothing else mattered to her now, nothing but being with him. There was no past, no future. There was only the present. And if she was lucky, she could make it last forever.

She toyed with the towel still slung around his neck. It was her white flag. She slid her hand upward and cupped his jaw.

"God . . ." Passion flared in his eyes, turning the irises to green flames.

A hint of warning clung to that one word, but she ignored it. She wanted to explore him. If she lost her nerve now, she might never have another opportunity.

His day's growth of whiskers rasped against her fingertips, sparking friction that raced down her arm, settling in her breasts.

"Your beard is rough."

"It's harmless—unless I were to get close enough to kiss you."

Her breath caught. Beside her, hanging on the wall, the lantern light flickered over the top half of his face, hiding the lower part in shadow. She couldn't see his lips, concealed by his mustache. But she remembered his mouth pressed to hers and longed to feel it again.

Slowly smoothing her hand upward from his jawline, she tentatively touched his top lip and smiled as the hair grazed the tips of her fingers. "This part is softer."

A slow half-smile exposed his white teeth, contrasting with his dark mustache and tanned skin. His tongue stroked the sensitive pad of her finger. Sparks sizzled through her arm to every part of her body. She moaned softly, the pleasurable sensation so intense she couldn't keep it inside.

He drew in a ragged breath. "Do you have any idea what you're doing to me?"

She crossed her fingers and nodded. Truthfully, she hadn't the least notion what was happening to him. She only hoped it was a fraction of what she felt. A knot of need that she didn't quite understand coiled in her belly, and she felt a warm wetness between her thighs. She inched closer to him, seeking.

He opened his legs wide and pulled her between them, on her knees. Then he touched her cheek and trailed his hand lightly over her right breast to the tip of her braid resting there. After untying the ribbon binding it, he untangled the length. She shook her head from side to side letting her hair fall loose and wild on either side of her cheeks. His ardent gaze heated her blood to liquid fire.

He tunneled his fingers through the strands around her face, then cupped the back of her head and drew her leisurely, inch by inch, toward him. She couldn't breathe; she couldn't look away. With excruciating slowness, he touched his lips to hers.

He tasted of man, his mouth steady and sure, the feeling sweeter than honey, more heady than wine. His wiry mustache stroked her upper lip, raising tremors that spread to her shoulders and breasts, settling in her abdomen. Firm and unhurried, his lips moved over hers before opening slowly. He traced her mouth with his tongue, then dipped his head lower and moved to her neck. Like wildfire, hot and unexpected, passion flashed through her. Her labored breathing pounded in her ears. Or was it his ragged breath she heard?

Bree flattened her hand to his chest and gloried in the coarse hair that made her fingertips tingle. He pulled back and stared. Her wrist brushed the towel, and he jerked the length of material from around his neck and dropped it on the deck beside him. Then he guided her palm back to his bare curved chest muscle, and she felt his heart slamming against his ribs. The hammering fell into rhythm with her own pounding pulse.

She explored the powerful contours of the wide expanse, the corded muscles that coiled and rippled beneath her touch. With the tip of her finger she brushed his nipple and felt it grow erect. He sucked in his breath and she froze. Her gaze flew to his, searching.

For an instant she thought he was hurt. How could that be? Her touch was feather-light. Then she knew the face of pleasure. Pain and desire, the two so close sometimes it was hard to tell where one left off and the other began. And she'd brought him that expression with a single stroke of her finger. What a wonder. She felt powerful, his equal.

But why should the force of a single touch surprise her? She remembered still the sensations evoked when he'd touched her breast, and her thigh with only her pantalettes separating skin from skin. How much greater the excitement of touching bare flesh.

With deliberate slowness she moved her hand on his chest, testing her newfound weapon. Green fire smoldered in his eyes and melted something within her.

His gaze lowered to her bodice, the open front of her cotton shirt, where the pink ribbons of her camisole peeked out. In her fascination for Tanner's naked torso, she'd neglected to fasten her own buttons. She glanced up and saw him devouring her breasts with his eyes. Then his mouth tightened as he closed his hand into a fist.

She sat back on her heels and took his wide wrist, placing it knuckles down on her thigh as she uncurled his fingers, one by one. Then she lifted his palm to her mouth, the calluses pulling at her soft lips before she brought his open hand to her breast. He dragged in a deep agonized breath.

Jeff savored the curved mound within his touch. How perfectly she fit him. How deeply this gift from her had touched him. Then he blinked, struggling to pull out of the erotic spell she'd spun around him.

"No . . ." His growl lured her smoky, heavy-lidded gaze back to him. "You don't know what you're doing."

He removed her fingers holding his hand to her breast and saw that his own were shaking.

Then he stood abruptly and moved away from her to the bow of the boat. He looked out into the wall of blackness, wishing it could swallow him.

He was an idiot, a fool. When he'd grounded them, he'd never intended to touch her. He'd only wanted to talk, convince her that he'd never hurt her again.

But in the lantern light her satin skin had beckoned, her lips had enticed. Her silken hair had pulled him to her as surely as the strongest rope. Even now, especially now, he felt the ache in his groin. He wanted her. She was a drug and he couldn't get enough. One touch increased his craving; one kiss and he had to have more. But if he continued touching her, kissing her, he wouldn't be able to stop. As it was, it had nearly killed him to pull back. But he'd sworn not to hurt her.

The lonely wind whistled past him, curling around his neck, cooling the sheen of sweat on his back. He drew in a deep breath struggling to control the raging need within him. Then a soft sound floated to him on the breeze.

He froze, listening. There it was again. Sniffling? "Oh, God," he said hoarsely. "Don't do this to me."

Almost against his will he turned, then dragged his fingers through his hair. She sat where he'd left her, on the deck with her forehead resting on her knee, a golden halo on the back of her head where the light kissed her. Black hair fell in a curtain, hiding her face and brushing the deck. He'd been prepared for her anger, but he couldn't fight her tears. The sound, the soul-wrenching anguish in her pose combined to break him. Slowly he moved toward her. Her body stiffened. Instantly she was on her feet and into the wheelhouse.

He reached out a hand to stop her, then let it drop to his side as he followed. "Bree, listen."

She shook her head, and her long hair caressed the back of her waist. "Don't say anything. I understand."

How could she when he didn't know what the hell was happening? "Don't cry."

She reached up and brushed a hand across her cheek. "I'm not crying."

"Dammit. Don't lie to me." He'd learned to count on her honesty. He gripped her shoulders and turned her to face him. Hesitantly her palms rested on his chest.

"You pushed me away," she said, then stopped and caught her trembling lip between her teeth.

"Because I don't want to hurt you."

"Don't I have a say?" She lifted her chin and glared at him defiantly. "I know what I'm doing."

More than anything Jeff wanted to believe she meant that. He wanted to kiss her. Every second he held back became a painful ache. He pulled her to him and lowered his mouth to hers. She came to him without resistance. Her lips tasted soft as clouds, sweet as the spring rain, and moved against his as she willingly accepted the pressure. Her eager response clawed at his self-control.

Slipping his hands beneath her shirt, he eased it from her shoulders and let it fall. With shaking fingers he untied the pink ribbon of her camisole, the flimsy barrier between him and her soft skin. He slid first one, then the other lace-edged strap down her creamy shoulders, baring her small firm breasts to his heated gaze.

"You're so beautiful."

Bree didn't believe the words, but the burning look in his eyes told her he wasn't lying. His expression made her *feel* feminine, that she was the only woman in the world. All that existed for her was his touch, his scent, his heat. Nothing else mattered. She wanted to give him everything.

Taking his hand, she led him to her mattress in the corner of the wheelhouse. She knelt and pulled him down with her. He splayed his fingers and weaved them through her hair, brushing it away from her face. He put his arm around her and lowered her, following her down. The un-yielding wall of his chest with its covering of coarse hair rubbed against her bare breasts, and her nipples hardened in response. Leaning on one elbow above her, he studied her intensely, his gaze burning into hers before he dipped his head and kissed her. Then he tasted her jaw and con-tinued the caress to the sensitive spot beneath her ear.

Pleasure ricocheted through her, the delight too great to bear. She stroked the thick, wavy hair at the back of his neck, then pressed, making the touch of his lips more firm on hers. The rough wetness of his tongue along the soft column of her neck raised goose bumps along her arms and legs. She trembled and moaned, arching her hips against him, instinctively searching with her body, asking for more.

When his lips moved lower and closed over her nipple, her breath caught as pleasure shot through her. It was the most wonderful feeling she had ever experienced. She held still as a stone, afraid she'd miss even a single ripple of delight. His tongue moved over the peak of her heated flesh, stroking and circling as pressure built in her belly and an ache danced in the core of her womanhood.

He moved his knee between her legs, and she instinc-tively rubbed against his thigh trying to ease the tension. He groaned and his breath fanned her breast and the moistness left by his lips. Her skin went cold, then hot, and the fire spread over her body until it stole her breath. A feeling so powerful it hurt, deep inside, grew until she couldn't bear it. Frustration swelled as she arched her hips against the hard evidence of his desire. Still she wasn't close enough to him.

A knot tightened in her chest until she couldn't hold it in and a moan escaped her. His hand squeezed her waist, then slid lower, over her denims, until his palm cupped her between her legs. White hot pleasure scorched her, and she rhythmically moved her hips, trying to cool the fire, and failing miserably. She didn't understand why.

"Jeff, I never imagined anything like this," she whispered hoarsely.

He stopped his exquisite sensual assault and looked at her. "Me, either," he said, his breathing ragged.

"I have so much time to make up for. I want to know what it's like. Show me."

Jeff stared at the blind trust in her eyes. Her innocent confession was as effective as a bucket of ice water in the face in bringing him to his senses. She was a virgin, untouched by another man. The reminder rocked him to his core. He knew what she needed. He felt the same ache in his gut. Somehow he had to find the strength to let her go. He knew it as surely as he knew she was the most desirable woman he'd ever met. If he touched her satin skin, the silky mound of her femininity the way he wanted, he'd be lost.

He closed his eyes, rolled away from her and sat up. One leg bent, he rested his wrist on his knee and refused to look at her. He didn't trust himself. He'd want to strip away her remaining clothes and feast his eyes on her beautiful body. But he'd never be able to stop there. He couldn't keep from burying himself deep in her waiting moistness and taking his pleasure from her. He'd be the liar she thought he was; he'd do what he'd sworn not to do. He'd hurt her.

"This is a mistake," he said, releasing a long breath.

"I don't understand—" Confusion and hurt intermingled with her soft, breathy tone and burned him.

He branded himself the worst kind of bastard. But at least he had enough control left to keep from making things worse. He wouldn't stoop to taking her virginity, then walking away. And he had to walk away from her. He wouldn't let himself stay. It was best for both of them.

"You were right about me. I'm a low-down, cheating, two-timing skunk." He chanced a quick look at her and saw that she'd pulled her camisole over her breasts. Thank

God. He picked up her white shirt and dropped it beside her, sighing heavily. "Go to sleep, Bree."

"But—"

"Don't argue with me," he said harshly. He wouldn't be able to turn her away a third time. That would take a stronger man than he. "Just go to sleep before I do something I'll regret."

She sucked in her breath.

He heard a rustling behind him and when he looked, she'd turned her back to him and curled into a tight ball.

"I'll keep watch."

She buried her face deeper into her arms.

Somewhere between deep sleep and full awareness, Bree stretched, then winced. Her back hurt, her chest ached, and her swollen eyes refused to open. There was something wrong, and she fought to push it away.

Then she heard the shrill whistle, and her eyes flew open. The *Elizabeth*. Suddenly she recalled where she was, and last night's painful scene came back with crystal clarity. She wanted to shatter the memory and sweep the shards away. She wanted to forget she'd ever laid eyes on Jefferson Tanner. She wanted to die when she recalled her eagerness to offer him everything and his coldness when he'd thrown it back in her face.

The whistle sounded again. She glanced out the wheelhouse door and tried to judge the time. By her reckoning it must be nearly nine o'clock. Cap hadn't wasted any time looking for them. At least that would save her long, awkward hours with Tanner while they waited to be pulled out of the mud.

After hastily tucking in her shirt, she looked around for her blue ribbon to tie back her hair, but couldn't see it anywhere. Wind must have blown it away. She shrugged, then grabbed her hat from the peg beside the doorway and stuffed her hair beneath it before leaving the wheelhouse. Even with the brim shading her face, the sun blinded her.

She stopped a moment to let her eyes adjust, and the hot wind caught her head on, sneaking inside her shirt and billowing it out behind her. Instantly her lips grew dry, and she moistened them with her tongue. The unconscious movement reminded her of the night before and Tanner, his mouth and hands doing wonderful things to her body.

Before she could stop herself, she looked for him. He stood in the bow, watching the bigger steamboat slow down and stop, just a short distance from them. She moved to the opposite side of the boat from Tanner, thirteen feet across the beam, as far from him as she could get.

He hadn't put his boots on yet and his bare toes curled up against the heat already radiating from the deck. Disheveled dark hair framed his face, and she imagined the rasp of a day's growth of beard as he rubbed his jaw. What would it feel like to press her soft cheek to his stubbled one first thing every morning? She shook her head to clear it, but her eyes strayed back to him as if of their own mind.

His white shirt hung loose over his denim pants and was open at the neck, revealing just a bit of the coarse hair on his chest. She recalled the muscled contours she'd explored only hours before with such abandon. A night of tears hadn't washed away any of her longing. She still wanted him. A scraping sound brought her attention to the stern of the *Elizabeth*.

Riley slid a plank from her father's boat to *Belle*'s bow, then straightened and grinned. "Every'thin' all right, missy?"

She nodded. "Just dandy."

Bree looked past him and saw her father at the big wheel on the *Elizabeth*. Then she watched two figures emerge from the wheelhouse. Cady Tanner hurried forward with Kane Carrington right behind her.

Cady stopped by the gangplank holding her yellow gingham skirts against her to keep the wind from catching them. The captain stood protectively beside her, his gold-trimmed uniform hat shading his eyes.

"Jeff, are you all right?" she asked.

"Fine. What are you doing here?" he snapped, staring intently at his sister.

"I was afraid something terrible had happened to you."

"Why is he with you?" Tanner nodded toward the officer.

Cady glanced at the man still holding her elbow, and Bree swore a blush colored her creamy white cheeks. "I met Captain Carrington in town yesterday. We spent the better part of the day getting acquainted."

A muscle in Tanner's jaw tensed as he observed the couple. "That doesn't answer my question."

"I came along in case Sean needed help," Kane answered. He met Tanner's gaze evenly, challenging.

Riley snorted. "Horse manure. Ain't a stuck boat anywhere Sean and me cain't pull out alone."

"He's here because I asked him." Cady shrugged sheepishly. "I thought you might need help."

The heavy thud of boots scraped the *Elizabeth*'s deck just before Sean stepped up on the gangplank and came across, a shotgun in his work-roughened hand. Bree rushed forward to hug her father and was surprised when he didn't return her greeting. Her gaze immediately flew to his face. In the shadow of his hat brim, gray brows gathered across his forehead like a threatening thunderhead. His mouth tightened into a grim, straight line. She hadn't seen him so angry since she was thirteen and had stowed away on his steamboat for the first time.

"What happened, Breanne?" he asked, resting the butt end of the gun on the deck.

Not now, she thought. She wanted to pull the boat out and talk about it later, privately. The last thing she needed was to be scolded like a child in front of Tanner and everyone else. "We ran aground, Cap. I need the winch—"

"Don't get smart with me, young lady. I've got eyes.

How did this boat get stuck? You haven't done that since your first season on the river."

"I'm sure it was just an accident," Cady said.

"You stay out of this, Cady," Tanner said, glaring at her. Then he turned to Sean. "It's my fault we ran aground. I deliberately miscalculated the depth of the river. I wanted to talk to Bree—alone."

"What the hell was so important to say to her that you had to pull such a harebrained stunt? Somethin' tells me talkin' wasn't what you had in mind." Her father's voice boomed out, reverberating against the riverbank and bouncing back. "You have a helluva nerve endangering her that way."

"I'd never hurt her."

"Cap . . ."

Bree was getting angrier by the second. How dare they discuss this as if she weren't there? She and Tanner had come awfully close to doing exactly what Cap accused them of. If Tanner hadn't pulled away . . . But he had.

Her father held up a hand to silence her. "Quiet, missy." His gaze never left Tanner's. "You *have* hurt her. After keepin' her out all night alone, she won't be able to hold her head up in town. But you're gonna fix it. You're gonna marry her."

"The hell I am." Tanner's eyes blazed, and he took a step forward.

Bree was stunned. She grabbed her father's arm and turned him to her. "Listen to me, Cap. Nothing happened. Tanner didn't do anything. I don't understand why you're going on about this."

"For weeks now the two of you have been sniffing around each other—nipping and fighting and making cow eyes. You show me a single person in the Territory who'd believe this was completely innocent, and I'll buy a round of drinks for everyone in Cactus Kate's on Saturday night."

"You're not going to drop this, are you, Sean?" Tanner

let out a long breath, then evenly met her father's furious gaze. "It makes no difference that she's the same as she was when we left Hardyville yesterday morning."

"I'd hoped she and Charles would marry. Never happen now." Her father looked at her, then moved his shoulders as if they pained him. "Doesn't matter what you did or didn't do. It only matters what folks *think* happened. She's ruined for any other man. You're going to marry my daughter, Tanner, as soon as we get back to Hardyville."

He picked up the shotgun and cradled it in his arms.

thirteen

Bree couldn't believe she'd heard right. Marriage? To Tanner? With a shotgun in his back? She'd rather throw herself in the river. If it were higher than two feet, she'd have done it and let the current carry her away. Tanner didn't want her. She'd offered him all that was hers to give, without expecting anything in return, and he'd turned her away. Reason enough not to spend her life with him.

She looked at Tanner. Anger, hot as the Arizona sun, blazed across his features. He was madder than she'd ever seen him. His hands clenched into fists at his sides, and his green eyes were hard. Pressure seemed to build within him; he looked like a steam engine ready to blow.

Obviously, the idea of marriage to her was something he couldn't abide. She wasn't a lady; she couldn't be his wife. Pain splintered her heart and worked its way to her soul.

She tried to hate him, but she was afraid her feelings had gone too far for that. Pride was all she had left, and she swore that he'd never know how deeply he'd hurt her.

She placed a hand on her father's shoulder. "Cap—"

"You stay out of this, girl."

"Captain Murphy," Cady said, "forced marriage is a bit extreme. Don't you think? My brother would never comp—"

"Butt out, Cady." Jeff glanced across the small distance

at his sister still on the *Elizabeth*. "The last thing I need is your big mouth making things worse."

"Now wait a minute, Tanner—" Kane Carrington placed one shiny military boot on the gangplank. "That's no way to talk to your sister."

Tanner looked at the army captain. "Don't tell me what to do, Carrington. I'm not one of your greenhorn recruits." His eyes narrowed. "Just how well are you and my sister acquainted?"

"Simmer down, you two." Riley elbowed Kane out of the way and stepped up on the gangplank between the two riverboats. "Anybody wanna hear what I think?"

"No!" Four voices chorused in unison.

"I'm gonna tell ya' anyways." He looked down at Bree. "Someone's gotta make ya' see reason. A weddin's the right thing—and not cuz you were alone with him."

Jeff stared at the creased and weathered faces of the two interfering old men. He could see reason six ways to sundown—until someone tried to force him into something. He was used to giving orders, not taking them. But that wasn't what had lit his fuse.

Sean had come right out and said that he wanted Charlie and Bree to marry. Was the man blind? Couldn't her own father see that she was afraid of him?

Righteous fury erupted inside him, and Jeff knew one thing for sure. That slick sonofabitch would marry her over his dead body. He'd promised himself he'd protect her, and he damn well intended to do just that.

"You win, Sean. I'll marry her—whenever and wherever you want."

Riley cackled. "Never knew I had it in me t'be so convincin'."

Bree's head snapped up and her eyes widened, round and blue and shocked. With her mouth open she looked from one man to the other. Her father's face wrinkled into a wide, self-satisfied grin.

Sean stuck out his hand. "Pleased you saw things my way."

Bree stepped between them before Jeff could shake on it.

"Does anyone want to know what I think?" She stopped and looked around at the five pairs of eyes focused on her. "I wouldn't marry Jefferson Thomas Tanner if he were the last man on earth."

"Now, Bree, honey. Be reasonable." Sean lifted his hat and wiped the sweat from his forehead.

"I am being reasonable." She grabbed the shotgun from him. "I'm going to put this thing away."

Bree brushed past him and headed toward the wheelhouse. Behind her she heard heavy boots. After placing the rifle inside the doorway, she turned to her father. His ruddy face was lined with fatigue and creased with confusion.

"Why the hell won't you marry him?"

"Because he's going to marry a lady."

"You're a lady."

"I'm a riverboat captain."

"Doesn't mean you're not a lady."

She laughed bitterly. "Look at me—my clothes. I'm more at home on a boat deck than a dinner party."

"Your mama taught you t'be a lady. And later, when Mary and I tied the knot—well, you recollect I tried t'talk you out of followin' after me. But you are the most pig-headed female—"

"See, Cap? Female. Not a lady."

"If only your mama was here. Since she's not, I know she'd want me to protect your good name. She'd want me t'see to what's right. You have t'marry him. I say so."

"Why now, Cap? Why are you acting like a father when I don't need one?" Her brows drew together. "I don't care anymore what people think about me. Nothing happened with Tanner, and nothing could make me marry him." Her hand slashed through the air. "That's the end of it."

Sean shook his head. "Where did I go wrong? It's not easy bein' father and mother to a girl with a mind of her own. I've always done the best I could."

"I know you have." Her anger melted away, and she softened her tone. "Marrying him would be a mistake." She glanced over her shoulder at Tanner. He moved toward them. She looked back at her father. "Trust me."

Jeff carefully read father and daughter, studied their serious expressions, translated the mixture of emotions that crossed their faces. Some of Sean's conversation carried to him, then he saw Bree gesture defiantly with her hand. He didn't have to hear it word for word to know she'd refused to marry him. That rankled.

"I don't get you," Jeff said, moving past Sean to stand in front of her.

"Don't much care whether you understand me or not."

"Any number of women would jump at the chance to marry me."

"So pick one and leave me alone."

"You're sure this is the way you want it?" Sean asked. "He's willin' t'marry you, girl."

"I'm positive." She looked down, uneasy. "This probably isn't the best time to bring this up, but you might as well know now. Tanner asked me to stay in his private car when it arrives today at the bridge site." She tensed as she heard what she'd said.

Jeff braced himself. He moved beside Bree, ready to back her up if Sean challenged her decision.

"I'm staying there with Cady, Cap. Not him. He's bunking with Dan," she added quickly.

Her father stared at her, then nodded slowly, his gray brows pulled together. His shoulders slumped in defeat. "You're going to do what you want anyways. I guess I have to trust you." He speared Jeff with a warning look, then pointed at her and jabbed his finger in the air. "Don't make me sorry."

"Don't worry. I'm a big girl. I can take care of myself."

She smiled at him. "Now help me get this boat out of the mud."

Sean nodded again, then, without another word, walked to the bow and crossed the gangplank to the *Elizabeth*. Bree followed.

Jeff moved closer to help and watched her work with Riley to attach the winch. He waited to feel a sense of relief that she'd refused to marry him. It never came. Frustration, annoyance, irritation—those emotions were closer to what he felt. Why the hell had she refused to let him save her from Charlie, not to mention her reputation? She was a big girl, all right. Now she had to face accusation and innuendo from the whole town. Because of him.

He kicked himself for not considering that before getting them stuck. All he'd thought about was himself and what he wanted. There had to be a way to make it up to her.

Bree pulled the frayed carpetbag from beneath her bed. She needed to pack some things to take with her to the Pullman. Most of what she'd need was stored downstairs in an old trunk in the master bedroom, but there were a few items tucked away in her armoire.

Placing the bag on the bed, she pulled the top wide and stared into the black opening. After everything that had happened, she wanted to stay at the construction site about as much as she wanted to tame a snake. The scene on the boat had embarrassed and humiliated her. She blamed Tanner for that. And if she'd had any doubts before about the way he felt, they were gone now. Spending his life with her was about as attractive as being staked out in the desert sun over a mound of fire ants. She wished she never had to lay eyes on him again. If only she hadn't given her word to stay with Cady. But she had.

She stared at the armoire and noticed that the doors were open and Tanner's white linen shirt peeked out of one of the drawers. He'd certainly made himself at home in her room. Then a thought struck her. For the next few weeks the shoe would be on the other foot. He'd be sleeping in a tent and she'd be living in his private car. There *was* justice, she thought grinning wickedly.

Behind her the door creaked open, and she closed her eyes. She'd hoped to be in and out of here before Tanner. She wasn't ready to talk to him, let alone see him in her room—unchaperoned. Then again, maybe it would be better to clear the air. They had to work together until the bridge was finished.

"I'll be out of here in two shakes of a lamb's tail," she said without turning around.

"Don't hurry on my account."

Bree whirled at the sound of Charles's voice. He stood full in the doorway, blocking her exit. Automatically she felt for her gun at the waist of her jeans. It wasn't there. She'd left it on the downstairs hall table, while she packed her bag. Fear knotted in her chest; panic pulled and snapped at the edge of her mind. She fought it down. If she lost her wits, he'd get to her.

Her gaze flicked around the room searching for an escape. The hot breeze from the window ruffled the hair on her neck, and she realized that was the only way out—if she was fast enough to elude him.

She gripped the spindle on the bedpost, struggling to stay calm. Was anyone else in the house? Tanner had helped Cady take her luggage down to the dock. Mary had gone to the mercantile. Cap? He'd said he needed to work on the boat's boiler gauge, and he'd taken Riley with him. She'd thought Charles was at Cactus Kate's. She named herself every kind of fool for letting her guard down.

"What do you want, Charles?" She swallowed hard, trying to keep her voice from shaking. Predators could smell terror. *Don't let him know your fear.*

"What I've always wanted." He hooked his thumbs in his pants at his waistband, long, slender fingers pointing down.

His hands looked white and weak, but she knew his steely grip and surprising strength. She shuddered, then pushed the thought away. She wasn't a little girl now. She was older, wiser. All she had to do was keep her head and wait for her chance.

"I don't have time for games. Tanner's waiting for me at the dock. If I don't show up—"

"You're not a very good liar."

"I'm not lying. He took his sister's things down to the boat. If I don't get there soon, he'll—"

"He'll wait. I have. If I asked him whether you're worth it, what would he tell me, Breanne?" His lips curled derisively. "I heard what happened."

"Nothing happened."

"It's all over town—how you were on the boat with him all night." He shook his head, chiding her. "But don't worry. It doesn't change the way I feel about you. And our folks are counting on a weddin' between you and me." His pale blue gaze lowered to her breasts, then moved to her abdomen, then sank farther. "No matter that he got there first." He touched his tongue to his thin top lip. "It only makes my turn easier."

"Get out, Charles. Leave me be." Brave words with nothing to back them up. She'd give anything to have her gun.

Bree despised the trembling that started in her hands, then spread to her arms and legs. It was as if she'd gone backward in time and was thirteen again. She remembered his mouth on her, wet and hot—his hands touching her everywhere, wild, frenzied. Fear squeezed her chest so tight she could hardly breathe.

"Why do you pretend so, little sister? You want me. That's why you wouldn't marry him." He took a step forward.

"I don't want anything to do with you. And if you come any closer, I'll kill you. I swear I will." She watched him carefully, her eyes burning when she refused to blink, every nerve and instinct poised to run if he moved again.

"And how would you explain that to Mother and Sean?" He smoothed back a loose strand of oiled hair. "He's the closest I've come to having a father. No, I don't think—"

Downstairs, the front door opened, then slammed shut. Heels clicked in the entry hall, then muffled on the stair runner.

"Dammit." Charles's mouth tightened, and he glanced over his shoulder, before his narrowed gaze returned to her. "This isn't over. My time is coming. Make no mistake, Breanne. A used-up prospector with a shotgun isn't going to keep me from getting what I want. No drunken old man who can't forget his first wife is going to stand in my way."

"Tanner won't—"

"Tanner's leaving." He pointed his finger at her, and she shrank back. "It's just a matter of time. And that time is coming soon whether we're married or not."

"Bree, are you ready?" Cady called out to her from the top of the stairs. "I forgot my—" She stopped short, a few steps behind Charles.

He leaned his back against the doorframe. "How nice to see you, Miss Tanner."

Cady nodded uneasily. "Mr. Perkins."

He looked back at Bree. His smile never reached his eyes. Anger and frustration smoldered there. "If you ladies will excuse me, I have to help Sean. The boiler gauge has been acting up." He moved into the hall, then glanced back. "Don't forget what I said, Breanne."

When he was gone, Bree exhaled, a deep, cleansing breath.

Cady watched his retreating back for a few seconds, then hurried into the room. "I don't know if I should say anything, but—" She hesitantly chewed her lower lip, a concerned look on her face. "I think if I were you, I'd keep my distance from him."

Bree tried to laugh, but the sound caught and nearly choked her. "I plan to."

Cady nodded emphatically. "I'm glad you're staying with me. You'll be away from him."

Bree smiled thinly. Away from Charles and close to Tanner. Out of the frying pan into the fire.

She removed her trembling hand from the bedpost. Cady saw the movement and frowned. The younger woman took her by the shoulders and sat her on the bed.

"Can I get you some water?"

Water couldn't wash away her terror, and the concern of a friend wouldn't help. She shook her head. "I'm fine."

She lifted her still-shaking hand, and Cady took it between both of hers. "Your fingers are like ice."

"Must be cooling off outside."

"It's stifling, and you know it. Bree, let me—"

"Don't trouble yourself. Really."

Bree searched for something to say, anything to change the subject. She didn't want to think about Charles. She wanted to pretend that everything was normal. Maybe then the sickening fear would go away.

"Cady, I'm sorry about what happened on the boat. My father was—"

"Don't give it another thought. I understand. My father would have done the same—unless of course one of my brothers got there first."

"You and Kane seemed awfully friendly. And I got the feeling your brother wasn't too happy about it."

Cady met her gaze, then her eyes lowered as her cheeks flushed beet red. "Kane's not like any man I've ever met." She looked up and her face brightened. "He's invited me to a formal reception at Fort Mojave on Saturday. Some dignitary is coming from Washington for an inspection. I've never met a government official before. Who'd have thought it would happen way out here in the Territory? I guess all those lessons from boarding school will come in handy after all."

"You must have made quite an impression on Kane. Where is he, anyway?"

"He was in a hurry to get back, but that reminds me. He wanted me to be sure and tell you about it. He'd like you to be there."

"A formal reception? I couldn't . . ."

"Jeff's invited, too."

Bree laughed. "And that's supposed to make me feel better?"

The other girl nodded and the golden-brown ringlets cascading from the crown of her head bounced and tickled her cheek. "He's already accepted. Only because he wants to keep an eye on me, of course." Cady's petticoats rustled as she sat on the bed. "You have to come, Bree. That place is crawling with soldiers."

Bree gave her a wry look. "It is an army post, after all."

Cady smiled sheepishly. "I know. But I just can't go by myself, and I'd really like to see Kane again."

The thought of the soldiers didn't bother Bree. She saw them all the time; she delivered their mail. But meeting someone from back East—a government official—was different. She wouldn't know how to act or what to say. She didn't have the right clothes.

"Cady . . ." She sighed, staring at her hands clasped in her lap. "I might as well tell you the truth. I haven't anything fancy enough to wear for a formal reception."

"Is that all? I can fix that. Easy as pie." She clapped her hands together like an excited child. "We're the same size, I think. I'm sure one of my dresses will fit you. So, it's all settled."

Bree hesitated, then shrugged. "I guess it is."

But in her heart she wondered if she'd ever feel settled about anything.

Jeff pushed back the flaps and left the tent he'd shared with his camp foreman for the last week. He'd missed the comforts of the boardinghouse, but it was worth it to see

Cady again and have her nearby. In spite of the primitive cot, the howling wind that snapped the canvas walls in and out with every gust, and the relentless dust, he'd slept like a rock.

He looked around the railroad camp, the makeshift tent city. Beside the Pullman Carrington's horse waited, restively tossing his head. Cady had stopped by to inform Jeff that the captain had come to call and she intended to take him on a tour of the site. He watched them now, a short distance away by the river. Their low voices carried to him, but he couldn't make out the words.

Billowing, gray-tinged clouds struggled over the top of the jagged mountains, then raced across the sky, casting moving shadows over the desert floor. The sun peeked in and out, and the wind gusted. But the young couple continued to chat, oblivious to their surroundings.

As hard as he tried, Jeff couldn't fault Carrington's manners. And in his crisp blue uniform with its polished gold buttons, he would turn any feminine head. He appeared to be a gentleman. But there was nothing gentlemanly about the way he looked at Cady. Jeff knew that look all too well, felt it every time he saw Bree.

He remembered the jealousy he'd felt when he'd assumed that Bree and Kane were more than friends. Now that he knew the nature of their relationship, he was relieved. But he observed Cady as she smiled up at the good-looking officer. His protective instincts intensified, and he glimpsed the enormous responsibilities faced by fathers of girls. Would he have behaved any differently than Sean if his sister had been out all night with Carrington? He'd probably have wrung the man's neck until he'd extracted a promise of marriage.

But he'd agreed to marry Bree. And she'd turned him down. That should have been an end to it. But somehow, he couldn't forget her refusal. He couldn't understand why she'd spurned him.

He had a lot to offer a woman—security, a place in so-

ciety. She'd never have to work again. Dammit. She could
do a helluva lot worse. Charlie's smug smile flashed
through his mind.

At least that bastard couldn't get near her—for the time
being. Cady had told Jeff about finding Bree alone with
her stepbrother and how frightened she'd looked. If Bree
agreed to Jeff's marriage proposal, he'd have the legal
right to protect her. But rights or no, if Charlie came near
her again, he'd regret it.

The wind lashed him across the face. He shoved his
hands in his pockets and hunched his shoulders against it.
Grains of sand rolled and shifted, like insects blown along
out of control.

Jeff turned to look at his private car, silent and still on
the unfinished section of rail. The bridge was nearing
completion, and the next step was to lay track across it,
connecting the lines on the other side of the river in California. When that was accomplished, he could get the hell
out of this godforsaken territory.

But what would happen to Bree then?

He glanced at the railroad coach again and wondered if
Bree was truly all right. In the days since she'd come to
stay at the site, she'd been uncharacteristically quiet.
Earlier that day she'd been tired and cross, so he'd sent
her to the Pullman to get some rest. He wondered if she
was feeling better now.

She'd told him to leave her alone. But he couldn't get
her off his mind. Besides, he had to get his frock coat for
the reception the following night. Cady had promised to
press it for him. He grinned. How many excuses did he
need to see her—besides the most important one. He
wanted to.

Jeff climbed the stairs and swiftly crossed the outside
rear platform, his boots ringing against the metal. He
rapped a knuckle once on the door, then opened it and
stepped inside.

Gazing around the coach, he experienced the familiar

satisfaction in its elegant air and furnishings. He looked at the ceiling and noticed the chandelier Bree's bullet had shattered the day they'd met had been replaced. But she'd left her mark in other ways.

Her blue ribbon rested on the cherrywood table between the two green velvet wingback chairs. Her denim pants and white cotton shirt lay in the center of the car as if she'd hastily stepped out of them. Her pantalettes and the dainty camisole with the intimate pink bow hung from the dressing screen separating the car's parlor and living areas. Beside the feminine apparel dangled a thick, white towel.

Splashing sounds came from the bathing area. A slender foot and ankle rested against the edge of the brass tub. He should've guessed this was where she'd be. Maybe he had, he thought smiling.

"Anybody here? Bree?"

The leg was instantly drawn back, and water slapped onto the floor.

"If you come any closer, I'll shoot you, Jefferson Tanner!"

"Then come out here so we can talk."

"No. Leave me alone."

He took three steps forward. "If you don't come out, I'm coming in."

"You're bluffing."

"You think so?" He moved toward her, and the floorboard creaked.

"You low-down, underhanded . . ." He heard the unmistakable click of the hammer on her gun. "One more step, and I'll see your bluff and raise you a bellyful of lead."

"I'll stay put if you'll tell me something."

There was a brief silence while she apparently weighed his words. "What?"

"Why did you refuse to marry me?"

He heard sloshing water and pictured her squirming uneasily in his brass tub, naked and pink and appealing. The image of her body slick and shiny, her full breasts barely covered by the water, caused sweat to pop out on his fore-head. His breathing accelerated; his groin tightened with the well-known ache.

"What's wrong, Tanner? Hasn't anyone ever said no to you before?"

"That's beside the point. You could do worse than mar-rying me, you know."

"I could do better, too."

"How do you figure?"

She didn't answer, then water hit the floor as if she'd shifted angrily in the tub. "This discussion is pointless. What do you really want?"

You, he thought.

Dammit. He'd only intended to talk to her. He hadn't meant to let his control slip, but where Bree Murphy was concerned, he had no control. He didn't have to see her or lay a finger on her to want her. The evidence of his desire pressed full and heavy against his trousers.

"Come out here. I want to talk."

"I don't."

He watched her towel disappear from the top of the screen, and his mouth went dry.

"Then you're different from the women I've met."

Her deep sigh floated to him. "How many women have you met who run a riverboat?"

"Only you," he said hoarsely. "Come out here so we—"

"No. Go away."

He exhaled slowly. "I guess you leave me no choice."

He reached out and opened the Pullman door. After hes-itating a fraction of a second, he shut it loudly without leaving.

A moment later she drifted around the screen with the large towel knotted above her breasts. Her black curls were piled on her head, with stray wet strands plastered to her neck like a lover's fingers. She was more beautiful than he'd ever seen her, and the realization slammed him in the gut. Flushed from the warm steamy water, her face looked innocent, seductive. Contradictions, yet each description fit her equally well.

Startled, she stopped abruptly and gasped. Then she hunched her shoulders forward as she crossed her arms over her chest. "I thought you'd gone."

He knew he should look away, but he couldn't, and the pressure between his legs throbbed painfully. He shrugged. "Like you said, I'm low-down and underhanded."

"You forgot sneaky." Her voice was husky as she stared at his mouth.

He took a step closer. "I stand corrected."

"You shouldn't be standing here at all." Awareness flared in her eyes, then her lids fluttered and lowered, spreading her thick lashes across her smooth, freckled cheeks.

"I'll leave, just as soon as I . . ." He bent forward slowly and lifted her chin with his index finger, intending to taste her soft pink lips—just for a second.

"Don't—"

Before he could convince her to hold still for his kiss, Cady entered the coach while Kane held the door for her.

"Oh, my God!" Bree screeched, then dashed behind the dressing screen.

"Jeff, what are you doing here?" Cady asked, frowning.

He cleared his throat. "I came for my coat. Did you press it for me?"

"It's right there." She pointed to the brocade-covered settee behind him.

He glanced over his shoulder. "So it is. I didn't notice."

"I wonder why," Kane said wryly, brows raised as he stared at the spot where Bree had stood in her towel. "If you're not careful, Tanner, there's going to be a shotgun wedding after all."

A loud, unladylike snort sounded from the other side of the freestanding divider. "Who's the unlucky lady?"

Jeff frowned at the screen that separated Bree from him, and watched her undergarments disappear one by one.

Then he glowered at the other man. "Don't start, Carrington. Why aren't you at the fort, anyway? Don't you have work to do, some bigwig from Washington to nurse-maid?"

"The undersecretary is arriving in the morning. Besides, I am working. It's my duty to make sure that your sister is safe and enjoying her visit to the Territory."

"Duty my a—"

Cady stepped between them. "I think both of you should leave—now—and give Bree some privacy."

Kane nodded and opened the door, waiting for Jeff to precede him outside.

"Hurry it up," Jeff said gruffly to his sister. "You'll miss supper."

Bree peeked out when she heard the door close. She'd hastily slipped into her undergarments and stepped cautiously out into the open, pistol in hand. Tanner had tricked her once; she wouldn't let him get away with it again. She looked at Cady, sitting on the settee.

"Are they gone?"

"Yes."

She glanced around one last time, just to make sure. After breathing a sigh of relief, she sat down on one of the wingback chairs and placed her pistol on the cherrywood table beside her. The luxurious velvet was smooth against her skin, and she settled herself into the green plushness with a small wiggle and a wide grin. A stab of guilt over the ceiling chandelier she'd shot chased away her smile. She hadn't learned her lesson; she'd almost shot at him again. But he'd tricked her. Was he sorry he'd asked her to stay in the Pullman with Cady?

She wasn't sorry she'd agreed. Even after several days of living in such affluence, she wasn't accustomed to the richness of her surroundings. She resisted the urge to pinch herself. The indulgence—comfortable bed, soft sheets, the convenience of a tub whenever she wanted it—

things she'd never dreamed of, extravagances she'd never have again.

Cady studied her speculatively. "What's going on between you and Jeff?"

"Nothing. I can't stand the sight—"

Cady held up her hand. "He was about to kiss you when Kane and I walked in."

"You're imagining things."

"No, I'm not. And judging by the look on your face, you were about to let him. It's obvious to everyone who isn't half-witted and blind that you two care for each other. Why did you refuse to marry him, Bree?"

She sighed and let go of her pretense. "That's what *he* wanted to know."

"What did you tell him?"

"I told him to leave me alone."

"Why?"

There were more reasons than Bree wanted to list. But it was easy to sum up her refusal. She wouldn't tie herself to a man who didn't want her. And Tanner had made it clear that marriage to her was intolerable. But Cady was right about one thing. She cared about him—and she wouldn't force him into a marriage that would save her reputation at the expense of his position in society. She wouldn't hold him back in the business world. "I'd only make him unhappy."

"Let him be the one to—"

"No. I've made my decision."

Cady tapped her index finger against her lip. "You should know something about my big brother. It might take him a while to know what's good for him. He's a man, after all. But when he makes up his mind—"

"It wouldn't make any difference."

"Yes, it would. When Jeff Tanner decides he wants something, it's only a matter of time until he gets it. And after I finish dressing you for the reception tomorrow night, well, let's just say that man's mind will be made up."

Apprehension sparked and flared, threatening to consume Bree. His mind would be made up all right. Once and for all Tanner would know that she didn't belong in his world.

fourteen

Golden rays of sun reflected off the brass tub behind the dressing screen as dusk slowly approached in the desert outside. Bree brushed up against the gold quilt spread over the bed as she sidestepped the glare, then nervously curled her bare toes into the rug covering the floor. How she wished she could dodge the evening's reception as easily. Steamy moistness from bathing and the perfumed scent of soap bubbles filled every corner of the Pullman. She couldn't put if off much longer. Soon Tanner would know how socially backward she really was.

Biting her lip, she watched Cady lay out stockings, corset, dress, and matching satin slippers on the coverlet beside her. Already dressed in emerald green silk, the other girl rustled elegantly as she bustled back and forth in the coach. Bree looked down at herself, partially covered in chemise and pantalettes. It wasn't too late to back out.

"Let's get busy," Cady said briskly. "Jeff will be here soon to drive us to the fort, and he hates to be kept waiting."

Bree sighed deeply, knowing she couldn't disappoint Cady. Obediently she sat down before the dressing table with its attached oval mirror situated between the identical quilt-covered beds. Cady stood behind her and picked up the ornate silver-handled brush.

"First things first. Let me help you put your hair up."

"Can you fix mine like yours?"

"Easy as pie."

Starting at her hairline, Cady ran the soft bristles back through the tangled thickness with monotonous, calming strokes, gently pulling Bree's head back with each one. Giving herself up to the relaxing movements, Bree felt the tension leave her shoulders. The other girl worked until her scalp tingled and the black strands gleamed.

"That feels wonderful. But I shouldn't let you do this," Bree said, making no attempt to stop the motion.

Cady paused, her brows drawn together in concentration, and removed a pin from her mouth. "Why?"

"Because you're not a lady's maid—you're a lady."

"If that means I can't be of help to a friend, then I guess I don't want to be a lady."

Bree met Cady's gaze in the mirror and returned her smile. What a notion. "Friend?"

"Yes, indeed. I hope you feel the same." Cady pulled Bree's hair up on top of her head and prepared to secure it with pins. "In fact, I've always wanted a sister. This is how I pictured it."

"Me, too." Emotion gathered in Bree's throat and grew until she swallowed hard to dislodge it.

"When you grow up with two hell-raisers like my brothers, I suppose it's only natural to miss having a girl your own age around."

"What's your other brother like? Tanner showed me his picture, but he's never talked about him."

Cady looked thoughtful for a moment. "Jackson is different—brooding. Jeff is easy to get along with—" Bree snorted, and the other girl laughed. "I know you don't think so, but truly he is. He acts hardheaded because he's determined to be a success, because of something that happened a long time ago—with our grandfather."

"He told me about it."

Cady nodded. "And I'm pretty easygoing, maybe just the tiniest bit impulsive, although I prefer to think of myself as spontaneous. But Jack is restless, searching, discontented. He's more like our father." She stopped with her hands full of hair, and a faraway look crept into her eyes. "I think my parents worry a lot about him."

"I can see that you don't." Bree watched her shrug as the worried expression was replaced by a sheepish smile. "You're close to your brothers, aren't you?"

"Yes. They'd do anything for me. And I feel the same."

Bree thought about her own family. She remembered Charles's taunts. His threats were more direct now, less veiled. Something in him had changed. She sensed his restlessness, the tension that seemed ready to snap, and somehow knew he'd make good on his promise. Tanner would be leaving soon. Riley would do his best, but besides him, she had no one to count on.

Even though she knew Cady chafed at the restrictions they placed on her, she envied the other girl's close-knit, supportive relationship with her brothers. Jeff Tanner took care of his own.

"Hold still," Cady said. "I'm almost finished. Then we'll get you into a corset."

Bree's eyes widened. "Is that absolutely necessary?"

"If you're going to do justice to my dress, you must wear one. And if that dress does for your figure what I think it will, Jeff won't stand a chance."

"How many times do I have to tell you that I'm not trying to impress him?"

"Oh? Then why am I going through all this?" she asked, her voice muffled by a mouthful of pins.

"Cady, this whole thing was your idea. You keep assuming your brother and I are interested in each other."

"Why do you deny it . . ." Suddenly her hands stilled and she stared into the mirror, her expression stricken. "You're not sweet on Kane, are you?"

"Aha. So that's how it is." Bree laughed. "Don't worry about me. Kane is my friend. Nothing more."

Cady released a long breath. "That's a relief. I wouldn't

stand a chance if you were." She critically studied her handiwork. "Your hair looks better than mine."

Bree stared at her reflection. She thought Cady's hair looked lovely. But she had to admit the other girl had done a masterful job on her own. Swept off her forehead, the dark mass was pulled back and piled on her crown with ringlets cascading over her right shoulder. The blue-black strands bounced and danced, making her feel feminine and beautiful.

"Now it's torture time."

"The corset?"

Cady nodded.

Bree stood and stepped into the white whalebone garment. She'd never worn one before; maybe it wouldn't be as bad as she thought. She held it in place beneath her chemise-covered breasts while Cady laced up the back— and slowly squeezed off a good portion of her air.

"There. Your waist is as small as anything now."

"I'm so pleased." Stiffly Bree took two steps. "I have to sit," she said, looking down at the bed as if it were completely out of her reach. Then she glanced up at her friend. "I don't know if I can."

Cady laughed. "You'll get used to it. Take small, shallow breaths."

"I have no choice," she said, clutching her ribs.

What would Tanner think about this contraption? After all, this is what ladies wore. But when they were alone on the boat, he'd seemed to enjoy the freedom of her body, especially when he'd removed her clothes. Then he'd pushed her away; the memory still hurt. Even more because, as much as she hated to admit it, his touch had driven her wild, pushed her to the edge where she wanted to jump off and experience everything.

Every time she came near him, her senses reeled out of control, her breathing became rapid and shallow even when she wasn't wearing a corset. All it took was the strange magic Tanner's hands possessed. She'd hoped that time would ease her reaction to his overwhelming masculinity. But the same thing had happened the previous day when the scoundrel had tricked her out of her bath and into the open. The memory of his heated gaze sent fire flashing through her, making her light-headed.

Cady held the dress for her. "I know what you're going through. Trust me, it'll be worth it."

Bree wasn't so sure. But she stepped into the garment, and Cady pulled it up while she slipped her arms into off-the-shoulder cap sleeves. After they concealed the straps of her chemise, she stood in front of the mirror—staring in awe. She forgot her discomfort as she gaped at her reflection.

The indigo silk was a shade darker than her eyes, and the smooth material glided past her cinched-in waist, swirling over her petticoats and around her ankles like a cloud. The low-cut gown left much of her bosom bare as the corset pushed her breasts upward, straining against the top of the dress. Did she dare let Tanner see her in the provocative gown?

Some shameless part of her wanted to see his expression when he saw her so elegantly clothed. When they'd first met, she'd vowed to shake him from his calm outward appearance or die trying. This could be her opportunity. She decided his favorable reaction would be worth everything—even the very real possibility of suffocation. If only the gown covered a little more of her . . .

"Stop trying to pull it up," Cady said, gently pushing her hands away from the neckline.

"Are you sure this isn't too . . . too—"

"Scandalous? It's the latest fashion. Relax and put these on."

Bree slipped her stockinged feet into the matching shoes, and Cady clapped her hands together. "Perfect. I just knew it would be."

"I can't believe it's me."

"You look a little pale. I can fix that." Cady pulled a

small jar from the dressing table drawer. "Sit down on the bed."

Bree sat, very carefully, absorbing the stabs of pain as the whalebone stays gouged her ribs.

Cady dabbed some stuff on her cheeks. "Close your eyes."

Bree felt something brush across her lids and then her lips.

"Now open. Look," Cady said, pointing to the mirror.

She stood, then moved to the dressing table and studied herself. Her lips were more defined. Her cheeks had a slight pink color, and she hadn't even pinched them. Her eyes appeared bigger, bolder—dark, mysterious.

"This is paint," Bree said, a little shocked.

"Only a bit. No one can tell if you're careful with it." Cady shrugged sheepishly. "It's not necessary to wear it like Ginger and Sally. Besides, a girl's got to use every weapon at her disposal."

"Does your brother know you have this?" she asked, meeting her friend's gaze in the glass. Two bits to a dollar Tanner had no idea his sister used face paint.

"What Jeff doesn't know won't hurt him. And if you say a word, I'll pull the laces on that corset so tight, you won't be able to breathe—let alone blab my secrets."

Bree sucked in a breath. "If you tighten this contraption any more, you're going to have a corpse on your hands. My painted lips are sealed."

"Are you going to wash it off?"

Glancing at her reflection, Bree knew she'd leave it. As wicked as she felt, she liked the way she looked. Besides, Cady was right. She needed every weapon at her disposal to deal with Jeff Tanner. And a gun seemed inappropriate for a formal reception. She giggled. "No. I'll leave it."

Cady steepled her fingers and tapped her lips as she studied Bree. "You look beautiful. I'm so jealous. If you weren't my friend, I'd be forced to hate you."

"If I look good, it's because of you." Bree smiled, then impulsively hugged the other girl.

"Are you ready to go?"

Bree nodded. But her stomach fluttered nervously as if butterflies flitted and flew inside her. Her abdomen was bound so tight, she wondered where they found room.

She slipped the lace gloves Cady had given her over her work-roughened hands. The delicate material caught on the calluses covering her palms. But for once she didn't mind. Every single inch of her was covered by satin, silk, and lace.

Jeff stood impatiently outside the Pullman and took his watch from his vest pocket to check the time. If Bree and Cady didn't hurry, they'd never get to the fort before sundown. They'd been at it for what seemed like hours. Bree was punctual to a fault. What the hell were they doing that was taking so long? He replaced his timepiece and decided to see for himself. If they weren't ready now, it was too damn bad.

He grabbed the coach rail and took the steps in two strides, swinging himself up to the rear platform. After knocking once, he waited, restless and irritable.

He saw a shadow behind the curtains on the upper half of the door just before it was opened. Cady stepped back and admitted him, a secret smile on her face. What was she up to? Dressed in emerald green that set off her eyes to perfection, she looked radiant. His heart swelled with pride and affection for his little sister. She didn't look so little just now, and once again he felt the weight of responsibility.

He quickly scanned the interior, but Bree was nowhere in sight, and he wondered if she'd backed out after all.

"Where's Murphy?" he asked, half afraid she'd gone back to Hardyville, even though he'd seen *Belle* docked beside the riverbank. He sat in one of the wingback chairs facing the dressing screen.

"She'll be right out." Cady studied him critically. "You look very handsome tonight, Jeff."

"You don't look so bad yourself."

"Eloquent praise like that will turn my head," she said dryly.

He grinned, ignoring her sarcasm. "I wouldn't want you to get too full of yourself."

There was a rustling sound, then Bree appeared from behind the screen. Slowly Jeff pushed himself to his feet, staring at the vision before him. She was stunning.

Shiny black curls fell over her shoulder and caressed her full, scantily covered bosom. Enormous sapphire eyes watched him uncertainly as she bit the corner of her full pink bottom lip.

He felt as if he'd been flattened by a runaway steam engine.

Cady moved beside him and took his arm. "Say something, silly. Doesn't she look wonderful?"

He glanced down at his sister and took a deep breath. But when he looked back at Bree, he was speechless.

"Men," Cady said, shaking her head. "Miss Breanne Murphy, may I present my brother, Jefferson Thomas Tanner."

Bree moved forward and held out her palm. He noticed that her fingers trembled slightly. If he didn't know differently, it would never occur to him that she hadn't attended a formal function before. He took her hand and hesitated, then bent at the waist and kissed her knuckles.

"It's a pleasure, Miss Murphy. I don't think I've ever met a more beautiful lady."

A pleased smile brightened her features. "Thank you, Mr. Tanner. You're very kind."

"No. It's the simple truth." He looked from one woman to the other and sighed heavily. "I can see I'm going to have my hands full tonight."

"Why's that?" Bree asked, lifting her delicate dark brows.

"It's an army post. There are men everywhere. I feel a responsibility to protect you both. Perhaps we should skip the reception and—"

"Not one more word, Jeff Tanner." Cady planted her fists on emerald-clad hips, and there was a dangerous glint in her eyes. "If you won't take me, I'll go by myself."

"Simmer down. I was joking."

"I'm not in the mood for your teasing. We're going to be late. I'll get our wraps, Bree." Cady glared at him before gliding around the privacy screen to the rear of the coach.

"Thank you for not making fun of me." Bree moved closer, near enough for him to reach out and touch her.

The perfumed fragrance of wildflowers filled his head. "Make fun of you? Why would I do that?"

"For trying to make a silk purse from a sow's ear."

"You're hardly a sow's ear. I've never met anyone more beautiful—East or West."

"Truly? Or are you teasing me?" She clasped her fingers together and earnestly studied him.

He held up his hand, palm out. "On my honor as a gentleman."

"I wouldn't go so far as to call you a gentleman. After all, in this very place, you tricked me—"

"You were being uncooperative and stubborn. But I will admit one thing."

"What?"

"As lovely as you are right this minute, I do miss the way you looked in a towel."

"Jefferson Tanner—" Her tone held a note of warning.

"And I'm grateful that there's nowhere you can hide your gun," he said, nodding toward the cleavage of her gown. He chuckled at her outraged gasp.

Cady reappeared, with two lacy shawls. "Let's go. I'm so looking forward to this evening."

Bree sighed. "At least one of us is."

Jeff took one of the shawls from his sister and stepped

behind Bree, draping the fragile material over her hair and around her shoulders. Then he stepped beside her and offered his arm.

"It's all right, Jeff. I can do my own wrap," Cady said.

"Fine," he answered absently, never taking his eyes from Bree.

She returned his gaze. In his black coat and matching vest and trousers, he looked every bit the successful railroad tycoon. And he'd never been more handsome. His wavy dark hair was neatly combed, and the masculine scent of soap drifted to her from his freshly shaved jaw. Her heart pounded painfully against her ribs. Surely he could hear. But she had to admit that the intense, admiring expression in his eyes was worth all the time and discomfort.

Despite all her misgivings, she felt beautiful. And he'd called her a lady. What a wonder. Confidence flowed through her. If she could be transformed, anything was possible.

But no. She refused to let herself hope. This was only one night. She'd enjoy the evening. No expectations today, no disappointment tomorrow, she cautioned herself. She must remember where they both came from.

Jeff took her hand and tucked it in the crook of his elbow. "Your carriage awaits."

Her heart fluttered wildly at the intimate contact with him. So much for caution, she thought as he opened the door and the wind gusted inside.

"Just pretend I'm not here," Cady mumbled behind them.

Tanner wrapped the reins around the whipstaff and jumped down from the seat of the hired buggy he'd driven to Fort Mojave. The conveyance dipped and sprang back as it was relieved of his weight, and Bree shivered, chilly without his reassuring warmth beside her. He turned, reaching up for her, and she placed her fingers on his shoulders as he spanned her waist and effortlessly lifted her to the ground. Then he helped Cady alight.

"It's about time you got here. I was ready to send out a patrol." Kane joined them, the light from the mess hall behind him outlining his tall form.

"They were in good hands," Jeff said.

"Hello, Kane." Cady looked up at the officer, handsome in his dress blue uniform.

"Cady," he said, nodding. "Where's Bree? I thought she was coming, too."

"I'm here." She moved out of Tanner's shadow into the arc of light from the doorway.

He stared for several moments, then whistled long and low. "I'll be damned—darned."

"Doesn't she look wonderful?" Cady asked.

"Beautiful. Where have you been hiding?"

"I haven't been hiding," Bree muttered, uncomfortable with all the attention. "Just never had much of a reason to dress up before. Cady deserves all the credit. And you haven't said a thing about the way she looks."

Kane turned to the younger girl. "My apologies, Miss Tanner. Your dazzling beauty has put me off my manners this evening. May I say you look splendid?"

"Should I believe you?"

Jeff snorted.

Cady ignored her brother. "Thank you, Captain. You look very handsome tonight."

Kane offered her his arm. "If you'd care to accompany me inside, there are some people I'd like to show you off—I mean, that is, there are some people I'd like you to meet."

"It would be my pleasure."

He cleared his throat, and she placed her hand in the crook of his elbow. Their footsteps crunched in the sand before they walked through the doorway.

"Just pretend we're not here," Tanner said to their backs.

Bree looked around. She'd never been to the fort at dusk before. Parallel to the building the Colorado flowed peacefully at the bottom of the bluff. In the distance it resembled a silver ribbon, twisting and turning, tying Arizona and Nevada together as the sun set behind the mountains. The spectacular sight fascinated her. She'd never tire of the rugged, wild beauty of this land and wished she could stay like this forever.

Tanner moved behind her, so close she could feel the heat from his body.

"I guess it's time to go inside," she said.

"In a minute. Have I told you how lovely you look?"

She nodded. "But I like hearing it."

"You take my breath away."

She laughed ruefully and stood straighter, cupping her ribs. "I know the feeling."

"Are you all right?"

She went very still. "Uh—no. Well, that is . . . My shoes, I mean Cady's shoes are too tight."

"Oh."

Jeff stared down at the dark curls on her crown, then his gaze lowered to her shoulders, bare since her shawl had slipped and caught in the bend of her arms. She exhibited all the trappings of a society lady, and a vague sensation of disappointment settled over him. He wanted back the honest, free, and soft woman that was Bree.

He drank in the creamy curves of her breasts, swelling just above the tempting neckline of her dress. He ached to touch her. But he didn't dare—not here, not now. Not ever.

But it was impossible to get her off his mind. She was such an enchanting mixture, part innocent, part temptress. It was hard to accept that the delicate beauty before him guided a steamboat up and down the river. If he hadn't seen her do just that time and time again, he'd never have believed it.

"Why did you decide to work on the boat with your father?" he asked.

He felt her stiffen, then she turned to face him. In the light from the mess hall behind them, Bree's face grew pensive.

"I'm just curious," he said. "I'd assumed it was to please him, to be the son he always wanted. But I heard what he said that day he came to pull us out. He obviously wasn't pleased by your decision to follow in his footsteps."

"He wasn't, not at first. But the river saved me."

"From what?"

"From . . ." She stopped, choosing her words carefully. "After my mother died, I needed to be with Cap. I—I suppose I was afraid to let him out of my sight, afraid I'd lose him, too. But I discovered something. I love the river, being on the boat. I enjoy the work. I'm good at it." She bit her lip and looked up at him. "But sometimes . . ." She hesitated, assessing him.

"What? Tell me."

"Sometimes I miss having a family of my own— children." She paused, glancing past him, then directly met his gaze. "A husband."

"You do?"

She pulled her shawl tighter around her. "I shouldn't have said anything. I knew you'd laugh."

"I'm not laughing."

"Yes, you are," she said defensively. "But everyone has dreams. Just because mine can't come true doesn't mean I don't have them."

She started to walk past him.

Jeff took her upper arm, then cupped her cheek in his palm. "I wasn't making fun."

"Of course you were. Who'd want a crazy woman who runs a riverboat?"

"I . . ." He looked into her eyes. Her soft, full mouth trembled slightly until she bit the corner of her upper lip.

Frustration knotted in his gut. *He* wanted her. And he didn't care what kind of work she did.

Sand and rocks crunched loudly as a man's footsteps moved closer, destroying the sensual spell surrounding them.

"Don't you two want to join the party?" Kane stopped beside Bree and grinned down at her, showing even white teeth in the awakening moonlight.

Jeff cleared his throat. "We'll be there in a minute."

Kane met his gaze. A current of understanding passed between them, and he nodded. "Don't be too long. The undersecretary is anxious to meet you. He has some questions about the bridge and the railroad."

"We're right behind you."

If Kane hadn't come out just then, Jeff knew he'd have kissed Bree after promising himself only moments before that he wouldn't touch her. He didn't know whether to thank Kane or thrash him for the interruption. But as he gazed into the open doorway and watched his sister smile brilliantly at the officer as he rejoined her, Jeff resolved to return the favor.

Jeff looked down at Bree and extended his arm. "Are you ready?"

She took a deep breath and slipped her small hand into the bend of his elbow. He felt her shiver and placed his other hand over hers. "You're going to be the belle of the ball."

"I don't know how I let Cady talk me into this," she whispered nervously.

"My sister can be very persuasive. The sooner we make an appearance, the sooner it'll be over with." He studied her intently. "Just remember one thing. You're the most beautiful woman in the room."

"How do you know? You haven't seen anyone else yet, besides Cady."

"I don't have to."

The mess hall was a long, narrow building with a canvas-covered floor. Bree had only been in this room once or twice before and had never seen it look so bright and festive. Lanterns lighted every corner, and chairs lined the four walls. At the far end of the room a group of soldiers prepared their musical instruments, fiddle, guitar, and trumpet.

There were several other women, probably officers' wives, besides Cady and herself. Tanner's sister stood by a table arrayed with a punch bowl and various kinds of food. She was surrounded by an eager group of soldiers, and Bree wondered where Kane was. She scanned the room and saw him with a stranger—a civilian dressed in a black frock coat and trousers, a matching tie resting on his rumpled white shirt. He looked solemn and dignified and reminded her of an undertaker.

Bree noticed Kane's uneasy gaze stray constantly to the corner where Cady giggled and laughed with the men. So he was as smitten with her as she was with him. When Kane finally saw Bree staring, he grinned sheepishly and motioned for her and Tanner to join him.

The butterflies milling in her stomach snapped to attention and began a double-time march. The man came from Washington, probably even knew the President. What if she said or did the wrong thing? Should she curtsy or bow when she was introduced? Should she shake his hand?

She moved forward and stopped beside Kane, with Tanner on her right.

The officer indicated his guest. "Undersecretary Smith, this is Breanne Murphy, of Murphy Navigation, and Jefferson Tanner, owner and overseer of the railroad project we spoke about."

"Miss Murphy." Despite his full, reddish-brown beard, the dignitary looked much younger up close. He didn't extend his hand, so that eliminated one worry. But she wondered if she should curtsy or do nothing. She was trembling so hard, remaining as still as possible seemed the safest course.

The stranger cleared his throat. "I find it difficult to believe such a beautiful young woman captains a riverboat."

"It's true, sir—that I captain the *River Belle*, I mean."

"Sir, the truth is I couldn't have built the bridge without her assistance."

The undersecretary's gaze lingered on her for a long moment before he extended his hand to Jeff. "A pleasure, Mr. Tanner. That project is quite an undertaking."

Tanner squeezed the other man's palm. "Yes, sir. It's been quite a challenge." He looked down at Bree. "But I'm pleased to say we're ahead of schedule."

The dignitary nodded approvingly. "One of the reasons I'm here is to assess the continued need for a military base of operations in the Territory. With the completion of the bridge, the country will be linked entirely by rails. Transportation to the West will be easier than ever before. I expect the civilian population to increase dramatically in the next few years. Expansion is just what this country needs. In my report, I plan to state in the strongest terms the need for the continued maintenance of Fort Mojave."

"My partners and I appreciate the government's help with the project. Without the subsidies . . ."

Bree looked at the three men. This was the first she'd heard about assistance from Washington. Even the United States government was helping to put her out of business. For more than thirty years military outposts had been supplied by steamboats. Now they'd exhausted their usefulness and were being eased out by the railroad.

"Apparently loyal service counts for nothing," she said bitterly.

The undersecretary lifted his brows. "Competition and free enterprise are the backbone of this country, ma'am. It stimulates progress and promotes change, for the better."

"Better for who? The railroad?" She glared at Tanner. "What about the small companies that will be put out of business?"

"Surely in a Territory the size of Arizona, there's room

for everyone. Progress creates new jobs and opportunities."

"We only know one thing. The river."

Bree felt Tanner tense beside her and saw his frown. She should have just smiled politely and kept her mouth shut. But she couldn't be a silent decoration at his side. Sometimes she wished she didn't care so much. She was bone-tired, weary of fighting everyone and everything. If she'd had any doubts before, now she was certain. She didn't belong in Tanner's world. When the bridge was finished, she wasn't sure she'd have a place anywhere.

Bree didn't want to hear any more. "Excuse me, I think I'll join Cady."

She looked around and saw her friend engaged in serious conversation with several soldiers. Maybe she shouldn't interrupt. Maybe some fresh air would soothe her.

She turned and walked toward the door. Charles stood there, and his eyes glowed when he recognized her. In his hand he held his coal black hat, and the silver band reflected the light. His white cotton shirt contrasted sharply with his black vest and pants. Matching boots covered his calves and scraped against the canvas floor as he drifted closer, stopping in front of her with his legs braced wide apart. He slowly let his gaze wander over her, lingering on her bosom.

Bree stood motionless for a moment, stunned to see him. She should have known he'd come; he always lurked nearby. She tried to move around her stepbrother, but his slick sideways move blocked her escape.

"I've never seen you look more beautiful, Breanne. Is that a new dress? I don't believe I've ever seen it before."

Shock and revulsion flooded through her, and she went cold all over. She hadn't realized how relaxed and free she'd felt not having to constantly look over her shoulder, waiting to dodge his leering looks, evade his grasping hands and surreptitious fondling. Not half an hour before, she'd told Tanner why she'd decided to work with her father on the riverboat. It wasn't a bad lie; needing to be with Cap was more truth than deception. All she'd left out was why she couldn't—wouldn't—be alone with her stepbrother.

Why did he have to show up tonight and spoil everything?

She was dressed in silk and satin, but that couldn't hide who she was and where she came from. And it wouldn't protect her.

"What are you doing here, Charles?"

"Captain Carrington was kind enough to extend his invitation to me and all the merchants in Hardyville." He brushed a slender hand along the side of his light hair.

"Where's Cap and Mary?"

"Unfortunately, your father was feeling a little under the weather tonight. Mother didn't want to leave him. So I was forced to come alone." He looked down at her breasts, his eyes drinking in the expanse of her bare flesh like a thirsty wolf slinking from the drought-parched hills. "I've missed you, little sister. Hardyville is lonely without you."

"I haven't missed you." His bold, calculated look made her sick, and instinctively, she wanted to cross her arms over herself. But she wouldn't give him the satisfaction.

"How can you say that?" His pale brows drew together, feigning hurt. "We're so close." He moved toward her.

"Stay away from me. Don't you ever come near me." She backed up a step; she hated that he made her do that. Giving him a wide berth, she walked outside without a backward glance. When she reached the darkness beyond the half-circle of light, she lifted her skirts and ran.

fifteen

Bree cursed the satin slippers and confining corset that slowed her down. She'd gone only as far as the officers' quarters when the stabbing pain in her side forced her to stop. Not a single lantern shone from the windows of the row of squat, square structures. After rounding the last adobe building, she leaned against it to catch her breath. The full moon kissed the barren desert beyond the fort with an eerie light, almost as bright as day. There was no place to hide. Charles would find her.

Footsteps crunched loud as thunder in the rocky compound just on the other side of the building. Her heart stopped as fear clutched her chest. She tried desperately to gulp air into her lungs, preparing to flee again. Her clothing was too tight; she wasn't ready.

Strains of music carried to her from the mess hall. If she screamed, would anyone hear? She swallowed hard.

"Bree? Where are you?"

"Tanner?" She peeked around the wall and made out his tall, muscular form. Then she leaned back against the adobe and closed her eyes briefly, nearly weeping with relief.

Seconds later he was beside her. Heat from his body and the masculine scent of him surrounded her, and she felt safe. Charles wouldn't touch her as long as he was there.

237

It was all she could do to keep from throwing herself into his arms.

"Why did you leave? I saw Charlie. What did he say?"

"Nothing. I'm such a ninny. It's just that I—I didn't expect to see him and—"

"He wasn't invited." His voice was tight, clipped as if he held his anger in check.

"Are you sure? He said Kane invited all the merchants from Hardyville."

"He lied."

"How do you know?"

"Did you see any of them? The Bellmores? Reverend Howard? Luke McLaughlin—or anyone else from town?"

She thought. There hadn't been many women there besides Cady and herself. And she hadn't seen any familiar faces from Hardyville. In a town of less than a hundred, there weren't many faces she didn't know except the transient miners who came down from the hills periodically.

"No." She looked up at him as fear crept along her spine. In the shadows his features were indistinguishable. But his breath fanned her face. He was warm and strong and she needed him so much. She reached out a trembling hand. "Why is he doing this?"

Jeff caught her icy fingers between his own. She was shaking like a leaf. This woman faced the most dangerous river in the West without flinching, yet one encounter with her stepbrother had reduced her to this state. He wanted to know why.

"Was Charlie the one who was with you that night on *Belle*? The night I found you so frightened?"

"What difference does it make?"

"Was it *him*?" He took her upper arms and squeezed, shaking her slightly.

"Yes," she whispered. Her voice was so low, he had to strain to catch the one, tortured word.

Anger exploded within him, red and raging. Her image flashed before him, a picture branded into his mind of her pale face and broken spirit the night he'd discovered her on her riverboat, partially disrobed and terrorized. He stared at her for several moments, remembering the panic in her eyes, then released his grip and dropped his hands from her arms. Rage spilled over the boundary of his control, and he started to back away.

"Where are you going?" she asked, fear lacing her voice.

"To beat the hell out of him."

"No—"

"You can't stop me, Bree. Not this time. I suspected it was him. Now that I know, I'm going to make sure he never touches you again."

"And what good will it do?" She took a deep breath. "Don't you see? It would only make you feel better. It won't help me."

He took a deep, calming breath. "There must be something I—"

"What do you suggest?"

"Tell your father—or Mary."

"Tell them what? That I don't like the way he smiles at me? Or the look in his eyes makes my skin crawl?"

"Then I'm going to take care of him."

"No. It's my problem and I'll deal with it my way."

"I want to help you. I want to make sure you'll be safe before—"

"Before you go back where you came from? Don't give it a second thought, Tanner. I was fine before you showed up, and I'll be fine after you're gone. I can take of myself."

She started to walk past him, then stopped and leaned against the adobe wall, clutching a hand to her ribs.

"Are you all right?"

"Yes." She took several shallow breaths, as if she couldn't get enough air into her lungs.

"Are you sure it's not something more? And don't tell

me your shoes are too tight. I saw you race across the compound."

"It's nothing." She glared at him. "Just drop it."

"Not until I know you're not sick. I'm going to find the post surgeon—"

"Oh, for goodness' sake—" She let out a huge breath. "It's nothing. Really."

He bent and lifted her into his arms. "We'll let the doctor decide that."

She gasped. "Tanner! Put me down."

He ignored her and started walking. She put her arms around his neck, and her soft breast pressed against his chest. The touch burned him, even through his clothes. The night was pleasantly cool, but sweat popped out on his forehead. The fragrance of wildflowers drifted from her warm skin, and he thought how right the scent was for her. Wild and free.

He shifted her more securely in his arms and felt the whalebone stays. That wasn't right somehow, not for her. He'd thought about it when he'd lifted her down from the buggy. And now he missed the feel of her soft, womanly flesh. He felt her attempts to draw air into her lungs, and a suspicion began to grow.

"Where are you taking me?" she asked.

"Back inside. Surely the surgeon's at the reception."

"No! I'll never forgive you if you make a scene."

"Then tell me what's wrong."

"I can't." She bit her lip and looked away.

"If you don't explain to me what's the matter, I swear I'll take you inside." He made a halfhearted move to round the end of the building into the compound.

"Stop. I'll tell you." She stared at the collar of his shirt. "It's this corset . . ."

"Corset?"

She nodded. "Cady loaned it to me along with her dress. I'm not used to it. I can't breathe. And my side hurts, f-from running." She watched him tensely and waited. "Go ahead and laugh. Get it over with."

"I'm not laughing. And why do you always think the worst of me? Have I ever laughed at you?"

She nodded. "You didn't believe I could captain *Belle*—or work on the bridge project."

"I was wrong. Have I underestimated you since then?"

"Give me time. I'll think of something."

Chuckling, he gently put her down and pulled her into the shadows, then turned her so that her back was to him. At least he could help her with this.

Bree felt his large hands unfastening the hooks on her dress. Horrified, she tried to pull away. He reached out and stopped her.

"Hold still."

"What are you doing?"

"I'm going to loosen the laces."

"But you can't. What if someone sees?" She felt his fingers untying the corset bow just beneath her shoulder blades. Down her spine, he slipped his finger under the laces and pulled them loose. He worked swiftly, confidently, and the garment expanded. She sighed and leaned her back against him as she gulped a huge, unconstricted breath of air.

"Feel better?" There was a note of amusement in his voice.

"Much. Now you're laughing." This time she didn't care. It was wonderful to be able to breathe normally again. Then a thought struck her. "That hardly took you any time at all. You must have had a lot of practice." She felt the rumble of laughter across his broad chest.

"A gentleman never reveals his secrets—especially to a lady." His warm hands caressed her arms as she held the bodice of her gown to her breasts.

Her a lady? Hardly. Her cheeks burned with embarrassment. Being half-undressed by a man was not the proper conduct of a lady. A sigh escaped her as she stared up at the sky. Stars on a background of dark blue velvet winked down. Even they were laughing at her.

"This was a mistake," she said at last.

"What?"

"Tonight—the reception. I never should have come. I should—"

"You can't hide because of Charlie."

"It's not because of him."

"Then what?"

"I don't belong."

"Nonsense. You're a bright, beautiful woman. The undersecretary couldn't take his eyes off you. Your ability to distract a man would be an asset—"

"Stop."

"Why? May lightning strike if I'm not telling the God's honest truth."

"You never say that when there's a cloud in the sky." She clutched the silk tightly to her. "I didn't want to distract him. I wanted to—"

"What? Why did you excuse yourself? You were upset even before Charlie showed up."

"You never told me government subsidies were financing the bridge."

"Only partially. Would it have made any difference if you'd known where the money came from?" His stroking fingers stopped on her upper arms and squeezed gently.

"No." She thought for a minute. "I'm still going to get *Belle* back, you know."

"I'll look forward to it."

"As long as you know where I stand."

"I know exactly where you stand," he said, his voice turning husky and hoarse as his hands slid upward.

He lightly kneaded the tight muscles in her neck and shoulders. His ministrations felt heavenly. She knew she should pull away, but she couldn't find the strength or the will.

"Do you do this for Emily after a neighborly dinner for two hundred of your closest friends?" she asked dreamily.

His hands stilled. She sensed his hesitation and waited expectantly.

"No."

"Oh, of course. How silly of me. Society ladies are never high-strung. They're accustomed to corsets, and important people, and fourteen forks, and everything else that it takes to be a lady."

"It's not that. I've never touched Emily—like this or any other way." His voice was tight with irritation. She couldn't tell if he was annoyed with her or himself.

His hands moved over her shoulders and down her arms. He slipped his palms to her waist, then around her abdomen, and pulled her tight against him. The warmth of his body seeped through her clothes, corset and all, to settle in her back and buttocks, sending tingles up and down her spine.

Ever so softly, his lips caressed her neck. "I've never done this to Emily."

"Never?" she whispered, her heart pounding.

"Never." He moved his hands higher to slide her chemise down, freeing her breasts. Cupping the burning peaks, he stroked his thumbs across the full, round flesh pressed upward by her undergarments. Her nipples grew hard from the calloused pads of his fingers.

"Or this, either," he said.

Bree wondered if she should be insulted. He wouldn't touch Emily because she was a lady, yet he had no qualms about fondling her in the most intimate way. Ripples of delight raced over her breasts and settled between her thighs, throbbing with need. The pleasurable sensations his practiced fingers evoked left no room for outrage. Just pity. Emily didn't know what she was missing. Bree knew if it was a choice between being a lady and knowing the joys of being a woman, there would be no contest. She simply couldn't resist him.

He trailed his lips up her neck and stopped beneath her ear, his mustache tickling the sensitive area and sending sparks scampering over her body. Closing her eyes, she tipped her head back against his muscled chest, surrendering to his advances. His hands, his masculine scent, weaved a spell around her, wrapping her in a cocoon of sensuality. His accelerated breathing ignited the fire in her blood.

Jeff pressed against her, seeking to ease the painful pounding in his groin. He wanted Bree as he'd never wanted a woman. Touch Emily this way? Never. She was ice compared to Bree's fire.

He caressed the soft mounds in his palms, creamy and porcelain-perfect in the moonlight. The dark buds of her nipples stood erect in his hands, and he smiled with satisfaction. She fought against him tooth, nail, and pistol, but she couldn't resist him when he touched her like this. He knew it; he counted on it. He couldn't keep himself from wanting her either.

Behind him, Jeff heard the crunch of boots in the sand. Listening intently, he lifted his head and felt Bree's back go rigid.

"So, this is where the two of you disappeared."

Bree gasped at the smug, familiar voice, and Jeff reassuringly squeezed her arms when she began to tremble. Fumbling with the fallen bodice of her dress, she tried to right her gown. He slipped off his frock coat and dropped it around her shoulders. Then he turned to face her stepbrother, keeping himself between them to block her from the leering look he knew would be on the other man's face.

"What do you want, Charlie?"

"Breanne, if you continue to put yourself in such compromising positions, you will ruin yourself for any other man."

Jeff moved forward until he stood directly in front of

Charlie—close enough to reach out and grab him around the neck. "Get the hell out of here before I—"

"Before you what?" The other man's thin face contorted with hatred and his eyes blazed. The cool control slipped and shattered. "I'm sick and tired of you throwing your weight around. You screwed her first, but you won't be last. I'll—"

"You sorry sonofobitch . . ."

Jeff lashed out with his right fist, putting every ounce of his power and fury into the punch. Charlie never saw it coming. His head snapped back and a surprised, almost comical look crossed his face as the blow connected and lifted him off his feet, sending him sprawling backward in the dust.

He shook his head, then leaped up and came at Jeff, head and shoulders lowered like a charging bull.

As Charlie grabbed him around the waist trying to take him down, Jeff braced himself, then grappled, waiting for an opportunity to get the upper hand.

"I thought you'd stay in the dirt where you belong," Jeff said through gritted teeth.

He felt the fury that shook the other man at his taunt and took advantage of it.

Seizing him by the shirtfront with one hand, Jeff hit Charlie in the face with his other fist. Then he let him go and watched him stagger backward a step, hesitating. When Charlie came at him again, Jeff was glad. The stupid bastard didn't know when to give up. It gave him an excuse. After what he'd done to Bree, Jeff wanted nothing more than to beat the living hell out of him.

Jeff caught the other man with a left jab to the gut, and when he doubled over, he nailed him with a right hook to the jaw. Charlie spun around and went down heavily, face first in the dust.

"Get up." Jeff wiped his mouth with his sleeve and braced his feet wide, hoping Charlie'd be dumb enough to come at him so he could knock him down again.

"Jeff—" Bree touched his arm, and he pushed her behind him.

"Stay out of the way."

She grabbed his elbow and turned him. "Can't you see he's had enough?"

"I haven't."

She gripped his arm with both hands and shook him. "This won't solve anything."

"Maybe not." He looked down into her wide, frightened eyes. "But you're right about one thing. I do feel better—a helluva lot better."

"I'm glad one of us does."

"He's been taken down a peg or two in front of you. He'll think twice before coming near you."

"Do you really believe that?"

"I've dealt with ~~men like him~~ before. He won't bother you anymore."

She shook her head. "After everything . . . I can't believe it's over."

"Believe it." He glanced at Charlie, still facedown and motionless on the ground, and smiled with satisfaction. "Doesn't it make you feel better, just a little, seeing him like that? He's not invincible, you know. He's flesh and bone. When he's cut, he bleeds."

She looked at her stepbrother and just a hint of a smile turned up the corners of her mouth.

Jeff tipped her chin up with his index finger and brushed her soft lips with his own. "Trust me. It's done with."

He stepped over the man sprawled in the sand and held out his hand to her. "I'm going to get one of the sentries to get rid of this garbage. Let me hook up your gown. You can't go back to the reception like that."

She nodded and walked around her stepbrother, then took off Jeff's jacket and turned her back so that he could refasten her corset and dress.

When he finished, she turned and looked up at him, her

eyes pleading. "Do we have to go back? Can't we go home?"

Home? The construction site? He'd certainly been more settled and content since she'd moved into the Pullman. Suddenly he was tired, clear to the bone, and all he wanted was Bree beside him in his bed, in his arms. But not with his sister there. Frustration forced the air from his lungs.

"We can go as soon as I find Cady. Just after you left, she disappeared. And Carrington was nowhere to be seen."

"Maybe you should leave them alone."

"Not on your life. I know my responsibility." He smiled grimly as he remembered Kane interrupting him, just after they'd arrived. "Besides, turnabout is fair play."

Dust from the buggy wheels had hardly settled in front of the Pullman before Cady turned on her brother. Sitting between them, Bree pressed herself back into the leather seat, uncertain whether or not to duck. But she decided her friend's anger was definitely better than the occasional sniffle that Cady hadn't been able to suppress on the drive back from the fort.

"How could you humiliate me that way, Jeff?"

"What did I do?"

"As if you didn't know. You dragged me away from probably the most important discussion of my life. That's what. And you were so bloody cheerful about it, too."

He grinned and his white teeth gleamed in the moonlight. "Discussion? Since when is what you were doing called a discussion?"

"I was being persuasive. There's more than one way to communicate. Right, Bree?"

"I think . . ." She thought she was the last person Cady should be asking. Her life was such a mess, and she had no business getting involved in this dispute. "I'm probably not—"

Tanner jumped briskly from the buggy, then reached up

to lift his sister to the ground. She ignored him and stepped down.

"What were you 'discussing' with the good captain?"

"How much he needs me."

He glared at her. "Cady Tanner, I ought to—"

"He does need me. He just doesn't know it yet. Stuck out here in the middle of nowhere—" She sniffled. "He said I'm too much of a lady. He said women in the Territory have a hard life, and I'm not cut out for it. He said it would break me, and I should just go h-home."

"Why, that opinionated—Who does he think he is?" Tanner flexed his hand and winced, then studied his scraped knuckles as if gauging how well his fist would hold up in another brawl.

Bree felt nearly hysterical laughter bubble up inside her. She wasn't enough of a lady, and Cady was too refined. There was just no pleasing men, and she was sick and tired of trying.

Jeff lifted his arms to help her down. The corset made grace and agility impossible, but she stepped to the ground without his assistance. "Kane's a man. He's pigheaded and unreasonable. If I were you, Cady, I'd just forget about him—or shoot him." She shrugged. "Doesn't make much difference which."

Bree marched to the Pullman and placed her hand on the side rail. A thought struck her, and she began to laugh. She couldn't seem to stop, and she wiped tears from the corners of her eyes.

"What's so damn funny?" Tanner asked.

Bree lifted her skirt. "Shooting Kane would certainly get his attention."

"And me a noose," Cady said. Then she giggled. The two women exchanged a look and started snickering again.

Tanner muttered an oath. "I'm going to bed. I hope you both will be more rational in the morning."

Bree placed one foot on the first step of the railroad car. "Don't hold your breath."

"No, hold your breath," Cady said and began to laugh again.

"Women," he muttered. He walked away, and the wind whisked the sound of his footsteps into the desert.

When the sight, sound, and smell of him had faded, and the breeze whistled in her ears, loneliness stole over Bree. She missed him already. A gaping, black emptiness swelled within her and threatened to squeeze out her soul. How would she bear it when he was gone for good?

In her plain, threadbare, cotton nightdress, Bree sat cross-legged on the bed across from Cady and brushed out her hair. The loose garment felt like heaven after all the confining layers of clothing.

"Do you think his feelings are hurt?" Bree asked.

"I don't think Kane has any."

"I meant Tanner."

"Oh." With a thoughtful look on her face, Cady removed the pins from her hair. "Maybe we were a little hard on him. But, gosh darn it, I'm sick to death of men making decisions for me. I want to run my own life."

Bree sighed heavily. "There's always going to be someone telling you what to do. Too many things are out of our control."

She recalled what the undersecretary had said about subsidizing the bridge project. She couldn't fight Tanner and the railroad, let alone the United States government. She'd lost. It had happened a long time ago, but she'd been too stubborn to realize it. Her only choice now was to salvage as much of her business and her pride as she could. She'd already lost a piece of herself to Tanner, a piece she could never get back.

"Bree, do you think Kane's right? You've lived here practically your whole life. Do you think I'm not cut out to be a military wife?"

"Wife? Aren't you jumping the gun?"

Pink flooded Cady's cheeks. "I suppose we haven't

known each other all that long, but somehow I know time won't change the way I feel. I've never met a man like him. And I have the awful feeling that I won't ever meet a man who can measure up to him."

Bree knew exactly how she felt. But sometimes two people just weren't meant to be together, no matter how strong the attraction. "Cady, I haven't had all that much experience with men. But I'm convinced it's better to stick to your own kind."

"You're talking about you and Jeff. Aren't you?"

"There is no me and Jeff. There never will be. We're too different. Our lives would never mix."

Cady steepled her fingers and tapped her top lip solemnly. "I've never seen two people more in love."

Bree snorted. "Don't be a ninny. That's ridiculous. He's arrogant and stubborn and overbearing—and snobbish."

"That description fits you as well."

"I'm not a snob."

"You certainly are. You're holding it against Jeff that he's wealthy."

"He's destroying my business. That's what I have against him."

"From what I've seen, even when the bridge is completed, there will be enough trade and river traffic to keep Murphy Navigation going. That's not why you're in a snit. Like I said before—you're in love with him and you're fighting it because he's rich."

"That's the most absurd notion I've ever heard."

Cady lifted a dainty brow. "Is it? You're afraid that his acquaintances will turn up their noses at you. And you take every opportunity to discourage Jeff so you won't be hurt. So—you won't give him the time of day because he's rich. Consequently, you're a snob."

Bree had never thought of it quite like that before. "It wouldn't matter if I did give him the time of day. He's engaged to Emily."

Cady held up a finger. "Not officially."

Bree sighed and dropped her brush in her lap. "This is all too complicated." Then a thought occurred to her, and she narrowed her gaze on the other girl. "I guess Kane's a snob, too. What are *you* going to do?"

Cady's finely chiseled mouth tightened. "I'm going to prove him wrong."

"How?"

"I'm going to do something with my life."

"What?"

"I wish you'd quit asking so many questions and start giving me some answers." Sparks in her green eyes glowed brightly for a moment, then burned out, and Cady sighed. "I don't know yet. But the long ride back tonight gave me time to think. I've decided to go back to school—not finishing school, but a women's college. I'll show that condescending captain that I can make a difference even if I can't build a cookfire!"

Bree grinned. "Good for you."

If only *her* problem were that simple, Bree thought. She and Tanner were about as different as two people could be. No amount of schooling could change things between them.

"Will you leave soon?"

"As soon as I can make traveling arrangements."

Bree's heart contracted. "I'll miss you."

The other girl's eyes sparkled with tears. "I'll miss you, too. And Bree? I'm sorry I called you a snob."

"Forget it. You were right."

More right than you know, she thought. She *was* afraid—terrified—of being laughed at. And Tanner would never give up his high society life for her. Neither belonged in the other's world. He was an engineer, constructing a trestle from the hardest timber and finest steel to cross the unpredictable Colorado River. But even he couldn't build a bridge strong enough to span the differences between them.

sixteen

Arizona Territory
September 1881

Jeff stopped at the top of the bluff and turned to his sister. He fought the tightness in his chest, the thickness in his throat, as he studied Cady in her brown wool traveling suit. Saying good-bye to her was harder than he'd thought it would be. Behind her, the rising sun washed the mountains with pink and lavender light as the chill of the early morning wind blew over them. He pulled the collar of her jacket closer around her neck.

Although he'd gotten used to having her around, he was pleased that she'd finally agreed to go back to school. That was two he owed Kane, but he wished his sister hadn't been so deeply hurt in the process. Then again, maybe it was better this way. Frontier life was difficult enough for a man, but it was hell on earth for a woman. He'd sweated and struggled for ten years so that his family could have the best in life. He wasn't sure he wanted his sister to face the difficulties of surviving the unsettled Territory— especially at a military post. Moving from post to post, wondering if the man she loved would come back after every patrol, unrelenting heat, bitter cold. But, in the end, all Jeff really cared about was her happiness.

There was a faraway look in Cady's eyes as she stared past him, downriver toward Fort Mojave.

He lightly stroked her cheek with his finger. "You going to be all right?"

"Of course. I'm a Tanner," she said, smiling too brightly. Since the night of the reception, there had been a shadow around the edges of her cheerful smile. She tried to conceal her unhappiness, and most of the time she succeeded. But sometimes, when she didn't know he was watching, a lovesick expression stole into her eyes, and he didn't miss the deep, sad sighs. Although he'd come to look forward to seeing her every day, a part of him was relieved that she was going home so their mother could help mend the pieces of Cady's wounded heart.

He cleared his throat. "Your bags are loaded."

"Hmm?" She dragged her wistful gaze from the river and looked at him.

"Bree and Riley are going to take you upriver to Yuma. From there, you're catching the train east."

She placed her fist on her hip, feigning affront. "I've done this before. Remember? I'm a big girl."

"Yes—well. Take care of yourself."

"You, too." Her lip trembled, and she looked away, down toward the riverbank where *Belle* waited, black smokestack spewing a cloud that caught in the breeze and trailed behind her like a flag. "And Bree—watch over her."

"I plan to."

"I'm worried about her. Charles is, well—"

"I've already taken care of him. I don't think he'd dare lay a finger on her after—"

"So it *was* you." Her eyes narrowed. "I thought so. You knocked the stuffing out of him. Didn't you?"

He grinned. "That's not exactly the way I'd phrase it."

"I wondered. Mary told me it happened in the saloon—that he stepped in to help a drunken miner who was outnumbered—but I didn't believe it. I saw your scraped knuckles the night of the reception." She shook her head. "You should be ashamed of yourself. He has a black eye, a broken nose, and cracked ribs. Why, he hasn't been able to chew anything tougher than mush for days now."

"Yeah. I'm real sorry." Sorry Bree stopped him was more like it. "He won't bother her anymore."

"When are you going to admit you love her?"

His head snapped up. Love? Bree Murphy? He glanced at her on the riverboat, stoking the boiler with wood to build up steam pressure for the trip upriver. Her hat covered the shiny dark crown of her hair, and her braid hung down her back. Leather gloves protected her hands, but he'd felt the calluses hard work had earned her. How different she looked from that night at the fort. What a fascinating contradiction she was—competent riverboat captain one day, stunning, fashionably dressed woman the next. He found her refreshing and challenging—never a dull moment. She was unpredictable, and he couldn't resist her.

He recalled unlacing her corset and smiled at the memory. His amusement faded when he remembered the sensation of her soft breasts in his hands and her ardent response to his touch. Every night since, he'd been restless and tortured with frustration. He'd admit he couldn't get her out of his mind. But love? He wasn't sure.

Leave it to Cady to demand straight out what he felt for Bree. Jeff started to laugh. "You haven't learned to hold your tongue, have you? I'd have thought your encounter with Carrington would have—Sorry. Didn't mean to bring up a sore subject."

Her mouth tightened for a moment, then she nodded knowingly. "Well done, Jeff. The way you avoided my question and went on the attack. You have no room to talk where affairs of the heart are concerned. You can't even—"

He pulled her against him in a bear hug. "God, I'm going to miss you."

"Me, too." Her muffled voice caught on a small sob as she clutched him tightly and, just for a moment, buried her face against his chest. She sniffled loudly, then pulled back and smiled up at him.

"Give my love to Mother and Father," he said huskily. "Tell them I'll be home soon."

She nodded. "Anything else?"

"Yes." He reached into his back pocket. "Would you give this to Emily for me?" He pressed the wrinkled envelope into her gloved hand.

"What's this?" Cady asked.

"What does it look like?"

"Why do you always answer a question with a question? Of course it looks like a letter. What does it say?" She stared at it curiously, then held it up to the sun to read through the layers of paper.

"That's none of your business."

"Maybe not. But—" She chewed the corner of her lip. "I haven't wanted to say anything, but you know that young lawyer you hired for the railroad? He's been spending a lot of time with Em and her father. Mr. Hollingsworth likes him a lot."

"That a fact? Am I supposed to be jealous?"

"Well, aren't you?"

He took the letter from her and stuffed it into the reticule hanging from her wrist. "Just make sure Emily gets this. And Cady? Do me a favor and stay while she reads it."

"Why?"

He shrugged. "Just in case she needs a friend."

The riverboat whistle sounded signaling *Belle*'s imminent departure. Bree looked at the two of them, hand on her hip in an impatient stance.

Jeff looked down at his sister. "Bree has a schedule to keep, and God help the man, woman, or child who gets in her way. You'd better go."

Cady nodded, then kissed his cheek. "Bye. I love you."

He grunted a reply, then she was gone, racing down the bluff, and he watched Riley assist her across the gangplank.

Several yards away the *Elizabeth* waited. Jeff had arranged for Sean to take him to the bridge site on the other riverboat so that Bree could see his sister to the train in Yuma.

The hoarse, staccato sound of *Belle*'s engine drifted to him, and he watched the riverboat ease out into the main channel of the Colorado. Sandbars lay uncovered in the shallow water and uneasiness flashed through him. He knew how dangerous the river could be, especially when the level was down. But he trusted Bree; she knew what she was doing. If anyone could get Cady safely to Yuma, it was Bree.

Out of nowhere, the thought flashed through his mind that he wished she made her living another way. He didn't like her facing the perils that lay around every bend in the muddy, red-brown river.

From *Belle*'s bow, Cady turned and waved. He returned the gesture and watched until the boat rounded the curve and steamed out of sight. Then he started down the bluff. There was work to be done. The bridge would be completed in a few weeks, if his luck held. Then what?

He'd go back home. His partners had kept him informed about the railroad business, and he knew there were expansions to be undertaken, especially in California. He'd probably head up another project. But what about Bree? What would happen to her?

In the cloudless blue sky a plume of smoke dissipated over the river channel. He stared at the last sign of her. A powerful wave of emptiness swept over him and threatened to pull him under. Every day for the last four months they'd worked together. Every day her laughter and bright blue eyes, her sharp wit and keen intelligence, had filled his senses, given meaning to his days.

She was the only reason this assignment in hell had been bearable.

He'd survived years of laying track and the loneliness of that labor because he hadn't known any different. Now that he'd experienced Bree's zest for life, her sweetness and strength, he wondered how he'd get through a day without her.

He thought about Cady and her unhappiness at Kane's rejection. A soldier's duty didn't easily permit taking a wife. But his own situation was different. If he took Bree home with him, her life would be filled with luxury. But would that make her happy?

She thrived on challenge. He smiled wryly. The strictures of society would certainly be that for her, and the biddies who made the rules wouldn't accept her easily, if at all. The night of the reception, she'd told him she didn't belong. But she fit nicely into a place within him that had been empty for a long time. A day without Bree in it would be the day he died completely inside. Was it fair to subject her to his way of life knowing how uncomfortable she was in society? Shouldn't he let her decide? He didn't want to end up like Cady and Kane. There were no easy answers.

He needed to talk to her, later after she returned. In the meantime, he had to get to the bridge site, and to do that, he had a boiler to stoke. Sean had told him that Charlie couldn't handle it. He'd take the river soundings, but they needed a strong back for the heavy work.

Jeff smiled grimly. He looked forward to it. Physical exertion was just what he needed to take his mind off the beautiful riverboat captain.

The riverboat chugged around the bend, and Bree stared at the dock she'd left early that morning. She was depressed and her body ached with fatigue. Saying good-bye to Cady had been like losing a sister. They'd both struggled to hold back tears, and in the end had been unsuccessful. What a fine kettle of fish that was, she thought ruefully. She'd worked hard to fit in, to prove that she was as tough as any man and able to handle the job. And there she'd stood, hugging her friend and blubbering like a darn fool.

On the return trip work had been a godsend. It had been rough, taking every bit of her concentration to keep the boat out of the many sandbars that waited to break her up. Riley was tired too. He stood in the bow with a willow switch, constantly monitoring the water level. Every now and then she watched him rub the small of his back. She knew he'd be glad to get home, too.

The sun was just dipping behind a craggy hill, and one brilliant, concentrated ray caught her full in the eyes. She lifted a hand to block the glare. Moments later the light was gone and the slowly passing riverbank bathed in purple shadow.

She scanned the dock, but the *Elizabeth* hadn't returned. That meant Charles and her father would be spending the night at the bridge site. That meant Tanner wouldn't be back, either. Disappointment unraveled within her, expanded and pressed against her heart until it was almost painful to breathe. She'd miss him when he was gone. She realized how much she'd looked forward to his heart-stopping charm, his handsome face, his lazy grin.

Bree shook away her distracting thoughts and forced herself to concentrate on docking *Belle*. Otherwise there'd be the devil to pay. The boat still belonged to Tanner, and she didn't want to explain to him that she'd broken up on a mudbank because she was preoccupied with notions of what his slightest touch did to her.

"Can I take her to shore, Riley?" she called out over the engine's loud chugging.

The old man dipped the switch and nodded, then glanced over his shoulder. "Slow and easy, missy."

Bree guided the steamer carefully to the riverbank, senses sharpened for any sign of trouble, the slightest scraping noise, a hint of change in the ripples of the water.

She breathed a sigh of relief when they were safely tied up.

Riley moved the gangplank into place, then poked his

head into the wheelhouse. "Reckon yer pa's stayin' down-river tonight."

She nodded.

"Charlie, too, looks like."

She nodded again and a grin threatened. She knew where this was leading.

"You'll be safe as a cub in its den. So, I reckon I'll ske-daddle to Kate's and see Ginger."

Bree leaned her back against the wheel and crossed her arms beneath her breasts. "I reckon that sounds like a fine idea."

Riley cackled, showing his gap-toothed grin through the abundance of whiskers on the lower half of his face. He pulled the battered, brown hat more firmly on his head, then turned away. She felt the boat dip and sway as it was relieved of his weight, then she lit a lantern.

After checking the fore and aft lines one final time, she crossed the gangplank and headed up to the boarding-house. As she topped the bluff, she noticed that the house was ablaze with light and several horses were tethered out front. A blue-clad figure approached her. As she came closer, she detected the gold trim of an army uniform, then recognized Kane. What was he doing here? If he'd come to make things right with Cady, he'd missed her.

She stopped in front of him on the path. His hat and trousers were covered with dust as if he'd ridden hard and fast. A grim expression hardened his handsome features. Lines of fatigue and something else that made her uneasy grooved his face from nose to mouth.

"If you've come to see Cady off, you're a little late. And you should be ashamed of yourself."

He shuffled his boots in the sand and looked down before meeting her gaze. "Bree, I—"

"You know, you were awfully hard on her. She's tougher than you give her credit for. You didn't even give her a chance."

"Something's—" He paused and swallowed.

"What have you got to say for yourself? I thought you liked Cady. I've never seen you act that way before. How could you let her leave without a word? It would serve you right if—"

"Stop it." Fingers of steel bit into her upper arms as he shook her. "Will you be quiet. There's been an accident."

"What?"

"The *Elizabeth*. There was an explosion about half a mile from the fort. We brought them back to Hardyville. Tanner's—"

Fear closed around her, as cold and dark as the brown water of the Colorado. He started to say more, but she didn't hear. Her mind seized on two words—*explosion* and *Tanner*. She broke free of Kane's grip and raced past him up the hill. *Dear God, let him be all right.*

Bree couldn't stop when she reached the steps of the boardinghouse, though her lungs burned from the strain. She dashed inside and paused in the hall, frantically looking from one side to the other, uncertain which way to turn. Hysteria clawed at the edges of her mind, but she fought it down.

She took a deep breath, drawing in air. "Tanner? Where are you?" She turned left, toward the closed door of the front bedroom. "Cap?"

Boots scraped on the wooden floor behind her. From the corner of her eye, she saw a dark blue uniform.

"Bree, listen to me," Kane said, but his worried frown told her more than words ever could.

"Where's Tanner?" She whirled and gripped the front of his shirt, the brass buttons biting into her palms. "Tell me where he is."

"I'm here."

She twisted and saw him in the doorway to the front room, leaning against the frame. He was alive! Dried blood streaked his face from a cut over his right eye, a fresh white bandage covered his ribs beneath his unbuttoned, bloodstained shirt. He was battered, but he was *alive*.

Relief washed over her, leaving her knees weak as a newborn colt. She wanted to collapse right where she stood and bury her face in her hands. Instead, she moved toward him on wobbly legs—just to touch him. She needed tangible proof that he wasn't just created by her fancy because she want so badly to see him again.

When she could feel the warmth from his body, she stopped, just an inch away. "I—I thought you were . . ." Lifting a trembling hand, she traced the jagged, bloodied rip in his shirt. "What happened?"

There was a creak on the stair tread. She glanced over her shoulder at Charles, leaning on the newel post at the bottom. Gauzy bandages covered both of his hands nearly to the elbow. There was a sadness in his face she'd never seen before.

She had a bad feeling, and she looked expectantly at Tanner. Something told her she didn't want to know any more. But *not* knowing was worse.

"Please tell me," she begged.

He closed his eyes for a moment and swallowed hard. "It was a faulty gauge, I think. The pressure built and—"

She shook her head. "I don't understand. Cap said that gauge was fixed. I need to talk to him. He'll know what happened. Where is he?"

Tanner hesitated and she took a step toward the front room. If he refused to tell her, she'd find her father by herself.

"No."

Jeff reached out to stop her, lifting his arm to bar her way. Stabbing pain shot through his left shoulder. He didn't remember injuring it. But he didn't remember anything except an earsplitting blast. His last thought had been that he'd never see Bree again, then blackness had swallowed him. He'd regained consciousness at the fort. While the army surgeon had tended him, Kane had filled him in, told him what happened. Facing Bree now was the hardest thing he'd ever done.

She tried to brush by him, but he sidestepped to block her way and her view into the room. "Let me past, Tanner. Or tell me what's wrong."

He held her upper arms in a bruising grip as he looked into her frightened face. Freckles dotted her nose, and pink spread across her wind-chapped cheeks. Dark circles of fatigue stained the hollows beneath her troubled blue eyes.

"It's your father. He's been—"

"Cap's hurt?" She struggled in his grasp, trying to break free. "Where is he? I have to see him. Let me go." Her voice rose, goaded by fear and panic.

She tried to pry his fingers from her arm, one by one, but he held her fast. She had to know before she went in the other room, before she saw ... He wrestled with the information that was eating him up inside, fighting to find a way to tell her without destroying her. But there were no easy words. There was no painless way to say it.

"Bree, your father was killed in the explosion." He stopped and pulled her hard against him, welcoming the sharp pain that shot through him from the wound in his side.

"Sean's dead, Breanne." Charlie's voice was soft. He was trying to be kind. "You and I will have to run the business now."

Jeff felt her body stiffen in shock. She pulled away and stared up at him, her eyes haunted, begging him to say it was a lie. A shudder rocked her as she glanced at her stepbrother, then her gaze came back to Jeff, and she slowly shook her head.

"He's lying. Tell me the truth, Tanner. Where's Cap?" She seized the sides of his open shirt and jerked once. "I have to see him. Don't do this to me. I know we've had our differences, but—"

"It's true." He'd give up his fortune if only he could turn back time and buy her father's life. In the face of death, earthly wealth and influence meant nothing. He hated his powerlessness.

"How?"

"I stoked the boiler. The needle hardly moved. Sean said the boat felt sluggish, needed more fuel. He said the boiler gauge was just stubborn, keep feeding her. But it worried me. I was on my way to get Charlie to have a look." His gaze strayed to her stepbrother still on the stairs. Shock and loss mixed with bruises from the explosion. "Before I got halfway to the bow, it blew." He swallowed hard. "I'm sorry, Bree. I should have—"

"Where's Mary? Does she know?"

He nodded. "The doctor gave her something to make her sleep."

She glanced at the closed door, then to Charlie, who was staring at her from the bottom of the stairs. "What happened to your hands?"

Charlie stared blankly at the bandages. "I pulled him out of the fire. He was already gone."

Jeff watched as Bree's face paled beneath the color the outdoors had painted there. The smell of the sun and the river emanated from her, clean and earthy. A muscle in her cheek contracted as she clenched her teeth, valiantly struggling for control. The pain in her eyes swelled and grew until it squeezed out her spark. Jeff watched helplessly as her spirit dimmed and blinked out.

The sight and sound and scent of violence and destruction filled his head and clung to his clothes. He wanted to pull away from her, to keep the ugliness from touching her, but she needed him. Even if she didn't know it yet, she needed him. Jeff braced himself, waiting for her tears, preparing to give her what small comfort he could.

She looked at his hands, gripping her upper arms. "Let me go."

He hesitated. "Are you all right?"

"I'm fine. I want to see him." Her voice, emptied of all emotion, was soft and a shade too composed.

"I don't think that's a good idea. Remember him as he was . . ."

She pushed his hands away and visibly straightened, her spine as rigid as the steel rails he'd laid across the bridge. "Get out of my way."

She moved past him and into the front room.

Charlie stood away from the banister. "Families have to stick together at a time like this. He's the only father I ever knew."

"I'd like to go alone," Bree said to him.

He nodded and walked slowly upstairs. Then Bree went into the room where her father's body lay.

Jeff watched her, dying some himself at his helplessness. "Dammit. If only there was something I could do."

"Go with her, Tanner," Kane said, crossing his arms over his chest. "No matter what she says, she shouldn't be alone."

Jeff nodded. "I owe you, for everything you did today. Thanks."

Kane angled his head toward Bree. "She needs help now."

When he entered the room, Bree stood hesitating a foot away from the canvas-covered body resting on a plank stretched between two chairs. The only illumination in the room came from the candle in the sconce on the far wall. As she inched closer, the light lengthened her shadow behind her.

Jeff moved beside her as she lifted the covering from her father. His expression was remarkably peaceful in death. Kane had told him that Charlie burned his hands pulling Sean from the wheelhouse. He'd expected the body would be badly burned, too. He'd hoped to spare her this. But he should've known she wouldn't take the easy way out.

Bree brushed the gritty gray hair from her father's brow. His features were hardly marked at all. Jeff was grateful for that, for her sake. He studied her small, pinched face and slumped shoulders. He wasn't sure she even knew he was there.

The corners of her full mouth turned up. "This is what you wanted, isn't it, Cap? You're with Mama now. I know you've missed her. I know how hard it's been for you. I tried as hard as I could. But nothing took away the loneliness she left behind. Not Mary, not the whiskey, not me . . ."

"Don't, Bree." Jeff stood behind her and squeezed her shoulders. "He loved you very much."

She shook off his hands. "Not enough to stop drinking. Only Mama could make him do that. She was the only one who could make him forget the bad memories, from the war." She turned her head, and the candle highlighted her profile and the pain etched there. "He was in the Confederate navy. Did I tell you that?"

"No."

"That's where he learned about riverboats. He was good, when he wasn't drinking."

"He was a fine river pilot and a fine man. We'll sorely miss him."

"I'll have to see about burying him."

"Not tonight. It's too dark. Tomorrow's soon enough." Jeff moved around her and replaced the canvas to shut out death. But the smell of it was all around, and the sound of silence pounded in his head. "I took the liberty of asking Luke McLaughlin to make something to rest him in."

She didn't say anything.

"Is that all right with you?"

"Does it matter?"

"Of course. He's your father."

"Was. I don't know if I can say good-bye. It's too soon. I'm not ready." A shudder raced through her, and she clenched her fists, pulling herself together.

"You're never ready for this. Dammit. If only I could do something . . .'

"But you can't." Her tone was cold and hard.

Better than anyone, Jeff knew how strong she was, but her iron control made him uneasy. He was well aware how deeply she cared for her father. She'd taken on running the business practically single-handed. She'd protected him from the consequences of his drinking and steadfastly refused to burden him with her troubles. The man was all she had in the world, and now that world had been blown apart.

"You must be starved. I'll get you something to eat." He took her elbow to lead her back into the hall, but she pulled away.

"No." Her dazed look vanished; her mouth tightened into a grim line.

"Rest then. Go upstairs. I'll find someplace—"

"Don't tell me what I need," she snapped.

"Let me help."

"If you want to do something, leave me alone. I wish you'd never come here. I wish I'd never laid eyes on you." She turned away and walked out the front door.

seventeen

Bree looked at the gritty sand piled beside the gaping hole scraped and chiseled from the hard desert ground. She turned away, wishing she could be anywhere else. But wishing wouldn't change the facts. And the fact was, she had to bury her father.

The small cemetery enclosed by a run-down picket fence stood on a hill behind Hardyville. Makeshift crosses with names and dates carved into the slats dotted the rocky ground. Tumbleweeds scratched against the fence, trapped by the barrier as the merciless wind pushed and prodded. Beside the fresh grave, she saw the familiar marker, and her throat tightened as she read the words once again: *Claire Elizabeth Murphy—1842–1874, BELOVED WIFE AND MOTHER.*

She clutched her wool shawl tighter around her. The sun shone down; she knew because she felt the rays when the wind died away. She missed its warmth when the gray-tinged clouds passed overhead. Darkness hovered around her, threatening to pull her in. A shiver began in her shoulders, then raced through her, until it took all her willpower to stand.

She heard the crunch of footsteps on the gravel behind her and turned hesitantly. Several men carried the coffin that held her father's body. Beside Riley, Tanner gripped the wooden box and helped set it next to the mound of rocky dirt.

Her heart leaped at the sight of him, but she tried to push the feelings away. She tried to summon her defenses, tried to remember how she'd felt when she'd first seen him and shot his hat. The thought made her smile a little, and she knew it was impossible to resurrect her anger. After everything that had happened, after he'd made her feel things she'd never felt before, it was too late to hate him.

She dragged her gaze from him and watched the townspeople drift up the hill. When she saw Ginger and Sally and Cactus Kate just behind them, a lump grew in her throat.

Kate approached, her whiskey-colored eyes sympathetic. "I'm real sorry about your pa."

Bree tucked a strand of hair behind her ear. "Thank you."

"Ginger and Sally insisted on comin', too. Said you was real decent to 'em and wanted to know if they could do anything."

Bree looked at the two women, one tall and auburn-haired, the other shorter and blond. She shook her head and willed them to know how grateful she was for the offer. "There's nothing. But thank you for coming. It means a lot to me."

Men with hats in hands filed by her awkwardly murmuring words of sympathy, the women smiled sadly and squeezed her fingers, then all formed a semicircle around the grave. Mary arrived last, heavily supported by her son, his hands still covered with bandages. A crumpled handkerchief peeked from her fist. In respect to the widow the crowd parted to let them through, and Charles stopped beside Bree. He stood between the two women, his black hat low on his forehead.

Bree sensed he was trying to be the man of the family now. She knew he shared her father's wish that she marry him. Although she was grateful that he'd tried to help her father, Bree knew she could never give him what he wanted. Her heart belonged to a railroad man.

But right now she desperately wished Tanner had never come. He would be leaving soon, and it hurt too much to lose someone you loved. She swayed and her stepbrother circled her waist with a bandaged hand. She smiled a little, then took a step away.

Reverend Howard opened his Bible and began to read. The words mingled together until they became an incoherent droning, and her mind wandered. She thought back to her mother's funeral. That day her father had stood with her. This time she was really and truly alone.

She remembered her mother's words when Bree had asked her if she was going to die. *Those we love live forever in our hearts.* Not long after that she'd lost one parent. She wasn't prepared to give up the other. Her father was too vibrant and healthy. She'd always known she'd have to face it one day—no one lives forever—but not now, not so soon.

She brushed wisps of hair from her cheeks, and her hands shook, the way they had earlier when she'd attempted to fashion her braid. She'd finally given up and simply tied the wayward mass at her nape. With both hands, she tried to tame the wildly blowing strands, but she could feel her ribbon slipping. Her self-control frayed, and she struggled to regain it.

When the reverend stopped speaking, she watched the coffin being lowered into the grave. She risked a glance at Tanner. His dark head was bowed, and his mouth tightened to a straight line nearly hidden beneath his thick mustache. Grooves of tension and regret were deep between his eyes and on either side of his nose and mouth. The cut over his right eye had begun the first stage of healing and his eyelid had colored bright purple. He could've been killed. She might be burying him, too. With all her heart and soul she wanted to cry out against the thought of losing him. But he was going away as soon as the bridge was finished. Why did she have to give up everyone she loved?

The first shovelful of dirt hit the wooden box with a gravelly thunk, and she flinched as if she'd been shot.

Bree looked at the place where her father would rest forever. A voice inside her railed at him. *How could you do this to me? Why did you leave me?*

Still clinging to her son's arm, Mary approached her. "Dear, I—I'm afraid I must lie down now."

"I know, Mary."

"Afterward . . ." She looked at the people talking quietly in groups. "Everyone will want to extend their sympathies. I don't think I'm up to . . ."

"Mother isn't strong, Bree." Charles pressed his black hat more firmly on his head with his right wrist. "She needs quiet."

"Don't worry," Bree said. Her mouth tightened when she looked at him. "I'll take care of it." Her glance darted back to her stepmother, and she softened her tone. "You go on back now and rest. We won't disturb you."

Mary smiled gratefully and allowed Charles to assist her down the hill.

"Couldn't help overhearin'." Kate moved beside Bree, followed by Tanner. "Everyone's welcome at my place. We'll give Sean a wake the likes of which this Territory's never seen."

The lump was back in her throat, and Bree swallowed hard. "I don't know what to say."

"Don't hafta' say nothin'." Kate opened her arms.

The smell of sachet, liquor, and smoke from the saloon clung to her, but Bree didn't care. The comfort offered by the older woman drew her like a bee to honey, and Bree gave herself up to the motherly embrace. The kindness, so freely and generously offered, threatened to dissolve her carefully constructed composure. "Thank you," she whispered, letting Kate pat her back reassuringly.

When she backed away, Kate cupped her cheeks, then

pulled Bree's shawl more snugly around her shoulders. "You're welcome."

Tanner cleared his throat and spun his hat through his hands. "I'll talk to the Bellmores and arrange for food from the restaurant."

"No need," Kate said. "Most everybody brought somethin' with 'em."

Bree tried to smile, but her lips trembled. She didn't want to break down in front of anyone. She had to leave before she completely fell apart. "I—I need some time by myself. Do you mind?"

"You take all the time you need, darlin'. Sally and Ginger and me will take care of everything."

Bree nodded gratefully and started down the hill. A large shadow blocked out the sun, and the sound of sliding rocks and sand penetrated her preoccupation. She glanced to her right. Tanner.

"Please go away," she said, increasing her pace. He was the reason she needed to be by herself.

She didn't want to see him or talk to him. Her feelings were too close to the surface, and her head reeled from the confusing emotions. When she thought he'd been hurt, or worse, it was fear the likes of which she'd never known before. Then he'd told her that her father was gone, and confessed his part in it. Everything had happened so fast, and she needed to sort things out.

But one thing was sure. She didn't want to need him any more than she already did.

She'd pull herself together without his help.

When he persisted, matching his long stride to her shorter hurried steps, Bree stopped. She touched her hand to her forehead, shielding her eyes from the sun when she looked up at him. "I didn't invite you along."

"You shouldn't be by yourself."

"Maybe not. But I haven't got a choice. My father's dead." She whirled away and hurried down the hill. This time he didn't follow, and she was relieved. But how could she force his handsome features and heart-stopping grin from her mind? His voice echoed in her head and held her fast, turning her stomach inside out.

Jeff watched the swirl of blue cotton skirts and a flash of white petticoat as she raced away from him. A tight band squeezed his chest. Buff-colored clouds of dirt churned up by her feet danced in the breeze behind her.

He slapped his hat against his thigh, and dust jumped from the crown. He absently traced the bullet hole as he hunched his shoulders against the chill wind pressing against his back, urging him to go after her. It wouldn't do any good. In her state of mind she wouldn't welcome his interference. She hadn't looked at him once during the service. He felt raw, inside and out. The gash in his side throbbed, and the scratches on his face were still tender. But that was nothing compared to the pain of being shut out by Bree. Last night she had said she wished they'd never met. But he counted himself the luckiest man in the world to have known B. E. Murphy. He wanted to tell her so, if only she'd let him.

"Don't take it too hard." Kate's smoky voice rasped beside him.

"I shouldn't leave her alone. She needs someone."

"Bree has someone." She motioned to the townspeople moving away to the saloon. "Let me tell you something, Mr. Tanner. Here in the Territory, things are different than where you come from. Shame it takes somethin' like this to bring neighbors together, but the fact is we take care of our own. Don't matter who you are or what you do for a livin', we watch over each other. We ain't got no one else." She took a deep breath and her large bosom threatened to overflow the low-cut black dress. "But changes are on the way. That bridge of yours is just the beginnin'. More people are comin' and the lines will be drawn straighter and deeper, but right now we're plain folks tryin' to make Bree's burden lighter."

Jeff knew she was right. These were kind, decent people. Out of the goodness of their hearts, they'd come to pay their respects to a fallen friend and offer sympathy to his family. Would *his* acquaintances do the same for him? He doubted they could be bothered unless there was a profit in it for them. Kate was right about something else, too. Everything would change when more settlers came west. Again he wondered—what would happen to Bree then?

"I want to help her. But she—"

"She has some things to think on."

"I can help," he said, starting after Bree.

Kate took his arm. "Come on, sugar. She'll be along when she's ready."

They started down the slope, and Kate's abundant breasts, straining the material of her dress, jiggled with every step. Jeff knew from her labored breathing that she wasn't used to anything more physical than a stroll around her place. But she was more than a flashy saloon owner. There was more to Kate than met the eye, something worldly and wise. She was straightforward and honest. He liked that and he liked her.

Bree had accepted Kate's compassion easily, and he understood why. But Bree's pale face, her delicate jaw so tightly clenched, the shadows of strain around her eyes, tiny cracks in the wall of her composure—all signs that told him how much she was hurting.

She wouldn't want anyone to see her break down. Self-respect was a quality she possessed in abundance, too damn much pride for her own good.

Jeff impulsively leaned down and kissed the saloon owner's powdered cheek. The skin was loose and soft, aging. "You're a good woman, Kate."

She winked at him. "Don't let it get around."

He patted her hand, then removed it from his arm. "You go on ahead. I'll catch up with you."

She nodded and continued down the hill, lifting her skirt and carefully picking her way among the rocks.

Jeff turned and went back through the picket fence to the grave site. Luke McLaughlin and Reverend Howard had just finished. They nodded solemnly and left him alone.

Dirt and death hung in the air, the taste of it thick and bitter. Two pieces of lumber, crossed and nailed together, marked Sean's final resting place. His name and the years of his birth and death had been hastily carved into the wood. Jeff promised himself that he'd arrange for something more permanent.

Jeff removed his hat and stared at the fresh grave. "I'll take care of her for you, Sean. You wanted her to marry Charlie, but he's not the right man for her." He looked at the sun and took a deep breath. "I am. I'll see she never wants for anything. I'd die before I'd let anyone hurt her. That's a promise."

He shifted his weight as the wind pushed against him. "No one knows better than you how stubborn she is. I'd be obliged if you could do a little something to help me convince her that throwing her lot in with a railroad man wouldn't be so bad." Jeff turned away and put his hat on, pulling it low over his eyes.

"Knew this was where you'd be." Riley stopped beside Bree and stared at the brownish-red Colorado for a moment, then rested a booted foot on the log where she sat. "Somethin' about this river that draws a body back without even knowin' why."

She nodded, a frown creasing her forehead. "I wanted to be by myself."

He squinted into the distance at the rapidly descending sun. "Left you alone all day. Now it's time t'talk."

"I don't feel like—"

"Don't much matter what you feel like doing. Time for brooding's done. Saw the way you high-tailed it away from Tanner at the cemetery."

"I don't want anything from that railroad man."

"You're stirrin' up resentment on purpose so you don't hafta' face what's in yer heart." He sat down beside her and rested his elbows on his knees. "River folk are used t' takin' chances. But the fact is, you lost your nerve. You love that railroad man, and it scares the hell outta you."

Love Tanner? Her emotions had come a long way from the animosity she'd felt when she'd first laid eyes on him, but love? She shook her head. "I don't care about him."

Riley snorted. "That's why you tore up the hill like a bat outta hell when you thought he was the one bad hurt."

She scratched her nose. "Kane's got a big mouth."

The old man cackled. "Maybe, maybe not. Point is, ya' don't act that way unless y'got a powerful lot of love for a man."

A man. One special man. Jefferson Thomas Tanner. Her heart pounded against her ribs. Riley saw right through her. She must be in love with Tanner. There was no other explanation for her behavior. But loving him made everything worse.

"Riley, have you ever been in love?"

He picked up a stick from the riverbank. "Once."

Her brows lifted in surprise. In her wildest dreams she'd never imagined him giving his heart to a woman. The revelation pricked her curiosity. "Does she live in Hardyville?"

"Used to. She passed away some years ago."

"Did I know her?"

" 'Bout as well as one person can."

"Who was she?"

"Your mother."

She gaped at him, stunned. "Did—did she love you back?"

He glanced at her. "As a friend, nothin' more. She didn't know how I felt."

"You never said anything to her?"

"Nope." The whiskers around his mouth parted, and a smile broke through. "First time I saw her, felt like my insides dropped clear to the soles of my boots. Claire was the prettiest thing I ever did see." He studied her. "You're the spittin' image of her."

"I wish I'd known her better."

"You're a lot like her. You've got her sweetness and her spark but also a toughness she didn't have. This land killed her. She followed Sean into hell itself, but her constitution wasn't strong enough for the Territory." He sighed heavily. "Desert burned the life right out of her."

Bree thought about Tanner. There were a lot of ways to lose someone. "Do you ever wish she'd known—how you felt about her, I mean?"

"Sometimes." The stick in his gnarled hands snapped. "Oh, I never woulda' made trouble 'tween your ma and pa—I don't regret that part. But I reckon if I'd just once told her, maybe this empty feelin' inside wouldn't be so big."

"I'm sorry, Riley."

"No need. It was a long time ago. But somethin' tells me you got that same kind of hankerin' for Tanner."

"For the sake of argument, let's assume you're right. Where does that get me?"

"Nowhere, if you don't tell him how you feel."

Tell Tanner she loved him? That would surely give him a big laugh. Or even worse, he'd pity her, be nice to her because she'd made a fool of herself. She couldn't abide him feeling sorry for her. "I can't."

"Thought you had some backbone. Guess I was wrong." He started to rise, and she placed her hand on his arm.

He smelled of tobacco and whiskey and sweat and dust, familiar, earthy odors that somehow brought her comfort. "Don't go."

"Then you talk to me true, missy."

"I just can't tell Tanner that I—don't want him to go. He's practically engaged to someone else."

" 'Almost' ain't 'done.' "

"But she'd be right for him. Emily understands what it's

like to live in his world. She won't embarrass him or make him miserable."

"Like you."

"Yes," she said, frustrated, unhappy, and already lonely. "I don't know the first thing about dinner parties and society and clothes. I wouldn't know the right things to say to those people or how to act in front of them. I'm contrary and outspoken. I can't stand mealy-mouthed by his side and not say what I think. He'd come to hate me, and I wouldn't blame him."

"Occurs to me he might not want a woman who don't speak her mind."

"We'd just fight all the time."

"Makin' up can be right pleasurable," he said, grinning. "If ya' get my meanin'."

Her cheeks grew warm in spite of the chilly wind blowing. She understood all right. She'd been able to think of little else for weeks. "He hasn't said he wants me, at least not for more than . . . Riley, I can't tell him. . . ."

"If you don't, you're always gonna wonder. That empty feelin' can get powerful big and mighty lonely. Think you can live with it?"

"That would be easier than seeing him grow to hate me. I don't know if I can risk it."

Riley paused and stared at the river as he snapped off another piece of the stick in his hands. "If your pa was here, what would he say?"

Her eyes stung from the sudden fresh tears that gathered. "He'd tell me he just wanted me to be happy."

"Then that's what I'm tellin' ya'. If ya' got a chance for that with Tanner, then grab on with both hands and don't let go."

"Do you really think so?"

"Yup."

"Oh, Riley." She threw her arms around his shoulders and rested against him. Coarse gray whiskers poked and scratched her soft cheek, and she savored the tangible proof of his presence. "What would I do without you?"

"Dunno. God willin' ya' ain't gonna find out for a spell yet." He patted her hand and stood. "Ginger's waitin' over at Kate's. You all right now?"

She nodded. "Go on. I want to stay a little longer."

Bree heard his footsteps fade as he trudged up the bluff behind her. While they'd talked, the sun had settled behind the hills for the night. In its wake the sky went from ominous gray to pitch black. Clouds hid the moon and stars, and the wind grew stronger. The temperature dropped, and she began to shiver. Her shawl gave her no protection at all, and she needed shelter, but she didn't know where to go or what to do. She needed warmth and security more than she ever had in her life.

There was only one place she knew for sure she could find that—in Tanner's arms.

When he'd broken the news about her father, only the sudden shock had driven her from the safety of his embrace. It had frightened her how much she needed him. Riley was right. She was afraid of her feelings, terrified of Tanner's rejection.

But now that she knew she loved him, it frightened her more to keep her feelings inside. Life was short and there were no guarantees. She'd lost her father. She couldn't stand the thought of losing Tanner, too, and was fairly bursting with the need to tell him how she felt. If he couldn't return her love, then she'd deal with that. But at least she wouldn't go through the rest of her life wondering if things could have been different.

Those we love live forever in our hearts. Again, her mother's words came to mind. And death wasn't the only way to lose someone you loved. She knew Tanner would be with her forever, in her heart, her mind, her soul. She'd always remember his green eyes, dark with passion, his smile—roguish one minute, achingly tender the next. She'd never forget his strength, and the feeling of protec-

tion she felt when she was with him. But she couldn't re-
call what she'd never had.

She wanted to remember him the way a woman remem-
bers a man.

If she could only have one night of memories, she
wanted to create ones that would last her a lifetime. During the hot summers and the long cold winters, she'd call
up a universe of sensation, a world where Tanner was the
sun and sky, the moon and stars. She needed to know what
it was like to lie in his arms, to touch him, be touched by
him, make love with him.

Pressure built within her. She felt shaky and unsure and
exposed. Yet no power on earth could keep her from him
now. The time for running and hiding was over.

Fate had taken her father from her. If she let the opportunity to love Tanner slip away, she'd have only herself to
blame—for a lifetime.

eighteen

Jeff scraped the last of the soap and whiskers from his chin and jawline, then dragged the razor across a towel. He hadn't shaved since before the accident. The abrasions on his forehead and cheeks were still raw. One deep cut over his right eye would leave a permanent mark. But he knew that would be easier to live with than the scars that didn't show. Beside the shaving basin, the flame of a candle glowed amber through a half empty bottle of whiskey. He almost poured a glass, but decided against it. Liquor wouldn't drive away his demons, only dull them for a while.

He wiped the last traces of lather from the lower half of his face before dropping the hand mirror on the table next to Bree's rocker. All these months he'd used her room and never sat in her chair. It was delicate, like her, and he was afraid of breaking it.

If he lived to be a hundred, he'd never forget the tragic image of her fragile form beside Sean's grave. Proud and dry-eyed, she'd endured the service and graciously received condolences. After she'd run away to be alone, he'd eventually followed her to the river, knowing that's where she'd look for solace. Though she'd wanted to be by herself, he couldn't just leave her. But Jeff knew if she'd spotted him, it might open fresh wounds. So he'd lingered out of sight on the bluff, just in case.

She'd knelt in the sand beside the Colorado, her head bowed with grief. He'd stayed and watched over her until Riley had found her. He had hoped the old man could give her some words to ease her pain. Afterward, he'd gone to Kate's and waited for her, but she'd never arrived. Now the sun had descended, and the night wind wailed over the desert. And still she hadn't turned to him, or anyone else, as far as he knew. She was all alone.

Worry gnawed at his gut.

Pacing the room like something wild and restless, he finally stopped in front of the window and stared at the glass. The unrelenting blackness outside mirrored his reflection. His bare torso showed the jagged gash where a piece of the deck had scored his ribs. He rubbed his shoulder, still sore from landing on it after the force of the blast had thrown him. The bump on his head was going down. But he was alive and Sean was dead. If only . . .

A knock sounded and he turned. Bree? His heart lurched. In three strides he crossed the room.

He yanked the door open and saw her there.

"Thank God." He wanted to pull her against him, to feel her warmth and softness and make sure she was more than an illusion.

"Can I come in?" Her voice was soft, unsure.

"Of course. It's your room." He stood back to let her pass, then shut the door.

"So it is." She looked around as if she'd never seen it before.

Her blue, cotton dress was dusty, and a triangular rip halfway down the skirt revealed her white petticoat beneath. The hem was darker, wet. A scent clung to her, desert and dust and the keen odor of damp earth. And lavender.

The ribbon which had tied back her long, black hair was missing, and the tresses curled in wild, windblown confusion around her pale face. When he looked closer, the pain he saw tore at his heart. Huge and hot and haunted, her blue eyes stared back at him. She'd not shed one single tear, not even when he'd told her that Sean was dead.

She looked at him and hesitated, then took a deep breath. "I've come to talk."

He touched a finger to her lips. "Good." He studied the hollows beneath her eyes, the tightness around her mouth. "I've been worried."

He still was. He felt the tension coiled tightly within her, the grief she still held inside. She was like a powder keg ready to explode from the slightest spark.

"Did it help—being by yourself?"

She shivered then, as if she'd been holding herself together with sheer effort of will and his words had shattered the fragile spell protecting her.

She nodded. "I needed to think things through."

Her trembling increased, and he pulled the pink and blue patchwork quilt from the bed and wrapped it around her shoulders. She clutched the sides together, and her knuckles turned white.

"You went to the river."

She looked surprised, then nodded. "Where else would I go?"

"There's a storm coming. I heard the wind picking up, and it's freezing outside. It's been hours. No wonder you can't stop shaking."

He went to the table beside her rocker. Next to his shaving basin, he picked up the bottle of whiskey and poured a small amount into a glass. He returned to her and held it out. "Drink this."

She shook her head. "I don't want any. It won't help— only make things worse." Her voice caught, and she bit her lip.

"It's just to warm you." He took her hand and closed her fingers around the glass. Then he touched the bottom and urged her to drink. He hoped she'd finally share her pain and let him comfort her.

She swallowed the liquor and started to cough. When

she controlled the spasms, she looked at him and a trace of a smile turned up her full lips. "No wonder it's called firewater. I do feel warmer."

"I aim to please," he said, grinning. Then he turned serious. "Is there anything else I can do?"

She handed him the glass and clutched the blanket at her throat. For several moments her gaze rested on the bed beside them, then she looked at him. The intensity in her eyes burned a path clear to his soul. "Love me, Jeff."

He nearly dropped the tumbler. Of all the things he'd expected her to say, that wasn't it. He swallowed hard. The silence in the room stretched between them. Wind off the desert gusted, and pebbles pelted the windowpane in a staccato rhythm.

"You don't know what you're asking."

"Yes, I do. For hours I've been thinking of everything I never said to my father, the memories I'll miss sharing with him." She closed her eyes briefly; her lips trembled. "I never had a chance to say good-bye. I never had a chance to tell him I love him."

He raked his hand through his hair. "He knew."

"You could have been killed."

"I wasn't."

"Don't you see?" She took a hesitant step forward, and her gaze traveled from his battered face to the gash in his side. A pained expression tightened her mouth. "I don't want to have regrets about you, too. I can't stand any more. I trust you. I want—" She stared at the bed again.

"Think about what you're saying. You don't know—"

"I need to feel alive. Inside me, it's as if I died, too. I don't want to look back and wish for something I can't have. I'm not asking you to love me forever. I know you're promised to someone else. I only want one night. Is that so much to ask?"

Jeff remembered the letter he'd sent to Emily with Cady. He knew releasing her from any implied promise had been the right decision for both of them.

Nothing and no one mattered to him right now except Bree and what was best for her. He didn't care what anyone else thought. He didn't care about the collision course of their two worlds, but would *she* regret it later?

His control slipped rapidly as his need to protect her battled with his desire to possess her. He turned away, but he couldn't shut her out. Her warm, womanly fragrance beckoned and teased. The scent of lavender surrounded him, battering down the wall he'd built, crowding inside him, clutching at his heart. He clenched his fists and closed his eyes. But her image followed him, floated to him out of the blackness—beautiful, beckoning, vulnerable.

"I shouldn't have come here." Behind him, her voice was hardly more than a whisper.

It felt like a scream.

He turned back as she quietly placed the quilt at the foot of the bed. Her hand brushed his shirt hanging from the spindle, and she flinched as if the cloth burned, then lifted the sleeve to her nose, inhaling deeply. She dropped the material and moved toward the door. The candlelight glistened off the shine of a single tear rolling down her cheek.

"Bree, don't go. Not like this."

She paused with her hand on the knob, her shoulders slumped. Her bowed shadow wavered on the wall. "I'm sorry I bothered you."

"Stay."

"No."

"We can talk."

"The last time we talked, alone on the boat, you almost had to marry me." She laughed softly, sadly. "I'll never forget Cap's—"

Her voice broke on a sob, and she turned to him as the gathered tears spilled over her lower lashes and down her cheeks. Her desolation slammed him in the chest. She could get to him—touch him—without laying a hand on him.

An anguished cry escaped her, and she buried her face in her hands, struggling to hide her grief. It was the first time she'd let him see her hurt. He'd seen her frightened, so angry he thought she'd rip his head off, proud, strong, and so damn desirable she drove him nearly out of his mind with wanting. He'd even seen her cry. But not like this—this absolute and utter sorrow.

Something inside his chest cracked. He hated that he couldn't do anything for her. The taste of defeat was bitter in his mouth; he didn't take it easily. He controlled a powerful railroad company, he could build bridges and lay track clear across the country, and he couldn't do the one thing he wanted most. He couldn't take away the pain of the woman he loved.

Gently he pulled her hands away from her face and drew her into his arms. Cupping the back of her head, he wove his fingers into her silky hair and pressed her cheek to his chest. He felt her tears, hot and wet, against his skin. "Let it go, honey," he crooned softly. "You don't have to hold it in anymore."

Her arms inched around his waist, and he held her as gut-wrenching sobs shook her slender body. As long as she needed him, he'd be there for her. Her abject distress destroyed his resolve. God help him, he'd do anything to put the sparkle back in her face, life in her eyes.

He loved her. He wanted her. He'd give her anything she asked.

Slowly her crying ceased, and she pushed herself away, sniffling. "I—I didn't mean to do that. I'll go now."

She put her hand on the doorknob. Before she could open it, he curved his hands around her shoulders, turning her toward him. In the candlelight he could still see the sparkle of tears in her eyes. "Please stay."

Bree leaned her back against the door and stared down at his bare feet, embarrassed at her show of emotion, unable to meet his eyes. He stood in front of her and cupped her face in his steady, strong fingers, brushing the moisture from her cheeks with his thumbs. Her skin absorbed his warmth like the sun's rays seeped into the desert sand.

She knew he didn't want her forever. He wanted her only for one night. But that was enough. "All right."

The room was dark except for the candle on the table near the window. Jeff placed his large hands against the door on either side of her head, trapping her between his forearms. His wide, muscled chest highlighted his strength and power. She reached out with both hands and touched him. His face was in shadow, but she felt his rapidly beating heart, the coarse hair covering his chest, heard the momentary catch in his breathing. His familiar scent encompassed her. A sweet ache settled between her breasts as he slowly lowered his mouth to hers.

The touch was like a bolt of lightning igniting dry brush. Flames raced through her and licked her lips, her breasts, her belly. She felt more than heard the moan that lodged in her throat. His breathing quickened as he moved his hips against hers, gently grinding, seeking. She felt his hardness and tensed as a flicker of fear coursed through her. He froze.

"Do you want me to stop?" His hoarse voice vibrated in her ear as he lifted his mouth from the sensitive spot on her neck.

This was Tanner. He wouldn't hurt her.

"I don't want to stop." Then a thought struck her. "Do you?"

He looked at her and she could almost see the flash of amusement in his eyes, just before they caught fire. "Lady, there isn't anything on earth that could make me stop . . . unless you asked me to." A fierce expression draped his features. "You are so beautiful, so sweet and soft. Don't ever wear a corset again."

"Don't have to ask me twice." She giggled, a healing laugh that shattered the shroud of sadness around her.

Bree wrapped her arms around his neck, sliding her fingers into the thick hair at his nape. She stood on tiptoe and kissed the underside of his chin, his jaw. The taste of soap was bitter on her tongue, and she wrinkled her nose, sniffing his scent, instinctively rubbing her body against him.

She pressed her breasts to his bare chest. She knew this rough covering of hair from a lifetime ago on *Belle*, and yearned to feel him again without the barrier of her dress and undergarments.

"You have too many clothes on," he said.

"How do you do that?" she whispered.

"What?"

"Read my mind."

A slow half-smile cut the intensity on his face. He took her hand. "It's a gift."

He led her across the room to the table and turned her so that the candle shone on her back. Then he unbuttoned her dress and pushed the sleeves from her shoulders, nibbling the bare skin in its wake. Shivers of delight frolicked down her spine. The garment landed in a heap at her feet, and she stepped out of the circle, turning toward him.

He reached out and pulled the end of the ribbon holding her chemise across her breasts. When they were freed to his touch, he quickly removed her petticoats and pantalettes. His eyes were like twin green flames as he sucked in his breath.

"I was wrong. *You're* a gift—and I'm honored."

"No. I—"

He silenced her with his mouth. His tongue eased past her teeth and stroked the untried recesses beyond. Her chest tightened with a need that spread to her belly, then lower. His warm palm cupped her bare breast and the contact sent her careening into a world inhabited only by Jeff Tanner. It was a place she never wanted to leave.

"Jeff—" She heard the pleading note in her voice.

"I know."

He lifted her into his arms and carried her to the bed, then gently lowered her to the sheets. Cotton caressed her bare back, and his masculine essence floated from the fibers. He quickly unbuckled his belt and removed the last of his clothes, then joined her. The mattress dipped from his weight and she half-rolled into his arms.

His warm skin caressed her; the thick mat of hair on his chest made her bare breasts tingle and swell with anticipation. She felt the rock-hard muscles of his thighs as he entwined his legs with hers.

She'd never been in this bed with a man. Not since . . . She stiffened.

He drew back and looked down at her. "What is it, Bree?"

"Nothing. Bad memories."

"What? Charlie?"

She nodded.

"Did he force you—"

"No," she said, closing her eyes to shut out the unwanted recollection. But the image focused, clear and terrible. "He would have—if Riley hadn't stopped him." She hesitated.

"Tell me. Let it go." He brushed the hair away from her cheek.

Rain, sudden and violent, pounded the roof and splattered the window. She shivered, and he pulled her into his arms.

She was safe with him. In the refuge of his embrace she could finally confess what had haunted her so long. Tanner had guessed most of it anyway.

"I was supposed to meet Riley. He was going to teach me to pan for gold." She swallowed hard. "But Charles cornered me before I could leave the house."

She felt his body tense as his arms tightened around her. His mouth straightened to a thin line, and a muscle in his cheek contracted.

Taking a deep breath, she went on. "I tried to fight him, but he was too strong. He—he ripped my dress. He touched me everywhere. And he kissed me. It was wet and horrible. I was thirteen."

But it could have been yesterday, the memory was so vivid. Her heart hammered painfully against her ribs just as it had then. It wouldn't have mattered what her age. The experience had been terrifying, degrading, shattering.

"But he didn't—" His eyes narrowed.

She shook her head. "Riley came looking for me when I didn't show up. He searched the house. I screamed."

"I wish I'd killed that sonofabitch when I had the chance."

"What good would that do? It's over. You said so yourself."

"If I'd known about this that night at the fort," he said angrily, "I'd have—"

"Don't." She placed her palm on his cheek and felt tense muscle beneath his freshly shaven skin. "Don't spoil this, Jeff."

"I like it when you call me that," he said, taking a deep breath. He lifted her wrist and brought her hand to his lips, kissing each finger. He studied her face, and his tender, concerned look slipped inside her and cleansed the wound festering there. "If you want to stop—I'll understand."

"No." Her voice was sharp. "I've been afraid for a long time, but not anymore—not of you. This is right." She turned on her side, her breasts caressing his chest. His body was warm—so warm and hard and strong. "I'm tired of thinking. And I don't want to talk anymore—at least not with words." She arched her hips against him.

With her right hand around his neck, she brought his mouth down to hers, kissing him with all the emotion and pent-up need within her. She pulled back and stared into his face, felt his accelerated breathing as his bare chest moved against her own. Her nipples hardened in response, aching with want.

She licked her top lip, and he groaned, just before he lowered his mouth again. He eased her on her back, cupping her breast, then stroking downward over the dip of her waist, over her hip and across her leg to her inner thigh. She held her breath in anticipation, waiting—wondering. Her skin grew hot as her chest heaved with desire. When his strong fingers gently entered her, she gasped in pleasure and lifted her hips toward him, telling him with her body that she welcomed his touch.

Trailing kisses over her neck and shoulder, he moved to her breast and took the sensitive peak into his mouth. The roughness of his tongue sent shards of delight spiraling through her body to settle between her thighs. Every inch of her skin vibrated with excitement, burned with passion. Her feminine moistness tightened around his finger as he primed and stroked until she craved more.

He moved away from her breast and kissed her mouth, his ragged breath hot and heavy. "I've wanted you for so long," he whispered, his voice raw with need. "I don't think I can wait anymore. Are you ready, love?"

"Yes," she whispered against his lips. "Oh, yes."

"I'll be as careful as I—I mean, I'll try not to hurt—The first time is—"

She placed a finger over his mouth. "I trust you."

In the dimness she made out the white of his teeth as he smiled. Gently he touched his mouth to her own, a sweet kiss filled with caring. Her heart swelled with emotion, so full she wanted to weep from it. Then he carefully settled his muscular body over her, bracing his weight on his elbows on either side of her head, letting her grow used to the feel of him. The coarse mat of hair on his chest teased her breasts, and she smiled at the sweet contact.

With his knee he spread her legs apart and eased himself between her thighs. She felt his hardness at the barrier of her virginity. With one swift thrust, she felt a tearing sensation and a sharp pain. Her breath caught, and her body went rigid. She closed her eyes and dug her fingernails into his shoulders.

"I'm sorry." He stilled and cupped her face in his hands, then stroked the moistness from her cheeks. "If there was another way . . ."

She closed her eyes and remained motionless until the discomfort eased. Looking at him again, she read his anguish in his furrowed brow, tight mouth, the lines on either side of his nose, deeper now than she'd ever seen before.

"Shh. I'm all right. It's better now." She pulled his face down and kissed him—his cheeks, his chin, his mouth—with all the tenderness and love she couldn't put into words. The intimacy was more wonderful than she'd ever imagined. This was Tanner and she loved him.

He began to move within her, and she savored the feeling of being one with him. She accepted his thrusts, then her hips moved with him in a rhythm as instinctive as breathing.

Perspiration gathered on her forehead and upper lip. Heat built within her, coiling and coursing outward to her legs, her arms, her cheeks—from the top of her head to the tips of her toes. Every lunge lifted her higher until tension knotted in her belly and advanced steadily downward, until her feminine core pounded with need. She was ready to burst.

One more movement, and she clutched him to her as white and orange and yellow light exploded behind her tightly closed eyelids. Wave after wave of physical pleasure swept over her, holding her immobile until there was nothing left but a warm glow where the fire had been.

Tanner pulled her tightly against his chest and held her in a steel grip as his body went rigid. He groaned and buried his face in her shoulder. She smiled, knowing that his pleasure matched her own. She gloried in her power to give him something so wonderful.

He rolled to the side and folded her in his arms. The room was quiet except for the sound of their still-rapid breathing. The worst of the rain had passed, and the remaining moisture trickled quietly down the window, each drop a diamond in the candlelight.

He kissed her temple. "Say something, Bree. Tell me how you feel."

She slid her hand across his flat abdomen and heard his quick intake of breath before she hugged him close. After kissing his shoulder, she rubbed her cheek against the thick muscle of his upper arm, supremely satisfied.

"I feel alive again. Not again. For the first time. Oh, I don't know how to explain it. I've never felt like this before."

His lips brushed her forehead, and his fingers stroked up and down her arm. "I know. I feel the same way."

"I'm glad it was you—I mean, the first time."

He tensed and his hand stopped. "Why didn't you ever say anything to your father—about Charlie?"

She sighed, reluctant to allow the bad memories into this sensual sanctuary. But he'd made it his business to help her; he had a right to know.

"Cap had just remarried. I didn't want to cause trouble for him and Mary. Anyway, I figured that I'd had a warning—forewarned is forearmed. I took precautions. I never put myself in that position again."

"He won't bother you anymore."

"I know. He really seems lost without Cap. I think he truly cared."

"In his own way he cares about you, too."

She didn't want to talk about Charles. Tanner was the man she loved, and after the bridge was finished, he was going back home to marry someone else.

She tried to sit up, but he held her against him in an unyielding grip.

"Don't go."

She didn't want to, not really. Like spurs to a horse's flanks, pride had goaded her to abandon his arms. The thought was about as appealing as leaping into the storm swept Colorado. But she couldn't stay, knowing he'd be gone soon. "I have to."

"No." He turned on his side toward her and nuzzled her neck.

Bree turned away from him and pulled her knees up to

her abdomen, curling into herself. His arm encircled her waist and pulled her tightly against him. She felt his arousal against her buttocks, and a shiver skipped up her spine. His tongue stroked the sensitive hollow beneath her ear, and tingles tripped over her shoulders and arms, down her thighs and deeper. He wanted her again, and she felt the same. With just the slightest effort he controlled her passion and commanded her body.

She knew it was because she loved him.

Cady had tried to tell her, but she'd refused to listen. Riley had made her see, and she'd come here to tell him. But there was no hope. Jeff was going away, and even if he wanted to take her, she'd never fit in his life. Words of love hovered on her lips, but she couldn't say them. She didn't want his pity. She had to get away from him.

"Stay with me," he growled into her ear.

His hand glided upward from her waist to cup her breast, and the rapture that raced through her was too delicious to be denied. Her resolve weakened along with the strength in her limbs. She'd always been helpless to fight his charm. And now that she knew how wonderful it could be, she was powerless to resist the ecstasy his masculinity could give her. She loved him.

Later, she'd leave. Later, he'd go back to his high-society life. But she had now, and the memories she made with him.

She rolled toward him and pressed her soft breasts to the solid wall of his chest. "Yes," she whispered.

She couldn't deny herself just a little longer in his arms. Afterward, she'd never be with him again.

nineteen

Bree lifted a handful of skirt on her cotton dress before sliding down the riverbank in the predawn light. She could just barely make out the drifting Colorado and its comforting gurgle over and around the rocks that would be hidden come spring. The smell of mud, wet sand, and rain drifted to her, a reminder that last night's storm had washed everything clean.

She hadn't bothered to tie back her hair, and the wind lifted it away from her face. It was a wonderful, free feeling, but she wondered if she'd ever be truly free again now that she knew what it was like loving Tanner.

She sat on her favorite log, the same place she'd talked to Riley less than twenty-four hours before. After he had confessed his unspoken devotion for her mother, she'd decided to go to Tanner. Would her old friend fault her for spending the night with a man who wasn't her husband? Somehow she didn't think so.

Her skin still tingled from the glory of Tanner's touch. And she welcomed the unfamiliar discomfort between her thighs, an intimate tangible reminder of sharing her body with him. She'd never dreamed giving and receiving from him could be so wonderful. If she had it to do over again, she'd make the same decision. Her memories of the night in his arms would have to hold her for a lifetime. He was leaving soon, and she'd never see him again.

She watched the dark flow of the Colorado and smiled sadly. How she loved the unpredictable river. Then she looked heavenward. "Lord, this isn't funny, not one single bit. Why did you let me fall in love with a railroad man?"

Behind her, she heard footsteps and the sound of sand and rocks sliding. It wasn't necessary to look over her shoulder to know that Tanner had followed her. And she knew something else, too. She didn't reach for her gun at every unfamiliar sound now; she wasn't afraid of Charles anymore. Thanks to Tanner, her stepbrother knew she wasn't his and never would be, no matter that their parents had thought they should marry. There was one and only one man she wanted to marry.

But Tanner could never be hers.

He stopped behind her, and she could hear his ragged breathing from his exertion sliding down the riverbank. She couldn't help remembering the way her touch during the night had produced the same breathless condition. She smiled. At least she had that to hang on to.

"Why did you leave?" Tanner asked.

"I wanted to be by myself. How did you know where to find me?"

"This river's in your blood, Bree. Where else would you go?" He sounded almost angry about her deep attachment to the Colorado.

"Funny. This river is fickle and dangerous, but I always feel at peace here." She watched the sky behind the jagged mountains go from purple to orange-pink as the sun started its crawl up the backside.

Tanner sat down beside her, close enough for her to feel the warmth of his body and smell the faint fragrance of his shaving soap. But not quite near enough for their shoulders to brush. He said nothing, just stared straight ahead at the river and the sunrise in the distance. His presence brought her a mixture of pleasure and pain that was almost a physical ache. She needed a clean break from him. It hurt too much to see him, smell him, sit beside him, and want him all the while knowing he was going away forever. She felt the pain of missing him already. The years ahead of her seemed like a great black emptiness. If she slipped any further into the hole he would make in her life, she'd never be able to climb out. Somehow she had to make him go away now.

"I thought you were sleeping," she said.

He glanced at her, then back at the mountains. "Missed your soft body next to mine. I woke up."

In spite of the cool morning air on her face, Bree felt her cheeks burn. "If you need me to help you sleep, you're gonna be one tired railroad tycoon."

"How's that?" He sounded more amused than anything.

"That's the first and last time you'll ever catch me in the same bed with you." She turned her head to see how he took that news.

Her heart slammed against her ribs as a slow half-smile turned up his lips. "That so?"

"That's so."

He rested his elbows on his knees. "I have to insist that my wife share my bed."

"I'm sure Emily will be happy to do that."

"I don't think her new beau would approve of her sharing my bed."

"Tanner, what in the world are you talking about?" For the first time a sliver of hope caught inside her and began to grow.

"I'm not now, nor have I ever been, engaged to Emily Hollingsworth. In fact, Cady told me she's been keeping company with a new lawyer her father hired." He picked up a stick from the riverbank and began to draw in the sand. "Just to clear up any misunderstanding, Cady took my letter to Emily explaining that I can't marry her when I'm in love with another woman. That woman loves me back. She's going to marry me."

"Give my sympathy to the poor, misguided soul."

"I'll do that." He rested the stick against his knee.

Jeff sensed that she was trying to pick a fight with him. He wasn't sure why, but he knew he had to handle her carefully. She'd told him in every way but words that she loved him. And by God, he'd get her to admit it out loud on the bank of the river that was his chief rival for her affection.

It was not more than a trickle now, and he wondered why it drew her. Did she get her strength from the muddy water? The flow of the Colorado constantly changed, and there was no way to plot its course, at times forceful and unpredictable. Just like Bree.

He turned his head and studied her. The rising sun showed him her face clearly for the first time since he'd joined her, since he'd made her his. This was the woman he loved. This was the innocent who had satisfied him so sweetly just a few hours before. Her lips were still slightly swollen from his kisses, her hair in wild disarray because he'd run his fingers through the silk.

His gut clenched with the force of his feelings. He had to show her she could have a life with him. Somehow he had to convince her they belonged together.

He looked heavenward and muttered, "Give me the words, Sean."

"What did you say?" she asked sharply.

He reached into his left breast pocket and pulled out a length of blue satin ribbon. "I have something for you."

"What?"

He put the strand of material in her hand. "I've had this ever since we spent the night together on *Belle*."

On the log she shifted slightly as she turned to him. He saw her wince and knew her discomfort. If only he hadn't had to hurt her to love her. He'd give her time for the soreness to pass, then he planned to spend a good portion of the rest of his life making love to her. From now on he'd give her nothing but pleasure.

She looked at the ribbon he held out, then brushed a

knuckle across her cheek, just at the corner of her eye. "Why would you keep this?"

He shrugged. "A reminder of the poor, misguided woman I love." He grabbed the stick again and continued writing in the river mud.

"But that's my ribbon."

"I know."

"You can't love me."

His grin slipped some. "Can't I?"

"You don't love me," she said, balling the ribbon in her palm and pressing it to her chest. "That's impossible."

"I reckon I can love you if I want."

"Why would you even think such a thing?"

"Damned if I know." A muscle in his cheek contracted. This wasn't going to be so easy. He sighed. Since the day she'd put a bullet hole through the crown of his favorite hat, nothing about B. E. Murphy had been easy. "I guess because I had the bad luck to fall in love with you. I want to marry you."

A gust of wind blew a silky strand of her black hair across her face, and she tucked it behind her ear. "You just think you want to marry me because you feel sorry for me. Because of Cap."

"Dammit, Bree, that's not true. I want you to be my wife because I want to spend the rest of my life with you."

She shook her head. "Jeff, I . . ."

He liked it when she called him by his first name. She'd done it during the night when he'd loved her so thoroughly. He planned to spend the rest of his life listening to her call him Jeff.

"Yes?"

"You love me?"

He nodded. "And you're going to marry me." He rubbed his hands together. "We have some plans to make. I thought we'd take the Pullman from Yuma to Phoenix, then east. The wedding—"

"East?" She bit the corner of her lip. "Where snooty society matrons with houses bigger than Hardyville have dinners for more people than I've ever laid eyes on?"

"No. Where my family lives so I can show you off."

"Your family?" A look of sheer panic stole the pink from her cheeks.

"I want them to be there for the wedding. You and Cady are already friends. My parents are going to love you as much as I do. And my brother . . ." He'd never been jealous in his life, especially of his brother, but the ladies seemed to like Jack. And when it came to Bree, he didn't trust any man. "I'm afraid he'll like you. Too much," he added half under his breath.

"It won't work. You'd only come to hate me."

"Never," he said, taking her cold hands in his.

Bree wanted to believe him more than she'd ever wanted anything in her life. She didn't dare. "I'm not a lady. I don't know how to run a big fancy house or plan a dinner party. I'd embarrass you in front of your friends, and I couldn't stand it if you came to despise me."

"I never figured you for a coward." He squeezed her fingers. "You won't give us a chance because you're afraid of what you think my friends will say. Anyone who doesn't accept you is no friend to me. And since when did you give a damn what people think?"

Since I first laid eyes on you, she thought. "Jeff, listen to—"

"No, you listen. I thought you trusted me. I told you I'd never let anyone hurt you. I took care of Charlie, and I promised your father that I'd take care of you."

"My father? When?"

"Yesterday. After the funeral. He knew we were meant to be together. That's why he tried to marry us after we spent the night alone on the boat. You don't really think he gave a damn what people would say, do you?"

"I don't know about that." She shook her head. "But one thing's for sure, I don't know how to act in society. I don't know a thing about the right clothes—"

"Don't you see that none of that matters? I love you—in pants, in a dress . . . most of all in nothing." He laughed when she gasped and her cheeks turned pink. "If you covered yourself in burlap, you couldn't hide your fine cheekbones." He ran a finger just beneath her eye. "Or your full lips." He traced her mouth. "Or those beautiful eyes."

"I'm not," she said, looking down.

"You are. But I don't care if you run a riverboat, shoot snakes, or eat with your hands." He lifted her chin with a finger, forcing her to meet his gaze. "I care about your spirit and strength. I once thought any man would count himself lucky to have a woman like you on his side." He tapped her nose. "I haven't changed my mind."

"I can't, Jeff. It would never work." Because he was right. She *was* a coward. She could face danger on the river, snakes and scorpions in the desert, and the two-legged kind of varmint. But she was scared to death of losing Jeff Tanner's love. She just couldn't marry him. "I'd be an embarrassment to you."

His mouth tensed until it was nearly a straight line. "If you can look me straight in the eye and tell me you don't love me, I'll walk away and never look back."

Oh, Lord, how could she do that when she was nearly dying for love of him? She had to try. She crossed her fingers and started to put her hand behind her back. "I don't love—"

He grabbed her wrist. "No fibs, Bree. Tell me you don't love me—if you can—and I'll never bother you again."

The pain in her chest expanded until a sob broke loose. His big hand encircling her wrist wavered as tears filled her eyes. "I can't."

"So you do love me?"

She nodded.

"Say it, Bree." He spread her fingers open and kissed her palm. "In front of God and the river you love so much. Say you love me and you'll marry me."

"I love you, Jeff Tanner." Moisture trickled down her

cheeks as a small smile turned up the corners of her mouth. "And I reckon that means I'm gonna have to marry you."

"Do you still think you're a poor misguided soul?" He pointed to his stick-scrapings in the river mud at their feet.

He'd carved a heart. Inside it said: "J.T. loves B.E.M."

She laughed and shook her head. "No. Now I think you're the one who's misguided. But since you made me say it in front of God and everybody, you better not back out. Or I'll put another hole in that hat of yours."

He cupped her face in his hands. "I'm scared, Murphy."

"Smart man, Tanner."

He gazed into her eyes. She knew that intense hungry look now for the love that it was. The same feelings grew bigger inside her. He finally lowered his lips to hers, and the feel of his mouth and the promise of his touch started a trembling that spread to every part of her body. She couldn't hold a gun on him if she wanted to. That was the furthest thing from her mind. She only wanted to love him.

epilogue

Arizona Territory
December 1881

As the cold wind whipped her blue wool skirt around her and white clouds skittered across the sun overhead, Bree stared at the impressive wood and steel trestle. The bridge was complete, a major engineering achievement. She thought she'd burst from pride.

"What a wonder," she whispered almost reverently.

Tanner's arm came around her waist. "Now what do you think of the mule-headed railroad man you married?"

"That you're still stubborn. And just about as smart as can be."

"Who said rivers and rails don't mix?"

Bree recalled saying that very thing the first time they'd met. "I can't imagine who was so shortsighted," she said, resting her cheek against his chest.

"Rails are going to help make this country great, Bree. They're the key to the future." He squeezed her closer to his side. "And ours is in California."

She touched her abdomen and glanced up at him. He was proud as could be about his part in building the Territory. Would he be as pleased with the life he was building with her? "Are you sure you're happy about heading up the expansion project from San Francisco? I know how hard you worked to make a place for yourself in the East. I—"

Tanner touched his finger to her lips. "That means nothing to me. I worked to make my name known in the railroad business." He leaned down and kissed her cheek. "I did that *and* I found you. As long as we're together, I don't care where we go."

She smiled, satisfied. "Before we leave, there's one last thing we have to do." Tanner nodded as he followed her gaze down to the riverbank where *Belle* was anchored.

She let her husband help her as they half-walked, half-slid down the bank and stopped at the gangplank.

"Well, lookee who's here." Riley O'Rear's desert-roughened voice carried to her from the boat. "Thought you two was gonna get on that loco-motive without so much as a by-your-leave."

Bree crossed the plank that connected *Belle* to land, then stepped onto the deck and moved up the starboard side to the bow. Right behind her Tanner kept taking her elbow as if she'd never been on a riverboat before, let alone captained one. Not so long ago she would have given him a piece of her mind. Now the gesture warmed her clear to her heart and on down deep to her soul.

Riley stood between the tall, black smokestack and the wheelhouse. When he grinned, the leathery skin on his cheeks, above his white whiskers, creased like a bone-dry riverbed.

Bree returned his smile. "You know we couldn't go without saying good-bye."

"Missy, you're pretty as a picture in that there dress."

She blushed as she smoothed the front of her expensive traveling skirt. The impractical little matching hat reminded her of the one Cady Tanner had worn when they'd first met. Tanner had taken Bree to Phoenix for clothes, although she'd resisted at first. But she had to admit, the beautiful material fashioned into the latest styles made her feel like a lady. When she'd said as much to Tanner, he'd laughed, then proceeded to make her feel like a woman. She finally realized that to him she was a lady whether she wore skirts or trousers or nothing at all.

"You really like it?" she asked, pulling down the fitted jacket she wore.

The old man swallowed hard as he nodded, and she swore his pale blue eyes were suspiciously shiny. When he sniffled and mumbled something about some mysterious ailment coming on, she felt her own throat grow thick with tears.

"Tanner and I have something to tell you," she said, looking up at her husband.

Jeff nodded and took a sheaf of papers from the inside pocket of his black coat, then handed them to Riley. "We want you to have the *River Belle*."

The old man looked at the bundle, then at Tanner. "The hell you say."

"You're the only person Bree trusts to take care of her."

"What about Charlie?" He lifted his battered brown hat and set it on the back of his gray head.

"He's busy helping his mother run the boardinghouse," Tanner said. "Never saw a man change as much as he has since . . ." He looked down at Bree, and she knew he was thinking about her father. "Since he's become the head of the family. He doesn't have time now for the army's freight runs."

"Might if he didn't see Sally so much. He sure has taken a shine to that little gal in Cactus Kate's. Ginger don't seem to mind, though."

"Like I said, Charlie's a new man." Tanner smoothed his mustache with his thumb and forefinger. "So what do you say? Will you take *Belle*, free and clear, from the railroad?"

"Hell, yes," he said, cackling. "Still don't know why you'd want me to have her."

"Cap would want it this way," Bree said.

"You were his best friend. And it's my way of saying thanks for watching out for Bree until I could take over." Tanner put the stack of papers into the other man's hand.

"So where are you two goin' in that fancy railroad car?"

"East to spend the Christmas holidays with Tanner's family. Cady and his mother are planning a wedding reception for us since he couldn't wait to get married. After that, we head to California. And it won't be too soon for me." There was a very good reason why she was anxious to put down roots.

The wind stirred up waves in the river that rocked the boat. Bree steadied herself, but couldn't quiet her stomach so easily. "I—I think I need to sit down," she said, taking a deep breath before resting her arms across her stomach.

"What's wrong? Are you sick?" Tanner gripped her upper arms and studied her face.

"There's nothing the matter with me. At least nothing that won't be all right in about seven months. I've been meaning to tell you—"

Riley cackled and shook his head. "You're still slow as mud, boy. Can't you see she's in the family way?"

Tanner blinked, then stared open-mouthed at her. She smiled at his shock. "I planned to tell you closer to Christmas and make it a present. But, yes. We're going to have a baby."

"A baby?" A slow grin turned up the corners of his mouth, making her heart race so that she forgot all about her queasy stomach. "We're going to have a baby. Did you hear that, Riley?"

"The way you're shoutin', folks clear down in Hardyville can hear."

"Hot damn. This is really somethin'."

"That it is," Riley said. "Wish I could stay and listen to ya' carry on, but I'd best get goin' while there's still light." He extended his palm. "Don't you keep her away too long, boy. I want to see that young'un when he gets here."

"Count on it." Tanner shook his hand, then stepped back. He stared at the jagged peaks far in the distance as if it was the most interesting sight in the world. Bree knew he would miss the old man, too.

Riley opened his arms, and she walked into them and pressed her cheek to his shoulder. "Never had me a daughter, but if I did, I'd want her to be just like you."

Bree felt tears burn her eyes as she hugged Riley goodbye. She started to say something, but the words wouldn't come out. He patted her back before gently pushing her away. She stood with Tanner on the embankment as the old man guided *Belle* out into the channel.

When the boat was out of sight and all that remained was a wisp of smoke above the river, she sniffled. A huge sigh escaped her before she could stop it. She was going to miss piloting that steamboat.

As if he could read her thoughts, Tanner turned to her and took both of her hands in his. A worried frown creased his forehead. "You're going to love the Pacific Ocean, Bree. Blue water as far as the eye can see. I'll take you out on the ferry, and if you want we can sail—"

"Stop." She smiled at him through her tears. "I'm not giving up the river. I'm choosing a life with the man I love." She placed her palms on his chest, over his heart. "I'll miss it. But having you and your baby growing inside me . . . I wouldn't trade that for anything."

"I'm going to be a father," he said, gently touching her abdomen where his child rested within her.

She smiled and covered his hand with her own. She'd wondered how he would take the news of impending fatherhood. His reaction had pleased her more than she could say. "The baby's going to be a boy."

"How do you know?"

"I just do."

"Is that so? And do you know what you're going to call him?"

She nodded emphatically. "I have a name that I'm sure your mother would heartily approve of. Lincoln Abraham Tanner."

"Linc Tanner," he said slowly. "I like it. So will Mother.

She's going to love you, especially when you tell her she's soon to be a grandmother."

"Do you really think so?"

"I know so. She's been after me for years to marry and start a family. She already knows about you," he said, lightly tracing the curve of her cheek with his finger. "But the baby will be a surprise."

"Then it will be an extra special Christmas present."

He pulled her to him and looked into her eyes. "Nothing could be better than the day I met you."

"If I remember right, I sent a bullet or two your way."

He grinned. "Through my favorite hat. Not to mention the chandelier you blew to kingdom come."

She met his gaze and grew serious. "I love you, Jeff. I love you with all my heart and soul, and I'd do anything for you."

"I love *you*, Bree Tanner. You don't have to do anything. Just be in my life. Forever."

"That's easy as pie." Bree pressed her cheek to his chest and sighed at the sound of his heart pounding. Her own matched it, beat for beat. The Pullman waited to take them east, and she couldn't wait to be inside, alone with her husband.

If anyone had told her she'd fall in love with a railroad man, Bree would have said they were crazy. Tanner was far from the ruthless man she'd expected. He was decent and kind and loving, in spite of the fact that he was used to getting his own way. They would probably disagree and fight. But making up would be downright pleasurable.

She was contrary and he was mule-headed. But she couldn't imagine sharing her life with any other man. He was all she ever wanted and more than she'd ever hoped to have. His determination to tame the reckless river had brought them together. The course of love would lead them to heaven on earth.

FREE
Romance
(a $4.50 value)

Send in the Coupon Below

To get your FREE historical romance and start saving, fill out the coupon below and mail it today. As soon as we receive it we'll send you your FREE Book along with your first month's selections.
